HUGH'S *of* BLUE

HUGH'S *of* BLUE

Christine Ellen Law

iUniverse®

HUGH'S OF BLUE

iUniverse books may be ordered through booksellers or by contacting:

iUniverse
1663 Liberty Drive
Bloomington, IN 47403
www.iuniverse.com
1-800-Authors (1-800-288-4677)

ISBN: 978-1-5320-0607-4 (sc)
ISBN: 978-1-5320-0608-1 (hc)
ISBN: 978-1-5320-0609-8 (e)

Library of Congress Control Number: 2016914723

Print information available on the last page.

iUniverse rev. date: 10/31/2016

For my daughter Nicole who brought Bryn to life.
For my son Robert who epitomizes Andrew's virtues.
For Elizabeth who read the first chapter and asked for more.

C.E.L.

Part One
THE HISTORY

I had not lost my patience, yet. Ladies did not lose their patience, especially with children, but there came a point in time when one's toler ance reached its limit. "Your name, boy!" I demanded, raising my voice more that I had intended. The child had tried to steal my purse, but being a no nonsense kind of person, I grabbed him by the ear and dragged him home with me. We came through into the kitchen and there sat my Lily, by the hearth, watching me and the boy, while Cook gave her a fresh baked cake. Nothing took Mrs. Fairchild by surprise, so she just continued on with what she was doing, knowing I would fill her in later.

I had to conceal a smile as the boy squared his thin shoulders and puffed up what little chest he had, "T o m m y . . . Thomas Hall".

"How did you find yourself on the street stealing ladies purses, Thomas Hall?"

"Well . . . mam", his dirty hand took a swipe at his nose. I noticed the child had some manners as he removed his cap. His hair was dirty and matted and my heart immediately melted. It was evident in the way his hands worried his cap behind his back, that he was frightened, but he had a streak of courage that was admirable in one so young. I could tell he was deeply embarrassed at being restrained by his victim, failure written all over his face. I am not a cruel woman, but he had done wrong and now deserved to stew a little in his own juice. I was actually trying to think of a punishment that would fit the crime. I was not naïve and knew of the dreadful conditions that children were forced to.

"Me da was a miner, took coal lung and passed on just these few months past. Mum took consumption and died some years gone. I didn't want a workhouse, did I, beggin' your pardon mam. I'm truly

3

not a thief, just hungry, that's what I am. Beggin' your pardon, mam, I don't rightly know how to tell ya, but I am afraid for the others. Since my Da passed, it's been feast or famine for me. Things had been all right before my mum died. After . . . we both missed her somethin' awful, but we made do. Da and me. When Da passed it didn't take too long for the do-gooders to come and shift me from my home. I couldn't do at the workhouse, so I escaped to the streets. There's lots of us so I didn't feel so bad. I ain't never been proud of the thieving; but I only took from those what's could afford it. I know my Da would be shamed to see me now. My Da was an honest man, a man who took what life dealt him."

Well, it was very obvious to me that Thomas could never know the affect his story had on me. Still, there he stood, with his chin held up high. I could see there would be no whimpering or crying. Oh God, what if he started to cry. It was like the little man could read my mind. He straightened his shoulders, looking me straight in the eye.

It was clearly apparent that the smells from the oven of fresh baked bread and cakes were becoming too much for the lad. He stood there almost breathless waiting on my mercy. Eternity passed and came around again as he held my stare. Lily, was fidgeting in her usual way, being very distracting. I could see she was putting on a pretty show for our current visitor. I was also aware that Thomas was hard pressed not to laugh and thereby encourage her. I always succumbed to Lily and her antics, so I did allow a smile in her direction, noting that her little fingers were covered in icing and the strawberry filling. This kind of excitement never happened in our quiet end of the street so she was definitely enjoying herself. Oddly enough, I perceived that she seemed to put him a bit more at ease and he shifted his concentration back to me, who stood silently in front of him. I could feel him sizing me up. Probably the way he had done shortly before he decided I would be a good mark. To be successful at his current trade, he would have to be a fairly good judge of character. Well, everyone makes mistakes. His embarrassment was palpable, as the color rose in his face. If I really wanted to hurt the child, I could call the constable. He would then no longer be my concern. Or, I could have my husband, Hugh, return him to the workhouse.

My maternal instincts were strong at this time, and it was unmistakable that the boy had not eaten well recently, but although a thief I sensed a strong moral background. I glimpsed the same fire in his eyes and the quick intelligence of my beloved husband. I felt the new babe stir deep within me. What if this was my son, I mused?

The room stayed hushed, as distracted, my thoughts drifted on my dream of a son for Hugh. A son for Hugh, the thought brought a sudden shiver of warmth tingling down my spine. What a blessing to be able to look twice into the same eyes of rich, warm mahogany. I envisioned Hugh taking the little one on his first ride, curls of golden russet bouncing in the breeze, my men off to face the world. I sighed as I remembered Hugh the day they met.

His back had been to me as he concentrated on the book he was reading. He was tall and I had admired the way his navy suit sat on his broad shoulders. I had noticed him on more than one occasion in the bookstore. Truth be told, since I had espied him, my visits to the bookstore had increased, much to my mother's consternation. I had confided little about my feelings, much preferring to privately savor the image I was building of this young man. I had moved closer to the shelf he was standing in front of and had drunk in his musky scent.

Having already picked my own book, I had opened it and was able to glance surreptitiously at him. As he read, I had admired his light brown hair that curled at the nape of his neck. He was tall, perhaps six feet I thought. I, too, was tall, especially for a woman, standing a full five feet and seven inches. My height had been a source of great agony as I was introduced to potential admirers I looked down to. Many was the handsome lad who had looked my way with admiring glances as I sat chatting, but they discreetly turned away the moment I gained my full height. It had occurred to me that this man need not notice me with my colorless eyes that had the audacity to change with the weather and my mutinous strands of mousy colored hair.

This ritual of following him in the store had been going on for weeks now and if he didn't say something soon I knew I would explode. I had determined this would be my last visit if he said nothing today. I had taken notice that he read books here at the store, but he rarely purchased them. He placed the books reverently back on the shelf. His long slender fingers lingered over the leather bindings. The books he read were of exotic places, Africa, India and the Far East. I purchased one and was swept away into the world of Genghis Khan and Marco Polo. I sensed a change in his stance and I looked up to find him staring directly at me. Here I thought I was being discreet. Truly startled at the intensity of his gaze, I had blushed to the roots of my head and had fumbled the book trying to bury my face in its protective cover. The book fell, binding open and we had both stooped to pick it up. As Hugh's hand covered mine, I had known, looking into his deep brown eyes; I had met the man I wanted to marry. I reveled in the memory of him asking permission to come calling.

Reluctantly I returned to the present, smiling a secret smile. I knew what I had to do.

"Okay, Thomas, Cook will see to your clothes. After you have bathed and eaten, I will make my decisions known." The relief was visible on Thomas' face. He managed to stammer out, "Thank you, mam".

While Thomas was in Cook's capable hands, I had taken Lily's hand and together we left the kitchen. Miss Abernathy was in the nursery waiting to receive Lily for her afternoon rest. Lily was curious about the boy, but I did not say anything about him and Lily knew better than to ask.

When Thomas was presented to me in the parlor, no one would have recognized him. His glossy black hair reminded one of coal from the mines he had worked in with eyes to match. He was small for eleven and gangly, his body not yet in tune with his age. Lily was not as inconspicuous as she seemed to think and I knew she peered slyly around the door that had not been quite closed.

The interview was brief, as I had already decided the boy's fate. "You are guilty of quite a serious crime young Master Thomas Hall." I paused for a brief moment to let the statement sink in, then continued. "You will work off your debt in service to my husband, Mr. Hugh Henley, learning your responsibilities from him. You also require tutelage. You will attend classes that are to begin for our daughter Lilyan. Help to Mrs. Fairchild, our cook, her household staff and Mr. Fairchild, our handyman, will also be expected. There is a room in the attic you may use and you will join the staff for meals."

The child had his pride, I had to give him that. But my heart skipped a beat when he replied, "I'm in your debt mam . . . Mrs. Henley. Thank you mam, I'll do me best, I'll make you proud." My daughter could not contain her excitement. In her seven-year-old mind, she had just inherited a friend, maybe even a big brother and she was thrilled beyond words. I knew she would be off to tell Hugh all of the day's events.

---

*L*ily came bursting into my private study, full of life and excitement. I had just been thinking of Emma and the book store. The image of a lovely girl with light brown hair popped into my head. I thought about her a lot during the day.

The birth of Lilyan had completed me. I had tried, unsuccessfully, to block out the memory of the terror I felt when Emma had delivered her. Then Elizabeth Anne came and the terrible, maddening wait for the cries that never came. I swore I'd never do that to my Emma again. Now a new babe was getting ready to test her strength once more. I was more than terrified. I had no need for others, only Emma. That the death of the small infant had left a scar on her heart was not in question. She seemingly had a spot to tuck such tragedies away in her womanly heart and move on. I never ceased to marvel at her strength.

I was pulled back to the present by the insistent tugging on my coat sleeve. I decided to make an effort to understand this latest excitement in my little Lilyan's life. Through Lily, I came to know the child Emma once was. It saddened me when I realized she would bounce from my knee forever, to seek love and protection from another man. I would lose her, but not Emma. My Emma would never leave me as others had. I never wanted to feel that lonely, helpless, or betrayed again. Not ever!

I again tried to focus on my little daughter but as usual, I found her excited chatter was muddled and confusing. However, I discerned that something had happened and my wife had decided on a course of action. That my daughter was obviously happy with whatever it was pleased me. Emma would tell me all about it shortly and it would make sense then. There were no secrets between husband and wife. "Not now Lily. You must go back up to the nursery before your mother sees you. There

8

you go lamb." Lily knelt on my lap and gave me a smacking big kiss. She slipped from my lap and gave me a conspiratorial look. She grinned at me and was gone. I could not restrain the chuckle that rose in my chest.

Emma entered the drawing room, sniffing at the air. My tobacco was made to my specifications and the aroma was sweet and tangy. I knew she liked the aroma of my pipe. I glanced up from my paperwork and smiled in true pleasure.

"Hello, my darling", I said as I rose to embrace her. Her fragrance filled me with desire.

"I take it some excitement has been afoot in the house today?" We both said, "Lily" at the same time and laughed.

"Well", started Emma, "I was the victim of a pick pocket this morning".

"Oh, my darling, are you alright? Did you summon the constable?"

"Yes . . . I'm quite alright and there was no need for the constable."

"But . . ." I stammered.

"No, no, it's quite alright. He's just a boy. I have spoken with him and Mrs. Fairchild has fed him, which he needed badly, and cleaned him up. His name is Thomas Hall and it occurred to me he could work off his debt, here in service to you. Would you like to meet him now?" I did not miss the glint in Emma's eyes.

"Lily was quite taken with the lad. Of course, I'll meet with him. I'm sure I could use the help," I agreed. If Emma wanted help for me then help I would get it, anything Emma wanted I would do. Emmaline released herself from my embrace with a quick but tender kiss, went to the door, and brought Thomas Hall in for his final inspections.

Emmaline had been right. It did not take Thomas long to catch on and adapt to life at the Oakley. He was fast becoming a fixture in our household. Everyone enjoyed his quick wit and his offer to assist with any task, however menial. Under Miss Abernathy's tutelage, Thomas and Lilyan thrived on the lessons. It was rewarding to see him dropping his guard as he began to feel safe and secure once more.

The months passed, and the time came when Emmaline would deliver the new babe. I was so anxious and tried valiantly to meet her every need. She had taken to her bed early in the morning and the doctor was called. Cook was in an uproar, trying to keep up with the doctor's orders for hot water and clean linens. Of course, Emma and cook had had these things organized a long time ago, but cook liked to issue more orders.

Lilyan's birth had been without serious mishap. However, I could not shake my trepidation as I remembered the birth of our second child, Elizabeth. Elizabeth was buried in the churchyard by the south doors of St. Jude's. I paced up and down, miserable with worry.

Late that evening the baby's cries rang out. A short while later the Doctor informed me we had a son. The grave expression on his face and somber voice alerted me to a serious problem. My Emma was not well! She had been well through most of the pregnancy. Occasionally though, Hugh had been very concerned when he would see the dark circles under her eyes. She had always laughed and said she was fine, excited to be having our child.

"Come Hugh, your wife wishes to see you. I'll not lie to you, it's grave, and she'll probably not last the night. She's too weak."

I took the stairs two at a time, forgetting all else except my need to see Emma, my beloved wife, lover, friend and mother to our children. The tears were already flowing as I approached our bed. Her eyes were closed in exhaustion. She was as pale as the sheet she lay on. I took her hand into my own and bent over to kiss her gently on the forehead. Her eyes fluttered open and we looked at each other for a few moments, each knowing the horrible truth.

"Oh Hugh, he's a beautiful boy, our son . . . Andrew Charles Henley. He has your eyes. Love him Hugh, and Lilyan. And never ever forget how much I have loved you." As she watched the tears flow from his grief stricken eyes she whispered, "Kiss me".

"My darling, I love you Emmaline Henley, with my whole heart." My heart shattered as I bent to our mutual desire and kissed her, sharing one last taste of each other. I held onto her hands tightly, struggling desperately with the pain of my breaking heart, "Don't leave me . . . Emma . . . please." I swallowed, trying to instill in my last ounce of energy. As that failed, I selfishly prayed that the Lord take me instead.

Then time stood still. Her hands lost the strength to hang on. Her eyes closed on a sigh as the hand of death came to take her to whatever lay beyond. My heart turned cold as the warmth of life ebbed from the hand I held. I could not face life without her. I stayed by her side for a long while. Finally, the doctor came back into the room and placed his hand on my shoulder. I resigned myself to my fate and whatever else would sustain me. Slowly I relinquished her hand, squared my shoulders, and rose. I glanced at the crib where our son slept, left the room, and never entered again.

And now there was her son . . . Andrew.

~ *Bryn* ~

The Letter, Missouri 1868

A letter for the Henley's was rare. It was addressed to my father, Mr. Andrew Henley, so Jake took advantage of the excuse to ride out to our ranch hoping to sneak a visit with me. While I was courteous to all of them, none seemed able to capture my interest. Although appreciative of his effort on my father's behalf, unsurprisingly, I offered Jake no encouragement to stay and visit. Discouraged, he only water and rested his horse before heading back out on his journey home.

I enjoyed being on my own, finding peace in the quiet solitude. This was the time in the day when my father and three brothers were still out in the back forty but would soon be making their way back in with empty bellies. They were always rowdy and it took time for them to settle from the day's work. The routine had been long established as the horses were tended and fed and then, after Drew made multiple attempts to drown Rob in the watering trough, they would become the civilized men they thought themselves to be; finding their places at the table. Drew was not always around these days. He helped out during the busy times on the ranch, but his heart was in town where he was starting up his own livery and stable business. My eyes caressed the burnish oak that shone with age and care. My father had built the table when they moved from the soddy into the homestead. The table was oak, its warm ivory color reflected in the years of wax and elbow grease. The table was my Mama's pride and joy and she never ceased to be grateful for its existence. She had watched Papa as he cut the planks and lovingly put them together. The fittings were perfect, not a rough edge to be seen. The knots that were the very essence of the tree stood out in stark splendor dark and aged. I cherished these moments. I loved to watch Papa, with his hair combed back and his big rough hands, as they came together for the grace.

The letter for Papa had arrived out of the blue. I missed Mama at this moment however, her absence could not be helped. She was away helping my eldest brother, Josh, with his two sick children. I was not expecting her to be home any time soon.

There were usually chores to finish up at this time of the day, but for once, I seemed to be more organized than usual and I found myself with nothing to do. It was hot and stuffy in the house even though the windows were open. The air was sultry and stagnant, resisting any silent beseeching to move as the relentless late summer heat bore down. My blouse stuck to my over-heated skin and the tendrils of hair that broke loose from my braid made wet ringlets that clung to the side of my face. There was no escape from it, only the shade of the porch. I sought the respite of the porch swing. Mama had seen a similar swing on one her travels into town and insisted one be built for our own front porch. I settled myself on the cool planks of wood and leaned back. I lifted the weight of my hair from my neck and basked in the breeze created by the back and forth motion of the swing.

I kept turning the letter over in my hands as I swung, pondering over the contents; my fingers luxuriating in the feel of the heavy cream color velum. There was a barely discernible postmark. The letter was weather worn; it had traveled a great distance. Mail was not uncommon, but word from the outside world was rare. Once a month, Papa would make the trip to town for supplies. My mother, Sarah, always made sure she ordered at least one book for the library in the front parlor. Mama and Papa were very proud of the books they had collected over the years. Mama also liked to look over the new fashion magazines, knowing they were out of date, but for her, the pleasure was in the vision. I turned the letter reverently one more time. The neat even letters held me spellbound; I didn't recognize the handwriting.

Succumbing to the heat, I unwittingly closed my eyes dozing and woke disconcerted with a sore neck and stiff back. "So much for the comfort of the porch swing." I said to myself as my neck had become wedged in the picketing. Sagging back into the seat, I massaged the soreness out of my neck. My fingers lazily made their way through the riotous mass of damp curls surrounding my face. The wild curls came from Papa. His often looked just like the picture I had once seen of a lion's mane. I had my Papa's hair, but while his was a beautiful warm brown with russet highlights that danced in the sun, mine was the washed out color of a wretched field mouse. I wished I had my mother's golden tresses. Not being one to lament on the things nature had given me and I could not change, I lifted both arms in a soothing, long stretch. I looked down at the outline of my rather long, gangly legs as the material of my skirt draped and fell to expose the white of my petticoat. I pointed my toes and once again lifted the braid from my neck. The air quickly cooled the sweat that trickled down my back. Pulling myself to a sitting position, I stared across the veranda to the small area of grass that had withered to a dry dirt bed under the scorching, summer sun. The scent of Mama's roses, still in bloom, wafted gently in the stillness of the afternoon. They were my mother's pride and joy and took a lot of hard work to keep them alive. I got up; leaving the swing to sway in my wake as I made my way to the railing. I leaned over, took a bloom in my hand, and plucked it. The petals were so delicate and yielded nothing to the unpredictable climate of Missouri. The scent would be welcome in the house. Shielding my eyes to the lowering sun as it prepared to bid the world a good evening, I picked enough to make a small bouquet. Evening was starting its shift as the daylight faded. It was finally starting to cool down. I stood, still a bit sore and tried to shake off the last vestiges of sleep. Not prone to napping in the afternoon, I didn't feel particularly rested. It was time to check supper preparations. Still in a stupor, I made my way to the kitchen, thankful for the years of my mother's training that fed my compulsion to prepare as much as possible in advance. As I got to the kitchen I looked in horror as I realized I had forgotten the cooling pies. They were on the window ledge and were a long time cooled. I rescued them to the pie safe, as the dinner table with no pies would not go unnoticed. My mother made the better pies with light flaky pastry, but mine would do in a pinch. Circling around once more I picked up a cloth and entered the dining room. The table was set, but as was my custom I fiddled with each of the place settings, straightening forks and polishing the knives. I had made a beef stew. I loved preparing the meat, and the vegetables, it gave me time to think. The dry sink had a window that looked out toward the mountain in the background. It wasn't really a mountain but it created enough of a show as to make the ranch feel secluded. Isolated in a way, I thought. It did not bother me, but was more of a fascination; no doubt because I did not feel isolated. There was so much to keep me busy I had little time to contemplate anything else really. Well, except when I pulled one of the books down from the shelf. Then I was really lost to this world and found myself in the next. The scent from the stewing meat permeated the house from the summer kitchen. I set the roses in Mama's favorite crystal vase in the parlor, the Henley women's favorite room in our home. The room always caught the first stirrings of a breeze in the summer and boasted the small library that we had taken pains to collect over the years. I ran my hands over the treasured volumes. Some of these had belonged to my Grandfather Henley, given to me by Aunt Lily. I never really understood the reluctance with which my father allowed these books to be added to our collection. My father never touched the books of his father. I took down one of my favorites and tried to settle on the settee. This was a book about the Orient, but what attracted me was not the content, but that it always dropped open to the flyleaf and the inscription written there,

"*To my darling Emmaline,*

On the occasion of our marriage, I will share the world of these books and beyond with you all the days of my life.

Eternally yours,
Hugh"

The inscription was faded from the gentle pressure of fingers tracing the words across the page; my own fingers had gently followed the pattern many times as well. I held the book comfortably in my lap and gazed off into nowhere. I was a daydreamer and I knew my family despaired of my flights of fancy.

For the second time today, I heard the sound of horses approaching. Carefully replacing the book, I picked up my wiping cloth and returned to the porch, giving a casual glance at my makeshift bed. There sitting on the swing, where I had lain it down, was the letter. I picked it up and put it in my apron pocket.

Earley, our foreman, and the boys rode past and touched the brims of their hats in friendly salute on their way to the stable. Father, Drew, and Rob rode straight up to the front porch. Each dismounted with the fluid grace of men who were one with their mounts, each hitching his horse to the post. For me, it was wonderful to see them together again. Rob's absence over the last nine years had been hard on the whole family, but especially my parents. Rob's arguments with Papa about the ranch had been emotionally shattering. Although difficult at first, Rob's return would make things right.

Rob had been gone for nearly half of my life, as I had been nine going on ten when he left. Papa, Drew and me were surprised and delighted when he suddenly showed up just the week before. As was his way, Papa took the high road, thinking it wiser not to make reference to Josh's reaction to the news of his twin's return. Rob was taken back into the hearth like the Prodigal son; though sometimes Papa could be caught watching Rob with an expectant look; a look often mirrored by Rob. Drew, too young to remember the arguments, welcomed Rob home without judgment.

I came out of my reverie as Papa handed me the dropped cloth. I remembered the letter held in my pocket. "Jake rode out earlier today with this for you." I smiled making no attempt to hide my excitement.

He took the envelope I held out to him, rubbed his callused fingers over the velum, and without so much as a glimpse, tore it open. I was surprised he could be so rash! As he read, Papa wiped the back of his hand across his brow, then slowly his fingers circled down to rub his bottom lip. When he had finished reading, he closed his eyes and tipped his hat back on his head. His hand dropped to his side still holding the letter. Dust clung to his large frame, fresh from his day out on the range.

The wide expanse of his chest still heaved slightly from the exertion of the long day and the ride back in. His broad muscular shoulders slumped slightly as he seemed to quietly resign himself to the contents of the letter. No one moved.

*S*lowly I turned, handed Drew the letter, brushing my hat against my thigh, mounted the stairs, passed Bryn, and settled on the porch swing. All eyes were upon me as I took my seat shifting into a more comfortable position. I understood myself to be a big man by anyone's standards having been told so all of my life. To my knowledge, no one ever crossed me, and I'm not ashamed to admit it would be to their peril if they did. I taught by example, day in and day out. I had my principles and stood by my decisions. In an earlier life, I had been a guide and frontier trader before I met my Sarah and settled down. People, in these parts, depended on me almost as much as my family did. Especially in times such as these, when water was in short supply and the grass was dried up with its roots cemented in the ground. I had been through droughts like this before and would see them through it again. With the majority of water running through my land, I went out of my way to ensure that none of the ranchers, or their cattle went without, averting a range war. I have always endeavored to be a steward of the land; including the wild country which surrounded us.

I shifted once again in my seat, settling my hat in my lap, I gazed into the far distance trying to take in the enormity of this request and all of its potential hazards for me and my family.

"Read it out loud, son. It's no secret, y'all know soon enough."

Drew unfolded the letter and began to read.

"Dear Andrew,

You will be astonished to hear from me, of this I am certain. I must convey news to you and am unsure how you will receive it. I have faith that despite your differences, you will, perhaps, want to know that your father has passed."

With that shock, I noticed that Drew hesitated to look at me and averted his gaze. Confused, Bryn moved across the porch and sat down beside me. She slipped her arm through mine and our fingers entwined, as was my comfort to her when she was little. Time stopped in that fraction of a second, I nodded at Drew to continue. In the wake of the stunned silence, the only sound was that of Drew's voice as it picked up again revealing the contents of the letter.

"We were in India at the time of a cholera epidemic. There has been a cremation, as is their custom. I was instructed by your father to finish his business, deliver his securities and instructions to Miss Lilyan and yourself. Andrew your presence is strongly requested.

With this letter to you, I have completed much of my assignment. The Wallace's anticipate my arrival shortly. If all goes well, I intend to be with Miss Lily and Mr. John to celebrate the anniversary of your father's eightieth birthday, August 18, 1868. If you are not present on the eighteenth, I have been instructed to divest to Miss Lily alone.

I, as you know, am aware of the difference of opinion you had with your father, however, I believe it would be expedient for you to join us. Trust me Andrew. Please come.

Your obedient servant,
Thomas Hall

~ *Bryn* ~

he heat of the day was forgotten. As Drew's last words faded away, the silence was deafening. I looked at my brothers, waiting for one of them to react to what we had just heard. Rob was pale and speechless, that was a first. Drew was also silent. Men!

"Well, will you go?" my blunt question broke the silence.

"That's something your mother and I will have to decide," Papa answered.

Drew finally shook his head and responded, "I'll take the horses to the barn. Earley can rub 'em down while I saddle fresh ones."

Papa calmly interrupted, "No. No need to rush. Nothing'll change by tomorrow and there's no point alarming everyone by riding over after dark. Tomorrow will do just fine. We'll all tend our own horses."

He rose and started across the veranda, then turned and told me, "Serve up supper, Bryn. The men are hungry."

With that said, he descended the steps and took the letter from Drew. He carefully refolded it, inserted it back in the envelope, and tucked it in his breast pocket. They retrieved their horses, moving off toward the stables.

Papa would say nothing to anyone outside the family until he and Mama had discussed the situation and reached their decision, so I knew I wouldn't miss anything while they were in the barn. He wouldn't make a move without Mama, but September 18th was not far off. I stood and made my way back to the kitchen. As I served up, I was anxious about sitting at the dinner table as though nothing was the matter.

Father, Drew and Rob followed closely behind. Dinner went much better than I expected. Conversation was always lively, but remained civilized. Mama would not tolerate cussing at the dinner table, or in the house for that matter; not that Mama need have worried. Table discussions tonight were centered on the tracking and killing of a large cougar that had been plaguing the herds. After dinner, everyone thanked me and took their coffee out onto the porch to catch the evening's cooling breeze and have a smoke.

Everyone, that is, but Earley. He helped clear the table, as he sometimes did when mother was away. Earley was a peculiar man in a way, wiry but strong. His bushy eyebrows and long mustache had always been a source of entertainment to me. I would imagine him in any number of scenes from unsavory... making a run for the border at Mexico, to my hero rescuing me from some unknown source of danger. When I was a child, he had always told the most exciting bedtime stories when mother would allow him to tuck me in. He would sneak me little biscuits which is how I earned the nickname "Biscuit". Like my father, he was not a man to mess with, but was blessed with compassion that only a few were fortunate enough to witness. Papa trusted him with his life and had been rewarded for his faith numerous times. That was where his nickname came from – he had always shown up "early" enough to help. Earley had had the first gift of land from Papa. Unfortunately, his wife passed during the birth of their first child and their child died with her. He never married again.

Earley had been there all my life. As we cleared away the last of the supper dishes from the table, I wondered if he might hold answers to some of the questions building up inside. Earley has that sixth sense that all cattlemen need to survive. This time he even stayed to wipe the dishes. He knew something was amiss, but waited, as always, for me to make the first move.

"Tell me about my Grandfather Henley."

Earley paused, looked down at the dish he was drying and in his usual, unhurried style said, "What about him?"

"Everything!" I exclaimed. I snapped my mouth shut, not wanting to appear as though I was catching flies.

"Ask your pa," he responded with a straight face. He was not trying to provoke me, however I didn't know I was poking a hornet's nest and was going to get stung.

"Oh Earley, I can't. Not now at least. A letter arrived today for him. After he read it, he had Drew read it aloud. I know he'll tell you all about it. I thought both his parents were dead. I thought Aunt Lily and Uncle John were the only relatives we have on his side, but the letter said that Grandfather Henley died recently in India. The letter spoke of an estrangement between Papa and Grandfather Henley. He's been asked to go to Aunt Lily's to meet a Mr. Hall. I'm not sure how he's feeling right now. He won't talk to me about my grandfather until he's spoken with Mama. Why didn't we see our grandfather or at least know he was alive? We could have written. You've known Papa forever! Tell me. Please . . . I need to know!" I wrung out the cloth in my hand and started to wipe the side board.

Earley finished drying the dish he held; then put the towel on the rack, the dish on the sideboard and went over to the table. He lifted his right foot up onto the chair and with accustomed ease, reached into his pocket for his tobacco pouch. He tamped the tobacco into his pipe while watching me closely - taking stock of my mood and the ramifications of anything he could tell me. He lit the pipe, leaned his elbow on his knee and drew several times. The tobacco smoke curled up around him in a familiar dance. Leisurely, he took another draw and finally responded.

"You want to know Biscuit, not need. Learn to know the difference." After his instruction, he paused to take another long draw before continuing. "I've known yer Pa a long time, that's a fact, but not forever," he chuckled. "Yer Grampa had ships, sailed 'em out of England all over the world. Yer Aunt Lily and yer Pa are the only two children. Yer Grandma, yer Pa's mother, died young and they say yer grandfather never got over it. I know yer Pa's got no interest in boats. When yer folks settled out here, that was the last time yer Pa and grandfather spoke."

"Did you ever meet him . . . yourself?" I asked.

He paused to watch the smoke gather into little clouds above his pipe before answering.

"Once, back east with yer Pa, I went to dinner at yer grandfather's. Had the pleasure of meeting yer Aunt Lily for the first time. "Fore we left, I saw Miss Lily and yer grandfather on the street. Tipped my hat to them, she nodded and smiled, but yer grandfather looked right through me. Reckon that's all."

From the look on his face I knew he had said all he was going to say on the subject. As I had done so many times in my childhood, I threw my arms around him and whispered my thanks in his ear. I kissed his cheek, and he completed the familiar routine by patting my shoulder before breaking the embrace. He made his way to the front porch while I did the final clearing away. Shortly after, I heard the men thank Papa for their dinner and leave for the bunkhouse. I could now move out to the porch myself. All was quiet. I stood in the doorway as I had so many other summer nights and watched the men of my family sitting, relaxing. Papa rocked, comfortable in his favorite chair with his head leaning back and his eyes closed. His hands rested on his chest, fingers intertwined. He looked relaxed and peaceful with his long muscular legs crossed straight out in front of him. His feet kept rhythm to a tune playing in his head and the chair rocked steadily with it.

Drew sat on the stairs by Earley, as was their habit. Rob, moonlight dancing off the red streaks in his dark hair, was lounging on the rail, his back resting on one of the pillars. He watched our father intently. For a brief moment, it seemed as if Rob had never left. It was, I was sure, because Josh often held that exact same pose.

Though they had been apart these last nine years, they were twins. They both favored our father's build; tall, lean, and strong. Rob favored Papa with his dark brown hair and deep chestnut brown eyes that carried the weight of the world inside them. Josh's coloring reflected Mama with soft blue eyes and strawberry highlights in corn silk hair that caught the sparkle of the sun and the sheen of the moon. Josh was the quiet twin while Rob was more gregarious. Their coloring and verbosity were the only differences. They had been inseparable best friends. My heart swelled with love for Rob at this moment. It had taken a lot of courage to come home and I was encouraged that the hard feelings between the men in the family might finally be resolved.

I sat in mother's rocker that was side by side with father's. I was contemplating the letter and how I felt about the secret father had kept. The coming of night had cooled the air to a level that was tolerable. I listened to the crickets making that rickety noise that never seemed to stop. There was a scampering noise under the rose bush, no doubt a mouse that was looking for a way in. I hated mice. I was alright with spiders and other critters but mice made my palms sweat and my heart race. The stars overhead were magnificent. The dark ink went on forever, dotted with the sparkling lights.

How propitious that Rob had returned just before this tragedy. He had ships of his own now and was doing well . . . our grandfather had had ships. As far as we knew, Rob had no need to return to the family fold, but here he was. That Papa was pleased was obvious, but they had still not been enlightened as to the real reason behind Rob's sudden reappearance. He was obviously not a man at peace with himself. He had been home for barely a week and he rarely put more than two sentences together. At first, I could honestly admit that it was nice to see Rob speechless. A quiet Rob was not my brother though, and now I longed for the return to the constant banter, arguments and teasing that I remembered from my childhood. Josh was sometimes at them, teasing and taunting; but Rob had always been a source of merriment and irritation. He was always after Drew and me mercilessly. Now his dark brown eyes had clouded over; he remained isolated and quiet. I took it upon myself to bite the bullet and asked "What have you planned?"

Father glanced my way; obviously, he had been enjoying the quiet. His eyes told me patience Poppet. I shuddered inwardly thinking, "When will I ever learn to hold my errant tongue?"

At last he spoke, "We'll ride to Josh's tomorrow morning. You boys . . . y'all go early, catch Josh in case he wants to head out. Bryn and I'll follow at sunrise. Earley will take the ranch."

Drew and Rob nodded their agreement.

"Good thing you're back son . . . whole family'll be together tomorrow. Earley, we best make some plans tonight before settling down."

Earley's nearly imperceptible nod was his agreement. He and Papa rose and walked out towards the barn. My brothers were disinclined to talk, so I decided to turn in for the night.

I was sure I would never get to sleep with so many plaguing questions. I didn't understand how my parents and Aunt Lily could ignore our grandfather's existence all these years and not a word. He must have been so lonely; my family was always so loving. How could they have been so cold? How could they exclude him? And Rob . . . so withdrawn, so changed from the brother I remembered and loved.

I slept the moment my head hit the pillow.

I slept well, surprising myself that I had not dreamed of the strange letter. I understood myself well enough to know that I had an over active imagination. The aroma of coffee stirred me to action as I pulled myself from my cozy blankets. I shivered slightly as my bare feet touched the finished wooden floor. It was very early and, to be honest, I was very tempted to crawl back into my little cocoon. As I washed and dressed in my riding clothes, I mulled the letter over in my mind. There were a lot of questions to be answered. Papa was keeping something to himself, and when he set his mind to something, nothing was going to change it. The stairs creaked with each step I made. It was virtually impossible to move around the house without being heard. I could hear the deep murmur of voices below. Papa and Earley were moving around in the kitchen, no doubt discussing cattle. When I made my appearance, Papa placed a warm mug of coffee in my hands. I packed some jerky in my saddlebag to eat on the way. The horses were saddled and hitched to the post at the front porch. Less than half an hour after I had risen, we were on our way; the dawn just coming over the horizon. The sun was peeking above the mountain in the distance. Not a mountain, by pure definition, but the folks in the area referred to it as such. It promised to be another warm day. The dust from the horses hooves hung in the still air, taking its time to float back to the baked earth. It was still a good day for a ride though. They would not be pushing the animals beyond their limits of endurance. Some grass was still growing, being very hearty, although sparse which was not unusual at this time of year. The path we were following was rocky and pebbly which presented a threat to the horses, so we travelled carefully.

I glanced at Papa a short distance from home and noticed sweat already popping up on his brow. I had made this trip many times before, however this time I was looking forward to having Papa to myself for a while. This did not happen very often as there were so many things to be accomplished in a day. Papa and the men were gone all day, and then in the evening I had to share his company with my brothers and, quite often, some of the men if they stayed later. When we did spend time together though, it was in quiet companionship; however, today we rode in total silence. Each was feigning enjoyment of the beautiful day.

The sky was a dazzling azure stretching out before us like a heavenly lake. Questions about the letter kept niggling at the back of my mind, bidding to be asked, but Papa sat tall and unapproachable in his saddle. I loved my parents dearly but it seemed strange to think of Papa with a living father of his own, and about whom no one ever spoke. It was at the very least fascinating to contemplate how two people of the same blood would be unable to communicate with each other; on the other hand, I realized I was now in the same dilemma.

If Papa and Earley had taught me anything at all, it was to be honest; while my mother always emphasized discretion. The horses kept to a steady walk. It was frustrating that once at Josh and Beck's, I would still have more waiting to do. Tinker, my mare, sensed my disquiet and was becoming skittish. Each passing minute made it more difficult to bring up the contents of the letter. I needed to break the silence.

"I could have kept up with the boys. I love riding out here."

Father didn't rise to the bait.

"Papa . . . I spoke to Earley last night."

"Figured you would."

We slowed. He shifted his weight in his saddle, and glanced at me. That closed look from yesterday had reappeared in his dark brown eyes. From my perspective, they looked black. I worried whether acquiescing to my curiosity by bringing up the subject had been the right thing to do. I knew this tactic worked for my mother and as a woman of twenty, I was finally learning a bit of her mother's patience and feminine wiles. My hands tightened on the reins as father turned, straightened up and continued on. I followed, disappointed and frustrated.

Finally, he exhaled long and low and then spoke.

"Curiosity's not a bad thing, Poppet, but timing and patience are necessary with it to survive. We should wait for the boys, but you've managed to wait a good while. It's a woman's thing, this wanting to know right away. Your mother would be the same. The boys would wait; men do." His voice was flat and completely void of emotion. Having concluded his brief lesson he continued.

"You have a right to know, but there's not much to tell. My mother died when I was born. Apparently, my father had loved her very deeply. He loved Lilyan too . . . in his own fashion, but my father and I were never close. We've never seen eye to eye. I like wide-open spaces. I needed to have the land beneath my feet. He wanted me devoted to his business; in his shipping offices and on his ships. Above all Bryn, I love your mother and our family. After we settled out here, your mother and I wrote asking him to come for a visit. I thought if he saw us settled and happy . . . only Lily and John came. I've not seen him since."

That said, he picked up the pace again. We didn't have much further to go and rode in silence again, each lost in our own thoughts. For the moment, I would have to be satisfied. There were still questions clouding my mind. Father didn't look at me again, just rode on, keeping a little ahead of me. He needed space and so did I.

The sun was now up and it had proven to be just as warm as Earley had forecast. The house came into view first, the outline of the barn behind it. The house was similar to our own with a wide welcoming porch attached to the front. When the men cleared the wide break of land for Josh and Becky's house, they wisely left a few of the bigger trees to surround and shade the house, as they had done with my parent's home.

I knew it would be pleasantly cooler on the porch than inside. Josh had built summer cooking ovens outside and for the last part of our ride we could smell the delicious aroma of Becky's fresh baked bread and fruit pies. My mouth started to water at the thought of them. Becky, like mother, had the hands for pastry. She, too, had tried to share the "secret" with me, but to no avail. .

We had come in at a steady pace and Becky heard our approach, alerted to our pending arrival by Rob and Drew. She came out onto the porch to welcome us. She was surprised by the whole family's sudden appearance and as we neared we could see the worried look on her face. Josh must've heard too because just as Papa gave a greeting to Becky, Josh appeared by her side.

I couldn't imagine one without the other. Josh had known Becky all her life. They went to school and church together and whenever there were any social gathering, Josh was always with Becky. The Callaghans and Henleys had been good friends for decades. The day they were married, I remembered Josh standing tall and handsome beside Becky, with her emerald eyes smiling and her chin jutted forward. She met his gaze as they pledged their vows to one another. It had been a beautiful ceremony. They quickly built a home and settled down. Before the second year was out, Jared was born. Josh was there to proudly become a father. But shortly thereafter war broke out; Edward and Josh were already gone. Josh did return though and little Jessica was born ten months later.

When Josh married Becky, he gave me the one thing I had always wanted, a sister! Our bond as sisters had strengthened over the years and I loved her more than a blood born sister. There was no sign of Mama. No doubt she was with the children. Josh looked as concerned as Becky and, with good reason. People didn't travel all these miles, unexpectedly, unless there was a problem. Becky tipped her head and glanced at Rob as he and Drew returned to the front porch, but the focus of attention was on Papa. Becky got the welcomes over with and tried to usher us all into the house. Still we found ourselves standing on the porch unable to move now that we had reached our destination.

Becky broke the silence first.

"I've got coffee brewing and there's fresh bread and butter. The men can see to the horses; Bryn, Josh will take Tinker. Come help me serve up and we'll talk out here".

It was a good idea. It broke through some of the tension and gave everyone a few more minutes to collect themselves before the story began to unravel. When we returned with coffee, Papa was gone having announced he was going to find Mama.

"No use in telling a story twice when once will do. I want y'all here when we get back. Josh, you and Becky may wish to read this. The others have. We'll be back presently," had been his parting words to Josh. Josh had waited so he and Becky could read the letter together. After reading and some silent communication between them, Becky joined me on the porch swing.

Josh, with his arms crossed, leaned back against the front of the doorframe and returned Rob's challenging stare. Rob, had eased himself back onto the rail, leaning against a pillar with his arms crossed as well. Drew found his usual seat on the porch stair. Once the air settled a bit, while Papa was still gone, I told them what I had just learned. Our parents finally came back to the house with Jared and Jessica tagging behind. Mama made short work of embracing and accepting the prodigal Rob back. I was glad to see her again. It had only been a week, but I still missed Mama at home. I served up more coffee while Becky hustled Jessica upstairs for a nap. It had been an exciting morning for her with going to the creek and the added excitement of the family gathering. Tired from all the activity, she went without too much fuss. Jared was set up to play out front where the family could l keep an eye on him. "Our happy wanderer," was Becky's relevant nick name for him.

Papa squeezed mother's hand in his, took the letter from Josh and replaced it in his pocket. Becky finally came back downstairs. The family was all together for the first time in years. I knew by the look on Mama's face that the story was about to be told for the second time. Father cleared his throat and began to slowly unravel the story behind the letter.

~ Andrew ~

"There's been a letter from someone I knew a long, long time ago. His name is Thomas Hall and he is my father's butler. My father died recently in India. He was in shipping and always did very well with imports and exports, as well as traveled extensively. My father and I have not spoken in about thirty years. I don't know the details of his death, but I do know that Thomas, following the local custom had him cremated. All his papers are being taken to your Aunt Lily's and I've been asked to attend when Thomas arrives. Your mother and I have decided that we will go. We'll be away for the next little while, but I intend to be back for fall roundup. Before I go, I will have some requests of you boys."

After a quick glance at each of my offspring, I took Sarah by the arm and led her into the house and up the stairs to her room. I watched the sway of her skirts as she slowly climbed the stairs. She looked at me with all the expectations of a new bride and I was happy to oblige her. Such was the nature of our relationship.

~ Rob ~

They still really had not learned anything new beyond what was in the letter. Bryn, of course, broke the silence.

"Why was Grandfather Henley's existence a secret? I thought both those grandparents were dead. What else don't we know? Josh, you're oldest. What do you know? Did you know? Rob, you've traveled . . . you've even been to the Far East. What do we do?"

At Bryn's reference to my trip to the Far East, I nearly jumped out of my skin. Controlling myself, I closed my eyes and took a deep breath. For the second time in as many days, my mind replayed an interesting scene from my last trip. I, too, had been startled to find out that my grandfather was still alive and well. It had happened quite by accident. Certainly, nothing had ever passed my parent's lips, nor Aunt Lily's or Uncle John's either.

I had arrived in port in Calcutta and was booking a room in the hotel. A man had approached me just as I finished checking in.

"Excuse me, sir. Please excuse my being forward; however would your name be Henley, sir?"

"Who wants to know?"

"Forgive me sir. I'm startled as you look the very image of someone I knew a long time ago. I am Thomas Hall, sir, at your service," he said with a polite bow.

"And why do you want to know?"

"Please sir, first. You are a Henley?"

"Robert Charles Henley, if you must know."

As my name was listed on the hotel register, it would not be hard to work this puzzle out so I allowed the man this information.

"Oh, yes, the resemblance is startling. Yes, your eyes, your cheekbones, you have his stature and are tall like him as well."

"Look, I have business to attend to. Who are you and what are you talking about?"

I did not want to be rude but this annoying man was irritating me and I was thirsty, hungry, and looking forward to rest, tiring quickly of this verbal sparring.

"Quite so sir, I beg your pardon. Please come by the compound at two o'clock tomorrow. Is that convenient? You're Andrew's son here from Missouri now New Orleans. Serendipity, there is someone you must meet, and he you! Here is my card with the address." Having not met with a negative response to his request, Mr. Hall had tipped his hat, turned and left. I knew I had not given out any details and certainly not mentioned my father's name or my homes. I kept the appointment the following day, my curiosity being piqued. Nothing in my past though, could have prepared me for what would happen that afternoon.

Dhir answered the door of the compound when I knocked at the appointed hour. With a half bow and murmur, he indicated for me to follow. I was used to the deep intake of air when people first saw me. There are other tall men, I thought, but less so in this part of the world. Dhir led me to the center of the compound and through the house to the covered back patio. There I saw an old man sitting in a chair with his back to me. Dhir, heavily accented, announced, "Mr. Robert Charles Henley, son of Andrew."

I knew I had not yet given my name. How did these people know me? His father? What was their game? My guard was up, but I was unprepared for the shock as the older man, with a full head of white hair, stood and turned to face me. My blood drained and my knees went weak, as I stared into the mirror image of myself, fifty years from now.

"Welcome, Robert Charles Henley… grandson. Come, you've gone quite pale. Sit down; you've had quite a shock. I have had twenty four hours to reconcile this. Thomas, some single malt, please."

I sat and listened as Father's and Aunt Lilyan's young lives unfolded through the words of my grandfather and Thomas. We had several more visits before my ship set sail once more. On each succeeding visit, I learned more about, not only my father, but my grandfather as well.

Grandfather had also drilled me with questions about our family and my father. In the end, I told my grandfather I would return home. Now the old man was dead. What a shock! Fate had taken a decided turn. I need never have returned to this place I had once called home. As soon as the thought struck, I felt guilty. It was truly a pleasure to see my family once again. But on the other hand, it did not change the present circumstance I found myself in. Although welcomed home with open arms, my father was just as unapproachable as ever.

My thoughts rejoined the conversation, "You're right Bryn. It's a shock, but not something we can't handle. We're a family and all together. I'm sure they had their reasons and he'll tell us in his own time and his own way. Until then, we wait."

I stood then, addressing no one in particular, and announced, "I'll be with the horses."

That said, I vaulted the railing and left, for the paddock. I felt Josh's eyes follow my progress until I was out of sight but he stayed where he was.

Part Two
THE JOURNEY

Becky dipped her head so her hair might shield her, closed her eyes, pursed her lips and clenched her delicate hands in her lap, a few tears escaped before she swallowed and managed to regain control. I had never actually witnessed the strain on Becky brought on by the ravages of war and her brothers' estrangement. I found it difficult to keep my own emotions at bay.

Josh stepped out of the way and off the porch as Becky and I made our way to the kitchen and started cutting bread, cheese, and meat for the noon meal. Neither of us spoke, but soon the familiarity of work began to ease the tension surrounding us.

Papa had an uncanny sense of timing. Just as we were getting ready to call everyone to the table, the two of them appeared, mother following father gracefully down the stairs. It was always a pleasure to see them together. They sat down at the table as Becky and I served up the meal. In the ensuing silence, even the children were quiet, seeming to sense the sudden tension surrounding the adults. Everyone waited anticipating the opening comments. Father bowed his head in prayer,

"Thank you Lord,

As we gather together as a family and for the meal before us. Grant peace to your servant, Hugh Henley, grandfather to my children. Amen."

Papa took his time and looked each one of us square in the eye.

"Your mother and I have decided to go to Aunt Lily's together and I will be glad of her company. I feel Lily may need her support and I will try to make some sense out of all this. I have no sorrow over my father's death and only attend in support of my sister." He paused to look at each of his children again before continuing. "I feel I need to be there for her and I owe Thomas as well. It has been many years and I, for one, am not getting any younger. I will discuss with each of you what needs to be done. Bryn, your mother and I have decided that you will accompany us. We intend to go over the plateau to save time. I want to be back in time for roundup."

The family discussed several other topics, the anticipated changes in weather and how much longer the drought was likely to last. Despite the sorrowful reason for the journey, I was thrilled beyond words to be going. It had been several years since I had seen Aunt Lily. I pulled at the curls sitting on my shoulder imagining the changes Aunt Lily would see. I mulled over what to pack, what to do with my hair, and how to wheedle information about grandfather. My thoughts kept me busy the rest of the meal and all the way home.

Lying in my bed that night, I realized I had been so taken with the fact that there would be no argument about my going and was so absorbed in my plans, that I had completely ignored Rob and Josh and the strained silence around them. I thought how much of our father there was in Josh, moreover, Rob, his twin, so very different now. Usually the talkative one and always playing devil's advocate, Rob had been quiet during the family gathering. He barely said a word, seeming to agree with everything that was going on through little nods of his head and sideways glances at Papa. I could feel the distance between them and realized that we hardly knew him anymore. It made me sad. I could not stop the tears before I finally fell asleep.

Papa and Earley established the route we would take. The weather on the plateau could be fickle at this time of year. Yet with round-up coming around the corner, Papa remained adamant in his decision to go over the plateau, risk the passes and save precious time. All in all, he figured going this route would take six to eight days. We could all ride our own horses, Tinker would love it. None of us were new to pack horses and Mama and I were able to manage an arduous ride. Mama had made this journey before but I was just an infant at the time.

Mama and I packed Papa's bag. We had a good laugh then Mama insisted on packing a tie and his only store bought suit. It was carefully folded into my dress for packing. I was guessing there would be some fashion of funeral or memorial service for my grandfather. It was late when all was finally ready.

I felt sure I would be unable to sleep for the sheer excitement of it all. I drew back the curtains that had helped to block the heat of the day so I could open my window. I stuck my head outside and took in deep gulps of the fresh night air. The moon was at its quarter, casting little light into the impenetrable dark that surrounded our home. I could make out the shapes of the barns, but all of the livestock were at their rest and invisible to my gaze. I lay down in my bed folding my sheet to the side, cozying into the down filled mattress. I laid there staring up at the corner of my room. Although I could not see them I knew my clothes were neatly ordered and hung in the wardrobe Papa had built for me when I was but a little girl. The heavy twill skirt for everyday work around the ranch was hung up under the cotton shirt on the hook at the back of my door. I had left the curtains pulled back; I could see the night sky and all the stars. It took a few minutes, but soon I was day-dreaming deeply about the journey and the excitement that would surely follow.

The break of dawn seemed to come earlier than usual. I opened my eyes, resisting the urge to roll over and go back to sleep. I could hear Mama moving downstairs and no doubt, Papa was already out getting the horses ready. My feet touched the floor and I reveled in the feel of the cool planks of the wood flooring in my room. The floor was always cold; winter, spring, fall and cool in the summer. The rag rug I had made to save my tender feet was tucked under the bed waiting for the cool of autumn. I closed the curtains, readied for the day and slipped downstairs.

"Mornin' sleepy head, I was just about to come up and get you," Mama said as she gave me a hug.

"I guess Papa has us nearly packed and ready to go. I just want some coffee and then I'll go up and get dressed. I won't take too long, if my hair cooperates."

"Whether your hair cooperates or not, we'll be breakfasted and on our way in under half an hour," Mama declared moving, to stand by the stove with a spoon in the hand that was resting on her hip. I poured myself a coffee and hurried back upstairs to comply.

When I finally stepped out onto the porch, not quite half an hour later, the sun was not yet fully up. Earley and Papa were talking; they had brought the horses up to the porch. They already had the food bags hitched. Mother came out with the final saddlebags. I handed Earley mine with my toiletries in it. He shook his head as he looped it around Tinker's saddle horn.

Rob and Drew joined us on the porch. They had gone to town yesterday from Josh's and came home late. They telegraphed Aunt Lily letting her know that there were three of us on our way. My brothers were going to stay and help Earley while we were gone. Work never stops on a ranch, and now was when the fences needed attention. Fences took the men away for days on end, depending on where they were located. Rob was not happy with the turn of events, but had promised Papa he would not leave while he was away. I stepped off the porch and gave each of them and Earley a hug. I was eager to start and knew Father was anxious to get going too.

My parents rode together a little ahead of me. For the moment I was happy to be left on my own. The stars had faded and the fiery horizon gave way to the rising sun. They started at an easy pace; there was no need to exhaust the horses. Papa had already decided where we would set up our first camp the first night out and had a tentative plan for the rest of the trip, which should last six, perhaps seven full days. I stifled a yawn and stared around at scenery that I knew like the back of my hand. I never tired of the beauty of this part of the ranch. We would be on our own land for quite a while. In the blink of an eye, the sun was up with the foothill before us, casting a shadow down the length of the rise. Billowing clouds lazed along the edge of a brilliant blue sky, in no hurry to reach their nameless destination. They offered a glimmer of hope that rain was finally on its way to the parched lands, but not yet.

We continued to ride along with no worries other than when to stop to rest the horses. Time is endless out here. There is no beginning or end, it just loops around causing night to become day and back again.

We stopped for a noonday meal. Papa built a fire for coffee and Mama handed around biscuits. We ate in companionable silence, each storing up our own reserves. This was only the first day out. Papa very carefully extinguished the remnants of the fire, ever vigilant about the dry land and lack of rain. The ground was tinder dry and the cattle would be in serious trouble if rain didn't come soon. He and Earley had been keeping an eye on the height of the river that ran through our land. The drought was bad and neighboring farmers were getting desperate.

It was not easy for a woman to do this kind of journey by horse. The men were used to being in the saddle day after day. I rode every day and Mama rode most days, but not this kind of distance or this many hours in the saddle. The continuous jarring in the saddle was irritating me along my inner thighs. On the last privacy stop, Mama gave me some rendered fat to ease the red, rashy welts that covered my legs. The fat was very soothing and I was able to tolerate the hours in the saddle a little better. It was only the first day but the grease had made me less reluctant to get back on Tinker. Papa wanted us to be on our way so that we could have a few more miles behind us before dark. Finally, we crossed the river late in the day at the shallow ford, on the eastern border of our land and the gateway to the plateau.

~ *Andrew* ~

"**W**on't be long now, ladies. We'll set up camp just before dusk. The horses are tired and you gals look like you could use the rest too. I'll make dinner tonight for my girls."

I was concerned about their comforts, but Bryn wasn't sorry to be stopping and he could see by the look on Sarah's face she wasn't sorry either. When we finally stopped, Sarah got down off Gingerbread, her sorrel, and walked carefully over to the little stream for some fresh water.

It didn't take long to get dinner going. Simple fare: we had beans, bacon and biscuits and finished up with coffee. Bryn could remember many campouts with me, nothing fancy, I'd say, but it always tasted delicious.

The first day had been somewhat easier as we made our way across our land; land that had been cleared or foraged. Also the river had been easy to ford with the water levels being at their lowest. The horses knelt to drink long laps of the cool, clear water that ran in little rivulets over the occasional rocks and large pebbles.

The next day brought us onto the plateau. The terrain turned alarmingly rugged all at once and we found our pace slowed in natural response to the change in the landscape. The horses had to pick their way across the broken landscape. Although I was an expert rider, I was happy to see her remaining vigilant; a misstep or any injury could be a calamity. Earley and I were always after Bryn to pay attention when she rode. Her tendency to daydream could spell disaster.

~ *Bryn* ~

W e kept moving, the elevation changing quickly and now we were high up and approaching the first pass. This was all new territory to me. The view from up on the side of the mountain was beyond words. I had to look very carefully to catch a glimpse through the trees. Though often struggling to be acknowledged as a woman at twenty, I was secretly aware of feelings of comfort at having my parents nearby. The air was so fresh and clean that I felt invigorated; such a lovely change from the heat of the ranch. We rode along, making casual conversation. We were deep in the forest and my mother was naming the flora and fauna common in this area. The terrain was rough and dense, with the high canopy, rich in oak, hickory, maple and beech trees. The scent of fresh pine assailed the senses as the hooves plodded through the dense undergrowth. The pines were as old as time and they were tall; their tops picking up any change in the air around them. Then again some were no better than scrub, short and rangy. Mama noticed the bountiful azaleas. She stopped to pick them for drying, remembering what her mother had told her. Mama would use them to make a tea she knew to be good for chest colds. The mass of plants stood out on their single stems with the clusters of red berries forcing the stem to lean with their weight. Deer were plentiful this time of year but made silent passage around the travelers camouflaged against the forest rim. I joined her but was daydreaming while I picked, and was brought up short for bruising some of the leaves. It crossed my mind when I looked at Mama to apologize that she was looking a bit pale. Papa had also made comment before he journeyed on ahead to hunt some dinner and scout out a campsite for us close by.

Mama had a way with herbs. All of my life I heard the stories of recipes passing from one generation to the next. Mama nursed all of us through our illnesses and injuries, always knowing which poultice to apply or which tea to drink. My brothers and I would wrinkle our noses when she brought out the liniment. The foul aroma would permeate throughout the house. It was all purpose, what was good for the humans was good for the animals too; words of wisdom from Papa.

"Don't forget your shawl, Bryn" Mama reminded me. I had taken it off earlier in the heat of the afternoon.

Papa had gotten a fair piece ahead of us. I said as much to Mama. "Don't worry, we are separated at the moment but I am sure he will be back for us shortly."

We mounted and started back on the trail. We were following each other closely, when we both heard the occasional clap of thunder. The sun was now playing hide and seek with the dark cumulus clouds that had come out of nowhere. They were gathering quickly and the air became charged. Rain would soon be following, no doubt. Mama continued on at a steady pace, but I could sense her unspoken fear. The cacophony of sound that had followed us all day was now silent. It was very eerie. Where had Papa gotten off to?

I strained to listen. I felt the first chill of the evening breeze creep across the back of my neck. Mama looked at me, just as puzzled. We both called out together. There was no response.

"No need to panic. We're separated, but that's alright. He'll double back for us. We'll make camp here." I stated this with a calm I was not sure I really felt. We had one of the packhorses with us. Papa had the other. In consideration of just this kind of eventuality Papa and Earley always divided the gear between the horses - each always carried shelter, food and ammunition.

Our horse had the blankets, clothing, and medicine. Papa's held most of the food and large tarps. Quickly, we took stock of what we did have. It was getting darker by the minute. There were matches, coffee, biscuits and there was a small stream we had just passed for water. I had a rifle and ammunition; wild animals were a concern at the moment and the fact that it felt like it would finally rain did not help. While I watered the horses at the stream and staked them so they could graze,

Mama used our small tarpaulin to make a lean-to shelter with room for all three of us between some trees and boulders.

I also gathered kindling and wood together for a small fire and spare for tomorrow morning. The temperature had dropped in a matter of minutes making the fire imperative. Lightening now preceded the thunder and it was frighteningly close. The wind was picking up. I filled the skins with water for coffee. We ate biscuits and drank coffee. Not what we had been looking forward to. Papa could not have been successful with fresh meat for dinner or we would have heard the report of his gun. Mama and I ate in silence, neither wanting to worry the other with gloomy thoughts. I banked the small fire, as it was starting to drizzle. Papa was still out there and we would go looking for him in the morning. It would be dangerous to split up now. We bundled and curled up under the tarp, purportedly to sleep.

Something woke me. I looked around groggily and tried to move, but was so stiff and sore it was with great difficulty that I made it to a sitting position. Mama was sound asleep beside me. It had finally stopped raining. The damp cold was penetrating, so that I felt cold and numb to the bone. Was it the cold that had woken me? I didn't think so. I heard something move just outside the camp's edge. I froze and tried to stifle the scream that was seconds from my lips; carefully, I started to reach for my rifle.

"Sarah . . ." Papa crawled into camp. I lunged out from under our tarp and rushed over to help him. He slumped forward into my arms. "Sarah . . . "He was barely conscious. Mama woke to his call and was over to us in a flash. She never wasted words when action was required. The two of us struggled to get his large frame under the tarp. I put my saddle under his head and rebuilt the fire. There was blood still oozing from a cut above his right eye, and there was blood coming through his right pant leg. We had no idea how much blood he had lost. He was wet, cold and shaking with shock. Mama got him out of his wet clothes, assessed his injuries and wrapped a blanket around him to warm him up.

Once he looked fairly comfortable, Mama started in, "Andrew Charles Henley, you've got some explaining to do. Do you know how worried we were for you? And look at you . . . just look at you," but by now he was slipping off into unconsciousness, and she fell beside him and started to cry. I put a comforting arm around her, Mama, not usually one for self-pity, pulled herself together before he came to his senses. I watched carefully as she tended to his head wound and re-checked his leg and then the rest of him. The rain held itself at bay, giving us time to react. I put more wood on the fire and spread more tarpaulins to cover them, in case of more rain.

"The gash on his head is mostly bluster but his leg is badly sprained. Even now I can see how swollen it is and the bruising is starting to show. By the way he is moaning, I'm thinking his ribs are hurt too. Better to mend him while he's unconscious. Try to get two sturdy, straight pieces of wood. We'll use them to brace his leg."

"Is he going to be all right?"

"He'll do Bryn. Get the wood please and we'll give him a broth, I will make a tea from the azaleas we gathered today. Go dear, while I set some water to boil."

He was still lying there unconscious, quiet and pale, when I returned with the wood for splints. Mama had put a bandage over the gash on his head. I held him while mother gently arranged the sticks around his leg as straight as she could and set it. Then I helped her hold father up while she wound strips of cotton around his chest for his ribs. Thankfully, he only moaned and stayed in a twilight sleep while Mama ministered to him.

It was a long night. Together, Mama and I worked side by side; inside the cramped quarters provided by the tarp. We worked in shifts, partly due to exhaustion and partly due to space. He was now very warm to the touch and we knew a fever was upon him. He tossed and turned his head with abandon. Every moan was agony for us as all we could do was watch. Mama had given him some laudanum, from the medical bag, to soothe him, and then patiently held his head in her lap urging trickles of herbal tea down his throat. He finally settled into a more even sleep by the time the sun was just coming over the top of the plateau. Mama was dozing peacefully with her head down on her chest. Unfortunately, she was used to this, having nursed all of us at one time or another and having just cared for Jared and Jessica. I managed to get in a few more hours of fitful sleep, but was groggy in the mid-morning. I got up

46

slowly and restarted the fire, then checked the horses. Sometime during the night, Phantom, Papa,s horse had found his way into camp. My reaffirmation of faith came when I saw the supply horse had followed him. Both appeared to be no worse for wear. I tied them to a tree with the others. I stood, turning in a circle to take in the whole sight.

Both of my parents were deep in exhausted sleep, five horses needed tending, firewood needed to be collected and food prepared. My nerves were taught like the wool on the spinning wheel in the parlor. My eyes blurred with un-spilt tears of helplessness and fear. My senses heightened in a way they never had been before. The gravity of the situation was obvious. We were in trouble. The horses were blowing and stamping in agitation. I could hear the occasional rumble of thunder again in the distance. I was chilled through; it was cooler at the higher elevation. A few weeks later and I would feel the need for my heavy wool coat and my fur lined bonnet. It was too soon for snow, but Papa knew thunderstorms up here were just as treacherous.

Now a watery sun was popping in and out of black tumultuous clouds. They lay so low I thought for a moment I may be able to poke my hand into one and swirl it around until it just disappeared. I continued to look at the clouds, trying to control the bitter gall that kept floating up from my stomach. In my heart, I knew it was imperative to control my growing panic. The surest way to disaster was panic! We needed proper shelter too, and quick! I found myself remembering important survival lessons from Papa and Earley. I steeled myself for the next step and brought myself back under control. Looking behind, I knew clearly we had come too far for us to go back to the ranch. In any case, that was out of the question, I would not even consider leaving Mama alone with Papa in such a tenuous condition.

Mama and I needed to gauge our situation. I went over to rouse her. She moaned and would not wake.

"Mama?" I felt a cold wave of terror run down my back when I looked at her, pale and sweating. I felt her forehead; she was burning up with fever. She had been pale and exhausted the last two days. Now I had genuine concern that she may have what the children had had. I did not try to wake her further. The rolls of thunder were getting louder and closer. With each new clap, my world shook with the terrifying horror of reality hitting me. I realized I was now in charge of our situation. Slowly, I stood up and tried to clear my head. I needed a plan. I shifted into action, as I realized the horses were becoming much more agitated. I swore I'd be soaked before I lost those horses and I needed proper shelter and nourishment for my parents as well.

~ *Lily* ~

I could not contain myself as I stood waiting for the train to pull into the station. The platform was full of other people, some families, some single, waiting patiently. It was beyond me to stand completely still, I fidgeted with my reticule. I had inspected its contents at least fifty times. I pulled at my satin gloves, wiggling my fingers and moving the fabric up and down my hand. My bonnet had a wide front brim edged with ribbon and lace protecting my delicate, some said porcelain skin from the harsh realities of the sun. It was open at the back allowing for the sweep of my hair. The ringlets that framed my faced were a dubious blessing. My husband, John, was used to my uncontrollable bundles of energy. He smiled down at me, his top hat sitting at a rakish angle. The whistle announced the train's imminent arrival from several miles off; the steam jetting from the stack visible in the distance. The power of the engine was awe inspiring. Three more blasts from the whistle and then the steam rose around the gigantic wheels as the engineer started to apply the brakes. I thought the train would never stop as the engine passed them in the middle of the platform, the engineer bringing the huge locomotive to a well-timed stop just opposite to the end of the platform. The engineer had his hat off waving it out the side window. The brakes screeched causing hands to rise up to cover sensitive ears. The steam hung in the air as the brakes were released and the big coal engine clank and clicked as it started to cool. John stood beside me holding my arm helping to temper my excitement.

"He'll get here with the train and not before Lily, be patient." John was chuckling as he uttered the remark.

"Oh John, I know he will, but the anticipation is killing me. It's been so many years since I've seen Thomas. I want to know all about what happened in India. Poor Father, I feel so guilty not having seen him in so long. Should I have tried harder with him on Andrew's behalf? Could Thomas and I have influenced Father?" I had kept up with my father through letters, but even though I had tried, I had never been able to initiate reconciliation between my two Henley men. Sadly, now I knew it was impossible.

John and I stood our stead waiting for the train to stop. The steam and smoke from the engine dissipated in the mild breeze and the track was once again clear for everyone to see. The platform was crowded. St. Louis was a busy terminal for people, mercantile goods and livestock. I thought it was just marvelous that people could travel so quickly, in a matter of days from the east coast. I enjoyed living in these modern times. After what seemed to be an eternity, people finally started to disembark and I stood on my tiptoes making a valiant attempt to see around the other people crowding the platform.

"There he is John, I see him. Thomas! Thomas!" my excitement as always was abundantly clear to those around me. I prompted many smiles as I made my way down the platform to greet Thomas with John in tow. John knew the wisdom of giving me my head, just following for the moment. Thomas caught sight of me just in time to set down a small travelling valise and brown leather satchel. I flung myself into his open arms and reached up to kiss his cheek.

"Miss Lily, how very good it is to see you again. It's been much too long. Mr. Wallace," he acknowledged holding out his hand. John and Thomas exchanged warm handshakes and then Thomas took control as he always had. He shifted to pick up his bags.

"I must go to see about the rest of my baggage, where would be a good place to meet up with you?" He enquired.

"Do you need our help?" John offered.

"No, no, I'll be fine. I've been doing this for so many years now. Let me do this bit of business and then we can visit. Shall I meet you at your carriage?" With a nod from John, Thomas turned towards the baggage being unloaded as John steered me to the carriage to wait.

~ *Thomas* ~

I had a vital reason for wanting Lily and John to wait for me elsewhere. For a split second, seeing Lily had chased all thoughts of the task before me from my mind, but reality came oozing back like the brackish waters of India. I was in control once again. I needed to organize Mr. Henley's baggage, and for that matter, I needed to organize Mr. Henley himself! Some things would never change. After all these years, I could not imagine life without this responsibility. Deep down, I admitted to myself that I really cared for the old man. But Hugh was sorely testing that loyalty these days, despite my growing skepticism; I fervently hoped that all would turn out alright in the end.

Thomas made arrangements to transfer Mr. Henley and his baggage to the Jefferson Hotel where his reservation had been made under an assumed name. To set Hugh up in residence in Lilyan and John's hotel was too risky, so they had settled on one a few blocks away while, I would move to their Grand Hotel. I would visit Hugh on the morrow to arrange a routine so Mr. Henley would know how to contact me. This made me a little less anxious. With this responsibility settled, I secured my own baggage and hired a lad to porter it to the Grand. I then picked up my valise and the satchel and made my way to the waiting carriage. John waved me down as he caught sight of me coming out of the station. I acknowledged the wave and strode over to the carriage. I gave William, the driver, the valise to be put up in the luggage compartment and got inside with the leather satchel.

I hated to admit it, I was exhausted. The effort of travel was one I was used to. I had no difficulties with time changing, different cultures or different food and water. This time was different though. I was going to do something very out of character for me and I knew it. I was still wondering how I was going to handle it all when Lily interrupted my thoughts. "I've been thinking Thomas, we're all adults . . . now that father is no longer with us, John and I would be pleased if you would call us John and Lily. You've been so much like a brother to me. Let's drop the servant/ employer relationship once and for all. You have been a trusted friend for as long as I can remember."

I wanted to pull my celluloid collar away from my neck as the sweat started to flow. "I would be honored …. Lily…. John. Thank you." And with that John tapped the door and William pulled away. Lily had decided that I should stay at their home.

"I know you made reservations at the hotel; however, I thought it might be nice for you to stay with us as a guest in our home instead. Is that amenable with you?"

"Miss Lil . . . Lily that would be very nice. I do not wish to offend but this is a lot to take in all at once. I believe right now I would feel presumptuous staying as your guest."

John interrupted, "I understand fully Thomas. We'll honor your reservations and once you are more settled, perhaps you'll change your mind and join us. You're always welcome in our home and our hotel." Lily smiled and held John's hand as she acquiesced, "Just so, I agree." With her accord, John called out the change of destination to William.

I followed Lily and John into the lobby of their hotel. As they crossed the expansive lobby, I could not help but take in the wonder of the atmosphere Lily and John had created. The rich dark, oak paneling on the walls and crown molding along the ceilings enhanced the beauty and splendor of the hotel as we made our way to the front desk to register. The gas lit sconces on the wall were large and had tear shaped globes of etched glass with various patterns from flowers to country scenes; the images gentle against the soft glow of the flames. There were comfortable chairs and several settees in the lobby placed for relaxed conversations. My head swiveled from side to side as I attempted to catch all of the enticing details, to my left stood the restaurant and an elegant bar. It was all very welcoming. I had seen my fair share of elegant hotels around the world, and this ranked with them. He looked up to the ceiling and felt the jolt of nostalgia. The lay light had been re-created in the exact style of the one at Oakley, the Henley's home in England, with a similar floral central design. "Amazing!" he thought to himself. Lily usually moved forward, taking the best with her and leaving the burden of pain behind, but in every home of hers, I had seen reminders of the home of her youth in England.

As we passed by the registration desk, Lily took the time to acknowledge Frank, who was ever alert behind the desk. After a short discussion, she retrieved a key. John took Lily's arm as she gracefully picked up her skirt at the foot of the staircase. She nodded back at me smiling as I followed behind them. We ascended to the mezzanine. Unhurriedly, we strolled along the mezzanine allowing me the opportunity to observe the lobby and restaurant below.

I continued to follow my hosts down the carpeted hallway. It was pointed out that the wool carpets had been made in India and Lily commented on the rich reds and green and the texture of the fiber. Lily explained that their private suite was the first two sets of doors on the left and I would be right beside it. She used a large brass key to open the third door on the left in the short corridor.

Once inside Lily placed the key on the large dresser and moved into the room. It was beautiful. There were matching pairs of comfortable chairs with a small table by the window. The yellow flowered chintz complimenting the dark woods surrounding them. The bed was a large four poster. The wood was the same wood as the furniture and dark stained oak. The rounded finials fixed to the long polished pole that shone with brilliance and care. Beside the dresser, there was an elaborate wash stand with a mirror gilded to match the wardrobe that exhibited beautiful craftsmanship with ornate leaves and roses. It was a room made for comfort. The down filled comforter on the bed was beckoning to me as I swayed slightly on my feet. I put down the leather satchel by the dresser.

"I'm sure it has been a long day for you Thomas, I'll contain my curiosity, let you clean up and rest for a while. John and I will return to share dinner with you. Shall we say seven this evening in our private rooms next door? Then we'll discuss my father's passing. I know we should wait for Andrew to arrive before discussing all the details but I simply must know what happened."

"Andrew is coming?" I asked with enthusiasm.

With a smile, Lily came toward me and embraced me with a peck on the cheek. "Yes, we received a telegram. He, Sarah and their daughter, Bryn, are on the way and should be here in the next few days. But I can't wait; will not wait until then for the basic details. Please humor me." In my ear she whispered. "It's so good to have you here. Thomas, I've missed you."

"I too have missed you, Miss Lil . . . Lily. I look forward to our dinner. Thank you for your kindness. I will be most comfortable here, I assure you." We released from the brief ceremonial embrace and smiled at each other. Old bonds of friendship resurfaced swiftly from the past. The old, easy part of our relationship was alive and well and we were at peace with this.

John followed Lily out, closing the door behind them. I retrieved the urn from the leather satchel and placed it on the dresser by my room key. Then I went and sat by the window looking out onto the busy street. I was alone again with the urn and with the increasing apprehension about the post dinner conversation and problems it would create. I splashed the tepid water over my face and straight away felt better.

I left the room using the key Lily had left to lock the door behind me. At this late date, I wanted nothing to happen to the urn. Its secrets were mine to keep, at least for the moment. I would not let down my guard. I went back the way I had come and stopped at the rail on the mezzanine. My primary concern was Lily. I was trapped.

I strolled around the lobby, once again, admiring the fine details. At one point I stopped in my stroll to study the lay light in the ceiling, and then resumed my walk to the restaurant. I decided a cup of strong black tea was just what I needed. I entered the restaurant and sat down. The bustle of the restaurant soothed me as I reflected upon my own situation.

Revived by the tea, I started to make my way back through the lobby to the stairs. I was in plenty of time to make myself presentable for dinner with Lily and John. In the meantime, I would lie down and contemplate what the evening ahead would entail.

Precisely at seven, Lily knocked on the door. I opened it to greet her. She beckoned me to join her in their suite where John was ready to offer refreshments.

"Do you feel rested?" she enquired as she sat down on the settee. It was placed just in front of the wide open hearth of the fireplace. The piece was French provincial and had been in her mother's sitting room at Oakley. I recognized it right away. Lily put her arm casually on the arm of the settee. She crossed her ankles and with her other hand arranged her skirts around herself. John took his place by her side and I sat in a comfortable chair opposite. The furniture created a cozy atmosphere and invited intimate conversation. I felt a stab of nerves, little beads of sweat popped up on my forehead and my palms were damp.

"Thomas, are you feeling alright? You look a bit flushed."

"Just the change in the climate, I'm used to a much different heat than this in India."

"You simply must tell us everything. All of the details about Father and your trip out here. I have hardly been able to contain myself, I'm so anxious to hear all your news." I was more than a trusted servant, I was her first friend and she knew in her heart I would deliver the details regarding her father's death gently.

I used my handkerchief to mop the sweat that threatened to run down the side of my face. It was as if I could read Lily's mind. She was a grown woman, but so unchanged from that mischievous little girl I had met all those years ago. Her clear blue eyes were wide with innocence and anticipation. I knew Lily was searching for closure and my heart was sore as I realized just what my betrayal would do to her. Would she ever be able to forgive me? Well, in for a penny as they say. I smiled back at her with all the love I held for her in my heart and hoped that she would understand it was not me solely who would bestow the pain that was inevitable at the end of this charade.

Another knock at the door relieved me as Frank entered with the dinner cart. This was Lily and John's private suite. It had been designed for this very purpose, intimate dinners with close friends or just as a getaway for the two of them. We all seated ourselves at the table, with John doing the honors for Lily with her chair as Frank served up a delicious meal. I wanted to keep Lily's questions at bay, so I engaged them in general conversation about St. Louis.

After Frank left, John poured the wine and we all raised our glasses for a toast. In a clear voice John said, "To old friends and new memories!"

The glasses clinked together and we all tucked into the wonderful roasted beef and potatoes that had been prepared for us.

Lily chewed thoughtfully, swallowing with a mouthful of wine, "Tell us what happened in India," her eyes glistened with unshed tears. "I'm aware it's not proper dinner conversation . . ."

"I understand Lily. Of course the events that bring me here were devastating; your father was his old scheming self, right up to the end. Over business I mean. You know what a fine instinct he had for business."

"Why did you have to cremate him? Was it cholera? I hope he didn't suffer too long. When did he actually die? Why couldn't you bring him home to us and we could have given him a Christian burial?" as she blurted out her questions she was overcome with emotions.

"Lily, my dear, dear, Lily, he didn't suffer. The Henley compound was near Fort William, and of course, the garrison commander held your father in high regard. He was able to enjoy many privileges that others could not. There was an outbreak of cholera in Calcutta, which was not really an unusual occurrence. It quickly grew to epidemic proportions though and the government quarantined the city and the ports. Most of the ships in port flew the yellow flag of cholera. It was a frightening time.

We were spared much of the ordeal as your father had been friends with Dr. Snow. The last time we were in England, in 1856, they hotly debated many of Dr. Snow's findings. He believed that the cholera was in the water those affected used. He had plotted the cholera epidemic in London the year before and with his information had determined the source of the cholera to be the Broad Street well, when the authorities removed the pump handle the epidemic petered out. Dr. Snow would only drink water that had been boiled. Your father introduced the precaution into his compound as cholera is an unfortunate fact of life in India. We used boiled water to drink, cook, wash, everything. The incidence of cholera in our compound was significantly less compared to other compounds during each local epidemic in Calcutta and your father believed it was because of the boiled water. We were scrupulous about it. Others were beginning to follow his lead with the boiled water to great success.

However, this last was a major outbreak encompassing the entire city, there was no choice. Anyone who died of cholera was cremated. Often there were mass cremations. There were no exceptions! The decision was not up to me. If I had my druthers I would have brought him home to you or at least to London. He never did say what his wishes would be should this happen. Although cremation is a devout custom in India with outbreaks of this sort, burning is the only way to rid the area of the plague, so there are no other options. Our house servant Dhir chose the urn. He wanted something that befitted a man of your father's stature. Dhir was really quite fond of the old man." I paused, not sure of how much further I should go, afraid they might pick up on my ambiguity.

John broke the awkward silence following my disclosure, "What's done is done. It's beyond anyone's control. Thomas, tell us of his estate. How it will all be dispersed. Surely Hugh made plans for this. He was not so young after all."

"Quite so, John," I acceded. "He has always had a plan in place for the disposition of his worldly goods, occasionally disbursement plans have been modified, but there has always been a plan. They are to be disclosed on his eightieth birthday, hopefully with Andrew present. Directions are in place for either contingency." I watched their reactions closely. Lily looked somewhat relieved for the moment anyway.

"I feel better knowing he had a plan. Enough of this, tell us about the rest of your trip." She said this so quietly, resigned and sad.

Now on safer ground, I spent the rest of dinner telling of my travels to St. Louis via London and Boston. I elaborated about the interesting and different people I met along the way, the things I had seen and some of the trials I had endured. "I remember quite distinctly one particular occasion. I was off on a business venture for your father to Dacca. Absolutely the best hand woven silks are produced there. It's a small town but the people are very industrious. Your father did a brisk business with them. There are unbelievable hordes of people and animals on the trains. Truly, people travel on the roof of the train and seemingly never fall off, even as it rocks backs and forth threatening to derail. I was very familiar with Dacca and took my regular room there. I was out and about on my first evening taking my usual stroll, when I was set upon by a couple of hooligans. Hit me right across the back of shoulders they did. I was so shocked I fell to my knees and they were on me. I was sure I was a goner. But like a flash this tiny man appeared and dispatched the marauders with ferocious efficiency. He helped me back to my feet and smiled disarmingly. I bought him a drink and he smiled at me once more and was gone in the blink of an eye. It was only later I was to learn he was from the north and lived in the mountains known as the Himalayans. Apparently they are well known for their fighting."

Dinner came to its inevitable conclusion. After a post dinner brandy by the fire, it all of a sudden seemed to be quite late. John stood up and stretched, Lily stood up taking John's hint to take their leave. They escorted me back to my room.

~ Bryn ~

The wind was picking up and whipping my skirts around my ankles. It made free movement difficult. My hair slashed at my eyes stinging, bringing tears that blurred my vision. I struggled a bit with some ribbon and then, at last, could at least see what I was doing. My hat would not stay in place on my head and kept blowing back the thongs choking me as the hat dragged down my back. The last thing we needed was for the horses to break free, so I re-picketed them first. The fire had been lost in the rising wind. I tamped out the rest for fear of flying coals. Mama roused a little, but was helpless and weak. I was able to lend her a hand to move her closer to father and settle next to him. A quick check told me he was still breathing. Now I was dreadfully worried about both of them.

Papa's packhorse had our two large oilcloths for just this sort of emergency. Struggling against the wind, I managed to get them off the horse. I had never had to set these up before and had not realized how heavy they were. The weight of them pushed me off balance and I toppled into the soft undergrowth. Pinned for a minute under the burden, I tried to catch my breath. I pushed the tarps aside, and struggled to gain my balance as I stood up, but my skirts were heavy with mud. Unhurt, I could plainly see, that I was the only healthy one and I would need to be more careful. A fresh roll of thunder persuaded me to get going and I was up with renewed energy and a sense of purpose.

Fortunately, I had set our lean-to in an advantageous position, between some huge trees. Several great boulders were wedged around on the side of the hill and this is where I had made our camp. As father had done many times while I watched, I now put the stakes into the ground and using the rope he always had fastened to his saddle, I lashed the oilcloths into place. With a struggle, I made a proper makeshift shelter around the two of them. There was just enough room for supplies and for me to squeeze in and tend a fire for warmth and coffee. I then fed and watered the horses, rechecked their tether lines and harnesses, content that they were now as settled and comfortable as I could make them. The first drops of rain had started to fall by the time I had gathered all the supplies from the horses and around the camp. I tucked everything around the inside edge of our shelter.

It was midafternoon, but it looked like midnight, by the time I was dragging in the last of the firewood I had collected. Then the deluge began. The rain fell in thick heavy sheets. I could not see out beyond the edge of our little shelter. Like my father, I had weighted both sides of the cloth with large stones to help prevent the wind from lifting the edges and to help prevent water from seeping in. It must have been late afternoon, but with no sun, it was hard to tell. I was thankful the fire started with no trouble. The warmth coming from the small fire was comforting. I was becoming unnerved again, but the fire bolstered my spirits enough to consider a plan. Warm drink was upper most on my mind. Movement was limited to crouching and turning on all fours to reach what I could. The first sip of coffee was wonderful. I got some coffee into Mama and Papa. There was nothing else I could do at the moment so I banked the fire and laid my own head down in sheer exhaustion.

When I woke up, it was still raining hard, and very dark. The banked embers from the fire made a faint shadow along the edge of the oilcloths. I could not bring my immediate surroundings into focus and was unsure of just what had roused me. Turning onto my side, I realized the problem. I was soaking wet, not just wet; I was lying in a puddle of cold water! My parents were in the same puddle. I could not hear their short breaths above the roar of Mother Nature going on around them; but leaning close I could see the slight rise and fall of their chests with each breath. I reached for some dry wood to stoke up the fire; grateful that I had put it up on the boulder under the tarp. It was still dry. With the fire back under control, I went to tend Mama and Papa. I was thunderstruck when I touched mother's forehead. She was even warmer than when they had settled down. That explained why the cold water she and Papa were lying in had not bothered her.

"Mama, Mama can you hear me?" I cried desperately shaking mother's shoulders.

She barely opened her eyes before slipping back to sleep. Putting on my slicker, I mustered my courage, braving the full fury of the storm to dig trenches around our camp. I did what I could to relieve the water situation, but all three of us were soaked to the skin. With the kettle on the boil again for coffee, I went to see about drying off my parents. Mother was awake by now and wanted to help, but she was weak and she started to cough, a deep, heavy, cough. It made my blood run cold. I'd heard that cough recently, when Earley had taken the pneumonia last winter. He had been so very sick. Papa had brought him into our home, where he had had the comfort of Mama and I caring after him. Worried about what I was going to do with these two out here, I started to fret! I could not get them both into the saddle. Even if I could, how could I keep them there? As it was already evening, the only thing to be done now was to try and get some sleep to be able to make sensible decisions tomorrow.

By early morning, father was easier to rouse. I could tell his leg and ribcage hurt something fierce, but he was able to keep his head up. I gave him some more laudanum and he was thankful for it. He was able to take a little more coffee. He asked for my assessment of our situation. From the look in his eyes and the set of his brows, I could see he had already sized it up but I gave him my report as instructed. He listened, deliberating before speaking.

"It's ok Poppet," the endearment helped calm me. "You've done well, but we've got a problem here. If we use our heads and don't panic, we should be alright."

His face contorted in pain as he tried to shift his position. He was still quite weak from his loss of blood and the pain. He laid his head back and took a deep breath as I readjusted his saddle and blanket under his head. He spoke slowly, carefully choosing his words.

"Too far out to go back. River's probably flooded anyway so you can't cross", his lips were pursed and his face was drawn and white with effort. "Its a few hours ride north east to the major pass, along the base of the ridge. MacLaren's up there, this side. He'll help. Probably aware we're here, but not our problems. Bank up the fire. Leave my rifle, ammunition, food, medicine, and wood in reach. Bryn, take what you need for two days and head east up the base of the ridge. Likely he'll find you or you'll find his cabin. Wait for him there. Bring him back. Shouldn't have to send you. Sorry Poppet, but we need his help, alright?" He looked for and received the nod of my acceptance.

"There really aren't any other options, are there?" He shook his head as I asked. After a moment's hesitation I continued, "I can do this, Papa. Don't worry, but I'm not taking the food. You two need it more. I'll bring him back. I promise. First, I'll make you some broth though, for the both of you. You need the strength."

"I'll not argue that one but you must take some food. We need your strength too. Go safely, Poppett. Godspeed!" He laid his head back and lapsed into an exhausted sleep. I sat there for a few minutes to collect my nerve. Mother was resting quietly now. The trenches I had dug earlier were now successfully diverting the rain. Another roll of thunder interrupted my thoughts. It was not going to get any clearer and probably get much worse. I quickly set up as father had instructed, and set a broth for them to be heated when they woke. I checked the horses then saddled Tinker bringing just the essentials in my saddlebags.

I was shaking as I mounted Tinker. Balefully, Phantom and Gingerbread looked at me, they were unaccustomed to being tethered for such an extended period of time but there was nothing else I could do for them. Soaked and extremely uncomfortable, I had all I needed, but was nervous about leaving camp. Even with the wide brim of my hat, the rain seeped down my neck. My hair held the cold wet to my back under my slicker and wet curls were pasted to the side of my face. I could not see very well, so I was depending on Tinker, my sure-footed Appaloosa, to keep to solid ground, while I concentrated on staying out of tree branches.

As we picked our way along the rough trail, I wondered about this MacLaren and what he did all the way up here. There was plenty of fishing and trapping, but father's terse comments provided no real clues. I had to assume I had never met the man. Had he ever brought furs or such into town for trade? Had Father known him and just never mentioned him before? More secrets! I wished Papa could have been more explicit. MacLaren… I didn't even know the man's full name. I had so many questions. In a few days, Aunt Lily would be getting worried too. So much to worry over; we plodded along at a slow but careful and steady pace.

Visibility was zero for rain and trees. There was no dependable way to know whether I was going east as father had told me. I began to think I was riding in circles. I leaned over putting my head down on Tinker's strong neck. Stroking her mane, Tinker whinnied reassuringly. What seemed like several hours passed. I sensed we were near the foot of the ridge on what may have been a trail, but the darkness was completely shrouding me. My level head told me I was near but my panic was still close to the surface and threatened to overtake me. I pulled on Tinker's reigns bringing her to a stop. There was not a star in the sky. I could just make out the churning black clouds as some had turned almost silver where the moon was playing hide and seek. The pass was close; father had assured me of that. I began to think about stopping for a rest when the branch I had pushed out of my way snapped back knocking me out of my saddle. I had no memory of hitting the ground.

Waking, with a pain in my head, beating in steady rhythm with the pouring rain on the roof, I struggled to open my eyes. They felt like lead. My feeble attempts were getting me no-where so I just stopped trying for the moment. I must have been dreaming because it seemed to me that I remembered being carried by a bear. It must have been a dream. It felt like I was tucked into a soft, clean bed. The smell of wood burning and the crackle of a roaring fire in the hearth comforted me. With a gentle touch to my forehead, my eyes flew open and I found myself staring into the eyes of a dark giant.

"So you're finally awake, lass?" He gently slid his arm under my shoulders and helped me to sit up. "Aye, here drink some of this. It'll help you feel better. You've a nasty bump on your head and injured your arm." The deep timber of his voice washed over me as I took a sip of the warm liquid. He was so close I could smell the earthy richness of him. His voice was mesmerizing, and I surrendered to his gentle examination, as his hands probed the bump on my head and my tender shoulder.

"Ow . . . ahh . . . yes. Who are you? Where am I? What the heck happened? Oh my gosh! Are you MacLaren?"

"Aye, Aleck MacLaren, at your service," he affected a formal bow. "You're in my cabin. You must've taken a spill from your horse. She turned up here late yesterday afternoon. Figured from the empty saddle someone was in trouble. So, I went looking. I found you out cold and brought you back here. Now 'tis my turn lass. What were you doing up here in the mountains by yourself? Aye,'tis no safe place for a woman alone."

"I . . . Oh . . . Aleck MacLaren . . . Oh I found you. Mama! Papa! Oh my gosh! How long have I been here? I need your help. We desperately need your help . . . my parents... my father's been hurt, my mother's ill! When I left, she was burning with fever. They're out there, in this storm depending on me to find you." Speaking of our situation my panic resurfaced. He cradled my head into his shoulder and let me cry. Reaction took me and I wept and shivered, he rubbed my back slowly. He calmed me, then whispered in my ear.

"Aye, you found me." He chuckled as he spoke. Then he sobered, "You've been here but one night," he sat me up and looked directly into my eyes. "Who are your folks, lass?" Over the sound of the pelting rain, I caught the soft edge of his muted burr. I had expected an old trapper or guide not a man who probably aged with my brothers, and so appealing to look at. He was looking at me intently, stroking his chin, as did father, when he was thinking. His eyes... I had to concentrate. What had he just asked me?

"Oh... Andrew and Sarah Henley. You will help us, won't you?"

"Josh's wee sister?" 'Tis a small world we live in. Aye, I'll find your folks."

"Please, there's no time . . . they've been out in this so long. And yes I am Josh Henley's . . . younger . . . sister! Oh please help me... them... us, please?" My tongue was tied in knots. I was sure I must sound daft.

"Aye . . . younger. Haste willna help your folks lass." Although his tone remained soft, with the hint of a laugh, there was no doubt that he would help.

"Now your folks, you say they are in a verra bad way. Tell me what happened, and how bad?"

I explained as quickly as I could. The intensity of the storm had not diminished. I could hardly hear myself think over the roar of the water sluicing from the roof. Apparently I was not making myself very clear as to my parent's situation, out in the open and subjected to the elements. Wobbly, I sat up in bed and threw my legs over the side. The heat hit my face with a vengeance as I realized my legs were bare. I tried to stand but with fierce waves of nausea, I was forced back to the side of the bed. His arms quickly came around me protectively preventing a fall. I felt so dizzy. My shoulder and arm hurt as well, the aching was one continuous throb. MacLaren noticed the grimace of pain on my face and started to gently massage the injured limb. It felt so good . . . the deep, soothing strokes were relaxing . . . I closed my eyes. He laid me back into the bed and tucked the covers up under my chin.

"Rest easy lassie; I'll go now for your folks. Must be a ways off the main trail else I'd have found traces of them, Aye." He mumbled to himself as he pulled on his rain slicker, picked up his hat and arranged his gear. He vanished out the door.

The door ricocheted back on its hinges as he reappeared. The noise startled me. I was awake and met his dark stare as he came into the room dripping wet. He hesitated, strode quickly to the side of the bed and leaned over placing his hands on either side of my shoulders. His eyes were a deep warm brown with an intensity that went right through me. Intrigued and mesmerized; I closed my eyes, licked my lips and waited. His kiss still warm on my lips, I heard the door latch; sighing contentedly, I drifted off to sleep.

I found myself, alone, running through the darkened forest. I could feel my heart thumping against my chest, my lungs heaving as I struggled up the incline. I turned my head in all directions lost, cold and frightened. There was one goal in my mind and that was to find the man in the cabin. I tossed onto my side and snuggled deeper under the warm quilts and my heart beating with anticipation and excitement. The fear had dissipated and had been replaced by the pleasant soothing voice of the man. Maclaren.... Aleck ... um. I turned into his warm embrace and acceptance evident in my eyes as I leaned into his kiss.

Sometime later I awoke thirsty and alone. A pitcher of water and a mug were on a table by the side of the bed. Remembering that Aleck

MacLaren was out looking for my parents, I saw to my own needs. I found the lump on the side of my head, and massaged it gingerly with my fingers. A simple exam of the rest of my body seemed to be in order. He had said all else was fine but I felt the need to know for sure. Nothing was broken or otherwise out of place, except I could not fathom where my clothes were. All I was wearing was his shirt! I took a deep breath to control the alarm that was threatening to take over. I pulled the covers back up again.

Alert now, I carefully turned on my side to get a better understanding of my whereabouts. From what I could see, I was in a one room cabin. Where is the door to where I am? To the right of the door was a dry sink built into an armoire for dishes and storage. Beside it, with a window above, was a small table, with two chairs for meals and preparation. On the long side wall was an immense stone fireplace flanked by a cook stove on the left, near the small table and to the right a window with a large wooden rocking chair in front. No curtains were on the windows, but the hardwood floor was finished and had been swept leaving the room neat and orderly. To the left of the door was a matching window and on the wall hung various weapons and paraphernalia. She could see two shot guns, ready for use. Directly beneath the shotguns was a large tall table. Though it was hard to see from the bed, it looked like some rifles that were perhaps in the process of being repaired, lay on top. My clothes were hanging on a line beside the workbench. Along this side wall was a dresser with a lamp and over the bed where I lay was another window. The bed . . . Aleck MacLaren's bed . . .I laid my head back and prayed he would find my parents and be able to bring them back safely.

The sun was warm and blazing down on my face. I was basking in that state between dreams and reality. I had been running through a tangled maze of trees and shrubs, chased by a huge cat with a coat of flaming red. Suddenly there were two great arms around me, sweeping me up, carrying me away and protecting me from whatever beasts were out and about in the world. I tried to tell this handsome stranger about the cat but he would not listen. He held me close until I was comforted by the heat of his body and his scent, the tenderness of his embrace made me snuggle closer. He scowled at the cat and it turned and leapt away. I wanted another kiss.

I awoke again to the sun coming through the window and the smell of fresh brewed coffee. My head was much better and I had less difficulty sitting up. Aleck was there at the stove frying bacon. I was famished and could not remember the last time I had eaten. I watched him work in the kitchen area. He was obviously quite comfortable and used to looking after himself.

He was very tall. His long black hair brushed across his back. His leather coat was fringed in a Native style. The beadwork had clearly been plied with a loving practiced hand. The intricate patterns of bright colors were stunning. The leather molded transversely to the broad muscles of his back. His legs fit snuggly into the leggings showing off the power that lay beneath. His feet were clad in fur lined moccasins. The rain had finally stopped and I sat up to take a look out of the window. It must be sometime around noon from the look of the light through the clouds.

We were surrounded by forest. There was a barn in back of the cabin and a small paddock that held eight horses. I was thinking he must be quite well off when I realized Tinker, Gingerbread and Phantom were there. My parents! I turned to survey the room and there they were two sleeping bundles of humanity.

I rose carefully, went over and knelt down beside them. I touched their hands. They were warm and their breathing was even as they slept as only the totally exhausted can sleep. Aleck had made them comfortable by the fire. They were dry with lots of blankets tucked around them. The gash to father's head had been properly cleaned and redressed; however, mother was restless with fever. Her skin was hot and dry to the touch. I placed my hand on mother's forehead and was thoroughly alarmed when she did not respond to the contact. I hung my head, folded my arms around myself, rocking back and forth on my knees. Hot tears coursed down my cheeks and trickled onto Mama's blankets.

I was keenly aware of Aleck's presence behind me. He put his hands on my shoulders in a comforting gesture, stroked my cheek, brushed the tears from my face and then lifted me into his embrace.

"Hush Bryn… calm. They should both be fine. Aye, we got to them in time," he crooned into my ear. The warmth of his body ran up my back, his arms wrapped snuggly around me, comforting more than I could imagine. We stood like that for several minutes. When I had been soothed, and heaved several hearty sighs, he picked me up and carried me to his rocking chair where he sat setting me gently into his lap, like a child. As he wrapped his arms around me again, he said softly, "Aye, they'll really be okay, my lassie," I turned my head just a fraction. His face was ruggedly handsome, but weathered looking above the soft creases of his mouth. I licked my lips. It had been several days since his beard had last seen a razor. But it was his eyes that held me spellbound. They were a deep, dark brown, warm with reassurance. He believed what he said. Relieved, I gave in to the desire to lay my head down on his shoulder and asked, "So . . . who are you?"

"Aleck Duncan MacLaren, at your service m'lady." I giggled at his formal response and sat up to see his face. He chuckled, "Aleck, because my mother liked the name and Duncan was the name of my father." At the mention of his parents, he closed his eyes, there was anguish there, but before I could ask, he cradled my head back against his chest and continued. "My parents came here after the Scottish Uprisings and the repercussions of Culloden. Settled here because this reminded them of the Highlands back home in Scotland." Aleck was obviously proud of his heritage. Done with his personal details he asked, "And you? Where were you and your folks headed lass? This is nay the time of year for Andrew to be up here and with his family too!"

"We're on our way to my Aunt Lily and Uncle John's in St. Louis. Aunt Lily's my father's sister. He got a letter last week telling him that his father had died. He was asked to meet a Mr. Hall at my aunt's. I didn't even know my grandfather was still alive. No one ever spoke of him. My brothers didn't know either. Very confusing, he was like a family secret."

I blurted out more than I had intended but continued anyway. "We're several days behind my father's schedule. My folks won't be riding any time soon, will they? Aunt Lily will be getting worried. What am I going to do?"

"I'm sorry Bryn, aye, but it does explain things." He read the surprised look on my face. I thought he had used my name before but now I was certain. Aleck caught on immediately. "Your father was verra worried for you lass, mentioned your name. Also, I ken your brother Josh and his only sister is you."

"Can we get a message out to my brothers or my aunt?" I began to feel a bit awkward and shy being rocked like a child and asking for his help.

"The trails will be washed away. I'd make it down, but it's tricky going off the trail. You found that out yourself the hard way, aye?" He tried to stifle his chuckle as his fingers gentled brushed the bump on my head.

His voice and gentle touch were sending shivers down my spine. I started to rise from his knee, my cheeks felt like flaming cherries and I was keenly aware of the proximity of my parents in the room; albeit, still unconscious. The bump on my head must have made me daft. I could not tear my gaze from his mouth. His eyes seemed to drift from my eyes to my mouth with pent up mirth. I couldn't help but wonder what he thought was so damned funny. Luckily, I knew he couldn't read my mind. In no time, I was cold and shivering and instead of giving credence to his peculiar sense of humor, I crawled back into his bed and snuggled under the covers.

I thought I was being discreet. I was just learning. I was no innocent when it came to the mysteries of life. Not only did I live on a ranch, but there were enough young men around that I had flirted with. I even might have stolen a kiss behind the barn. What I was having difficulty with right now was the immediate impact that Aleck had made on me. It came as no surprise to me I could sink into those dark brown eyes forever, but as a women, I did not want to give my game plan away in one brief kiss, no matter it had set my body on fire with feelings I had never felt before. Without knowing it, Aleck had opened a whole new door to me and I was wanted to go through.

He told me about what had happened out there and thinking about what could have happened terrified me. I was reflecting on the conversation, his voice soft and low with the rhythm of the rocking chair, mesmerizing as he told me about the mountain lion and the danger I had been in. My heart hammered in my chest as I thought about the "what if's" of the situation. He relayed his own concerns when he saw the rider less horse and came to the conclusion it was a woman's horse. Bad enough to be a man in trouble up here but a woman would have very little chance on her own.

When I had returned, I knelt beside Bryn, who lay motionless on my bed. Hastily, I had covered her with a blanket. This was a new frontier for me. I was well familiar with the ladies and had a good idea of what I would like to do, but this woman was young. It would never occur to me to defile her or any other woman. I liked and respected women in general. So it was with great effort that I gritted my teeth and averted my eyes as I carefully removed her wet clothing and did a proper search for injuries. Her skin was translucent and unmarked except for the nasty bruise coming forth on her shoulder. Her eyes were closed and thick dark lashes lay upon her cheeks. The wet clothing I surmised was more of a concern that her other injuries. I did not want her cold.

I had slipped one of my clean shirts on her still protecting her modesty then stoked the fire putting two more good size logs onto the flame. I wrapped her in blankets then gently combed her hair. Her hair was matted and tangled with leaves and wet pine needles from the forest floor. The curls sat in tight ringlets around my fingers and I delighted in the fine softness of it as it ran through my fingers. That seen to, I had cradled her in my arms and rocked her letting her curls lie over my arm and dry in the warmth of the fire. Unable to resist, I had kissed her forehead several times and cradled her close. Finally, I laid her in my bed. Satisfied with her condition, I had then gone out into the night and cared for her horse and her gear. Returning to the cabin, I banked the fire, wrapped myself around her blanketed form and for the first time in my life slept the full night beside a woman.

Her face was an open book to me. She wanted me to kiss her; I wanted to ravish her mouth, but she was Josh's sister. I laughed to myself and stifled a groan. The cabin had suffered no damage in the storm. It was sturdy. It was made of logs and built into the side of the mountain. The trees were so thick it was easy to miss the fact that there was any human habitation up here. The native people told many stories about this area and the spirits who inhabited them. If this was true, I must be at peace with the spirits for they had protected me well. And now they had brought Bryn to me.

I was in a turmoil not really knowing what to do. This young woman had overcome amazing odds to get as far as she had and I admired bravery in any human I came in contact with. Obviously, she was someone who would do what was necessary in order to survive and to protect those she loved beyond her own life. I saw myself as an outsider looking in. I did not consider myself shy but pragmatic. It was better for me to live in quiet isolation. The War had done that to many men. They no longer felt welcome in polite society. But from the moment I had brought her here, I had experienced a feeling of comfort and protectiveness about her. And I knew when she left . . . it did not bear thinking about.

Andrew was rousing. I demanded in a tone that brooked no disagreement "Andrew, we've got to tend that leg aye. Yer no up for it man. Here you'll be needin' this for strength," and I poured two large shots of whiskey down Andrew's throat. When Andrew stopped sputtering and choking, I gave him a strip of leather. Andrew gritted it in his teeth, nodded and then directed Bryn on the next steps to be taken to help me bind her father's badly mangled leg.

Bryn rushed to pull me back. "You're hurting him!" she screamed.

I turned back to her and gently released her arm from mine. I kept my voice firm trying to be gentle, "Lass, he knows there is no other way. It has to be done and quickly." With hot tears of anguish streaming down her face, Bryn relinquished my arm. She went to sit with her mother.

Andrew let out a bellow from behind the leather and thankfully passed out. Bryn was distressed by her father's reaction. Then we wrapped his ribs too.

~ Bryn ~

*A*leck changed the sheets on his bed and moved Mama and Papa into it. By early afternoon, I was able to wash myself and change my clothes behind a makeshift screen Aleck had hung from the rafters. He had washed her muddy clothing and hung it to dry. It felt nice to have my own clothing on, clean once more. But I missed wearing his shirt with his comforting scent.

Later, when Papa woke, he was able to eat the meal Aleck had prepared. I could not help but be very worried about Mama. Despite Aleck's best endeavors, mother was not doing well. I had boiled the fresh azalea berries we had picked on the way up and made a tea for her, but she was not responding. I could get only small amounts of the tea and broth into her and she was very weak. When she roused her voice was hoarse and her cough was loose and sapped all of her energy. I sponged mother's aching body and fresh clothes helped her to be more comfortable. Aleck had boiled some willow bark and made a tea that was good for taking down a fever. He had learned this from the Kickapoo whose village was a day's ride from the cabin. I had never in my life seen my father so agitated. He felt responsible for our situation, that much was clear, and was beside himself with guilt. Papa and I exchanged glances. I was helpless to alleviate his suffering. I bundled mother up once again. For the moment, she seemed to be resting better.

Sitting on a stool in front of the fire, I started running my fingers through my hair to untangle my ornery curls, such a tedious task. Aleck went to the window ledge to retrieve my hairbrush and to the table for my comb. He pulled his rocker up behind me. I reached for the brush with a "thank you" ready on my lips, only to have my hand swatted away. He proceeded to slowly untangle the mess from the tips to the crown, no yanking or pain. He then brushed the freed strands until they were soft and shiny. I luxuriated in the pleasure of someone else tending to the task. Afterwards he set aside the brush and simply ran his hands through my hair. I felt I could purr like a contented kitten.

Much later in the afternoon, as I checked on mother once again, I was elated to find that her fever had broken. With that news Papa perked up as well. He conveyed to us how he had been doubling back, when the storm broke. Phantom had reared at a streak of lightening that struck a nearby tree. Panicked, Phantom had stumbled, throwing Papa off balance in the saddle. He had fallen and ended up rolling down a hill for a short way before a tree trunk stopped his descent. Papa relayed his loss of consciousness and on coming back around, he needed time to reorient himself. It was dark and during the tumble he had hit his head. The pain shooting from his leg let him know the damage and he understood the cost.

It would be a while before my parents were saddle ready. Papa was nowhere near ready to put any kind of weight on his leg. There was the continuing worry about Mama and there were people waiting for us to arrive in St. Louis. Time was of the essence and this waiting was torture. A move needed to be made one way or the other, either to stay here in the cabin and wait out the long winter or move on to St Louis without my parents. After much consideration, I settled on a very straightforward plan. With Papa alert and Mama on the mend, it was time to voice my tentative solution.

"We need to let everyone know we're alive and I've come up with a plan." I said this as I walked over to stand behind Papa and Aleck who were back at work on the guns. Neither spoke but turned and watched me, waiting. Mama looked over from where she was resting on the bed and smiled at me encouragingly. I took a deep breath bringing me up to my full five and a half feet, clasped my hands behind my back and looked Aleck straight in the eye. "If Aleck will return me to our previous camp, I'm confident I can find my way back home. If we leave early in the morning, I can be home in three days; from there I can telegraph Aunt Lily and let her know what has happened.

"NO!!" both men spat out in unison, as they slammed their hands on the table and glared at me.

"And why not? It's a sound plan." I countered just as forcefully. My eyes locked with Aleck's but I could feel Papa's heated stare.

"I've already told you, lass, these mountains are no place for a woman alone. Aye, you'll not go out there without me!" countermanded Aleck with barely controlled passion. I saw father's gaze shift to Aleck.

"And just what do you propose?" I snapped back at him.

"He proposes nothing," Papa managed between clenched teeth. "This is my problem. I will go on to Lily's and return for my girls when everything has been settled. I'm sure Aleck would let you both rest here 'til my return." Pain was etched on his face and his jaws clenched so tightly you could see the muscles twitching in his face. Aleck shook his head. He knew pain clouded Papa's judgment but for him to head out in his condition was ludicrous. He knew he needed to smooth Father's ruffled feathers but wasn't sure if it would be possible. Aleck spoke gently, "think again man. I've known you a long time Andrew and in all that time, never heard you called for a fool, aye, but I swear at this moment, fool you be! The only ones fit to sit a saddle are Bryn and me."

~ Sarah ~

I sat calmly listening and felt Andrew's pain and pride as he reacted to this situation with love and fear for his daughter, logic flying out of the window. It had ever been so for Andrew where Bryn was concerned. Familiar with the habits of my husband, I could not hold my silence, "Andrew love, you know neither one of us is ready to ride. Your leg and ribs need more time. There's difficult riding ahead. I agree that Aleck and Bryn are the ones who should go."

"Over my dead body!" Andrew exploded.

"Oh Andrew if you go on like that it may just be the case. Please see reason," I rebuked.

"There is no reason to see". He countered me. "Aleck and Bryn will not be alone together and that's all there is to it." He was getting worked up. He knew he wasn't strong enough to make the ride but how could he let his baby girl go with Aleck. Andrew had seen the way Aleck's eyes followed Bryn around the cabin.

~ Aleck ~

*I*t was as if I could read his mind. "Do you no trust me, Andrew?"

"With my life, yes, but not my daughter's reputation!" Bryn had never witnessed her father so impassioned. He was seething with frustration.

I absorbed the truth of the comment. I was not a father but I was astute enough to realize the situation Bryn would be put in. And yet there was really no other way around it. I would have to steel myself against my growing attraction to Andrew's daughter.

The ensuing silence allowed the four of us to catch our breath and think. Bryn returned to the rocker by the fire and I saw her meet her mother's glance. Andrew steadied himself and was the first to speak. Resignedly he said, "You're right Aleck. Like your father, I'm counting on you to be a man of your word. You will make sure Bryn arrives safe and sound at Lily's but . . . "He heaved a great sigh and said quietly," Aleck MacLaren I entrust my daughter's safety into your hands . . . but beware if you dishonor her or your word, if anything happens to her... I'll track you to your dying day! Mark my words!"

The tension had been released and I chuckled, "Aye, and if you had gone on alone as you first thought you'd have left her here with me. Alone in my home. And your wife in no condition to intervene. T'would be worse that, aye?" Then I sobered, clapped Andrew on the shoulder, met his eyes clearly and promised, "I give you my solemn word that to my dying day I will see Bryn safe and I would give my life for hers. Aye, I'll care for her." Bryn's eyes popped wide at the vow of protection.

I turned to face Bryn. My eyes met hers and she felt drawn into the deep brown depths as I took her hands in mine, "Bryn, your father is not able to ride, nor your mother. Your aunt will surely be worried. Aye.

I will see you safely to your aunt's but you must travel with me willingly yourself and abide by my judgment in regards to your safety, lass. We can prepare your folks so they can get by on their own for a little while, 'til I get back. Will you come with me Bryn? For if you'd rather, lass, I'll go alone for him."

~ Bryn ~

*C*ould I possibly say no? He held me spell bound! I could not breathe but somehow managed to stammer my reply. "Yes . . . I'll come with you."

I heard Mother's sigh as Father growled. "Then it's arranged. Keep her safe man, from all! Mark my words; I am not happy about this!"

Aleck dropped my hands, turned to Papa and nodded. "I understand and am honored. I'll not fail you."

I could see Papa was exhausted from the effort. Mama called him to come and sit with her. She had to ask him twice. I too felt the need to separate the men as if a huge struggle had just been fought. "Will you take me to see Tinker? Please," I asked Aleck. He glanced at my parents and with mother's nod of permission, we walked outside and over to the paddock.

Once outside Aleck asked, "Are you sure, lass, that you are willing to come with me? There's still time to say nay. I would not fault you. You've nay known me long." I shushed him. Boldly I reached out gently pushing him up against the paddock rails, stepped in and wrapped my arms around his waist. His arms came around me and I couldn't help but sigh contentedly into his chest and snuggled. Aleck leaned his cheek into my hair and groaned.

Once again, on this mountain, I would leave my parents behind and strike out. Only this time with a man I had only just met as my guide, companion and protector. I succumbed to the excitement to be on our way. If my brothers knew, they'd be as enraged as my father. We spent the rest of the day readying things for my parent's ease and our travels.

I was conflicted. There was a part of me that was keen for the adventure. The burgeoning young woman had no fear of the unknown as I watched Aleck prepare for the journey. On the other hand, Papa was only just hobbling on a crutch and Mama although better, remained congested and lethargic. How could I leave in good conscience?

I came and sat with Mother. Mama took my hands in hers'. "Mama, I feel this is the right thing to do, but I feel giddy." I confessed.

"I understand, Bryn, I was young once too. I see the way you look at Aleck." Mama stroked my hair smoothing it on my shoulders. "Just be careful, my love. Use your own common sense, it won't let you down." Mama gave me a squeeze.

It was hard to say good-bye. I gave Father a hug and he patted me reassuringly on the back. "It'll be alright, Poppet."

~Lily~

I kept my eyes closed as I warmed to the memory of Thomas and my youth. I vividly remembered, reinforced by the retelling from Thomas himself. Mother, marching through the door with a scraggly, filthy, grimy faced Thomas Hall in tow. He had tried to steal Mother's purse. Thomas told me she had grabbed him by the ear, literally dragging him home. I chuckled to myself as I saw the little girl I had been peaking around the parlor door so I could eavesdrop in on what was being said regarding the dirty boy. In retrospect, I now understood my Mother to be loving, sensible and intuitive. Mama must have sensed the innate goodness in Thomas, for he was cleaned up, trained and kept on as butler to Father. Sadly, I remembered very little else specific about her except always believing she was loving, fun, kind, generous and very pretty with an infectious laugh.

I was only seven when Mother suddenly passed away. That was the day I had gained a brother, but I lost the mother I adored. As I continued to reminisce, I realized I had lost my Father that day as well. He withdrew into himself in a way that I was never able to reach. The child Lily I remembered as frightened and confused as they had closed the lid of the coffin on my mother in the parlor where Father had held vigil. Thomas had stayed with me and Andrew as the adults took her Mother's coffin to her funeral at the church and then to grave. The family never returned to the church again. It was about a decade later, a week before the family was to set sail for America that I ventured near the grave. I was overwhelmed by the beautiful stone, father's testament of his eternal love for the wife he had lost so young. I was surprised and delighted with the pretty garden that held audience at the head of the grave. The verger was pottering about that day and at my request he explained that Mr. Henley arranged for the garden every year and had left an endowment to cover the cost for many years to come. But no the verger did not know if her father ever visited and I knew I would never ask him.

The day Mama died, so did the laughter and the love in our home. But every cloud has a silver lining. I now had a baby brother, Andrew. I adored him and I spent most of my time with him. Through my mother's charity, I had been given Thomas and he had become a good friend. I grew to love Thomas over the years. To my younger self, Thomas, like an older brother was the most wonderful boy in the world. That my world at this point in my life was very small did not concern me. The three of us were inseparable.

Thomas thrived in the household under cook's ministrations. The food and care quickly filled him out. The scrawny lad became strong, his muscles firm, his new found strength evident in his every move. His responsibilities developed his confidence. He learned quickly and no task was too menial. He loved us. Thomas was busy but always made time for a hug, to sit and listen to me chatter and to answer my never ending flow of questions. It was not unusual either to see Thomas crooning to Andrew when he was upset or carrying the baby around while he did his chores or keeping him entertained while others were busy at their tasks. Thomas always brought Andrew while he and I took our lessons, sharing his burden with Miss Abernathy when he needed to write. Thomas grew into his position and Father never regretted Mama's decision regarding the lad. More and more responsibilities were delegated his way. He proved himself to be the essence of discretion and integrity. Father never noticed the growing closeness of Thomas with us. He had simply lost interest in everything but the business.

I remembered that Mama had occasionally slipped into the back of the room where Thomas and I took our lessons. I remembered that I had been welcome in my father's lap any time but less so after the death of Mother as he was so seldom around. It seemed so very long ago now. I stifled a choked breath as I summoned up the shattered pieces of my life after mother had died. I was grateful to those who remained behind. Thomas, the Fairchilds and Miss Abernathy as they endeavored to fill the void that Mama's passing had left. I could look back now with a smile in my heart. The years had eased the pain of yearning for things that could never be changed. But I still missed mother and always would and now father too.

It was through Thomas' stories that I had caught little glimpses of who my parents had been; always having dinner together, lunch together if Father could manage it, playfulness around the house, carriage rides in the park, the look of adoration from one to the other, unconcealed displays of affection, hands held and kisses given and Mama's excitement to be carrying another child. There were occasional formal dinner parties but they were few during her confinement and non-existent after her death. Thomas retold again and again of their nightly trip up to the nursery to peek at their sleeping lamb, before they retired. He told too of Father's occasional trips up after Mother's death to peek in on me and, indirectly Andrew. Thomas had loved Mama with all of his young heart. He did his best to keep the memory of her love and laughter alive for her two small children.

Every need was provided for - a lovely home and good schools but with only Thomas, Miss Abernathy and Mr. and Mrs. Fairchild in the large household, we were so desperately alone. Thomas had carefully watched over and helped to guide Andrew and I as we grew into, responsible young adults.

I, in turn, had watched Thomas grow and mature into a fine young man. He had been an honored guest at my wedding to John.

Now too, Thomas was older. It had been too many years since I had seen Father and Thomas. He had remained with him all these years and now Thomas would be free to do as he chose.

"Lily love, where have you been?" John asked as he entered the room noticing my absent stare. He had broken the spell and with a sad smile I turned toward him.

"Oh . . . lost in memories. It seems so strange to have Thomas here with us. I just can't believe Father's gone. Oh John, I just want to weep for him, he missed out on so much. I'm worried about Andrew too."

"Don't worry about Andrew. He's too practical to have regrets over the loss of that paternal relationship."

"Oh John, I know that, I meant I was worried more with the storm."

"Now Lil, Andrew knows what he's doing and he'd never jeopardize Sarah and Bryn. He's probably got them safely sheltered up somewhere and won't risk moving out again 'til the weather's settled. I know you're eager to see them, but you'll just have to be patient." We were interrupted by a knock on the door.

"Excuse me, Miss Lily, Mr. John," it was Frank who worked the front desk and at quiet times tended bar at their hotel. He nodded to me and continued. "That Mr. Hall wants to see you. He's awaitin' in the lobby."

"Thank you Frank. We'll be down directly."

~ *John* ~

I too was concerned about Andrew and his family but I did not want to alarm Lily any more than she was already. The storm that had ravaged the town had moved over the plateau where Andrew, Sarah and Bryn would be travelling. I had been on several hunting trips with Andrew and his boys over the years. I found Andrew to be good company and a reliable, responsible outdoorsman. I knew Andrew could handle most of whatever came his way. But still, no one, including Andrew, was infallible.

Unlike Andrew, I was not a rugged, outdoorsy kind of man. I had always taken care of myself and was very fit but had never enjoyed great quantities of time out of the cities. Lily and I owned a string of grand hotels together. It was not a difficult life, as we made good business partners as well as being a devoted husband and wife. My interests had been expanding at the time I had met Lily. My father had been a railway man and his fortune was quite expansive. I had kept my hand in the railway, but thought about hotels as adjuncts to the railway business and the bet had paid off in spades. I had the business acumen, foresight and charm. Lily, while breathtakingly beautiful, had the gift of finance and social graces to go with it as well. She was, I felt, the most amazing woman I had ever met. We are a formidable team.

I turned and followed Lily downstairs to find out what Thomas, who had dropped rather unexpectedly into our lives, wanted. He had always seemed a decent chap. Certainly, Lily thought the world of him. I wondered how Thomas had tolerated the old man all these years. Lily had told me countless times about the day Thomas had arrived at their house. Lily, he knew, thought of him like her older brother.

~ Thomas ~

"I came to see if there has been any word from Andrew." I shifted my position. It was awkward but I would never waiver until my duty to the old man and his family was done. After all, for all intents and purposes, these people were my family! The family I had adopted as much as they had adopted me. I owed my life to Miss Emmaline and before all of this was over I would make sure Miss Emma could once again be proud of me. I was not comfortable with the role I was now playing. What my partner in this venture had planned was inappropriate and I now felt terribly responsible for Andrew's situation.

"No word as yet, they should have been here about two days ago, but then if they were caught by that weather, I would have to wonder how any of us would know at least for a little while yet," Lilyan said the words though without much conviction.

"Yes, what you say has merit. I suppose we could wait a few more days." But even as I spoke the words, I showed no sign of relief.

"If there has been no sign of them in the next few days we'll arrange a search party. I think it would be prudent to wait, but not too long." John added.

That evening Lilyan decided she could wait no longer. With John by her side she telegraphed Josh and Drew the next morning telling them that the family had still not arrived.

I was floating in that peaceful dream world between nighttime's sound sleep and morning's early rousing. I didn't want to open my eyes, so I gave myself the pleasure of a lazy stretch and turned onto my side to face Andrew. I reached for the solid warmth of him and could not control the sigh of contentment that issued forth. I scooted up behind him cuddling my body into his. I was beginning to feel like a pampered cat. I let my thoughts run free, as I adjusted the down coverlet back over my shoulders. Finally, after a few days rest and recovery, I was feeling much better and felt my old energy returning.

There was no doubt about it. We were lucky. We had both wrestled with the devil and won. I snuggled closer to my husband wiggling my cold feet up against his warmth. Andrew was on the mend too. I had been positive he had broken bones but fortunately I was mistaken. It did not make matters any better though, he was still unable to put his weight on the leg. Thank God for Bryn and Aleck. I knew I should get up, but Andrew had other ideas.

"Morning, my darling," he grinned as he rolled to face me. He only grimaced slightly as he shifted his weight over his injured leg and ribs. The pain was a reminder of the seriousness of our predicament in the storm and the guilt he felt for having left them in the meadow to scout ahead. His mouth met mine in a morning ritual spanning more years than either of us cared to think about; our mutual desire in harmony. My hands touched the crisp hair on his chest. A look of mutual consent passed between us and I was in his arms giving myself to him with carefree abandon. At these special moments, we knew each other so well; the love making was always fresh and intense. Sated, we lay together as the heat of our passion slowly abated. Each knowing there was no other, soul mates people called it. Together we watched as the sun lifted up in the sky pouring its golden warmth into the room. Cozy in each other's arms, we relaxed in the mystical spell that we cast when we made love. Neither one was anxious to end the bliss, but we knew that very soon we would have to make the decision to leave this Eden. With no words spoken, I moved gently away from Andrew and started to rise.

"Whoa, my darling! What's the rush? Bryn and Aleck will tell Lily and John what has happened. They should be there by now. Thomas is a good man and he'll know how to handle our absence. Besides, when was the last time you and I had this much time alone together? Umh?" Andrew queried.

"Before Edward was born," I answered in a tight whisper. Andrew's playfulness ceased for the moment. A small shiver passed through both of us as we thought of our first born taken during the War. Six years gone. The silent thread of agony tore through them at the same moment. It wasn't right, war never was. Parents weren't meant to outlive their children. Andrew touched my shoulder and I knew we shared the same pain. Sometimes it was too much to bear and Andrew was always there for me, my source of strength. I patted his hand in a loving gesture.

"I really must move, Andrew. I'm stiffening up like an old woman and I'm vain enough not to want to admit it! That chest cold took more out of me than I thought. Of course, spending the night in the pouring rain with thunder and lightning and being swamped I'm sure didn't help either!" I moved to the side of the bed, "and you do want your coffee, don't you?"

"You know I can't resist . . . your coffee," he paused emphatically and gave me a pinch on my rear. I playfully slapped his hand away. I gave his hand a squeeze as my feet touched the floor. I had forgotten how high up we were as I felt the chill run up my legs. I hugged the blanket closer to my shoulders and moved to stoke up the embers in the fireplace and in the woodstove.

What a beautifully compact, but efficient place this was. I took a look around, taking my time to get my bearings. The floor of the cabin was wood planked, scrubbed and sanded feeling like velvet beneath my feet. The cabin was square and well-sealed. The windows were small but clean allowing in the natural light. As I looked around the room, it was evident that there was a place for everything and everything was in its place. It was definitely a man's home with no feminine touches, but I could feel the love that had gone into the structure. There were well cared for tools hanging along one wall. I took my time and absorbed the atmosphere. I made my way across to the armoire and stopped to look out the window. The outbuildings were also well constructed and the paddock appeared sound.

I had watched Aleck pick up after my absentminded daughter, a ribbon here, a brush there, a drying cloth left on the table. He didn't seem to mind as her brothers did. He had made a space on the armoire for her treasures so she could find them. Supplies were carefully stowed and the dishes were all neatly stacked with only a few chips. My curiosity got the better of me; I opened the armoire and pulled down a small bowl I had seen Aleck tuck away. I fingered one of Bryn's ribbons and several strands of her hair that Aleck had braided and tied in a careful knot for safekeeping. I had been watching him watch our daughter . . . despite all the banter I had noticed the resigned sorrow in his eyes when they had left four days ago. I knew in my heart he would give his life to keep her safe. My heart went out to him.

Andrew and I had been here recuperating for four days on our own. I had to acknowledge I was still feeling tired, but that was a huge difference from the day before. I knew I had never been that sick in my life. The storm kept going over and over in my mind, I had truly been terrified. So many ifs and I knew better than to dwell on them. "We are not as young as we once were that's for sure." I grimaced and that started a coughing fit.

"Hey, be careful over there," Andrew called from the bed. "Hurry back to keep me warm, woman!" he teased. He was concerned about my cough; we were quite a pair at the moment.

I turned to face Andrew. I sat down in the chair next to the fireplace, and smiled at him. "I'll be there in a minute, you!" I countered. There was a water pump right there in the cabin. All the modern conveniences. I filled the kettle and put it on the stove. Then I crawled back into bed with Andrew to wait for it to boil.

The kettle came to a rumbling boil and I got up slowly to make the coffee. My balance was back and I was not as dizzy as I had been. I was pleased to feel the solid strength of the wooden floor beneath me as one surface and not having it float up and down to meet my every step.

I approached the bed with two steaming mugs of dark, black coffee. I watched Andrew as he dozed. I knew he was not asleep, but like me was feeling the effects of his injuries and the accompanying exhaustion. This was the first time in our lives together that we had lain about in bed for so long. I could feel myself drooping as I thought about the chores that were not being done in my own home.

I sat beside Andrew and snuggled up against him. We sipped our coffee, enjoying the fragrance of the warm, soothing liquid, in comfortable silence, enjoying the physical closeness of each other. I rested my head on Andrew's strong and always reliable shoulder. He draped his arm across my back and pulled me close. The solace I received from this had no words. I always felt safe with Andrew. I rested my eyes and a shiver went through me, someone crossing my grave my mother used to say. Visions of the wild, unrelenting storm assailed me and I trembled at the memory. Both of us had witnessed Mother Nature at her worst many times but always managed to stay unscathed in our home.

"You alright, hon?" Andrew patted my shoulder in a gesture of comfort and reassurance.

"Yes, for a moment I was back facing the rage the storm was spewing upon us and it was so real. I wasn't sure if I was dreaming or not. I was so frightened for you, Andrew. You were hurt so badly; and I could do nothing. I was so afraid and worried for all of us. Bryn was so brave!" I hesitated then... "What do you know about this Aleck? I know you trust him . . . but she's our daughter and now a young woman. I know they should be safe in St. Louis by now. Oh I don't know!" I felt the warm tears of reaction start to flow down my cheeks in a steady stream.

"Sarah, she'll be alright." He said this as he hugged me, understanding my real concerns and trying to alleviate some of the strain he sensed in me.

"The boys and I have met him several times over the years. Apparently he and Josh know each other quite well from the war years. Josh speaks of him with high regard and I have to say I value his assessment." Voicing his own apprehension would only make my concerns worse and that would be no help to anyone.

We lay at peace together, neither one willing to move. Andrew loved the feel of me next to him. It was always special, this vibrant sensitivity between them that had a life of its own. We completed each other, there was no question. With absolute abandon we had frittered the day away and at the end of this honeymoon day, we watched as the day passed into the night, but the trip that lay ahead was on our minds. We slept as always snuggled close together.

~ Andrew ~

The next day brought a beautiful sunny, breezy day. There had been a sudden drop in the temperature which was the norm at this elevation at this time of the year. Overnight the leaves had started there subtle turn, clearly announcing the season was changing. I could never explain why this particular season was my favorite. Certainly, it was the one that carried the most risk for my family, injuries were not uncommon during the round up and branding was dangerous, strenuous work. Dust was continuously swirling around the men as they balanced, directing the cutting horses with physical strength and skill. The heat and sweat was exhausting, making a long day seem longer. I then enjoyed the quiet peace of winter. It was my opportunity to work at fixing things around the homestead, getting ready for the spring drives; looking forward to the quiet was disconcerting for me. I was spending a lot of time lately wondering about my age.

I was elated that Rob had at last come home but I also had reservations. It was well understood that Rob was very successful financially. Nothing less would have been expected of any of the Henley boys. It was just too ironic for me to swallow Rob's success in shipping. Delighted as I was to have more help to mend broken fences, I could not help but wonder about an ulterior motive. In more ways than one, the apple had not fallen very far from the tree.

I, like many men, did not like to dwell on the past, so when I did take the time to ponder Rob and his business dealings, I had to consider my own arguments with my father. The outcome had been the same. There was an unspoken estrangement and tacit understanding of the reasons why. Hind sight was always near perfect. In the way of fathers and sons, both of us had been stubborn and adamant concerning who was right and who was wrong. It had taken years to bury these thoughts deep enough to keep them silent, but now I was being forced to face the consequences of the guilt I had burdened myself with all of these long years. I had learned the lesson the hard way years back at Father's knee. I vowed always to look ahead to the future and concentrate on the things I had the power to change. I promised myself I would never live in the past. Sarah was usually so at ease with the past. It must be her woman's heart; so strong and courageous and definitely in my opinion, underestimated.

I had mastered the crude crutches Aleck had made for me. I was stiff, but I was restless with the need, to be up and about so I went to check on the horses. Aleck had taken care of them but I was thinking their feed would be running low about now. I, against Sarah's wishes, hobbled out to the small stable at the back of the cabin. Aleck had wedged the door to the paddock ajar so the horses could enter and exit at will. I could not help but admire Aleck's craftsmanship. Both the cabin and stable were sturdy and well insulated and both made from the pine of the forest. He had created comforts for himself and those in his care; I admired his ingenuity. Aleck was a good man.

I checked the horse's feed. I hobbled over to inspect the saddlebags and saddles. All were in good order. They were hung up neatly and away from the dampness of the ground. While I was taking stock, my thoughts once again turned to Rob and Father. Something in the look on Rob's face when the letter arrived was not fitting for some unknown reason. It was just off. The silence of the building surrounded me and fueled by the solitude my emotions got the better of me. I surprised myself as I sat down on a bale of hay, my elbows on my knees and my head in my hands. I would apologize to Rob and rekindle our fragile relationship.

My shoulders shook and I cried like I had never cried before. I cried for all that had gone on, but most of all I cried for my father. Tears of regret, hot against my cheeks, burning like punishment for all of the times we flew at each other or ignored each other. Two guarded and territorial men always wary of the other, never able to trust and confused by the bonds of blood and love that stood between us. I wept for the mother I had never known and killed as surely as if I had taken a gun to her. I believed that with all of my heart. I sobbed for Sarah and all that she had gone through for the father-in-law she would never meet. I cried for Bryn and prayed that I had not underestimated Aleck's worthiness.

It was no surprise that I did not hear Sarah approach. I felt her arms come around me and the light in my life shone once again as she consoled me. She crooned softly in my ear as she ran her fingers through my hair. She took me to her breast like a child and held me through my torment. We would move forward together as always and all would be well. I could not live without her. The dawn of understanding for Father's loss and the suffering and loneliness he had endured began.

Sarah's soothing hands caressed my face, and then she squeezed my arm with reassurance. "I love you Andrew Henley; always will," she whispered, "You are warm, kind, generous and fair. He was beyond your control. Grieve as you must, then let him go."

"He loved her wholeheartedly as I love you. My mother was his life. Oh my God, Sarah, I can't imagine fifty years without you. Hell!"

"Andrew! Andrew Henley, watch your mouth! You are getting maudlin too much sitting around. There are things that need to be done and perhaps we best get at them. I think it's time we get going. We'll plan today, stay tonight and think about starting out tomorrow or the day after? What do you think? Take our time but we should go on to Lily's before we go home. This estrangement with your father and its memory eats at you and needs to be dealt with. I believe Lily can help."

I shook my head. "My darling, it's too late, he's gone."

"It is never, never too late to heal a wounded heart Andrew. You must reconcile your memories and the attached guilt that plagues you. I'm serious! Lily will help."

I nodded my agreement. With that, we helped each other return to the cabin. We would take and enjoy one or two last night's together in Eden.

~ *Aleck* ~

I had never been exposed to the tumultuous emotions of a woman. My self-sufficiency had stood me in good stead throughout my life, at least to this point. There were no brothers to come to the rescue, no sisters to protect from the unguarded passions of other men. There were the fading memories of my mother, an ample woman who always smelled of apple pies and open fields. She had always been happy and a loving mother. Even after my father had disappeared, she had never given in to dismay, although as my memory stirred I remembered the weight of the sadness in her eyes several years later as she prepared me for her final departure. She had been ill for many months, the impish gleam in her eyes had dimmed, the sheen of her copper hair had faded and her face paled and shrunk, her skin outlined the bones of her face. She made me promise to take for myself her one earthly treasure, her chain with the MacLaren medallion attached to it. It was the mate to my father's. With tears that could not be contained spilling from my eyes I gently detached the heavy gold strand from around her neck.

At the time, there did not seem to be any reason for me to stay. I was young and so I travelled back east to stay awhile with my aunt, my Mother's sister. I was big for my age, but had a gentle streak that belied my underlying strength. I was aghast at my uncle's tyranny and abusive comportment. I managed to land a job as merchant sailor, taking me all around the world. I had been to ports from China to Africa nevertheless the longer I was away the more I seemed to long for the soothing beauty of the cabin. I vowed one day I would return.

After the war, I had come home. I had rebuilt and improved the old cabin, with the intention of resuming the search for my father, but as the years have passed, this need grew less. Mother had always maintained

Father had died on the far side of the ridge. At first we had searched together, even though I was really too young to know exactly what we were looking for. Day after day, we would go out. On these sojourns, I learned well the ways and patterns of the mountains. She had shown me land marks that had not changed for as long as the ages had been counted. And I learned just how fickle Mother Nature could be. Also from her, I had learned to respect the animals of the wild, to soothe and nurture those who were injured.

At the moment, though, I had a lot to keep my mind occupied; I had relished the short time with Bryn in my home and knew it would be empty ever after without her. However, more importantly, Bryn's palpable anguish ate at me and I was unsure how to soothe her. The only solace I had provided until now had been the comfort of my embrace. It had seemed enough but out here on the trail, I was lost.

I had never been bothered by the rituals of death, wills and such things that trapped people and bound them to the restrictions of a society I had chosen to resist. Andrew was of somewhat the same mind, a bit of a maverick but now with a family to love and care for, it was different. Andrew's words were logical. He had discussed with me the decision to go to St. Louis and had told me frankly that it was not for him but for Lily and for Sarah and their children. They had never known his father and he was hoping that his father had found it in his heart to forgive him, although he doubted it. He had even shared Thomas' letter and I understood why Andrew had agreed to this trip. I thought I might have done the same myself if I had a family of my own.

I had always had a liking for Andrew. He was blatantly honest like myself and had a reputation to be a good man to have at your back. But, I confessed to myself, Andrew's greatest accomplishment was his daughter Bryn! I had met up with them on one of their famous hunting trips. Bryn was just a young girl at the time, pretty and spunky and full of promise. Now she was grown up with long brown hair rippling across her back with red fire gleaming like a halo as the sunlight caught it through the leaves. The curls she hated so much circled her face like a porcelain doll. The sensuous lips that graced her mouth were enough to make a man forget himself. I knew it had been hard for Andrew to accept the intrigue he recognized in my eyes.

The track we were following was well worn. I had used this route myself many different times. It was growing colder and we would definitely need shelter for the night. We would make St. Louis within two days. I knew just the spot to stop tonight, by the small pond that had a small waterfall that emptied into it. There was a cave well off the trail that I had taken refuge in over the years. I kept a good supply of wood there and furs for emergencies, as I did in several locations. But this was my favorite place and I wanted to impress her.

The trail was narrow and restricted us to single file. I wanted to look back to see if Bryn was all right now, but I did not want to intrude on her thoughts. I also did not want to face the stricken look in her eyes, so we rode in silence.

~ Bryn ~

I had been disheartened to leave my parents behind. Then again, I calmed down as the repetitive movement of Tinker soothed me. Mama was able to say good-bye, and Papa, although injured, would be able to look after her. My frame of mind firmly settled, I was comfortable enough to turn my attention to the handsome man who rode just ahead of me. From his well-worn black Stetson to the black hair that drifted loosely at the base of his neck, his broad shoulders slightly hunched as he sat relaxed in the saddle, I could envision the reins gently flowing across the palms of his gloved hands. With gentle but firm control, he guided his horse through the narrow pass. I noticed he sat tall in the saddle and had to duck frequently under the low lying branches that I simply rode under.

We traveled on like this with two light stops. We stopped under the sheltered shade of the trees with a fire big enough to boil water for coffee. We ate the bread and jerky that had been packed by Mama. Well, here I was in the middle of nowhere, with a man that I barely knew. My present situation was based on my father acquaintance with him. Still I could not help but feel reassured by his presence, but it was difficult to gage Aleck's mood, not knowing him very well. I thought Aleck was annoyed. In all fairness, I had to side with him, acknowledging the sudden change in his plans, whatever they had been. He had willingly changed them for me. Maybe that was why he was so solemn. At the moment he looked positively thunderous. I already understood Aleck to be a man of few words but the look on his face was bewildering. The hours rolled by. I was becoming aware of the chill in the air and hugged my shawl up around my shoulders. The storm's attack had been fierce and unyielding, conversely, after such a release of energy the world settled back to its routine; the calm after the storm. Our pace was slowing, I was way out of my own territory now and I realized we appeared to have left the main trail. I was unnerved to realize just how dependent I was on Aleck, a man I hardly knew. I began to understand Father's intense concern. My thoughts came to an abrupt halt when I suddenly realized he was looking for a place to stop. For the night! I had completely blocked out the fact that we would be spending the night together. My heart started racing. My stomach tightened in anticipation. I was blushing and was scared to death.

Aleck spotted the opening to the cave. He brought his horse around on the narrow track. "This is a good place to stop. Aye, you look a little tuckered out," he said as he helped me down. I eyed the mouth of the cave, trying in vain to quell my mounting trepidation. Several hours ago this did not seem like it would be difficult, but now I could feel the color mounting in my cheeks. I walked to the opening of the cave and pretended to survey the interior carefully. Saddle stiff, it had felt good to move my legs, shift my rear and give my body a good stretch. I had forgotten how hungry I was.

While Aleck looked after our horses, I ventured into the mouth of the cave. To my surprise it was not very deep, but would give ample protection from the outside elements. I had the overwhelming feeling that I was intruding into someone's home. Against the far wall, wood was neatly stacked and the rocky outline of a cooking fire lay ready in the center of the floor. It was neat and cozy. As I spied the furs folded by the wood pile I thought we might starve to death but we would not be cold.

~ Aleck ~

Meantime, I stood at the mouth of the cave admiring her perfect figure. Her back was so straight, and the folds of her riding skirt guarded the turn of her ankles from lusting eyes. I was struck by feelings I thought I would never have. I wanted to protect this woman, keep her from harm and have her by my side.

She jumped as she realized she was not alone. "You frightened the life out of me Aleck!" She said more accusingly than she meant.

Two long strides had me standing directly in front of her. I placed my hands on her shoulders. I noticed how vulnerable she looked standing there, exhausted from her ordeal and unsure of me with the night to come. Her hair was askew, sitting in damp tendrils around her face. She lifted her head in a graceful movement displaying her slender neck and the pulse that beat rapidly. Her face took on a flush, as her heart beat wildly in her chest. She did not pull away as I drew her to my chest and my lips met hers.

After that light kiss, her arms went instinctively around my neck. It was a tender kiss born of exhaustion and pent up passions. My day old beard rubbed against her cheek. Her lips remembered the taste of mine, so now she knew she had not dreamed that first kiss. Balanced on tip toes, she brazenly pulled me closer. My eyes bore right into hers as my mouth covered hers. My arms molded her tightly to my body as my tongue swept inside and plundered her mouth. She clung to me, overcome as I could feel her legs give way beneath. I felt her excitement and naiveté as she tentatively reached her tongue out to meet mine. I suddenly stood upright and placing my hands on her slender waist pushed her away from me. The spell was broken.

It was a few moments before I spoke. "I've staked the horses. Let's walk for a bit. I want to show you something not far from here. Aye, a beautiful waterfall where we can both freshen up and then I'll start a fire so we can eat." Shaken by the magnitude of my feelings for her, I had to break away but I knew if I let go she would fall over. I had to get control for both of us. Innocent that I knew her to be, she could have no idea what her response to my kiss had done to me. I wanted to claim her right here and now.

~ Bryn ~

I could feel the heat of his hands as they held my waist keeping me upright. I was rooted to the spot, and stood staring at him like he was a ghost. I had not understood a word he had just said. I was reeling from the intensity of his kiss. I had never been kissed like that before. Oh, I had been kissed, but those kisses had not left me feeling so heated, so hungry and wanting more. My lips still felt the pressure of his and my arms knew the roll of his shoulders as he stooped to kiss me. He was so tall. He reminded me of Rob and Josh, and with that, an onslaught of homesickness passed over her. Yes, of all of my brothers, he looked most like Rob with his dark rugged good looks. But his demeanor was all Josh, quiet with a quick wit and reliable character. Not one of the local fellas had ever made me feel this way before. I needed a moment to reconnect with reality. I blinked rapidly and then as he removed his hands from my waist he grabbed my hand. Tugged along, I followed Aleck out of the cave.

I followed him down the path. As we neared, the sound of the falls drowned out the call of the birds. I stopped at the edge of the water and gaped at the splendorous beauty of the scene before me. I had never been on this side of the mesa, never been through the pass. I had accompanied Papa and my brothers on hunting expeditions, but I had never witnessed anything as miraculous as this. I sat down on the edge of a huge rock and hiked my skirts to my knees, pulling off my boots and stockings

~ Aleck ~

I once again found myself fighting for self-control. Her shapely calves and dainty feet were enough to make me wish I were elsewhere. My mind focused furiously on the solemn promise I had given her father. She dipped her feet into the cool water and the look of utter contentment was arousing. Bryn wiggled her toes and swished her feet in the water; it looked like she had just found heaven. I could see the blisters on her feet where her boots had rubbed the delicate skin.

~ Bryn ~

*A*leck was beside me. I could see satisfaction written all over his face. He had wanted to impress me and he had. This secluded area was beyond description, but then Aleck stripped out of his shirt and took off his boots. I could not hide my admiration when I saw him. His broad chest covered in dark, curly hair that narrowed to a "V" where his pants were now resting on his slender hips. I didn't know where to put my face, so I just continued to stare and hoped I did not look like I was gawking. His hand came up to check the safety of the medallion he had around his neck before he turned and in one purposeful stride dove into the water. He surfaced in the middle of the pond below the falls and shook his head. Silver raindrops flew in all directions and like a prism caught the light in pinks and blues and yellows. He was laughing. "You really should come in. It's so nice" he cajoled me. I shook my head rapidly. The water was cold and soothing on my blistered feet, but I did not want to be alone with him in water that was over my head. He swam back to me with quick powerful strokes, and was out of the water, sitting beside me before I could collect my thoughts. His hand, once again came up to the medallion. I was intrigued; the gold chain was heavy with exquisite, cryptic tooling evident on the surface of the metal. I was about to ask him about it when I noticed the goose-bumps on his arms. The water was streaming from his body. The last thing I wanted was for him to catch his death of cold. I had already had enough of that with Mama this past week. His hair was dripping down the smooth skin of his shoulders. I followed the stream along its path to where his pants were tight across his waist. I was horror struck at the collection of scars, a long time healed, across his back. I could not stop the escape of air as

I uttered what I was feeling. Aleck quickly rescued his shirt from the tree branch it was hanging from. I searched his eyes for an explanation.

"Lessons from a long lost youth," was all he said. "We better get back, it will be dark soon and we have at least another full day's ride ahead of us tomorrow." He was up and offering me his hand. I took it and pulled myself up easily. We left the pond his hand in mine.

We were content to walk back to the cave in companionable silence. The noises of coming dusk just beginning. The rustle of the bushes, crickets with their continuous call escorted us as we moved through the brush. It had grown chilly and he put of the fur rugs around me until I felt cozy and warm once again. He looked after the fire and made dinner for us from our rations. Food always tasted so good when I was out on the trail. We had bacon, cheese and bread. Aleck toasted the bread over the coals. We were both hungry.

"I have ridden every day of my life, but my goodness I am tired this evening from the saddle." I was sleepy but content. Aleck sidled up beside me and casually put his arm around me. I was too tired to be flirtatious. He jumped up and went to my saddle bags and brought out some of my toiletries. He took my brush and bade me to sit in front of him. He patiently brushed my long wiry curls. I couldn't help it, I sighed like a contented a cat with each brush stroke.

~ *Aleck* ~

"**O**h, Aleck, that feels sooooo good." She purred, no longer able to keep her eyes open. I settled her down on her side and pulled her close to me. Just for warmth I thought. I kissed her eyes, proceeding down along her ear to her creamy white and slender neck. Her fragrance was of flower and spices. I was going mad… I had to stop. I would not be able to sleep at all if I continued. I gave in and laid down on my side and she lay with her back toward me. I pulled her close, perfect fit, but I already knew this in my heart. My arms went around her, like it was the most natural thing in the world to do, and she snuggled closer, and in this fashion we fell into a deep sleep.

The fire had died down to warm, glowing coals that cast eerie shadows on the wall of the cave. I awoke, my hand instinctively reaching for my gun. Something had alerted me. I gently eased myself away from Bryn, and was glad she had no roused. I placed her rifle where she could reach it if necessary and moved quietly to the side of the mouth of the cave. I saw nothing but the swirling of the trees in the wind. I gulped in the fresh air. I stood at the opening for a minute, my eyes becoming accustomed to the dark. The moon was shielded by clouds. Then I heard it, the wolf's sentry howl, two succinct hoots to be exact. I crouched down guarding each footfall as I crept into the darkness. I circled around to where the sound had come from. I knew this side of the mesa like the back of my hand. Within a few minutes, I found the cause for concern. One man I could see sneaking clumsily towards the tethered horses, while another was blundering through the underbrush. Quickly, I dispatched the one at the horse's side. His victim's gurgle, there was one more low howl from the vicinity of the cave. It was not difficult to fine the other culprit and felled him where he stood. A low all clear yip reached through the night, I answered with a yip of my own, then dragged the bodies well away from the cave and our horses. I then scouted the surrounding area and circled back feeling secure that there was no further imminent danger.

The threatening growl was enough to stop me by the clearing before the cave. He made his presence known. The large wolf then trotted out from the shadows at the side of the cave, passed me, and disappeared into the night. Content with our safety, and feeling the cold chill of the night air, I moved back into the warm shelter of the cave.

I stood over Bryn, watching her sleep. Her hair spilled around her, the fur pulled up to her chin. I lay back down beside her once more, and kissed her yet again. This time she roused and in her dream state, she kissed me back. I was not expecting the pleasure that passed through me. I groaned, knowing my lust would not be satisfied, not like this. Not with Bryn, and not to Andrew.

I had given the man my word, and by all I held dear, I would keep it.

*I*t was the smell of coffee drifting in the air that captured my senses and brought me fully awake; then I felt the rumbling in my stomach. My stomach then announced my famished state with a huge embarrassing gurgle. I prayed that Aleck had not heard it. Slowly, I opened my eyes and let them adjust to the dim light in the cave. Aleck had been so attentive last night. I did not want to wake up as I was having the most delicious dream, that Aleck was kissing me. It seemed crazy, but in my heart I knew I had found the man I was looking for. Just as he had done at the cabin, he stood with a mug of steaming black coffee for me. He settled in beside me, draping his arm over my shoulder. With a sudden growl and a shake of his head he leapt to his feet. His terse, "Time to get a move on," stunned me. He sounded so... harsh. I was unable to hide the hurt I felt at his sudden turn. He turned and started breaking up camp, giving me time to gather my things.

We saddled up. Aleck brought my saddle over and I took it from him. He gave me a questioning look. "I am fully able to saddle my own horse, Mr. MacLaren," I said as I set the saddle down and picked up the saddle blanket. I smoothed the blanket into position on Tinker's back, then hefted the saddle into place. I pulled myself into the saddle and left Aleck to pick up the final remnants of our camp.

~ Aleck ~

I stared after her wondering what had gotten into her. I finished up and was in the saddle in a matter of minutes. Women! I had the distinct feeling I had done something wrong, but for the life of me I could not figure it out. I replayed the morning in my head and seeing nothing untoward, once again wondered what had gotten into the warm, beautiful woman who was now a good half mile ahead of me. At least Splash was with me. I caught up to Bryn, took the lead and wisely gave her some space.

It was getting on to noon. The sun was high overhead and a warm, comforting breeze was rustling along the side of the slope. I decided to break the awkward silence that had developed between us. "There's fixins' for lunch. I'll have to hunt for supper. I'm thinking we'll be one more night out." I sat back in the saddle and adjusted my hat to cut the glare of the sun.

Bryn answered me with a cool, "that would be fine, Mr. MacLaren."

"Ahhh Bryn, my beauty, what's wrong lass?" I was now halfway between frustration and anger. My intuition warned me I was in dangerous territory, with no experience to fall back on.

"I don't want to talk about it, not at the moment anyway. A noon break sounds good though."

Surely she knew she was over reacting to whatever it was. I watched the tears well up in her eyes before she turned away from me. It struck me then, that my terseness over coffee this morning was the probable cause of her distress. I suddenly turned my horse and was at her side.

I wiped the fresh tears from her eyes as I crooned, "I'm so sorry, my beauty. I promised your father I'd protect you from all men including myself. I'm not doing a verra good job of it, am I? Aye and I've hurt your tender feelings. I'm so sorry."

~ *Bryn* ~

Relief had flooded my veins and I launched myself off Tinker and into his arms. He had laughed out loud as he caught me and held me close. "I take it my apologies accepted. Aye?" I had laughed with him, "Aye, yourself, you daft man. Kiss me, Aleck." Pleased with my response he silenced my laughter with his kisses. He now understood the hurt he had caused and would not make the same mistake again.

We rode on a little farther and found a natural clearing. Aleck set up the camp and I unsaddled the horses. I staked them nearby and let them graze. With the fire started and the coffee pot ready, I sat down. I watched every move that Aleck made. The sleek line of his body, the graceful movements of everyday living seemed more pronounced. He concentrated on his labor not so much as sneaking a look at me. I gratefully accepted the coffee he offered me.

"May I?" he asked.

"Of course," I smiled as he made to sit right beside me. Instinctively, I knew Mother would have told me I had been too harsh in my judgment this morning. And truly I did not like being upset with Aleck. We finished up the rest of the food, while admiring the beauty that surrounded us. Birds were singing in the trees and both of us looked skyward when we heard the haunting screech of a bald eagle. It swooped so close to me I felt I could have reached up and touched it. Its talons came out in front of him as he lunged for and caught a running rabbit. He flew away with the rabbit held firmly in his grip. "Well there goes dinner," Aleck chuckled. We laughed together.

We packed up the camp having spent more time than we ought to have. Once again back in the saddle, we settled down to a steady but careful pace. The storm had left its mark all over this side of the ridge and the horses had to take their time to secure their footing. Large boulders and trees littered the uncut pathways leaving them in awe of nature's wrath. Neither one of us wanted to disturb the unsettled tranquility that now consumed the forest.

I followed Aleck, conceding to his knowledge of the area. I still did not really understand what had happened to make Aleck jump away from me like that earlier in the morning. I looked intently at his back wondering how I would have handled the situation differently if it had been one of my brothers who had asked what the problem was. The path was so narrow it was impossible to ride side by side and was not conducive to a conversation. Besides, I thought Aleck seemed to be deep in thought himself. I wondered what nightfall would bring.

~ Aleck ~

usk comes rapidly up here. Sunset at this altitude is rapid, as daylight is chased away by the darkening skies. I was lost in thought. I was searching for a place to set up night camp. We were far away from the comfort provided by the cave. Tonight we would be out in the open. I was not worried about myself but I was concerned about Bryn. It had only been a week since the storm and I speculated on whether or not she would be skittish. Night was settling in quickly, meaning it would be dark very soon. I was thankful I had killed the two rabbits I had seen earlier in the afternoon.

"I know the place to stop, by a branch of the stream that comes off the falls where we stayed last night. It'll give us some cover and water. Aye, we should be there soon." I called back to Bryn.

"That sounds good! I'm famished!" replied Bryn.

"She's got a healthy appetite," he whispered under his breath.

We worked in synchronized harmony. Two days out and we had learned each other's rhythm. Bryn got the coffee going while I skinned out the rabbits and set the meat on sturdy pine sticks for roasting. Nothing ever tasted as good as the meal that was eaten after a long day's ride. We sat together facing the fire but avoided staring directly at the flames. The fire was for cooking, warmth and safety, to stare into the hypnotizing flames caused night blindness which was a definite disadvantage out in the wild. Then Bryn got up to freshen up before retiring. She took her saddle bag to the stream. She was within seeing and hearing distance of me. She intuitively knew I was watching her. She washed her hands and face and rinsed her mouth out. The water was cold, clear and refreshing. She came back to camp. I had banked the fire and put out our bedrolls. I put my arm out for her and she sat down beside me. It was so easy, so natural to nestle close, my body was warm, my arms strong but tender around her.

We sat in companionable silence for quite some time. I was stroking Bryn's hair, running my hand down her back. It felt soothing. I rolled one of the blankets lengthwise for us to use as a pillow. Both sated and tired, we curled up together. I whispered into Bryn's ear, "Good night, lass, pleasant dreams." I kissed the back of her neck. Bryn shivered in response even though her eyes were already closed. I attempted to close my eyes too, but was unsuccessful. I turned my head gazing at the stars in the cloudless sky. I asked myself the same question I had been asking myself all day. How did I come to be so lucky to have such a woman as Bryn Henley walk into my life? I must have done something right somewhere, because I could not really think of any reason why I should be so bewitched. It felt so good and so right for her to be in my arms, trusting me to be her protector. I could walk away and not cause her any pain right now, but I did not want to do that. But then the pain would be mine alone to bear. I made my decision. I would see her to St. Louis safe with her family and then I would return to the refuge of my cabin alone.

~ Drew ~

The simmering waves of heat continued. The sun rose early and set late, a big burning ball of fire usually welcome, but at this time of year, with so little rain, it was tantamount to disaster. We were all right so long as the river held but a couple more dry weeks and all the ranchers would be in devastating trouble. I left town for a few days to help at father's ranch. The livery was in good hands with Jake Richards working it. Business had been slow, so I took the opportunity to lend a hand. I did have an ulterior motive, and that was to get to know my brother Rob once again. It was Rob's turn to stay out with the other hands to watch the cattle. Earley and I had returned to the house for our two days' rest. It was dusk, signaling the end of another long, arduous day. The break in the heat as darkness began to fall was welcomed relief. Seasoned veterans of this area, we were alert to any signs of smoke which indicated a threatening fire. It was dry and the smallest spark could spell disaster. The house was empty and lifeless with only the two men to occupy it. Usually Ma would be fussing around the kitchen, singing to herself. Sometimes Pa would come in and they would dance around the kitchen together as if at a barn dance. Other times Pa would be putting up tack and puttering around the barn or the house fixing this and that. He may even be found in his favorite chair reading quietly or finishing up the household books. Bryn would be dancing around the table, disciplining the knives and forks, leaving little treasures in her wake; with my brother gone; only me and our parents were there to pick up after her. There was a basket by the front door where all the little odds and sods she left in her wake could be placed each day. It was her daydreaming. She would be off in another little world of her own and things would just get left behind. Usually it irritated me, but now with Bryn gone, I missed the silly habit. I felt a pang of loneliness and decided to abandon this line of thought before it ruined the rest of my quiet evening.

It was peaceful after dinner. Earley and I sat out on the porch in Ma and Pa's rocking chairs. The breeze had picked up, still gentle but with a hint of chill leaving no doubt about the season's change that was just around the corner. We both lit up our pipes. Earley carried his for those quiet peaceful moments on the trail but I never carried mine with me, reserving it for evenings on the front porch, so it was with great pleasure and anticipation that I tamped the tobacco into the bowl of the pipe. We sat in companionable silence; the creaking of the rockers keeping time with the rhythm of the chirping crickets. It was that in-between part of the last hours of the day, the finite time that lies between dusk and dark, when all creatures took stock of the day and prepared for the coming of the morrow. The pipe smoke curled in lazy clouds as the bone weary men sat in quiet contemplation of nothing and everything.

Earley sensed it first and then I saw a rider coming in hard from town. Dust flying from the hooves, as the large animal thundered along the path to the house. The rider was low on the horses' back as he urged every last bit of energy and speed from the huge beast. "There's a man with a mission," said the understated Earl. We came off the rockers as one and came to the edge of the porch as the rider approached. From a distance, I recognized Jake with one of the horses from my livery. Jake brought the horse to a skidding halt. The horse's hind came up under him as he pulled back hard on the reins. The horse bellowed out its displeasure. Lathered and exhausted from the hard ride, the horse bellied up to the trough and took deep gulps of the water.

"Telegram from your Aunt livin' yonder. Sorry." I snatched the telegram from Jake's hand and read it out loud.

"Josh, Drew stop Do not want to worry you stop Family have not arrived yet stop Bad storm five days ago stop Will await your reply stop Love Aunt Lily"

I stood still holding the paper in my hands as if to reread; Earley did not like the look on my face. I sent Jake to the barn to tend his horse and saddle a fresh horse for his return to town. No use in running a good horse into the ground. "Not bad news boy, just worrisome.

Nothing at the river to indicate trouble, even the cattle stayed quiet," said Earl. "Put your mind at ease, we'll ride out in the mornin' and do some scouting." He put his hand on my shoulder in an uncharacteristic display of affection.

Earley and I sat down and talked it out. "I'll send Jake back with a response for Aunt Lily. Josh can't go on account of Becky and the youngsters. I'm happy to have you with me Earley." Earley just nodded at me, and continued to listen to me ramble. "I think Rob should stay here." Earley started to laugh, a deep rumbling chuckle. I just gaped at him. "What's so darned funny?" I demanded.

Earley could hardly contain himself, as he said between gasps, "Rob is your brother, a Henley, you don't go tellin' a Henley to sit by while his family might be in danger. You got some growin' to do boy." He patted me on the shoulder then added, "I want to see this first hand."

We disappeared into the dark house to get some much needed sleep. I spent a restless night, the hours dragging by. Finally I gave up, got up and packed for the trail. I was not surprised to find coffee already brewing and Earley waiting for me. The horses were soon saddled and provisions loaded. We headed out well before sunrise.

The air was cool in the early morning hours as we mounted. The heat wave was nearly over, but neither had time to make comments about the imminent change in the weather. The sun was just breaking over the horizon in a glorious splendor of reds and pinks as we approached the river campsite to let Rob know what was happening.

Josh was a steady quiet man, much like our father. After meeting with Rob and the others, Earley and I would ride to Josh's to deliver the telegram and confer with him on our plans.

~ *Rob* ~

*A*s they "hallooed" the camp, they saw I was up and stirring around. We had been lucky once again as the water level at the river, although low, had maintained itself throughout the heat wave, making water available to our cattle. It had been a major worry for Pa. The water level was once again on the rise, the worst was over. It had been many years since I had to worry about the herd. I thought I truly hated it, but then I had that serendipitous meeting with Grandfather in India. What a strange, self-serving man he had turned out to be. It was because of that reunion that I had come back as soon as was possible. I found it more than interesting that Pa and I had had the same argument only in the reverse. I had been afraid that we would repeat the unnecessary, wasted history. But I chose to break the bitter tradition and so I had returned to my family home. My own business was being run by an associate and I felt I needed some time to collect my thoughts and approach Pa. Of course timing is everything and mine looked as if it was just a tad off these days. Not a time to gamble, I thought. The arrival of the letter had completely thrown me. For the past week I had been waiting, gauging the time to approach Father with the news about Grandfather. There had never been a good time. I had arrived during the heat wave. Papa and Earley were out every day watching the river, mending fences and keeping count on the herd. We had weathered the whole thing rather well, with only a minimal loss. Some of the other ranchers with smaller herds in the area had not fared quite so well. The main water supply ran through Henley land. It was the water that had attracted Pa to this area. It was not all free range but Pa had assured the other ranchers that their cattle were welcome to the water. I followed this wisdom. No need to start a range war, I had known these folks since I was a small boy.

"Looks like the heat's finally broken and rain soon too," forecast Cookey as a cool breeze blew the steam from his cup of coffee. He gave his hip a slight rub too. The other hands were rising wearily. The night guards were coming in and were ready to eat and drop their heads onto their saddles for some nice peaceful shut eye.

"Yup, 'round up's acomin,'" Cookey spat into the grass. He was an old timer veteran of cattle herding for the Henley's; in his opinion too many drives to count. The problem was Cookey never learned how to count or read and write but as a camp cook he had no competition. Like Earley, he had been with Pa from the beginning. So long in fact most folks didn't know his real name. They only knew him as the camp cook affectionately called Cookey. He had watched each one of us Henley children grow up. He loved us like his own. Course he did not have any of his own either. I could not remember a time when Earley or Cookey had not been there.

It did not take long to break camp. Horses were saddled; breakfast eaten or finished while mounting. In the middle of all this shuffle and dust, Rob was alerted to two riders approaching from the direction of the ranch house, their dust wafting in clouds behind them as they approached the camp at a better than fair clip. Trouble... just what, I could not begin to guess. It must be Drew and Earley, but what had brought them back out here and so early in the morning.

"Hey Rob," yelled Drew.

"Hey yourself, what's up? We weren't expecting you two back until morning after next." I hollered back, but watched for Earley's reaction. He looked uninvolved but ready to intervene as he had so many times when the boys had been young and gotten into fights. "We're a search party on the mountain, here read this." Drew pulled the telegram from his shirt pocket and handed it to me. Then he and Earley dismounted, loosely holding the reigns.

A look of concern sullied my face. I, too, dismounted and slowly handed the telegram back to Drew. We stood shoulder to shoulder. The sun was sneaking further up into the sky. After a brief hesitation, I grabbed my saddle bags. "Give me a minute to get everyone organized here and I'll be ready to go. I'm coming with you. Three can search better than two." Earley was biding his time but Drew readily accepted his brother's decision to accompany them. Sliding into the saddle, I called Fergus over and set the wheels in motion for the ranch to be run with Josh as the only Henley at hand. Pa had trained his men well and treated them even better. Although he had never left the ranch completely unattended before, there was no question of its care in his absence. I knew that all would run well while we were gone. There was little time for talk as the three men headed out. Three men, one thought. We headed to Josh's at a fast pace, only mindful of the need to keep the horses in shape for the strenuous ride ahead.

Fergus and Cookey stood watching the dust fly. Cookey muttered, "I'm sendin' ya up a prayer Lord, for my friend Andrew and his kin. He's one of the good ones, Lord, take care of them, please 'n thank ee!"

~ Josh ~

I was just finishing up one of Becky's scrumptious breakfasts; fresh eggs and bacon with fresh baked bread. It just did not get much better than this. I still remembered army fare; I grimaced and promptly gave my head a shake. With coffee in hand, I wandered out to the porch. Becky had gotten her usual early morning start and the wonderful smell of baking bread was drifting through the house. The children, now better, had left the house to complete their chores, Jared to do them, with Jessie following and getting in the way. And if Jared, the happy wanderer, decided to stray from his routine, Jessie would simply sit down and wail at the top of her lungs. I laughed silently at the picture that brought to mind. Sounds drifted out here for miles. We paid heed to these sounds as our lives may depend on it. Father had taught us about the power of listening. Even in the quiet, there were sounds that could be separated from the normal. It was as I was finishing this thought that I heard the pounding of the hooves. In a matter of minutes Drew, Rob and Earley pulled up to the front hitching post. Wasting no time or words, Drew handed me the telegram with a worried nod of greeting.

"This is serious, Drew. Go and get fresh horses and I'll fill Becky in. Meet me back here." I ordered as I turned into the house for Becky.

I wanted to be involved with the search for our parents and sister, never-the-less as eldest, I knew I was needed here for both ranches now. I knew Fergus could handle Ma and Pa's ranch, especially knowing I was here if the need arose. Drew and Earley were more acquainted with the high lands than I was and Earley was definitely the best tracker. Reluctantly, I let go the notion that I take part in the search. I returned to the top step of the porch with Becky at my side.

Rob nodded indicating me to join him around the side of the house, then left leading the way. I set my jaw, squared my shoulders, clenched my fists and followed. The others watched us from around the corner and waited with baited breath. All was quiet, too quiet. It was quite a few minutes before we returned. Me first, returning to Becky's side, draping my arm protectively over her shoulder. Rob returned a moment later.

"I'll take my own horse. But thanks for the offer. I want Thief under me." Earley was virtually inseparable from his Appaloosa. He and Pa were as one about the abilities and qualities of the Indian bred horses.

"Right, Earley may your name be fitting for the task at hand; I hope the signs are there for easy tracking." Then turning, I looked directly into Drew's eyes "Travel well, travel swift, watch closely." Then I turned to Rob, our eyes locked as we finally looked each other in the eye. I reached out and shook Rob's shoulder, concluding "May God be at your side and keep you all safe. I'm well pleased you're here to help. Bring our family home safe if you can. "Godspeed!" Rob nodded, clasping my shoulder in return, an old ritual resurrected.

I watched anxiously as they rode away, but was comforted by Becky leaning into my side.

or the second time in as many weeks, I stood on the porch and watched my family ride away. But this time, I was worried. I consoled myself with the thought that the men could handle most anything. I wondered, for an instant, if I should have urged Josh to set off with the search party. But I too knew Josh's responsibilities would be here and I was secretly delighted as I was loath to be separated from him again. The brothers were speaking again, albeit strained, hopefully . . . I nearly laughed as I realized that Bryn's daydreaming was starting to rub off on me. Josh sent one of the hands to retrieve my eldest, unmarried brother, Ian, so that he could pitch in. I had always hoped that Bryn and Ian would hit it off the way we had. But so far, my scheming had come to naught.

~ Earley ~

I was acknowledged to be the best scout and tracker for miles around. I knew Andrew would have crossed the river at the shallow ford bend, easier for the women and would then head back up into the hills. I did not have to be as considerate of the search party, so I took the shorter route and was presently rewarded. Andrew had obviously camped on the far side of the river the first night out and I had no trouble tracking the family this far. I also knew Andrew planned to use the pass on the afternoon of the third day. We had discussed this route before they left. Hopefully they had been near enough for shelter with MacLaren. We headed east into the hills. Without the women and the pack horses to slow us, we made much better time.

The riding was becoming rough. We had no idea about the severity of the storm until Lilyan's telegraph. Seeing the devastation first hand was awe inspiring, if not terrifying. Trees, wider than the breadth of a man, down and many completely uprooted. Ditches created by the run off were wide enough to create flowing unnatural rivers that carried rocks and other debris like cotton balls for miles down the sides of the long hill. Boulders shifted on the now unstable surface of the mesa. It was difficult to hold to any trail, let alone stay with the nearly obsolete track Andrew had followed up here. The temperature had dropped dramatically with the elevation from the sheltered valley, sitting cozy and protected far below us. The sun sparkled through leaves, still damp days later, the dancing shadows making visibility difficult, but beautiful. We fanned out, but were always in voice range of each other. But there was nothing.

"Getting' on to dusk we should set up camp here. The horses are tiring and there's no sense in enervating good animals. We'll head for

MacLaren's in the morning. He may know something of them." I, as eldest and tracker, assumed the role of leader. We set up camp, ate and settled quickly for the night. There was no chit chat or idle fireside banter, we all wanted to sleep as the sun would be up early and we would be ready.

The dull red halo of the sun was just peaking from behind the pitch of the mountain. I deduced that Drew and Rob had slept restlessly by the way they both had tossed and turned during the night. If it was due to chasing their own demons, no one was confessing. I slept with a clear unencumbered conscience. We were anxious to pick up the trail. Riding was slow, nerve racking and dangerous. The horses were all trail hardened and picked their way carefully over the loose stones. A stone in one of the horse's shoes could spell disaster, so the riders watched very carefully. We were making our way toward the base of the ridge when we picked up the campsite. If it was not for the piece of rope Drew found fluttering from a tree, we might have missed it. The storm had destroyed most of the recently dug trenches but the rocks that had encased the fire still remained. On further inspection, we found tattered bits of cloth, not a good sign. Drew and Rob were vaguely familiar with the location of Aleck's cabin, having hunted in this area occasionally with their father and brothers years ago. I also knew where he was headed but it still took us the better part of the early morning to find it. The strain of waiting and watching was immense. We were prepared for a lot of things, and none was easily shocked. However, the several scenarios we had envisioned were not pretty pictures. What we did find was beyond all of us.

Drew was on the porch first, followed closely by me and Rob. We peeked through the window and there sitting, picture perfect, were Andrew and Sarah enjoying a mid-morning coffee by a cozy warm fire. Both looked up in alarm as the men stepped in through the unbolted door. It was not like Andrew to let anyone get the jump on him.

~ Andrew ~

I broke the shocked silence first. "What in the devil's name are you doing here? And who's got the ranch?" The second question grated along my teeth through a clenched jaw.

"Anda howdy to you too," reproached Earl. It broke the tension and soon all were listening to me as I quickly filled them in on the basics of the events since our departure twelve days before. "As if the storm weren't enough, I was injured and worse, your mother was so ill, I thought we were going to lose her." The emotion was thick in my voice, and for a moment I was overcome by the memory. "Bryn saved us. She had a lean-to set up and got the tarp over us and some hot food into us. Then she went on ahead to find Aleck. She located him all right he had to rescue her from a fall from Tinker horse. She's okay now and then he came back for us."

"Where is Bryn? Is she alright?" Drew demanded.

"She took a bump on that daydreaming hard head of hers, but she's alright, son. We knew Lilyan would be worrying. Your mother was in no shape to travel and to be honest neither was I. So we sent her on ahead of us."

"You sent her on ahead by herself in this mess. Don't you know what you've sent her out into? She could really get herself hurt." And then he was speechless. The dawn of understanding rose on Drew's face. "You didn't send her by herself did you? You sent her with . . . him? Was she alright with this? I'll kill him with my bare hands if he lays one hand on my sister." Drew was flushed with anger and gripped his balled up hands tightly at his side. Drew honestly could not believe I would ask such a thing of Bryn. Rob and I held our peace for the moment. Neither was happy with this turn of events, I would never willingly risk anyone of my children, especially my daughter.

I sat back and assessed the situation carefully. I was very aware of the boy's ire, their faces and posturing told of their restrained anger. I did not want to end up on the wrong side of a fight with them. "She'll be alright with Aleck. MacLaren's word is solid and he'll keep it. It was essential she make it to Lily's as soon as possible. She'll be sick with worry."

We awoke to a day that was dull and gray, with a mist that swirled around the horse's hooves as we trekked slowly letting our mounts have their head. The fog hung like moss from the trees, curling and ever moving as we pushed on ahead. Navigation was dangerous before the storm but with all the trees down and the earth churned like a field for planting, there was a great deal of fresh debris to negotiate. The storm's aftermath left me with a strange feeling about my own comfort, security and future. Had I any right to fall in love with a woman like Bryn? Yes, I had to admit to myself that I had fallen in love with her. I had no idea it could happen so fast, but it had. I had had occasion to be around lots of women over the years but none affected me like Bryn. I had realized as we left my cabin that I wanted her in my home with me, but I could not ask her to live there, so isolated from everyone. She was used to family around her and friends; the secluded nature of my cabin in the mountains would be too much. Truly there were too many unanswerable questions going irrationally around in my mind. Certainly, she had implied she thought me handsome; and she returned my kisses with a passion I felt she was too innocent to pretend. Her body felt so right curled up to me in the night and I'd not tell her any time soon how she sighed contentedly each time I pulled her in close. Most women seemed afraid of my intense dark looks but Bryn had brushed my hair and run her fingers through it after I had brushed and braided hers last night. And I knew she was fascinated by my mouth, she seemed to vacillate between staring into my eyes while we had talked then licking her lips as her gaze dropped to my mouth. She liked my kisses. This morning I had groaned in pleasure when I saw her lips were still swollen from last night. I had afforded myself one lingering kiss this morning and then carefully, slowly reined myself back under control. I had made my pledge to Andrew and I would keep it.

I had been firm but considerate while I gained control over my ardor. In point of fact, it had damn near killed me but the reward was worth it. She was smiling and happy as we mounted and headed out. Bryn was completely unaware that her face was an open book. If she felt it or thought it, it was no secret to those around her, especially those who knew her well. So here I was, wondering if this wonderful young woman would ever forgive me for something that had not even happened. She was an innocent. I would make her my own one day, or die trying. This I promised myself.

~ *Bryn* ~

$\mathcal{W}$e made our way with care. The mist of the early morning had cleared, but the sky remained dark and threatening. The sun hung in watery pale shades of yellow, looking lost against the graying sky. Content and following Aleck at a comfortable distance, I felt secure, so I allowed my mind to wander.

Aleck had said it would not be long now before St. Louis appeared on the horizon. I was struggling to remember the lay out of the town. I vaguely remembered Main Street and, of course, the levee with its steam boats. I remembered from one of Aunt Lily's recent letters that St. Louis had really grown in the years since I had been there last. There was The Grand Hotel owned by Aunt Lily and Uncle John and now there were three more. There was also a new General Store, Aunt Lily wrote about the many bolts of material that were usually in stock. And the owner also kept all of the latest ladies gazettes. I was so excited about going through those periodicals. Aunt Lily had also hinted that the materials were all very fashionable and the ladies of St. Louis were quite pleased with the selections. New clothes! Fashionable clothes! Oh I really would need to sweet talk Papa into some purchases. Aunt Lily was favorably impressed with the new millinery shop too. She had described several of her new hats. She felt the couple who ran it were engaging and quite creative. A pretty new hat would be just the thing to bring back to the ranch to wear to our next barn dance. I stopped my musings while we stopped for a light, early repast.

"I've never been this far over that I can remember. My father would bring us up to camp and hunt but not this far." I initiated the conversation.

We were interrupted by the sight of an eagle that had just taken flight. Eagles rarely ventured over as far as the ranch preferring their own higher elevations and hunting grounds but up here they were common. This one's wing span was enormous, wider than I could spread my arms. Aleck broke in, "They're magnificent creatures, aye? I set the broken wing of an eagle once and his span was as tall as myself. When he was healed, I sent him back home. He comes by to visit every once in a while." The eagle suddenly and sharply made its dive down the backside of the cliff. As he rose into the sky we knew he would not go hungry this night.

The horses were calm, grazing in nearby grass as we talked about the beauty of the wildlife Aleck had pointed out along the trail. I loved listening to the timbre of his voice as he lovingly described some of the beauty and dangers we had seen. I shuddered, "I was just thinking, I had the eerie feeling we were being followed."

"Aye lass, we were. The forest up here is full of eyes that miss nothing that changes. The wind, the trees, the very air tells them a story about their surroundings. To co-exist with the animals here you must respect them and their home. Disrespect is not tolerated and the consequences are usually severe. There was a pack of wolves following us today. They have full bellies so they were more or less just curious about what we are doing in their territory. You may have heard them the other night at the cave. Had they been hunting, we would need to be more alert."

"Aren't you lonely up here all by yourself?" I could not imagine a day without someone to talk to.

"Yes and no. I have my moments and go into St. Louis if I have a need. Otherwise I enjoy my own company. And then there is the odd bit of excitement that assures me I'm in the right place!" he gave a sly grin.

"You do seem to be very self-sufficient, but what about vegetables and things that you need besides meat?"

"I have a small garden in the back of my cabin. It's hard to keep though, because the rabbits and deer come and enjoy before I have a chance to harvest. I'm in the process of building the garden up and putting up a sturdy fence. It may keep out the deer but the rabbits are going to go where they want, when they want. Aye, I can't trap enough of them to make a difference. There are other things to eat besides cultivated vegetables that wait ready for me in the forest. My mother showed me how to dry them out so they would keep throughout the winter months."

After the horses had rested, and were watered at one of the many streams that remained swollen and engorged from the storm, we were once again on our way. We had forded several of these streams at the top, although they were running, fast, they were still narrow enough to cross fairly simply. However, as they gathered force down the slopes, they could become quite nasty as several merged and showed their watery strength. Under the heavy skies and with the threat of more rain, I finally caught my first sight of St. Louis. It seemed a long way off in the distance, but Aleck assured me we would be there later today. I could almost feel the warmth and smell the scent of the bath water swirling around my aching, dirty body.

St. Louis was a bustling town full of chaotic activity. There were ferry boats crossing the mighty river. Although I could not yet make them out, I could imagine people crossing back and forth in front of wagons and horses being brought up short to avoid collisions with oncoming foot traffic. I could imagine dogs barking in the street and chasing after horses that could not be bothered to fight. Business brisk as women bartered for materials and general store goods. Most things, I knew, were put on a monthly running tab and the townsfolk and surrounding farmers paid their tab down monthly. To a farm bred girl like me, St. Louis was a booming, big city.

St. Louis was in a perfect location for commerce on the Mississippi River. Uncle John had been instrumental in bringing the railroad to the east side of the river. Now he was working on the "push to the Pacific" as he called it. The ferries were necessary as there was no bridge as yet. However, Uncle John felt they would come and so he was concentrating on taking the railroad out to the west. St. Louis was nestled in a fertile valley with prosperous farming that spread out from the town. Usually the farmlands were protected from the more severe weather that was experienced on the southeast side of the mesa. The fields were being harvested; men and plow horses dotted the outlying vicinity. Aleck and I had a spectacular view of the entire area from our vantage point on the crest of the ridge.

Neither seemed interested in breaking the silence but then something startled our horses. We were both caught totally unaware. Aleck's horse stumbled backwards in an attempt to regain its balance. Its startled and frightened neighing increased as it floundered no longer sure of its footing with the soil crumbling beneath its hooves. In desperation the helpless animal made one last valiant attempt to find some purchase on solid ground, and when that failed, horse and rider slipped over the edge. Tinker successfully backed up away from the edge as I grabbed wildly at thin air trying in vain to catch Aleck. He now had both hands on the reins and I felt the material of his shirt slip through my fingers. I watched in horror as they both disappeared from view.

I backed Tinker up even further; then quickly dismounted. Finding some stable level ground well away from the edge, I tied Tinker to a tree. Papa would be proud as I remembered to tether her with a knot that she could rear and break free from in the event of another disaster. With my rope, I secured myself to the tree and tied the other end around my waist, leaving just enough play to get to the edge. I had been screaming Aleck's name but the only response was the sickening whickers of his horse. Cautiously on all fours, I approached the spot where only seconds before we both had stood. I was down on my belly and inched forward to the ledge and peered over the side. Trying to keep myself together, I scanned below and spotted them. Aleck's horse was lying bent in an unnatural pose; its screams of pain were intolerable for me to bear. Aleck lay absolutely still.

"Aleck!!!" I screamed again, fear rising like bitter gall in the back of my throat. My heart beat a wild tattoo. He did not respond. Through tears, I looked around wondering how I would get down there. For the second time in a week it was all up to me. As I crawled back from the edge, I remembered yet again that panic equals disaster. Calming myself with deep breaths I thought this was becoming a habit I would just as soon break. By pulling on the rope I made sure that the tree I was tied to was a sturdy anchor and would support my weight as I lengthened my tether. Using a sequence of long learned knots I tied one end of Papa's rope to the pommel of Tinker's saddle. I gathered up the supplies I thought I would need when I got to Aleck. Making sure the canteen and rifle were secured to me I approached the edge again. I sent the rope attached to Tinker over the side to rest near Aleck. Then I took a deep breath and slipped over the side myself. I was unnerved by the unexpected swing of my body and grabbed the rope tightly quelling the queasiness that had started in my stomach. My four brothers had all taken turns teaching me how to climb and descend, taking great delight in my inability to control the shaking that always accompanied my fear of heights. My hands were slick with sweat inside my riding gloves but I was able to hold on without sliding. The slope of the ridge was steep, but thankfully not long.

Although it seemed like an eternity, in a few short moments I was down on the ledge with Aleck and his horse. Aleck was out cold. I put my hand to his forehead and then tried to rouse him. "*PLEASE! OH!* Please be alright," I pleaded with his unconscious form, but Aleck continued to lay oblivious to my pleas. His horse had stopped thrashing. He lay with his big soft brown eyes glazed and staring at Aleck. A weak whinny now escaped him. I tried to swallow, but my mouth was as dry as the sand we were on, as it dawned on me what I now needed to do. A quick check of Aleck showed no broken bones, so I repositioned him as well as I could, wiping back the steady flow of tears that now clouded my vision. I took up the rifle, holding it as steadily as my shaking hands would allow. Papa had had to do this many times, always out of necessity. But that was Father, not me. I looked at Aleck's horse knowing I had to do it right the first time. I took careful aim and pulled the trigger. He never flinched, his great bulk lay still. Openly sobbing with reaction, I turned to look at Aleck, still not a flicker of movement from him; I needed his comfort but it was not forthcoming. Wiping the tears from my face, I sat down and raised his limp hand to my cheek. Fresh tears started, I kissed his hand and held it to my breast for comfort while I tried to figure out how I was going to get him back up to the ridge.

I took a strip off my petticoat and soaked it with water from the canteen and applied it to the rising bump on the back of Aleck's head. There was no blood; that had to be a good sign. We had tracked along the top of this ridge for maybe half a mile and I could see no end in sight so the best way up was the path he'd come down. Tying the rope under his arms and up behind his head, I tugged him into position to haul him back up the slope of the mudslide. There were fewer obstacles in his way but the ground there was still very unstable. I tied my jacket around his hat to protect his head the best I could. My tears continued to flow freely as I removed his saddlebags from Splash and tied them to the end of the rope that went under his arms. We would need those supplies if I managed to get him safely back up onto the ridge.

Once I had myself back under control, using my own rope, I carefully made my way back up. Gravel and loose rock fell behind us which I found to be most unnerving. I hesitated to look back down and continued forward. Finally back on the ridge I lay trembling with reaction and fear. I must admit though, I was proud of myself, but I was not finished. My breath was coming in rapid short puffs, my body numb. Carefully, I inched away from the edge. When I reached firm ground, slowly I got up clearing pieces of debris that could rain down on Aleck. Tinker was standing waiting fretfully for my return. Readjusting the rope around the pommel of the saddle to take up the slack, I mounted Tinker. We backed up slowly and Tinker held her ground when told, as I had to keep getting down to check Aleck's progress. Slowly, his large frame slid back up the slope to the ridge. We dragged him well away from the edge. I moved the ropes to trees even further back from the edge and re-secured them and Tinker. Making Aleck as comfortable as possible, I again checked him for injuries. Finding no broken bones, just the nasty bump to his head and scratches, I finally lay down next to him. He would be sore and bruised later. I wrapped my arms around him and gave in to sobs unleashed by emotion and exhaustion. A short while later, I woke somewhat refreshed. We needed nourishment. Maybe some coffee would help rouse him. I untied myself and went in search of firewood.

~ Aleck ~

I grimaced in pain and tried to move. I could feel my eyes heavy as I struggled to open them. Desperately, I tried again to open my eyes and was rewarded for the effort by the blinding light. My eyes squeezed shut of their own volition against the brilliance of the daylight and the pounding in my head. I had a vague recollection of what had happened, but was quite disoriented. With a jolt I realized Bryn was nowhere to be seen. My head hurt like hell, splitting with the pain. I brought my hand up to gingerly feel the bump on my head. The movement caused a wave of dizziness and nausea. I laid back and tried to assess the damage. My shoulder hurt, but did not seem to be broken or dislocated. In fact, miraculously, nothing felt broken. I had to find Bryn! I was aware of my fall, accordingly I clamped down on the waves of nausea that engulfed me as I rolled over and carefully inched my way to the crest of the slope. I was baffled as there was a rope tied around me impeding my movement. I saw Splash, but no Bryn and my heart turned over. The pain in my head was now a steady pounding and I tried in vain to bring myself to my knees.

"NO! Stop! Get away from that edge! What are you doing? Good Lord the ground's not stable!" Bryn was screeching but could not stop herself. "Aleck get away from that edge! You're hurt, oh Aleck please." She dropped the wood and crawled to my side. Carefully, she maneuvered me back from the edge.

"Is that always the way you greet the crawling wounded?" I whispered shakily. "What happened? One minute my horse is under me and now I'm here, no horse and you screaming like a banshee. Aye! a banshee! I wish the ground would stop spinning."

I dropped back into a sitting position; then laid my head against Bryn as she pulled me into her embrace. I closed my eyes and drifted. The banshee stopped her caterwauling and began to utter soothing words of comfort instead as she pulled me down onto her lap gently stroking her fingers through my hair. I fell into a light sleep. This time I could see my mother, I thought I had heard her before. She was speaking to me; I was so pleased to hear her soft, sweet voice again. I stood staring in fascinated awe at the specter. Her hands reached out in a gesture of comfort, her smile sad yet understanding. Somehow I knew I was not to join her yet. She smiled at me. "I love you true son, but it's no your time . . . the lassie needs you, go back to her." Then she started to back away. "NO! . . . Stay!! . . . Mother!! . . . I love you! . . . Come back!!" I called out to her in vain as she continued to back away. "No son! She needs you . . . go back to your lassie. I love you too, but go back son, go now." That was all she said and she was gone. I stared into the empty void her presence had left, feeling her loss all over again like it was yesterday. There were so many things I wanted to say, wanted to ask.

~ *Bryn* ~

*L*eaning back against a tree with his head in my lap and Tinker staring down at us, I watched as tears ran through the dust on his cheeks leaving wet trails. Wiping them away I stroked his cheek, comforted by the steady rise and fall of his chest. I hadn't realized how exhausted I was. The climb had been taxing, but not nearly as draining as worrying if Aleck was going to be alright. Staring down at his now calm face I caressed his cheek hoping, to sooth him. His eyelashes sat full and black against his eyelids. I dozed fitfully and woke to his movement in my lap.

~ *Aleck* ~

I opened my eyes slowly to find the earth had finally come to a stop. My eyes found Bryn's; I lay with my head nestled in her lap. I did not want her to stop running her hands through my hair. My whole being was on fire for her and her alone. I managed a lopsided grin.

"So you've decided to come back to the land of the living have you? Aye, you had me a bit worried there." She mimicked my words to her from the cabin.

Reluctantly, I tried to sit up, but the sharp jolt of pain that shot through my head changed my mind. Bryn disengaged herself from me and offered me some water. "Here drink some of this. It's bound to make you feel better." She waited while I savored the wet cool liquid. She gave me a helping hand and I was finally able to come to a sitting position. I sat for a while leaning heavily on Bryn for support. Except for the headache, I decided I would live.

"Thanks for staying with me, rescuing me actually, and seeing to Splash. Aye, a great horse he was, and he loved to play in the water," I attempted a chuckle and thought better of it as I caught the flash of pain in her eyes. I had had to put a number of horses out of their misery over the years. You never got used to it and you remembered each one, however one did learn to accept it as part of life's passage.

"Are you a bit better now?" she asked tentatively. "Do you need some coffee? Something to eat? Do you think you might be able to ride in a little bit? We're so close."

"When this headache goes, I'm sure I'll be just fine. Aye, eat something yourself if you will but naught for me at the moment. Give

137

me a few minutes rest then we best get started. How long have we been here?"

"Several hours, but there is plenty of daylight left, we should make it to St. Louis I think. You are alright Aleck? You are, aren't you? You can ride with me or you can ride and I'll guide Tinker."

"Together lass, you ride in front, aye." I did not miss the rise in her color and I knew headache or no I would not mind the ride at all!

He put his hands on his temples and rubbed firmly. "I hate to put this on you lass, but I'm thinking there needs to be a warning of some kind for folks who may come up after us."

Bryn nodded and added, "I will put up some branches as a deterrent."

A small fire seemed in order, so I retrieved the wood I had collected earlier. The strong coffee and a few biscuits helped revive me. I gathered the ropes, apologizing to Tinker as I added the burden of Aleck's saddlebags with mine. There was not much to do to break camp. I mounted and Aleck seated himself carefully behind me. He was still weak; he put his arms snuggly around my waist and tucked his head onto my shoulder. "Right where it belongs," I thought. Aleck dozed while I concentrated on getting us down off the ridge and to St. Louis. I focused on the trail and seeing Aunt Lily and Uncle John. All would be well again. Several times Aleck roused enough to shift his position, but he never seemed to lighten the hold he had around my waist. Several times I could not stop myself from loosening a rein and gently rubbing his arm where it clung to my waist, his presence alone was comfort.

I knew our descent, with all the added weight, would be especially challenging for Tinker. It was alarmingly steep and the trails were unknown to me. Simple pressure was all that was required to send her in the direction I wanted. Tinker moved cautiously making sure each step held her hoof before moving to the next. I navigated the maze of debris, balking only twice at the surety of the ground. I trusted my instincts, backing up and changing our path. We would need all of our skills combined and focus to get into town without further mishap.

This would have been a challenge for a rider alone, but Aleck's weight, although comforting, did throw my balance. The strength of his massive body surrounded me. Normally ramrod straight, his body was curled up to my backside. His strong arms continued to encircle me and hold on tight, his head tucked at the nape of my neck. It did not take long for my shoulders to ache with the constant pressure of his drowsy head and upper body resting on me.

Occasionally he would stir and nuzzle my neck then drift back off to sleep. I longed to turn, be wrapped in his embrace and feel the passion of his kisses from last night. St. Louis and my Aunt Lily and Uncle John would see the end of that freedom. I was mystified by a sudden aching for completion and satisfaction. It was both physical and heartfelt. I longed for him to always be this close. The path before us took a turn interrupting my contemplation. At a good pace with two riders and Aleck who knew the trail leading, we would soon be in town. This unfortunately was not the case, we were moving very slowly. Dusk was coming on quickly but Tinker was still in good shape despite the extra effort. The time spent up there with Aleck out cold had given her a good rest. I could not help but wonder if I would ever be in control of my own fate. I was confident the answer to my dreams was sleeping on my shoulder, but how could he . . . with concentration I again marshalled my wandering thoughts to focus on negotiating the trail before us. And then we were down.

~ Sarah ~

I looked at my two sons, husband and his best friend. Intelligent men all, but everyone was upset about Bryn being with Aleck by herself. They all cared for me, but now I felt they were really being irrational.

"Settle down, all of you! Sit down while I fetch some fresh coffee and get biscuits. Then we'll discuss this like adults. You must trust Bryn!"

~ Earley ~

With a subtle nod of my head and a brief hand gesture, I stayed Sarah and went to make the coffee and fetch biscuits myself. My senses were warning me there was more to this scene and I wanted a few minutes to assess. Andrew had obviously been unable to travel. But in all the years I'd known her, even with nursing all those who were sick; Sarah had never succumbed to the fevers and illnesses herself. I knew Sarah would have gone in Bryn's stead, leaving Bryn to care for her father if at all possible. So, although she looked well, but pale, perhaps Andrew had not been exaggerating the severity of Sarah's illness. I was concerned for her.

Trusting Bryn was not the issue as far as the men who loved her now felt. It was more a case of the man she was with. But, we knew worrying never solved any problems. We sat and, over coffee, Andrew gave us the full details of the many trials the three of them had endured. "This whole situation has wreaked havoc for my family." Andrew glanced at Sarah and took her hand. "Sarah really put a scare into me. I knew the journey was going to be burdensome, but for all that is holy, I never figured on that storm." His feelings of guilt blossomed from his open collar to his face. "We are born of strong stock, aren't we, sweet heart?" he grinned sheepishly in front of them. "The letter from Thomas still sticks with me; all these years and nothing and now everything."

Sarah finished Andrew's statement by adding, "And so you see, he's still not fit to sit a saddle, and I must admit, though much improved I don't feel so spry myself. Bryn and Aleck had to go on alone. She'll be fine. You'll see."

Drew suddenly remembered the telegram and, pulling it from his pocket, gave it to his father to read.

"No wonder you were so anxious," he conceded as he handed it to Sarah. "In hindsight, I'm not surprised that Lily got in touch with you." He finished. There was not much else to say. Sarah was right, and they had made the only decision that was available to them at the time. They had never considered that Lily would send a cable.

The search party was still not satisfied: Bryn was still alone with Aleck and these two did not seem too anxious to change their location. Granted, Andrew was still in bad shape and would be for several more days. Even now, it was obvious he was still swollen and had bruises that were just beginning to turn color. Right at the moment, although still pale, Sarah was the picture of normal, good health, coddling Andrew as always. No doubt about it, women were an enigma. Andrew was not the kind to be molly coddled, but to Sarah, he was jelly in a bowl. Many a culpable man that faced Andrew Henley did so with palms soaked and shaking knees. There was no mistake to be made in understanding that from here on, they would be on their own. Andrew made it quite clear that he would bring them both down when he was good and ready to do so. The cabin was secure and there was no need for them to do anything but recuperate and enjoy each other's company for a while.

~ Andrew ~

"Pa, what was it about Grandfather that caused such a rift between the two of you? You've never spoken of him for as long as I can remember." Rob's question had come out of the blue and took everyone by surprise.

"That's a long story son; one I had thought best forgotten. I think perhaps it would be best if I waited and told you all at once. Confound that man and all the trouble he has caused this family." I said this almost to myself.

"No, I would prefer not." With a scowl and with an order that brooked no opposition Rob concluded, "I want to know the truth! Now!"

Startled by Rob's forthright demand they all turned to me. I too had caught the tone in Rob's voice and decided to tell the story twice. It would not be any better or worse the second time through. I looked to Sarah for strength and received her nod of support. I waited as she moved before me and gracefully dropped to sit on the floor at my feet, mindful not to bump my bad right leg. She placed her hands in mine and looked straight into my eyes. With a loving smile exchanged between the two of us, I began,

"My mother, Emmaline, Emma to my father, died hours after I was born." I paused as a flash of memory tore through me. "Although he never said it in so many words, it was made abundantly clear that my father held me responsible for the death of the woman he loved more that life itself. He was distraught, I am told, so he did what he did best, he shut down and turned to his shipping business to the exclusion of all else. Oh…he did those things necessary for Lily and me when we were children. We went to the best schools, had a fine home, fashionable clothes and good food. When, as a young woman, Lily assumed the role of hostess for his business, he condescended to bring me in and make me a part of his business as well. It was a very unpleasant experience for both of us. I was not at ease with the ships and commercial activities. Although he acknowledged my ability with the books, the strain of being in the same offices with me was intolerable to him. It was on a trip to America that I saw the expanse of land just sitting there for the taking and I knew what I wanted. I did not feel any kinship, or really any business obligation to my father; and ships are just so unsettled. I love the feel of the land beneath my feet and the wide open ranges. I got involved with a good guide. The rest as they say is history. I valued being able to move from one place to another. I welcome the contentment of an Appaloosa under me on the trail. While on one of the expeditions, Earley and I found the place for our homestead. Then I met your mother, love of my life, and we never looked back. I briefly explained to Bryn how we had tried to get him to come for a visit but he wouldn't. I did not disclose that Thomas broke rank and privately replied to my correspondence congratulating us and wishing us well. Even sent your mother the beautiful crystal vase she keeps in the parlor. My father did not deign to correspond, never even acknowledged your mother. That was unforgivable, so I buried it and moved on. I have never spoken nor hardly thought of him since.

Your Aunt Lily was appalled by our father's negligence and in-deference to my wishes has not mentioned him with any of us. I know she has stayed in contact with him, seen him, has even kept him apprised of all of you and your accomplishments. I was not interested in anything to do with him. Don't get me wrong, I don't hate him, I just don't feel anything for him. It's as if he didn't exist. I have never regretted it until now. The thought of his death is a little unsettling."

"And Thomas?" Rob demanded. As an afterthought he added, "Please."

"Thomas is Thomas. He was always closer to Lily, but he was very good to me, treating me like a little brother. Lily accepted him as an elder sibling and I just followed in her stead. I often had the impression he thought ill of how my father held me responsible for my mother's death. However, I am responsible, if it were not for me . . ." Andrew stopped and drew a deep breath, then continued, "Thomas has been very loyal to my father. Thomas was orphaned and taken in by my mother and trained as my father's valet. Thomas felt indebted, but more than that, he became family. Our cook, governess and Thomas were always in our home and effectively raised us. Our father was never there, always at his offices. Thomas occasionally tried, valiantly, to restore the relationship between my father and me. I can see him making this journey, honoring a last request from the old man but in actuality, I believe he is doing this is on behalf of my mother. Lily often told me she really believed he was a gift from our mother. That, I'm afraid, is the whole sorry tale." Sarah raised herself up onto her knees and stroked my face then leaned in for a hug.

All was quiet for a few minutes as everyone digested the information, then Rob responded, "Amazing . . . well, a confidence for a confidence. There are several things I have to tell you, and now is the best opportunity I've had so far." Sarah exchanged a grimaced smile with me before she resumed her seat on the floor between my knees, once more we held hands.

nce they were resettled I continued. "First of all, I must tell you I'm happy to be home. I've missed all of you. But I had a need to see other places. Through Aunt Lily, I know you're aware of my shipping company. It's never been a secret. I love it! Like Grandfather, I've done well and with a good partner, it has flourished and now it operates pretty well independently. Any business decision I make can be relayed by mail or telegraph to Toby, my partner. These are modern times we live in!" I was now starting to falter over my words. I knew where I needed to go with this monologue; however, my stomach was telling me to switch things around, stalling for time. I stood and started to pace. I looked into my father's intense eyes, and saw compassion and query. My mother's blue eyes filled with sadness as she recognized my personal agony and willed me the strength to get out the words that would carry me over this hurdle. Drew and Earley both watched quietly, waiting. As Papa looked at me, I remembered Drew reading the letter that had started this whole escapade. He nodded to me and that seemed to be the act of permission. All was quiet save my voice filling the cabin.

"I wanted to tell you when I came back, but there was never a quiet moment. What with the worry over water and the heat. By the way, that should be resolved by now. The air was cooler and rain clouds were forming as we left. Josh and Fergus should have everything back to normal soon. I think we made it through without too many losses." The conversation had taken a turn and Rob was content to follow it.

"How many did we lose?" Papa acknowledged the change of subject and recognized the need for more time.

"About twenty head, not too much to worry about, right?" I, looked to Earley for the anticipated nod of confirmation. The actual count was not in yet, but that was a respectable estimate.

"OK, that's bad but we can survive it. Things are progressing toward round-up, I assume?"

"No worries there, everyone knows what they are doing. Fergus is there and Josh sent for Ian." Now, more comfortable speaking to my family again, I moved back to the topic that had been so heavy in my heart for the last half year. "So as I was saying . . . well . . . it was . . . difficult after The War, so I travelled. I knew you'd never understand but I can't be tied to the land. It's alright but I enjoy the adventures of the sea. On my last trip to India, Thomas recognized me in a hotel in Calcutta. Of course, I had no idea who he was but he knew about you and bade me visit. He piqued my interest so I acquiesced. To say the least, I was shocked to meet our Grandfather. We had several visits before my ship left port. He is.... I mean was an eccentric, self-centered old man. He's one of the reasons I came home. I didn't want the same hard feelings between you and me. I still remember our last . . . discussion and to be honest I didn't know how my home coming would be received, but I came anyway. I'm sorry for the grief I've caused, really sorry."

*F*or the first time in a long time I was speechless. I stared at Rob stunned and all of the years of self torment came bubbling to the surface. Sarah scooted quickly out of the way as he stood up unsteadily and wrapped my arms around my son. I had never recognized how much Rob was like myself.

"Oh my God, Oh my God, I am truly sorry for putting you through this! Welcome home son! Thank God you came home," my voiced cracked under the strain of the emotion. "I never meant to drive you away; perhaps I'm more like the old brute than I thought. I never meant to do to any of you what he did to me. I'm so sorry – it's your life to live as you see fit. As long as it's an honest life, I'm content." I paused. Shaking my head I added, "We'll all go to Lily's now. I have been running from the truth myself for too long." Sarah, tears in her eyes, smiled up at me, still wrapped around our son. I felt her love assuage my guilt over the hurt I had caused Rob and by extension our whole family. I had never minded sharing Sarah with all of them but I had not had Sarah alone to myself like this in years and though it had been heavenly, and wasn't likely to happen again for a long time, I realized now it was time to move on. There were wounds I alone had caused and must now heal, starting with Rob.

I caught the look that passed between Sarah and Earley, there was more to Rob's story. In the emotion of the moment I had missed the signs, a sure indication I was not myself.

With confidences revealed, everyone settled down to a quick but hearty meal and we made our plans. The boys and Earley would leave now and try to catch up with Bryn and Aleck. I know it had been a blessing for her and I to have had this time together. Alas, it was time to get back to the world we lived in. I also knew she missed our grandchildren and her own routine. Perhaps it was also time to heal some ancient wounds.

The gray morning light had given way to filtered sun coming in through the windows. It was still going to be a wet ride but Drew and Rob were eager to be off after Bryn. The horses had been watered and fed; ready for their second ride of the day. Mud was going to be the enemy, as the horse's hooves sucked the earth into their crevices. I had given them last minute instructions on what to tell Lilyan. I would abide by whatever my family wished and provided my sons with a letter to that effect, assigning them responsibility to act on my behalf under the extenuating circumstances. The boys hugged and kissed their mother and shook hands with me. Earley gave me a slap on the shoulder, with a dire command to be careful and a friendly nod to Sarah. They gave a final wave and were off.

~ Earley ~

*A*s they were headed directly to St. Louis, it made sense that Bryn and Aleck would try to stay to the now nearly non-existent main trail. So although they were three days ahead, tracking them was not difficult and we made swift progress. We found one of Bryn's hankies caught in a bush. It had been well used and wrung into a knotted mess. The devastation on this side of the pass was incredible. We had to pick our way carefully over the magnitude of fallen debris. The miles turned into hours as, at a steady pace, we cast weary eyes over the storm ravaged trail watching for indications of Bryn's passing.

Many hours after starting out, I drew up my reins and came to a halt. "Hum, they've changed direction. Through this way," I said almost to myself and dismounted. I was deep in thought, and raised my hand to scratch at the beginnings of a beard. I mounted again, and continued on after a few moments speculation. Drew followed close behind, while Rob brought up the rear. By late afternoon we were at the mouth of the cave. The fire was cold, but it was obvious someone had been here recently. There were two sets of recent footprints and I was certain the smaller ones were Bryn's.

"Well I'll be, this is quite the nice little place," Rob growled. I could see his ire rising and it took a good deal of gumption to dampen my desire to find Aleck and beat him to a bloody pulp. Rob would be wondering how many other women Aleck had seduced in this cozy little hide-a-way. I walked over to the stack of wood noticing the furs neatly put back into place.

"Listen! Hear that?" Drew called as he pointed down from the mouth of the cave.

"Waterfall, let's go." I led the way. It had been an arduous ride. The pond was sheltered and secluded. We staked our horses, stripped to our long-johns and jumped into the frigid water of the falls. It was revitalizing, there was no getting around it, but we did not linger. We made a quick fire for coffee in the peaceful valley. The warmth of the coffee after the refreshing swim invigorated us. We were anxious to get back to the trail. We could get another hour, maybe two in before having to camp for the night and we all knew none of us would rest well in the vicinity of the cave. As we passed the cave, I called a halt and tracked off to the side into the brush. At my loud expletive the two brothers dismounted and ran to my side. There was no mistaking the fact that these two bodies had been left unceremoniously in the last few days. Aleck had indeed protected Bryn. We pressed on. Just the thought of Bryn alone and defenseless with a man like Aleck had made the brother's, otherwise calm, dispositions boil. With the discovery of the two abandoned bodies, our drive was intensified.

We made good progress since the cave but now dusk was approaching. I called a halt to the search for the night. We set up camp quickly, had a hot meal and coffee. We wanted an early start in the morning, so we sat around the campfire for a while, resting our weary bones before turning in. I lit my pipe and looked miles away in contemplation. It was not long before Drew's rage got the better of him and through gritted teeth he spit out his concerns.

"MacLaren left the trail on purpose to go to that cave. He knew where he was going. They could have gone much farther in a day. If they'd continued on instead of leaving the main trail maybe they wouldn't have met up with those two. It could have turned out real bad. I don't like it!"

Quiet was the only response, until after a minute or so I exhaled long and low. I replied in a slow calm tone, "Yer sister, from what yer folks told us, had a blow to her head. She was better off than them, but was she really alright? I don't know. MacLaren could 'a set the first day's pace slower to see how she was. Remember, it's Bryn we're talking about. He probably had to go slower until she got over her crying, half hour at least I'd say. We're used to sitting a saddle day in and out, Bryn's not – her pace'll always be slower than ours. Lastly, we don't know the weather they faced either and he may have wanted proper shelter for her. It was not that far out of the way. It may all been out of consideration for yer sister," I paused, unaccustomed to such long speech. "Those men could have met up with them anywhere along the trail. MacLaren dealt with them. It's enough." Drawing on my pipe, I then looked both men in the eyes. "Remember in this country, a man's innocent until he's proven guilty. I know ye're both riled, so am I, but MacLaren's always been an honorable man. We make no moves on him 'til we know the truth. Understood?"

Both Rob and Drew nodded their acquiescence, surprised by the long lecture. My points were sound and although it didn't cool the brother's tempers, they had no choice but to accept the wisdom of my logic.

We were off at the break of dawn and quickly came upon the spot where Aleck and Bryn had spent their second night out on the mountain. We were moving along the trail at the top of the ridge at a good clip, perhaps the storm had not been as severe here. A flash of color caught Rob's eye and he called a halt. He dismounted and made his way into the bush. He crouched down beside the mangled bush and was rewarded with a brightly colored hair ribbon he knew was Bryn's. Shaking his head, he recognized it as one he had picked up for her since he had returned home. He knew they were on the right track. Rob fingered the soft material thoughtfully, before tucking it into his saddle bag for safe keeping. After a bite to eat we started up again. Drew was rounding the bend after me as Rob was remounting. As I had rounded the bend, I was unprepared for the terrifying sight. I let out a vehement "Christ Almighty! Whoa Thief! Atta boy!" I screeched back to him.

I reined Thief in tightly, hooves leaving the ground as the heaving horse fought for a foothold. Thief whinnied in terror as loose gravel and dirt slid beneath his hooves. The nimble footed horse was able to frantically back his way around the corner onto firm ground. I dismounted yelling at the boys to stay away from the edge. I pulled Thief well back into the brush and calmed him.

Rob and Drew dismounted and pulled their horses back from the trail as they instinctively followed my act of self-preservation. We calmed and tethered the three horses. If Rob hadn't spotted Bryn's ribbon, stopping them, one minute more, and all three of us would have rounded the bend and slid most likely to our deaths down the slippery slope one on top of the other.

We moved back into the woods and came carefully at the slide from behind rather than the edge. There were signs of a lot of activity on this side of the slide. Horse's shoes, small footprints, Bryn's for sure, as they were left by a lady's boot. Not much else. Drew had made to rush to the edge, but Rob and I restrained him. I went back for his rope. I tied myself to a securely to a tree, then I crawled carefully to the edge and taking a deep breath looked over the side. Thank God! My shoulders relaxed slightly. Drew and Rob both relaxed slightly as they read my reaction. Still on my belly I scanned Aleck's horse, noting he had been put out of his misery. I spotted the trail where a body had been dragged up the side of the slide. Then upon close inspection he could see signs of activity on the far side of the slide. I edged back and reported my findings to the others. We carefully made our way to the far side of the slide. Here, we found the gathered wood where Bryn had dropped it, traces of a rudimentary fire, well extinguished and several pieces of Bryn's petticoat that she had no doubt used as bandages. We all came to the same conclusion. With St. Louis now in sight, Bryn had pressed on. Aleck had been injured, but not so badly that he could not ride. One horse took the two of them out. The tracks on the far side of the slide clearly indicated a heavier burden for her horse. She should have reached St. Louis by now.

~ Rob ~

e were now burning with a fury to get to our sister but common sense prevailed as Earley reminded us in a day or two our parents would be following this same trail. We went back to the other side and blocked the bend in the trail so no one else would succumb to the horse's fate. We brought our own horses around. Earley was planning to go down to retrieve Aleck's saddle and anything else of use. I denied him, taking the responsibility upon myself. I was surprised he didn't argue. I secured myself as Earley had and then slipped over the side and down to the horse's corpse. The shot to end the animal's misery was well placed and I was sorry my sister had had to do it, however I was proud that she had found the strength in her heart to pull the trigger. It must have been terrifying for her. I turned my attention back to my tasks and struggled to remove the saddle and blankets, then tied them to the rope tossed down by Drew. Drew, mindful not to send more debris raining down on me, carefully hauled them up. I cut a hank from the horse's mane. I had seen the knots of manes in Aleck's stable and felt from the looks of the slide his horse had died but his body had probably broken Aleck's fall possibly saving his life.

It was a gruesome but necessary task, and we now returned to our quest. Aleck would not want to lose a good saddle or bags. The blanket was a tribute to beauty, as it had obviously been hand woven. It was my guess it would have some sentimental attachment to it. It was getting late in the day but we felt that we could make St. Louis tonight if we got down to the plains. We hastened on. The death of Aleck's horse had tempered my anger. Dusk was rapidly engulfing us. As luck would have it, we reached the plain as the light faded, but the moon cast enough light to help us make our way.

I was beside myself with worry that there was still no sign of Andrew. We had heard back from Drew by lunch. So quick these modern conveniences, only twenty-four hours had passed since I had sent him the news. So he and Earley were already on their way to track Andrew, Sarah and Bryn from their side. Josh would mind the ranches. Why was it that anything to do with Father always ended up hurting Andrew? He didn't deserve it. My thoughts were thusly occupied when John entered the room. He had not changed one bit since the day we had met. Well, there were some small changes. The beautiful head of hair he had in his youth was all but gone. However, he stood straight and tall and to me, he was the most handsome of men.

"What brings you to the office at this time of day, my dear?" I enquired, "and dressed for a ride."

"I thought we'd go for a picnic, Lil. Thomas is driving us all to distraction. He is down there now looking lost. I'm sure he's feeling guilty as it was his letter that brought Andrew, Sarah and Bryn out on this trip but I for one just can't stand it anymore. I see you so stressed by this situation and it worries me. I need to get you away for a few hours. Then we can plan what our next steps are."

"Oh, John! An afternoon with just the two of us would be heavenly right now. I know exactly what you mean. I was just thinking how anything to do with Father always ends up hurting Andrew and this is beyond anything we've experienced. Even in death he haunts my poor brother. It's so unfair."

"Sweetheart, God never promised that life would be fair, just that he'd be with us every step of the way. Come away dear, business will keep." John took my elbow to move me out the door.

I knew a ride would clear my head; I truly needed some peace and quiet for a little while. I also knew that together, John and I made better and wiser decisions. He was right, we would ride and plan. I turned a warm smile in his direction. God! How I loved this man. "I'll need a few minutes to change clothes. Please get Frank to pack some bread, cheese and the canteens." From the grin on his face, I knew it had already been done. Perhaps a little distraction in the beauty of the outdoors would relieve some of my tension. It had always worked in the past.

Frank handed the picnic basket to John who slid it over the pommel of his saddle. Frank bid us a safe ride and told us not to rush back. He stood and watched as we rode off side by side. We left Frank in charge, as we often did. The hotel was not a problem, Frank was used to that, but Frank did not know what to make of Hall and his worldly ways.

~ Frank ~

*A*t first, Hall had been a good topic of conversation but now nothing new was happening with him and I barely understood a word the man had to say. Miss Lily had a similar accent but had been in America for many years and her twang had mellowed. Mr. Hall was right off the boat and he sounded like he was talking through his nose.

I had been watching Hall since his arrival in our fair city. He went out regular as clock work and had no particular destination in mind. I followed him twice. Both times Hall went to the Jefferson Hotel a few streets over. Hall would be there for a couple of hours, then would return to The Grand, have his dinner and retire to his room. In the beginning, Hall had that urn with him in his rooms, until John convinced him to store it in the vault at the hotel for safekeeping. Personally, I wasn't at all sure I liked the idea of having somebody's burnt body stored in the hotel vault but nobody asked my opinion, which as far as I was concerned, was unfortunate. Who'd steal a body anyway?

Now, the urn itself was something to behold. It was rather large, and obviously came from a strange and mysterious place. It was the most mesmerizing emerald green I had ever laid my eyes on. It looked as though the color had been fired into the enamel. The shape was odd, but wonderfully symmetrical, like a tear drop that came to a narrow opening that was rounded around the lip. There were burnt red and gold leaves inlaid on the surface completely surrounding the urn. There were unusual configurations of people in robes that Frank had never seen before. The fact that Miss Lilyan was not that enamored by the urn made me feel somewhat better. I simply did not like things I did not understand.

~ John ~

*L*ily and I cleared the edge of town in no time. We were leaving in the quiet of the afternoon. The bustle of deliveries, and ladies out doing their daily shopping had long since passed. The urgency of our plight had not been forgotten, but on a day such as this, it was hard not to be aware of the surrounding glories; so familiar but always changing. We would not pass anyone. The farmers were well out in their fields. Of course having lived here for so many years now, we knew everyone. The Carter spread was the first farm we would pass. Lilyan was good friends with Rachel. We maintained a steady measure. It felt good to be in the saddle. We had been so tied up with repairs from the storm and the persistent worry over Andrew these last few days.

As we passed the last farm, I turned to Lilyan and indicated my intentions. "I'd like to strike up a search party and start looking for them from this side of the mountains."

"But John, you don't know these mountains. You could be lost, get hurt . . ." The look on her face told me all I needed to know. She had spoken from her heart not her head, and I know she saw the flicker of hurt cross my face. She had inadvertently hurt my feelings. We liked picnics on Sunday, and I enjoyed the shade of the big maple tree on our front lawn. I was not a man who was prepared for the wilderness; I belonged to the city. I was brave though, or so I thought, and I know that it tugged at her heart as she tried to recant her statement. "John, I couldn't bear to have both of you out there. It's bad enough as it is. I can't bear the thought that you would be away from me too!"

"Lily dear, do you think I don't know that?" I knew Lilyan had not meant to hurt me. I offered, "If we hire the right people, are properly prepared and take our time, I'm sure we would be successful. We always are my dear."

Realizing the recovery option I was giving her she said, "You know me too well John Wallace. Where you go, I go! We will plan it out this evening." I leaned over to give her a kiss. "Oh, Mr. Wallace, perhaps we won't be going anywhere!" giggled Lilyan. We dismounted and had our picnic.

The sun had nearly set and the moon was visible in the evening sky; we knew we must end our little tryst and return to town and the problems that awaited us there. Before mounting, Lilyan turned for a long, last look toward the mesa, willing her brother and his family safely to her side.

I stepped up to her back and wrapped my arms lovingly around her. I could not protect her from the pain she was experiencing but I could aid and succor her. I could not fathom how everything her father did had such a negative impact on Andrew and yet Andrew was not bitter. I knew she resented her father for the pain he had caused her brother and her heart broke every time she realized that no matter what Andrew did, it would never be good enough for their father. It had been years since Andrew had tried. He was lucky to have Sarah by his side. Andrew only recognized Lilyan as kin, Emmaline the glue that bound them together. Andrew did not recognize his father and out of love and deference to her brother's wishes, Lilyan never mentioned their father around Andrew or his family.

But I knew she had mentioned her brother and his family in her letters to her father. Just little snippets at first then gradually in more detail as she felt a relaxing of the cold wall built around Andrew in her father's heart. And yet again, even in death their father had placed Andrew, and this time his family, in great jeopardy. I was outraged at Hugh's barbarous behavior. Lily moved in my arms turning, she presented her lips for the kissing. As I bent to answer her desire with my own, movement caught his eye.

"John . . . what is it my dear?"

"Sorry Lil, I thought I saw something move," she turned to follow my gaze. "I could almost swear I see dust over there," I pointed just west of our position.

Together, in one synchronized motion, we shielded our eyes, concentrating on seeing into the distance. Lily saw it as I said, "Yes, definitely someone on their way into town, only one I think. We had better be careful, but I think we should ride out and see if there's any news." As we mounted, I checked and holstered my gun, then we rode off to meet the inbound rider.

Part Three

THE PLAN

*T*hrough weary eyes, I caught sight of the two riders in the distance. I could have wept with relief if I had not been so dog tired. That they could be total strangers and could be dangerous whizzed in and out of my thoughts. Cautiously, I picked up my stride to meet these would-be rescuers.

I felt Aleck shift, "How are you feeling?" I asked through a blur of tears.

"Not bad at the moment. My headache is lessening. I was aware of Tinker's change in gait. It's a little hard to focus," he said. I was conscious of his hand slipping to his gun. It made me feel a little safer. Aleck hunched closer as the two riders made their approach.

It did not take long even in the dim light of the late evening for me to recognize my aunt. "Aunt Lily, Uncle John, ohhhh, you don't know how happy we are to see you!" With relief, I burst into tears. By this time Aleck was fully alert, sitting up, towering over my shoulders, his one arm stayed protectively wrapped around my waist while the other remained cradled on his gun.

"Bryn? . . . Bryn! . . . Oh Bryn honey, are you alright? Oh my dear? . . . Where are your parents? What happened? Did you get caught in that storm? . . . Who is this? Where's his horse? Have you seen your brothers? . . . They're searching for you." The questions came all at once, that trait alone helped convince Aleck that this really was Aunt Lily. We both chattered when stressed.

My tears stopped as quickly as they began but I was speechless with relief. I was suddenly very conscious of the man slumped against my back. Without warning, he felt the need to answer for me, "All are alive, and Bryn's alright more or less, aye Bryn?" I nodded in the affirmative letting him continue. "They were caught in the storm. Andrew took a bad sprain to his leg, Sarah's had fever. Bryn struck out and found me. They're recovering in my cabin, but knew you'd be worried. We rode out after the storm. My horse died in a fall. Its verra treacherous on the trails or should I say lack of trails. The land is unstable especially on the slopes." Aleck felt me shudder at the mention of Splash's death. He kissed my hair and crooned to me, "It's alright lass, you're safe now. T'would be wise to get Bryn indoors, please. Aye and I'm Aleck MacLaren at her service."

Abruptly I found my voice. "I'm not '*safe now*' thank you very much Aleck. With you here, I've been safe all along."

*J*ohn and I watched with fascination at the change in our niece's demeanor. We took in the desperate looking scene. Dirt covered both from head to foot. Aleck's hat sat slightly askew, while we took in Bryn's torn, blood covered garments. They looked exhausted despite Bryn's excited greeting followed by her outburst. Tears smudged the dirt on her weary face, making trails down her cheeks. Bryn sank back into the stranger's chest as her hands still holding the reins had dropped to hold his arm. Her hair was tied back but escaped strands straggled about her face. She was too spent to push them away. Her hat was still on her head but more by good luck than good management. My poor darling girl! What trials had she endured!

The stranger, Aleck MacLaren fared no better, perhaps worse. His calm but vigilant manner around Bryn had not escaped our notice, but his pain was evident in his bearing. Apparently having said his piece exhausted him as he sagged again into Bryn's back. Although he was covered in dirt, the nasty cut on his cheek was evident and would likely need attention. The blood had dried dark black and it looked like he was sporting a huge leech upon his face. His hand stayed steady on his gun as he squinted to try and keep his vision clear. We wisely understood the danger in his gaze. He would kill to protect Bryn. But so too would we.

I am an extremely good judge of character, if I do say so myself, and I recognized I need not worry too much about this stranger with my niece and sighed with relief. There was no noticeable danger to Bryn, so I relaxed my hold on the reins. "You're right, we have been dreadfully worried. Come, let's get you two home."

John offered to take Bryn onto his horse with him; Bryn shook her head as Aleck barked out a crisp, "NO!" Bryn was not bothered by the sharp denial, so John let it drop.

I was content to be under Aunt Lily and Uncle John's care at the moment. I felt confident that Aleck would be well received. Now as we rode, I could not stop the recollections of the mudslide. I could not tear my mind from the scene turning it over and over in my head. Nothing I could have done would have halted the cliff from caving in or the consequences it wrought. Tears spilled silently for the life I had had to take. I was aching in places I never dreamt of. My shoulders burned and felt like they could fall off. No amount of work on the ranch had ever made me feel this way. Besides scrambling around the slide, Aleck had now been a dead weight on me for hours and I was paying the price. But I would do it again in a heartbeat.

Once home, while Lilyan fussed over Aleck and I, Uncle John assumed responsibility for the horses and sending a telegraph to Josh. It was late and he knew the telegraph office would be closed, however he also knew that Abe would not mind being pulled from his rest for this kind of news. Uncle John did not have any siblings, but he knew Josh would want to know that I had arrived safely and that Andrew and Sarah, although injured, were alive.

I knew Aleck's head was still pounding but with a hand on my shoulder, he was able to stand upright without keeling over. He refused to enter the house this filthy. Reluctantly, he relinquished me to my aunt's care as William, their butler, appeared and at Aleck's request escorted him to the water pump by the side of the house. I paused before going indoors.

"Please take good care of him William, I have an idea he won't confess to the pain he's in at the moment."

"Very good Miss Bryn," William acknowledged with a smile and a wink.

~ Aleck ~

The hair on my body stood at attention as the frigid water hit my skin, but it felt good on my aching, bruised body. Once sure that I would suffer no harm, William left me to my own ministrations to secure towels and a pair of John's pants and a shirt for me to wear until my own clothes could be tended to. I was thankful for the loan of the clean clothes.

"I will show you to your room now, sir. You may rest. I will come for you later. My Rose is preparing dinner for all of you." said William with a slight bow.

~ Bryn ~

*I*followed Aunt Lily to the pretty room I remembered from my last visit. Rose came in with an armful of fresh towels and a ewer of hot water I could use to rinse off the worst of the dust and dirt. Lily excused herself to get me some fresh clothes. Then Lily and Rose filled the tub in the adjoining room with hot water, Rose swirled in Epsom salts to help ease my aches while Lily laced the water with her own scented lavender oils. Once they were gone, I rinsed my hands and face. Then I gave my hair a good scrub. Finally, I washed my feet before stripping and stepping into the deep tub. I sank with a sigh of pleasure at the luxury. Lulled and calmed by the bath, I finally took the French milled lavender soap and washed my body, head to toe. Before the water cooled too much I submerged my head and massaged my scalp and hair to pristine condition. Finally, I rose and stepped quickly from the tub to dry off. The air felt chilly on my wet body but the cleanliness soothed my mind. As I dried myself, I delighted in the thick pile of the cotton towels.

I wrapped the big towel around myself and took a look in the mirror. There were multiple bruises up and down my arms that were making themselves known. As I examined my poor, beaten up body I was shocked to see the deep purple marks that covered my arms and legs. They were excruciatingly painful to touch. They would heal, but not fast enough. I moved to the dressing table and picked up the silver handled brush and comb. Carefully, I combed out the worst of the gnarls and tangles with a lot of facial grimacing. I laughed at myself for being such a baby. Aunt Lily had laid out some fresh clothes for me and even provided some of her favorite lavender scented creams for my skin. I gently massaged the cream over my entire body luxuriating in the silky sensation. We had moisturizing creams at the ranch but nothing this luxurious and certainly nothing with the intoxicating but relaxing scent. After pampering myself, with determination I ignored the pain and got myself dressed for dinner.

I looked in the mirror again. Aunt Lily wore beautiful clothes and she had given me one of her favorite day outfits. I turned in the mirror thinking I looked gawky and awkward. The silk chemise Aunt Lily had provided was soft against my tender skin. The deep blue linen skirt was short on me but not uncomfortably so and the beautiful petticoats made it fall just so from my waist. The blouse was silk and felt like a whisper across my skin. It was the color of cornflowers, my favorite color. Short in the sleeves I rolled them up to three quarter length. I sat on the bed and pulled on my boots. William had washed the soles and buffed the soft leather to a dull gleam. Then Rose had dusted them out with corn starch and more lavender. They looked better than I remembered them looking when they had been new. I had always loved the look of aged leather boots and this pair are my favorite. Tomorrow I would unpack some of my things and I would have proper shoes to wear in the house.

The letdown after the trying day had left me exhausted and shaky, but the bath and soothing scents had revived me enough to make me aware of my hunger. Though it was very late, I was anxious to see Aleck. The gas lights in the house had been lit. I was struck by the beauty of my surroundings as I came down stairs. I made my way into the sitting room to find everyone including, Aleck, already there.

"I was just going to come up for you my dear," said Lily.

Aleck got up slowly and made his way toward me. This was the first time I had seen Aleck out of his buckskins and I was pleasantly surprised at how handsome he looked. The black pants that had been borrowed from her Uncle John fitted him snuggly, accentuating the strength of his legs while the crisp white shirt showed off his dark coloring to his advantage. I envied the way his black hair curled against the white of his collar. I was struck yet again by how breathtakingly handsome he was. I was speechless, drinking in the look of him, as if I had never seen him before.

~ *Aleck* ~

---

*M*eanwhile, I couldn't take my eyes from her. She was sensational. I had thought her beautiful before but cleaned up with lovely clothes, I was awe struck. I tried to remember to breathe as I escorted her following Lily and John into the dining room.

I pulled out her chair, mimicking everything John did for Lily. "Thank you," Bryn smiled. I had been worried about her, but she looked stunning as she seated herself at the table. She smelled so good and the outfit she wore fit her in all of the right places. I fumbled my way into my own seat unable to take my eyes off of her. We dined on cold meats that Rose and Lilyan had put together on platters. There was French wine and beer made on the premise by Rose and, her husband, William. The brew was well known and served in the hotel.

"A toast," announced John. "*To the safe arrival of our Bryn. Many thanks to you Aleck and for the continued safety of Andrew and Sarah.*" We all raised our glasses and drank.

After dinner, we retired to the drawing room. There was a fire burning low giving off a glow filling the room with soft light. I sat down in one of the comfortable arm chairs and Bryn came and sat on a footstool between my knees. She handed me the Wallace's silver brush and comb from her pocket. I accepted them readily and as I had done before I patiently untangled the rest of the knots and brushed her hair dry to a silky shine. I looked at askance to John and Lily, but neither seemed to be alarmed by the request. I was intoxicated by the gentle scent of lavender that wafted around her.

While we sat, Lily and John listened to my accounting of the storm and the troubles Sarah, Bryn and Andrew had endured. I told of our time together at my cabin and how they had started to heal. Lastly, I described our own journey down from the mountains. Bryn was startled when she heard of the two horse thieves and the wolf from our night at the cave. She was taken aback when she realized she had slept through the entire episode. "Aleck MacLaren, how could you keep such a horrible secret? I'm not a child you know, I can handle these things very well, thank you very much!" Her lips were pressed into a hard line. She was not impressed with my withholding. I had neglected to mention it to her. "Hold on Bryn, dinna fash yourself. I swore an oath to your father to protect you, there was nothing said about discussing it after the fact." I could hear the lilt of my mother in my voice. It happens to me when I am nervous or embarrassed. I am very quiet by nature so any company can be inhibiting. I softened my voice to a whisper to cover. "I thought you had enough to worry about. I want it to come out now and here so if there are repercussions I can deal with them." I noticed I had hit the mark, as Bryn was almost nodding off. I caught our hosts' eyes meaningfully before glossing over the mudslide and the aftermath.

After my recounting John had only a few questions as I appeared to have covered the whole story quite well.

"So, Aleck, you say you and Andrew concocted this plan? It seems a like a rather large leap of faith on Andrew's part does it not?" John trusted Andrew with his life, but I was coming here on second hand trust. This was his niece after all.

"Aye, that's exactly what we did. John, I understand your concern, but Bryn is safe with her honor intact. I swear on my life. If that is not good enough, I will take my leave, sir." I was grinding my teeth. I understood where John was coming from but by God it made my insides churn just the same.

"There is no need for such drastic action. Surely you understand my position. Bryn is like a daughter to us and her safety and happiness are our main concern"

"As it is mine, I assure you,." our eyes met each knowing the truth of the other.

John ended the family discussion saying, "Lily, tomorrow morning I will inform Thomas that Bryn has arrived safely and explain that Andrew and Sarah are alive and recovering. I'll arrange for you to have lunch in our private quarters with him at the hotel. I think you and Bryn would enjoy that. I'm sure he'll be fine with those arrangements."

Then John and Lily talked quietly over their after dinner drink. I took pleasure in the warm cozy atmosphere of people enjoying each other's company without any expectations.

"Bryn, lassie, before we retire for the night, we owe Tinker a visit." my eyes were glowing with my need. Cannily, I kept my face averted from John and Lily. I had no doubt they would know what else I had in mind, the question was how much would they mind.

Bryn gently agreed, her eyes registering the carnal intent in my own. "Just let me get a treat for her." Bryn got up and we excused ourselves to go out to the stables. We were not challenged.

We walked hand in hand from the kitchen. Rose had been glad to offer carrots and an apple for Bryn's dear horse. The two stable boys had walked and brushed Tinker down nicely. She was happily ensconced in her stall munching oats and had a bucket of fresh water. Tinker recognized her mistress and whinnied for her to come closer. Bryn went and affectionately rubbed the velvet soft nose. Tinker moved in closer. Bryn held up the carrots and apple she had and started to feed them to her one at a time. I could not resist the need to examine the animal that had carried us so well. After careful inspection of Tinker's back, legs and hooves, I was satisfied that she had incurred no injuries during the descent off of the mountain. With two riders, Tinker had been under tremendous strain. Tinker warmed to the attention. I could see she had been properly groomed and stabled, I could find no cause for concern.

"You can tell you and your Aunt Lilyan are related. You are so like her with your curiosity, chatter and concern for others."

"Is that a back handed compliment, Mr. MacLaren?" queried Bryn. She did not see herself as meddlesome which she assumed I was implying.

"I'm not implying interfering or meddling, no such thing if that's what you're thinking. I was making an observation of kindness, caring and consideration. It's a fair assessment and a good one. Aye, your aunt's a good woman." I shook my head with a smile and crooked my finger, bidding her to come to me.

"Oh," she stammered and moved to stand in my embrace.

The next day found me willing to rest. I knew I had sustained a bad blow to the head so at the moment I was quite content to surrender Bryn to her Aunt Lily's care. Rose brought me some toast and coffee. That sat well with me and I settled back to rest with my eyes closed. The compress that Rose had made up for my forehead was very soothing and calmed the obnoxious, continuous ache in my head. The lump on the back of my head was extremely painful, forcing me to lie on my side. I wondered about Bryn and Lily's lunch with Mr. Hall and what else they would do to fill their day. Bryn was safe with Lily, knowing this I succumbed to my rest.

~ *Bryn* ~

I recovered from the physical events of the trip rapidly. But, I had dreamt about Splash, the nightmare bringing me awake, my face wet with tears, my throat sore with aching. I got up and splashed some water on my face from the ewer patting the water from my face with a scented towel left by Rose. I sat back down on the edge of the bed and watched the breeze move the gauzy curtains at the window. The moon shone into my room like a lantern, casting eerie shadows across the bed. However, knowing I had done the right thing. I had been able to go back to sleep.

I was up early the next morning. I shook the sleepiness from my body and gave a long stretch. I had always loved the view of the gardens from here. There was a small balcony outside the French doors. I put on the light robe and went out to enjoy the fresh beautiful morning. The sun was flitting in and out of the white fluffy clouds in the brilliant blue sky. The breeze caught the fine cotton of my night dress as it swirled around my legs and ankles. I returned inside and found that Rose had been in with a tray. I loved Rose; she was very good to me. I was definitely being spoiled, just as I had been on my last visit here. I finished my breakfast and completed my toilet. I was dressed and ready when Aunt Lily came to the door.

"There you are, up and looking lovely. Did you sleep well?" she enquired.

"I did indeed. This room's so lovely and quiet. The bed's so comfy. I slept like a baby," I did not want to burden Aunt Lily with the nightmare.

"How do you feel about some shopping in St. Louis? I'll have William bring the carriage around. We can go anywhere you'd like. John has business in the city and won't be back until later this evening, so we have the whole day. Our only obligation is our arranged lunch with Mr. Hall. I'm anxious for you to meet Thomas. This will be such fun."

~ *Lily* ~

ruth to be known, it was my stance that Bryn needed to be spruced up. Her clothing was good, solid clothing that would last years on the ranch. In my opinion, Bryn needed something frivolous and feminine. I had not missed a thing when she noted the look in Aleck's eye and Bryn's obvious contentment with it. I still looked at John that way and always would.

Me being me, I drove the carriage myself into town. People were not quite sure how to take such independence from a high standing woman, but that didn't bother me. I drove sitting straight up in the carriage with my hands held high on the reigns and the horses under control. Bryn sat beside me, taking in all of the sights that were new to her.

"Emmett... yooou whooo... Emmett," I called.

"Howdy! Miss Lilyan. And who is this lovely young lady?" Doc answered.

"This is my niece, Bryn. You remember her, don't you? She's Andrew's daughter."

"Well my goodness, is this that sweet little girl, so grown up now. It's very good to see you again Miss Bryn."

I halted the carriage and got down with Emmett's gentlemanly hand assisting me.

"Wait here Bryn, I won't be but a minute."

"Emmett, Bryn was in the company of one Aleck MacLaren when she arrived last night. Andrew, Sarah and Bryn were caught in the middle of that storm we had last week. They were fortunate that Mr. MacLaren was able to help them out. In fact, Andrew and Sarah are still up in his cabin. You'll need to see to both of them when they arrive. In the meantime, Mr. MacLaren has had a bad fall. His horse went over a

179

cliff and he with him. Would you take a look at him to make sure he is alright? And, you know Emmett, for me you could do some digging to find out who this man really is. He is obviously taken with our Bryn and for that matter she with him. William will introduce you."

"Be glad to do it. I'm on my way out that end of town. I'll drop in and check him out for you. No problem. If I have any concerns, I shall leave a note with William. Would that suit you?"

I thanked Emmett and got back into the carriage. We went first to the new mercantile shop for a short browse. At noon, we stopped into the hotel to meet Thomas for lunch. Bryn did not have any idea of what to expect and I could see she was a little nervous.

I spied Thomas across the lobby. I crossed the lobby to him with Bryn in my wake.

"There you are Thomas," I gave him a hug. "May I introduce you to Andrew's daughter, Miss Bryn Henley. Bryn, this is Mr. Thomas Hall."

"It's a pleasure to meet you Mr. Hall," Bryn responded.

~ *Thomas* ~

I was thunderstruck. My knees went weak and sweat popped out on my forehead. Miss Bryn was the very image of Miss Emma. I took my handkerchief from my coat pocket to mop my brow. Further guilt, more personal recriminations for the lies I had told. I despaired there would be no recovery from this dilemma.

"Whatever is the matter Thomas? Are you un-well? You look like you've seen a ghost!"

"No . . . no Lily I am just fine, just taken aback. Miss Bryn has anyone ever told you how much you favor your grandmother?" I was quickly recovering from the shock. "I am so very glad you have finely arrived safe and sound. I understand your father and mother have sustained some injuries but are recovering. I was heartsick when I thought you might have been caught in the storm. I am so terribly, terribly, sorry for your troubles."

Lily looked at me with a puzzled expression. Lily had only been seven when her mother passed away. I realized that her only recollection of Emmaline would be from the formal portraits. Not expecting it she would not have noticed the striking resemblance of Bryn to her mother. When I really thought about it, I understood that I was the only one of them who was old enough to remember what Emmaline really looked like.

"Lily you have the portraits from Oakley upstairs here. I saw them at dinner the other night."

"Yes, in our rooms where our lunch is waiting. Shall we go?" Lily opened the French hand carved wooden doors that led into their private suite. It was spacious and decorated in Lilyan's trademark yellows and blues. The big four poster bed took up the center of the second room

181

visible through the large pocket doors. It was spotless and neat as I would have expected. And there, on the far wall just beyond the fireplace, hung the portraits side by side. I remembered the days of sittings when those portraits had been painted. Emmaline was not far along in her pregnancy with Andrew and was not showing the increase in girth brought about by impending motherhood. Several times she had been laughing at Lily and her antics as she twirled around the room dancing and although the portrait was of a serious Emmaline, the artist caught the sparkle of mischief and humor in her eyes and the gentle upturn of her mouth. I smiled at the memory. Hugh's portrait held the warm human side of him as Emmaline was often in the room during Hugh's sittings. His love was there written into his face and lighting up the gold flecks in his brown eyes.

After lunch, I quietly went out for a walk. My head was spinning from having seen the resemblance of Bryn to Miss Emma and I was thankful that lunch had been spent with Lily and I pulling memories of Emmaline and Hugh Henley for their granddaughter.

The portraits were set off by a beautifully carved walnut table. There were fresh flowers in the large vase. Aunt Lily loved to have fresh flowers and they were everywhere. The three of us stood before the portraits. I was taken aback as I felt myself to be looking into a mirror. I subconsciously touched my hair as I was held spell bound by the picture. I had never seen what my grandparents looked like. And then I was back to my favorite book at the ranch and the inscription that lay there, worn with time and oil from Emmaline's fingertips. I straightaway felt a strong connection with this woman.

"Well, as God is my witness. I wouldn't have believed it. These portraits have been here all along but now that I see you standing next to her, it is incredible. The resemblance is beyond my imagination," Aunt Lily sat down in the chair in front of the table and stared at me. I stared at the portrait; I did not believe I could be that beautiful. I looked at the portrait in awe. Certainly, it looked like my hair, my eyes, my features but my grandmother was exquisite. Then I turned my gaze to my grandfather's portrait. I saw my father as a younger man, there was no mistaking the resemblance there. Sorrow overcame me at the opportunities lost through no fault of their own. I did not understand the silence that had surrounded these grandparents.

Once we all recovered from the shock, we took our seats for lunch. Aunt Lily could not wait to tell John of our discovery. There was gentle friendly chatter throughout the entire lunch, full of stories of my grandparents from Mr. Hall.

Aunt Lily and I went back to the mercantile and then on to the millinery shop. I had an amazing time looking at the fashionable gazettes containing all of the latest fashions in clothing and shoes. My eyes popped as I took in all of the colors and textures of the materials on the bolts. The patterns were in vogue and I was also able to procure a beautiful pair of kid leather shoes. They were not practical for the ranch, but I would love to wear them to dinner and while we remained here.

When we returned later that afternoon, William greeted us at the front drive and helped us down. He would see to the multitude of boxes and the carriage. Aunt Lilyan and I entered to the delicious smells of Rose's cooking permeating the house.

Once back in the house, I could not keep my excitement under control. "I can't wait to wear my dress from the dressmakers to dinner with Aleck, with my new shoes and hat too. And it'll be ready the day after tomorrow. Unbelievable! Mama will be so surprised. I can't wait to show her the material we got too! Mama may be jealous of all my lovely things. I can't thank you enough, Aunt Lily. I feel like such a spoiled child with the lovely undergarments and creams too. Such a luxury, I think I can't believe it's really me under all the finery. I feel so special, almost pretty."

"It was my pleasure my dear, dear Bryn. And although you may not believe me when I say it – you are beautiful!" Aunt Lily declined to mention that she had requested several additional items for her niece. They would be surprises and Lily could hardly wait to watch Bryn's face as she opened the boxes over the next few days.

"If you don't mind I think I'd like to go and see how Aleck's doing."

William entered under a stack of boxes just as Bryn was mentioning Aleck, "He is in the stables with your horse, miss."

"Thank you William."

~ *Aleck* ~

It was abundantly clear to me that Bryn was going to be my one and only. But what could I offer the lass? I had never given pause to the notion of marriage. It didn't frighten me. I had just never met a woman to ponder over. Ah! But Bryn, with hair of fire when the sun hit just right; her daring impish eyes that changed in the blink of an eye. She was somehow the missing piece of my puzzle. I wanted to explore the very depths of her and how her kisses drove me crazy.

I was not a vain man, so it had been a long time since I had taken a long look at myself in a mirror. Pleasing was not a word I could use to describe my face. In all honesty, more than one lassie had shied away at my direct stare. I ran my hand across my day old beard, dark as night. And now a new scar would grace my cheek. My hair sat black in wavy curls around my shoulders. The curls I could thank my mother for. I peered closely into my own dark eyes, looking for answers to questions I had not yet thought to ask. All I saw were dark eyes surrounded by dark lashes with no answers.

So what did Bryn see in me? I could only guess. I narrowed my gaze seeing only the physical flaws I understood were there, pulling at my cheeks with my fingers. Trying, in vain, to see myself as Bryn saw me was a personal conundrum.

"Enough," I whispered to the man in the mirror. "She'll have me or no!" I promised the same man. I shaved then combed my hair, pulling it back off of my face with a leather lace. I went to the stables to find ease of mind. I was always able to find peace with the animals.

---

hen I reached the stable, I could see Aleck leaning against a post. As I approached him, I took in his full stance. His arms were folded across his chest and his legs were crossed as he leaned on the post of the door. He heard my footfalls and turned; a big smile lighting up his face.

"It's good to see you up with some color again," I started.

"Aye, but it's so much more delightful to see you, my beauty. I'll no say I want another bump to add to the other ones on my head, but the ride was worth it. Your aunt's friend, Doc Jones, came to visit. He looked me over and told me it was a verra good job I had a hard Scot head, otherwise I would be dead!" he spread his arms in a welcoming gesture. "Come here lass so I can greet you properly with no prying eyes?" He took my hand and led me farther back into the stables. It was cool and dark with the rich smell of horses and hay floating in the air. When we neared Tinker's stall, he took me into his arms and kissed me deeply, my response was warm and demanding. He had to pull back, he knew he was playing with fire and he really did not want to be burned; nonetheless before he was able to complete the thought I had pulled the leather lace, freeing his hair, then wrapping my fingers in his black locks I pulled his head down into range for a long searing kiss.

"You little vixen, I made a promise to your father and I'll no break it," but I just smiled and held him close. He silently groaned his pleasure. We only returned to the house when William came to get us in for dinner.

~ Aleck ~

*L*ater that evening as I prepared for bed, I decided I needed some advice, but from whom? I was not over run with comfortable male friends. I considered this for a moment. I lived a very solitary life. I had acquaintances, although friendly and jovial enough, were after all businessmen, the men I traded goods with on a monthly basis. No help there. I immediately dismissed the Henley men. I realized I didn't know much about courting, however I was no fool either. The Henley men would not be overjoyed at my interest in their daughter and sister, marriage or no. That left John. I had been covertly watching John and Lily. It brought back vague memories of my own parent's happiness together. I slept on that thought.

Late morning I left my room, again wondering how in the devil I was going to catch John alone and then broach the difficult subject. I did not have long to wait. As luck would have it, John's appointments had ended early and he had returned home. He was making his way across the front foyer, his boots falling heavily on the shining marble floor. John stopped to pick up the morning's mail that was sitting on a table with a huge bouquet of cut flowers just as I reached the top of the stairs.

"Hold up there, John," I called out. John looked up and waited as I quickly descended the elegantly curved staircase.

"John, I was wondering if I could speak with you on a matter of some delicacy."

"Certainly, let's step into my office for some privacy," I followed John down the long hallway. John opened the big, solid oak door and entered a room that was distinctly John's. Bookcases lined two of the walls floor to ceiling made of dark, rich walnut. A third wall supported a massive fireplace and lovely stone hearth. The furniture was fashionable and well used; the chairs and settee, though upholstered in leather, were plush and comfortable to sit in. I made myself comfortable in a large wing back chair and John took the one opposite. The fireplace was clean and in place of wood stood another huge bouquet of flowers in a wicker basket. The iron grate stood upright in its place at the front. John waited patiently for me to disclose the reason for this meeting.

"I . . . I'm really not sure how to begin," I paused and took a deep breath. I continued, "I have a favor to ask of you regarding Bryn. I don't know how to say this, but I have never met a woman like Bryn before. I'm unsure. . ."

~ *John* ~

I leaned back in my worn leather chair. Aware of Aleck's obvious discomfort, I could not and would not withhold the smile that touched my mouth. First Thomas, now Aleck. I brought my pipe up and lit it with slow deliberation and watched the smoke swirl above my head. Lily picked my tobacco and it was very fragrant, from the East as I recalled. Aleck disappeared from my view as I closed my eyes and thought back thirty years to the lovely young woman with blonde curls done up with jeweled hair clips sparkling in the candlelight. She was so excited to be in attendance at this particular ball on that particular night, her birthday. She was very animated as she greeted her father's business guests with a graceful curtsy, her left hand gloved and poised waiting for the customary kiss, while fluttering her fan in her right hand. It was love at first sight for me as I caught her eye going through the receiving line. I did not think it possible, but I had managed to steal Lily away for the whole evening. "And the rest, so they say, is history," I muttered to myself.

"Pardon," Aleck thought perhaps he had missed something.

"Sorry, my man, just thinking out loud," With that I looked Aleck squarely in the eye and requested confidently. "Would I be correct in assuming you are unsure of your merit regarding my niece? You know, about how to entice or secure her interest?"

Aleck sighed heavily, bracing his fingers beneath his chin with a grimace. "Afraid you're right on target. Aye, I've her attention right now but what do I do to win her, to keep her? I have no idea."

I interrupted, "How long have you known Bryn? Let me rephrase that, when did this infatuation begin?"

189

"We met last week in the storm when her horse wandered into my clearing and I had to go rescue her and then her parents. I could barely leave her to search for Andrew and Sarah. I knew of her as a child, met her a few times over the years. But now . . . I cannot bear to be parted from her, aye, can't tear my eyes away from her. I know I'm a lost cause. A woman like Bryn, what would she want with a man like me?" After his query he sighed, closed his eyes and leaned his head back in the chair. "Aye, but I love her, can't imagine my life now without her."

"You know Aleck, your situation is not dissimilar to what I experienced with Lily. I knew of her, had seen her several times before we actually met. She was not only popular, but beautiful, inside and out, I might add. I didn't think I stood a chance with her. But here we are thirty years later and still in love." I said amazed.

"If it's my advice you want, be honest, be yourself. Bryn likes you the way you are, for who and what you are. To change yourself for the sake of how others might see you is cheating, not only yourself but Bryn. You're not a love sick adolescent. Go to her as yourself and offer her what you have. Bryn will know her own mind; she's like my Lily that way. It's a Henley trait. It will be what it's meant to be. By the way, I don't give this information lightly. We've noticed the attraction between you two. You should know I've been asking around about you."

"Was sure you'd notice, figured you'd investigate. Aye, I'd have been appalled if you didn't. "So this is what I have found honest…, fair and trustworthy but a bit of a loner, a maverick some say. Fought for the Union and good man to have at your back. A blood born Scot which tells me you're probably very loyal. That's it so far. Is there anything you should tell me?" I queried.

"No John, I have no dirty secrets. What you see is what you get with me. But . . . there is a confidence you should know of . . . as you act in Andrew's stead. Aye, the only thing most people won't know, nor be able to find out for that matter must remain in strict confidence." At my nod of acquiescence he continued, "I operated an intelligence gathering unit during the war for the Union with a series of informants placed strategically throughout the South. That's as secret as I get and my only reasons for not disclosing that information to anyone is to protect those who aided our cause. And I do not share my private information loosely." Aleck had lowered his voice to a whisper.

After the disclosure, we sat in silence for several minutes before I added, "As for the war, your secret is safe. With Bryn I wish you luck, Aleck. I know I could never love another."

"Aye, neither I, my thanks, John," Aleck stood up ready to leave, but I stopped him.

"Then sit back man, relax and have a drink. You can plan in peace and quiet," I poured us each a healthy dram of my finest single malt. "To your success and our Bryn's happiness with it."

Several minutes later, Aleck again broke the silence. "By the way, I've need of some new clothes. And I'm verra comfortable with your taste." Aleck chuckled as he added, "Suits me, aye and maybe a haircut. Can you make any recommendations of your local establishments?"

I had seen the look of admiration in Bryn's eyes. I had to admit Aleck filled out my clothing handsomely. "I'll refer you to my haberdashery. My tailor can work some wonders for you, just don't get too gussied up. Keep it simple. And our Rose can give you a better trim than the local barber." I stroked my own bald head and added with a smirk. "I so dislike to have to admit this but you have the hair so don't trim too much off, Bryn seems to like it." Aleck remembered the wonderful feel of her fingers in his hair. They both laughed at the notion of Aleck being all dandified like the men of St. Louis.

~ Aleck ~

I sat back and relaxed, warming to my plans to capture Bryn's complete attention. I found myself staring at the flowers in the fireplace. They were beautiful but so out of place in John's masculine office. I liked them there. I understood. John and Lily were everywhere and always together even when they were apart. I wanted the same thing with Bryn. We sat and shared a quiet drink until William came to call us for lunch. As we left the room, John clapped me on the shoulder, "Good luck then my man. Be good to her, treasure her. But break her heart. . ."

"Aye, if you got a chance behind all the Henley men," I interrupted. We were laughing as we left John's office.

I reflected on my conversation with John. It was apparent to me that John was more than just a good man, he was also wise. Vague recollections surfaced to a similar kind of sage advice being given to me as a young boy. It sometimes bothered me that I could no longer conjure up a clear picture of my father in my mind whereas I could easily summon the image of my Mother. For a long time I felt guilty about it, but now I accepted this fading memory as a fact of life. I had been but a wee lad when my father had disappeared.

I feared that my mother's image would also fade. She had always been my comfort in trying times. Her ghost stood at my side during the whippings from my uncle, her angelic hands cradled my face giving me the strength not to whimper my agony and when the beatings were over, I sensed her tears in the cool water my aunt had used to cleanse my flayed back.

It was Mother's soothing words that had spilled from my mouth as men died around me in the war, the last earthly sounds they would hear.

Then the memory of her honesty and empathy would hearten me as I wrote those dreaded letters to the wives and parents of the men who had died. Her compassion helped me to share the final words of love that had been uttered and wherever possible an anecdote about each soldier. My letter might precede the arrival of the body and in many cases had to suffice for the lack of a body to bury at home.

Like the beatings, I was grateful that this particular time in my life had finally passed. I hated the war as had most others. Looking back, my youth had passed by quickly although the days and months after my father vanished and the time spent at his aunt and uncle's, seem to have taken forever. The illusions of youth, one minute young, the next a man, full grown.

I was nearly back to my full strength. The aches and pains were dissipating; the headache finally disappeared although I would carry the bruises for a while yet. I took extra care grooming this morning. I carefully scraped away the beard that always grew back overnight. With my fingers, I ran water through my hair, combed, and as was my custom tied it back with a leather thong. I leaned over the wash bowl, splashed water on my face rubbing roughly with the soft flannel to remove any traces of dirt. In the mirror I watched the color in my cheeks ebb and flow.

I went down the back stairs in search of Bryn. I spoke with Rose and William but neither had seen her yet this morning. I went first to look in the stable. If she was up, she was probably paying a visit to Tinker. Bryn was nowhere to be found and I was missing her. Since the night I first laid eyes on her soaked, unconscious body, we had been together constantly and this enforced nighttime separation was irritating me. I wondered if she might be missing me or was she relieved to have me out of her hair. She always appeared happy to see me but what did I really know of the ways of women. Well, he could wait to find out, not for long but I could be very patient when the need arose. I would accomplish my plans for the day and search her out, and then I might know for sure.

I saddled up one of the Wallace's horses. They had been more than kind to me. But once John had become confident of my honor and intentions around Bryn, he had offered me the open hospitality of their stables. John was an excellent judge of humans and horseflesh. I appreciated the generosity of my hosts as any of their horses would be an excellent mount. As I rode into town I acknowledged to myself that what I was missing was the wilderness that enveloped me and my cabin. On the other hand, I was also candid enough to admit I was enjoying my stay with the elegant Wallaces far more than I ever thought possible. I knew it was my attraction to Bryn that gave rise to the contentment and I marveled at how quickly I had succumbed to her capricious but feminine charms. She made everything enjoyable, made life worthwhile.

St. Louis had grown since my last stay. There were more streets, more people and I could sense the urgency of the city in the bustle of its daily business. It took me two turns to find the store John had recommended. Distrustful of the possibilities a city offered, I could not in good conscience leave John's horse to the mercy of a hitching post on the street. After carefully securing the horse at the livery, I made my way back to the shop and stepped inside. From the doorway, I took a circumspect view of the whole area and the goods it contained. To my right was an overflowing hat stand. I felt every style of hat ever created must surely be represented there. On the wall behind the hats were shelves filled with shirts. Straight ahead five paces was a table displaying pants. The back wall contained an inset where hung the dress trousers that I knew would be worn by the likes of John on a daily basis. Jackets and waistcoats were to my left.

I made my decisions without a fuss and when I left the store I was the new owner of two pairs of brushed cotton pants, a black Stetson to replace the one ruined in the fall, two pairs of working gloves, four shirts and several pairs of socks and two pairs of drawers. These would be delivered this afternoon once the pants had been hemmed and the shirts adjusted. Bryn would hopefully be pleased with the choices I made. Although I could not see myself dressed comfortably in such fine clothing, I would return tomorrow for a final fitting for dress trousers, a fine shirt, tie and a waistcoat I had ordered. This was an acknowledgment to courting her. The tailor whom John had recommended assisted me with the fitting assuring me they would be ready tomorrow afternoon and with his expertise would likely not require further alterations.

The mention of John's referral and the Wallace address for delivery had provided some special considerations regarding the choice of clothing as well as the proper fitting of these, including the shirts. I was sure that shirt fittings were rare, I'd never heard of having a shirt fitted. My shirts were all large loose fitting garments that allowed for ease of movement. With pleasure I remembered Bryn being swallowed up in one that first night in my home. I paid for my purchases and left. The last thing on my clothing list was a decent pair of leather boots to be worn on special occasions. These too would be delivered to the Wallace's home this afternoon. I had one more chore.

I walked with purpose up the street to the theater. There I purchased two tickets for the Saturday evening performance. It was to be a concert in the fashion made popular by Jenny Lind more than fifteen years before. I remembered escorting my aunt to see Miss Lind perform in Boston and how we had both enjoyed the music and her singing. Last night I had confided my intentions to Lily. She had been overjoyed to be included in the planning and had immediately offered to reserve a private table for two at the hotel before the performance and offered the Wallace box. I had graciously declined the box, so she recommended good seating choices. William would be at my disposal to drive us in the carriage. I accepted her generous offer thinking it might delight Bryn to be so indulged. I would take Bryn out for an evening of fine dining and entertainment; romantic even, if I could manage it.

The afternoon was still and hot. Unhurried, I walked back toward the livery gazing through the shop windows as items vied for my attention. As I passed the millinery shop, I was bewildered how Bryn kept springing to mind with such ease. I stood confounded by the latest in women's fashionable bonnets. I wondered if my mother and father had thought of each other nearly every minute of the day. John and Lily certainly gave that impression, although when I looked back at my life with my aunt and uncle there was no sense of love or respect there. I rubbed my forehead with my hand to ward off the possibility of a headache from such reflection. Bryn haunted me with blue eyes dancing with merriment and an underlying promise of mischief; it was driving me crazy. The curls that always framed her lovely face, the sway of her hips, the pulse that beat at the base of her throat when she looked up waiting for my kiss swam in my mind whenever I closed my eyes; even the simple thrill of finding things that she had absentmindedly misplaced so I could enjoy the delighted smile that these items evoked with the feel of her warm hands on mine when I returned them to her.

Once back at the Wallace's, the first thing I thought about was to find Bryn. I found her in the library. No surprise there, she loved to read and this was an extensive library. I understood many of the books had been brought over from Lily's home in England. I crossed the room and Bryn greeted me with a broad, welcoming smile. "What have...," I caught her mid-sentence sweeping her into my arms for a penetrating kiss. The book she was reading slid to the floor between us. She was breathless as she finished, "you been up to?" her voice a hoarse whisper. The emotion in her voice challenged me, almost to the point of no return. Yes, she appeared pleased to see me. I kissed her again more gently this time and set her gently down still in my embrace.

"I've been out shopping, you nosey wee lassie," I teased. "I have a surprise for you Saturday if your social calendar will allow." I released her and backed up. From my shirt pocket I retrieved the two tickets and teasingly waggled them in front of her as I asked with a trace of trepidation. "Would you allow me to escort you Saturday evening to dinner and the theater?"

Without a second's hesitation, she threw herself into my arms and excitedly whispered, "Oh I'd like very much for you to escort me Saturday evening. I've never been to a big city theater; I'd like it very much." Then she enticed the leather lace from my hair and twining her fingers in the dark locks tugged me down to her level for a kiss.

"Ah my vixen lassie, I'd be honored to take you."

*E*arley's brush with the mudslide unsettled the three of us. The trail we had been following was narrow so we had been riding single file. If Rob had not called a halt, sighting the colorful hair ribbon off to the side in the brush we would likely have continued around the bend and caused another larger slide. Earley certainly would not have been able to back up. Thief and he would have plunged down the slide to the shelf below. More than likely, we would all have cascaded down the slope on top of one another and the prospect of the chaos and injuries sustained from the jumble of horse and human bodies stunned us all.

After blocking the trail from both directions and retrieving MacLaren's saddle, we rested over coffee and discussed Bryn's courage and resourcefulness. It had been a startling revelation to think of Bryn in the role of rescuer, again. From Papa, we knew she had bravely struck out on her own, following Pa's instructions to find MacLaren. But this fiasco! She had put an animal out of its misery, secured and dragged an obviously unconscious man back up the slope, nursed him back to consciousness and gotten them back underway. She'd even remembered to rescue his saddle bags. This whole sorry episode garnered newfound respect from all of us. Bryn was no longer the helpless, flighty, scatterbrained girl we had been so used to taking care of. We were impressed, and had to admit, she had grown up to be a resilient, although scatterbrained, young woman.

After coffee we pushed on. Reining the horses back, we negotiated the final slopes reaching the plains leading to St. Louis just as the final vestiges of dusk faded. We watered and rested the horses and ourselves. Stars in the cloudless sky would provide enough light for us to make our way into town, however with the already late hour and still a distance to go we, decided it was probably better for us to go to the hotel than to wake the whole Wallace household. We kept the rest short with the promise of real beds tonight.

We sidetracked to go past the Wallaces but all main floor lights were out as expected. Managing not to wake the stable hands, Earley quietly checked out the stable. He reported that Tinker was safely installed there, which meant Bryn had arrived and was in our aunt and uncle's care. With weary sighs of relief, we set off on the last of our trek. It was very late when we finally arrived at the front doors of the hotel. Rob went in to register, fortunately there were rooms available. Once the horses were cared for, set up with feed and stabled at the livery, we made our way up to our rooms. Tomorrow would be a busy day.

~ Rob ~

I was up and ready to start my day at the crack of dawn. I had always been an early riser much to the annoyance of Josh who needed to be pulled from under his warm covers to start our morning chores on the ranch. I went down to the lobby to see if I could rustle up some coffee. The hotel staff was just starting their day and Frank had the coffee pot ready. I took my first sip and recognized myself as human. Frank remembered me from my stay years before with Lily and John. He had spotted my name on the register as he had tidied up last night's accounts and was watching for me to descend from the private rooms. Of course, he was only too eager to fill me in on all the exciting news that had transpired over the last week. Frank didn't miss a beat as he cleaned through the desk. He was enjoying the fact he had an eager listener. I poured myself a second cup of coffee. It was with a touch of relief I saw Drew and Earley coming down to join me.

Over a satisfying breakfast of farm fresh eggs, bacon and toast, I succinctly filled them in on what I had learned. Thomas was already here and staying at the hotel. Bryn and Aleck had arrived, Bryn was fine, and Aleck was concussed but much improved already. John had telegraphed Josh to let him know the family was alright. Good news all around. We were ready to see Bryn, Lily and John. After a short lecture from Earley, we also felt ready to confront Aleck. While on our way to the Wallace's, we telegraphed Josh of our safe arrival in St. Louis.

William led us into the parlor and bade us wait. Moments later, Lily made her entrance graciously welcoming us to her home. We stood in unison as she entered the room. "Welcome, Rob, Drew how wonderful to see you again, I gather from William you stayed last night at the hotel. He'll collect your things a little later this morning and set you all up here." She hugged us close and kissed our cheeks. "And Earley, so nice to see you again after all these years, thank you for your help with our family crisis." She took his hands in hers and kissed him on the cheek as well. "You'll stay here as family too, please."

"Good ta see you too Miss Lily. Yer welcome, needed ta search for my friends. Wouldn't have it any other way," He stammered with a quiet voice. "I can stay at the hotel. You'll have a full house with all yer family."

"Please, call me Lily. And we insist you stay here with us. You belong, as part of our family." Earley reddened as he acquiesced with a slight bow of his head.

"Please have a seat. William, would you please bring us coffee? Thank you. John, Bryn and Aleck will be down shortly, and then you can tell us everything. You can imagine, until Bryn and Aleck arrived, we had been beside ourselves with worry." Lily noted the eye contact between me and Drew. "Alright you two, I know something's up. Would you care to share?" She enquired.

Drew responded hotly, "We want to know about MacLaren! We're worried about Bryn."

"Take it easy young man. Aleck's a good man. John's an excellent judge of character and he's satisfied with his conduct around Bryn. We know Aleck would protect her to the death. Surely you know your father wouldn't willingly entrust Bryn into the care of anyone he didn't trust completely. He'd have bid Aleck to come on his own. Your brotherly concern is touching, but at this point unnecessary. Aleck's intentions about Bryn are quite clear and honorable. Take some worldly advice. Leave them alone," Aunt Lily wore her no nonsense look, glaring at Drew.

"Your nephews have arrived sir, in the parlor," We heard William announce our location as John strode into the room. "Good morning. So glad you've arrived safely. Welcome. Thank you for your search efforts."

"Get your hands off my sister!" Drew roared his interruption as Aleck walked into the parlor with Bryn's arm tucked through his. In one swift movement Bryn was swept behind him as Aleck assessed the threat. "You're trying to protect her from me! You swine!" hissed Drew as he launched himself off the settee. Earley grabbed Drew from the side as John blocked his path saying, "Hold on, son." Earley quietly commanded, "Drew, control yourself!"

Drew spluttered as Bryn peeked around Aleck with a shocked expression on her face. "Aleck it's alright, it's Drew, my brother," She squeaked as Aleck pushed her back behind him. Drew could see her fingers boldly holding Aleck's hips for balance. The intimacy added fuel to his over powering rage.

"Aye lass, your brother he may well be but he'll have to kill me to get to you at the moment. He's verra angry. Once he has himself under control, you can see him."

"You're protecting her from me?" Drew raged.

"Yes he is and we're all protecting him from you," John spoke in a calming tone. "Now sit down Drew and let's start over again in a civilized manner. Or do you need to take a short walk to cool down?"

I tugged Drew back onto the settee. "He's cooled off, let's try again." I could feel Drew bristling beside me and gave him a brotherly poke in the ribs to get him to settle. John measured up the situation and gauged that the moment had passed. He moved to sit with Lily as Earley reclaimed his seat. Aleck carefully surveyed everyone in the room, starting and ending with Drew. Sure that tenuous peace had been restored, Aleck finally released Bryn. She stepped around him, smiled up at him and went over to welcome us and Earley with a peck on our cheeks and a hug. She returned to Aleck's side, took his hand and pulled him closer to introduce her family. "These are two of my brothers, Drew and Rob. This is Earley, our father's right hand man. He's part of our family. And this is Aleck MacLaren. He saved Mama and Papa, then fixed Papa up and brought me safely here . . . to ease Aunt Lily's mind."

"When did you two get here?" I began the questioning in a friendlier tone as I gave Drew yet another poke in the ribs. For good measure I told myself as I enjoyed taunting my little brother.

"Three days ago. Aunt Lily and Uncle John have been looking after us since then. I'm sure you saw the mudslide. Aleck went over the side and had a bad concussion. He's much better. Except for some cuts and bruises, you'd never know. Tinker and I didn't fall. I guess you figured that out, didn't you?" She looked to Aleck asking, "Can they call you Aleck? You can use their first names."

"That's verra generous of you Bryn but that's their offer to make." Turning to face the men he offered. "Andrew's a good man, as his kin you are welcome to call me Aleck. Bryn, Lily and John do."

Earley and I nodded while Drew remained mute with menace in his gaze. Aleck remained on his guard as William arrived with a fresh tray of coffee. "Mam, Rose has prepared a breakfast table if you are interested. Shall I serve the coffee in here or at the table?"

"At the table would be lovely William, thank you. Please come and share as we break our fast." We rose and followed Lily and John into the dining room. Drew attempted to intercept Bryn on her way across the hall but Aleck quickly cut him off. John guided Lily into her seat and Aleck moved to do the same for Bryn. Drew again attempted to intercept, then changed his mind and quickly sat himself next to Bryn so Aleck would have to sit across the table from her. He smirked with his triumph but confusion crossed his face momentarily as I gave him a look of disapproval.

Mindful of our manners at the table the conversation was polite, non-committal and very strained. From our seats on either side of Aleck, Earley and I could see Bryn's smile and lingering gaze on Aleck. Drew was moodily silent as he was aware that Aleck had eyes only for Bryn. I soon realized that Lily and John were comfortable with the attraction between Bryn and Aleck as the four had a relaxed conversation about their stay in St. Louis, bringing us newcomers up to date. As they talked around me of Bryn's lunch with Thomas and described the scene when they had realized how Bryn was the image of Lily and Pa's mother. They discussed Thomas' sudden illness and confinement to his room at the hotel. Bryn's excitement was almost contagious over the new dress she purchased while out with Aunt Lily. She caught Aleck's slight shake of the head and forbore telling them about her outing to the theater this coming Saturday.

At the conclusion of the meal, Aleck suggested Bryn might like to take a break on the front porch or in the library. She was surprised when her, "Yes let's" was met with, "No Bryn, you go, perhaps Lily will accompany you. I need to speak to your brothers in private." She had assumed he would accompany her, but as she made to object Aleck firmly said, "Lass, the front porch or the library. I'll join you shortly."

With a huff and a muttered "men!" Bryn was led out of the room by Aunt Lily. Impressed, Earley watched as Aleck then turned to her brothers and directed to Drew. "Well, let's have it out then, aye, the stable perhaps?"

As they rose, Lily stuck her head back through the door. "John dear, I know there's a fight brewing. I expect you to keep it fair and no major damage to anyone or you will all answer to me. Got it?" John looked intently at his two nephews as he said clearly, "I expect it to be a fair fight. Aleck would you like me to see to your back?"

"Aye, if you've a mind to. I'd appreciate the support."

The stables had just been mucked out and were strewn with fresh straw. I stood second to Drew as John stood to Aleck. Earley declined allegiance. We leaned against a stall and waited as the two adversaries prepared for the fight. Aleck removed his shirt and hung it over a stall door. He chose to fight bare chested rather than ruin a new shirt, especially as Bryn's eyes had shown how she liked it on him. Drew threw the first punch which Aleck deflected easily. Each landed several well placed blows but the fight continued with neither scoring a clear victory. Drew had the fury while Aleck had the finesse. As the fight went on I whispered to my uncle, "I don't think he's fully unleashed. What say you?"

"I've never seen him in a fight before but I'd have to agree," John whispered in reply. The fight lasted far longer than it should with neither adversary able to claim a clean win. Both were sweating and bloody but wouldn't give up. John finally called the fight to a close. "Enough!" he bellowed so each would clearly hear. Aleck backed up, but Drew advanced. "Enough I said! End it!" As Aleck stepped out of range in response to the order Drew suddenly lunged forward and threw a punch that lifted Aleck into the air throwing him back into a pile of hay.

Before John could react Earley stepped forward and cold cocked Drew. "Bin itchin' to do that for a couple of days. Kid's too hot under the collar, letting anger cloud his thinking. Andrew'll have a talk with him about fighting fair and bein' a man." Satisfied, he turned to Aleck and offered a hand. "Admired yer restraint. Name's Earl, yer free to call me Earley like my friends here." Once he had Aleck back on his feet, Earley left the stables.

I offered to take care of my hot headed little brother who was still asleep in the hay. Aleck looked at me I straight on through a now swelling eye. "Aye, have you anything to add to this?"

"No, I'm thinking you did more than just the basics caring for our folks and then getting Bryn here safely. She doesn't look like she's been abused or Uncle John would've killed you with Aunt Lily's blessing. I too admire your restraint. Name's Rob, You're at liberty to use it. I'll just say this. I know you two are interested in each other but if you hurt her. . . ."

Aleck interrupted, "Aye, well line up with the others then. You'll all want to kill me. Now I best clean up and go see her before she really starts to fret."

John and I thought she'd be more than fretting, she'll want to kill Drew herself when she sees Aleck's face. Drew was coming around so John and I helped him to his feet. "That was uncalled for and ungentlemanly. I'm disappointed. You best stay out of Bryn's sight for a while," I chided and offered to get him into the house away from her wrath. John nodded his consensus of disapproval, turned and left me to deal with my brother.

~ *Bryn* ~

ncle John found me ministering to Aleck in the kitchen with Lily and Rose looking on and offering advice. He was trying to get away from all my fussing but I was having none of it. I had a cold compress held firmly over his eye and was giving him the dickens. "Why didn't you just knock him out straight away? I'm sure you're more than Drew's equal. Really Aleck, now you're a mess and he probably is too. Was this really necessary? Why do you men always think you have to solve everything with your fists? And then we have to fix you up! Why do you have to fight it out? Can't you use reason and discuss it? No! You have to beat each other up. It's despicable. I just don't understand. You should have known better. He's just a kid."

Uncle John was just about to speak when Aleck said. "Lass, he's a man, not a boy." When I shook my head Aleck reached for my hands, holding them below his chin, he looked straight up into my eyes and reiterated. "Aye Bryn, he's man, just not as experienced yet. He wanted to defend your honor. He thinks I've ruined your reputation. And maybe I have but most seem to understand the predicament and have made allowances. He needed to vent his fury. This was the easiest way for everyone. And these, they're just bruises, they'll heal. I'm alright lass and so is he. Let it go. You're parents understood, as do your aunt and uncle. It's their opinion that matters Bryn. Can you no understand lass?" He gently pulled me into his lap.

With a crook of my finger, I gave John my come hither look and we stole quietly out of the kitchen with Rose in our wake. In the hall, as William joined us, John summarized the fight mentioning Drew's fury and Aleck's restraint but neglecting to mention the final two blows delivered. From the look on William's face, John knew he had watched the entire fight, probably from the entrance to the stables. But with William's silence, it appeared as if Drew's disgraceful conduct would remain within the family. John was sure Drew would not make the same mistake again.

At my invitation the two couples moved to the front porch. The air was still and hot. Rose brought a fresh jug of iced mint tea from the front hall and William carried out the tray with glasses. He served them each, passed the women a fan then took his seat. Lily had never liked the idea of having servants. She preferred to think of Rose and William as friends whom she and John employed to take care of them. This had been the arrangement for so long now that they were all comfortable together. However, Rose and William usually refused to be that familiar when the Wallaces had company and Lily had learned to respect that. But the events transpiring now were exceptional and I had been assertive that they join us on the veranda. Rose and I put the fans to good use as we sipped our mint tea and discussed the reunion with the Henley children.

I knew my brothers well, but even so, this brew ha-ha with Aleck was beyond my understanding. It was not easy being the youngest, and a girl. What was it with men anyway?! It was unfathomable to me that they could not see what I saw in Aleck. Through the kitchen window, I watched Rob and Drew leave the stable heading to the pump. Drew's shirt was in shreds, his nose bloody and both eyes would be swollen but there they were, both were killing themselves laughing over some private joke that only they shared. Just like the old days when they would beat each other to a pulp over some misunderstanding and then laugh. Mama would just roll her eyes and tend to their wounds. Not even the threat of Mama stitching up wounds could deter them from releasing all of the pent up energy a good fight would release. My thoughts were interrupted as Aleck took the cold cloth from my hand, placed it on the table and gently drew me into his embrace again. He was more interested in a different medicine for his aches and pains that only my lips could impart.

A short while later the front double doors slammed open. I jumped up out of Aleck's arms but he beat me to the kitchen door, once more pulling me safely behind him.

"Wind must have caught the doors," William said with a wicked grin as he came down the hall towards us. "There's a special delivery from Abigail's Dress Shop for Miss Bryn."

I pushed my way around Aleck. "That would be me, but I didn't order anything." My jaw dropped in confusion when I saw the number of boxes that were being carried in by William and John. Seeing my bewilderment, Aunt Lily smiled offering me the card that accompanied the boxes. They were in all shapes and sizes. I definitely identified two hat boxes. I knew I had not made these purchases. I read the card.

Our dearest Bryn,
We are so enjoying having you here with us.
Our shopping trip was delightful. I appreciated how your
eyes lit up as some of these articles were shown to us.
Darling Bryn, please enjoy them.
Love
Aunt Lily and Uncle John

Flushed, I looked up at my aunt. "Oh my gosh! Aunt Lily, Uncle John! I don't know what to say. Thank you so much! You shouldn't have. What will Mama say? Thank you. Oh, I'm so excited. Thank you!" I flung my arms around them holding them as close as was truly possible. I loved them with all my heart.

With a soft laugh William said kindly, "I'll place these in your room, Miss Bryn."

"Thank you William. Oh! Thank you Aunt Lily," I looked around lost as to what to do or say next. Aleck gave me an affectionate pat on my rearmost steering me towards the staircase with the command, "Go on up lass. Inspect your treasures." I needed no further prompting.

Once in my room I carefully opened the pretty boxes one by one. Reveling in the excitement of the moment, I took my time and tried on each outfit. First came two skirts with matching blouses and a coordinating deep blue fitted jacket. I ran my fingers over the fine white lace collars of the blouses. With my eyes closed, I caressed the side of my cheek against the soft pile of the cotton. Then I moved on to admire the fitted skirt which flared dramatically below the knee in ivory with deep blue vertical stripes and a matching high collared blouse. The cording at the seams was the same deep blue as the jacket. The other was a full, medium blue skirt with pinch pleats running around the hem of the skirt. The intricate detailing was in the pinch pleated bodice with picot lace tucked in each pleat. The demure Peter Pan collar had picot lace trim as well. The simple navy day dress with pagoda sleeves that ended with lace trim that accentuated my delicate wrists was also trimmed in matching lace at the collar and hemline. The outfits were striking. There was even a black bolero style jacket with a sage green riding skirt and a fitted crisp, white cotton button up blouse. Aunt Lily loved lavenders and wore them at every opportunity so I was thrilled that she had chosen these outfits in my own favorite shades of pale to deep blues.

The last dress box contained the most beautiful evening gown I had ever laid eyes on. In my wildest dreams I would never have imagined myself wearing such a delicate, feminine garment. I caught a tear just before it left its mark on the ice blue taffeta. I gently picked up the gown and brought it out of the box. Holding it closely to my body, I held out the gently flared skirt and danced in front of the mirror. The face that reflected back held a promise of tomorrow; there was joy in my smile and my blue eyes glittered with excitement. The fabric of the dress intensified the color of my eyes.

The gown was fashioned of pale ice blue taffeta in a full length coat style. The top was tightly fitted with long pagoda style sleeves. Cinched at the waist, the skirt flared out to create an elegant silhouette. The cuffs, collar, hem and front edging were deeply ruffled in the same fabric. The inset bodice had a fashionably low décolleté. Mama would be astonished. I had never seen nor could I even imagine my mother in a gown like this. I carefully pulled it over my head. It was heavy but so soft and luxurious to the touch. I could not keep my hands from smoothing the skirt into place. Later I would count them but I was sure there were over a hundred small upholstered buttons in the same fabric, that went from below my waist to the nape of my neck I left the back of the dress gaping. I would need to enlist some help when the special night came.

I was in heaven and could not wait until Saturday to wear the elegant dress for Aleck. I would be on pins and needles with excitement until I was able to see the look on his face when I came down the stairs to greet him. I took the dress off carefully intending to lay it back in the box. More tissue at the bottom of the box caught my attention. I pulled it out to reveal a reticule and dress slippers of ice blue taffeta with white, silver and pale blue ribbon embroidery that coordinated with the pattern in my dress. Lastly, I discovered an ice blue taffeta cap with silk net to match my gown and a pair of white crocheted gloves to complete the ensemble. I collapsed on the bed in my under garments unable to control the contented sighs and the visions of myself in my lovely new wardrobe with Aleck always at my side.

Overwhelmed, the tears started to flow. I was aware it was partly reaction from the events over the past few days, but also there were tears of joy over the happiness I had discovered with Aleck.

I let them fall and ease my strain. Finally spent, I wiped my eyes and nose and rose from the bed. There were still the hat boxes to explore and I loved hats, I had always wanted a silly, frivolous, impractical hat.

The hats were my favorites. One was in varying shades of medium blue to match my outfits. It was a day hat to wear shopping and to church. The other was more formal, adorned in black Belgian lace. Three ostrich plumes sat back in a rakish style in the black velvet band. The smaller boxes contained more personal items. I loved the feel of the silky lingerie as I gently stroked the delicate fabric, such a pretty luxury! I had never owned anything like them. Then I held up the corset for inspection. Normally, I would not have any occasion to wear such an uncomfortable contraption. I was sure a woman would never design such a device. However, I supposed to be a fashionable young lady, one had to make compromises. I wondered if my aunt wore one of these under her elegant evening gowns. I could not wait to thank Aunt Lily again. I sat on the edge of the bed for another moment, reveled in my blessings then I got up and tried everything on again admiring myself in the long looking glass in my room.

The sun was starting to make its dip into the west; I realized it was time to collect myself for dinner precisely as Rose knocked at her door. "I'll be down as quick as I can." I was anxious to see Aleck after this long, exciting and harrowing day. I freshened up and chose the navy dress for the evening. As usual, I struggled with my unruly curls but with the silky undergarments and the lace petticoats, I felt very special as I made my way downstairs.

I heard someone in the dining room. When I entered, Rose was putting the finishing touches to the table. I felt a pang of homesickness. This was my job at home. Since arriving in St. Louis I had been nothing but frolicsome. Suddenly, it did not sit well. Normally, I was an energetic helper. I had stood side by side with my brothers and father for as long as I could remember and when it was required Mama was right there with us. Also, Mama and I ran the kitchen. The days here were luxuriously long and lazy. Aunt Lily, bless her, wanted nothing but the best for me, but then my parents were on the same page. I realized I had been luxuriating in the spoiling but now the practical part of me cried out to be involved in something. Like Aunt Lily was.

"Dinner will be served in about ten minutes, Miss Bryn. Perhaps you would like some sherry while you wait?" William enquired.

"No thank you William, I'll wait in the library."

No sooner had I settled myself with a book when William announced dinner. I was delighted to see Aleck just behind William and took up his proffered arm.

Aleck pulled my chair out for me and gently positioned it at the table as he pushed it in for me he whispered in my ear, "You look verra beautiful tonight." I blushed to the roots of my hair at the compliment as he took his seat beside me. Neither one of us missed the look that passed between my brothers. I had discussed this with Aleck while I had cleaned him up after the fight. We had decided to ignore Drew's foolish behavior. After all, I pointed out the more you pay attention to their antics, the more you encourage them to continue. Aleck had held his tongue as she had explained what he was sure was just common knowledge, at least among young men. But it had actually been a hard won lesson for me, who as a young girl was continually running to my mother or father to complain about some infraction perpetrated by one brother or another. When Mama had passed on this bit of maternal wisdom the penny dropped for me and life was much more bearable. Aleck forbore mentioning it was mostly Drew, not both my brothers who were being irritating. I attended to my napkin and smiled sweetly at everyone at the table. Aleck stifled a grin at my prim and proper performance. My heart went out to Aleck as he had no experience to fall back on. I noticed him subconsciously raise his hand to touch the bruising above his eye, a sure sign of his discomfort.

~ *Drew* ~

We were both a little battle worn at the moment. I was having the most difficulty and looked the worse from the morning's episode. But nothing was being mentioned and secretly I was glad. I was ashamed of my actions after my dressing down from Rob and Uncle John. And Earley, I knew Earley had decked me. Thoroughly humiliated, Drew remained sullen and fidgety. I wondered if Aunt Lily and Bryn knew about my disgraceful conduct. I was unable to lift my gaze and meet anyone's eyes. If I had taken the time to examine the reason behind my anger, I would have been surprised. Bryn had been there for me all of my life. She cared for me, looked after my skinned knees as a boy, my broken arm as a teen and too many cuts and scrapes to remember. She was my best friend and now that position was being contested by this Aleck. I felt guilty that all I could think of was who would care for me now? I slumped down in my chair and was rewarded with an elbow from Rob. I grimaced and sat up straight, relieved that dinner was being served. Now I had something productive to do with my hands other than itching to give Aleck a matching shiner on the other eye.

~ Earley ~

The stilted atmosphere at the table was not lost on me. Drew's uneasy slouch made everyone uncomfortably aware of his personal misery. Though swathed in a friendly environment, the elegant formality of the Wallace home was making my head ache. I needed to get away. "Drew, we'll be gettin' ourselves an early start in the mornin'. You an' me. Goin' back ta get your Ma and Pa?" That said and with the firm conviction that our departure ought to fix things up for both of us, I tucked into the delicious dinner Rose had made and William was serving. The objective being to separate Drew and Bryn! And get myself back in the saddle. Not wishing to create another scene in front of his Uncle, Drew reluctantly agreed. "Yes sir, I'll be ready."

I nodded in satisfaction and finished my dinner in peace. Conversation picked up and the awkwardness passed, though I remained silent through the meal. Drew and I excused ourselves and retired directly from the dinner table. The remaining five withdrew to the front porch for an after dinner drink, gentle conversation and to watch the stars come out as night settled in.

I gulped down the last of my coffee. I stood and moved to face Lily, my nervous hands working over the brim of my hat. "Miss Lily, we thank you for yer hospitality but Drew and me, we best be on our way. Be easier for Sarah if we're there ta help Andrew. Else he'll do too much. We'll guide and keep watch." I turned my head and nodded as I added, "Drew."

She rose saying, "you are most welcome Earley. You're part of our family and don't forget it. Please be careful going back. And please, please, please bring Sarah and Andrew safely home to us. Godspeed!"

She clasped my shoulders and kissed both cheeks. She gave Drew a hug and a kiss, twice for good measure.

We left for the stables to saddle up. Lily's eyes twinkled as she realized the return to the formal Miss Lily was only because I had rehearsed this long nervous speech. She knew I was feeling out of my element. It was a relief that we would be there for Andrew and Sarah. I had seen Drew and Rob talking quietly together just outside John's study this morning. I felt sure Bryn's peaceful time with Aleck, so rudely interrupted yesterday was not about to resume without some issues. I thought to raise the topic with Rob sitting so quietly beside Bryn but realized he too was ruminating on issues of his own so I wisely decided to leave the siblings to work it out.

"Drew," I called, "where are ya boy'?"

"Back here with Tinker, just thought I'd look in on her. I'm ready, let's head out." We rode around to the front of the house and with a salute to Lily and Rob, we were on our way. We donned our hats and rode down the lane at a steady trot. Drew was chuckling to himself thinking how annoyed his sister would be when she discovered Rob was left behind to chaperone. "This city is too darn big," I lamented to myself or anyone else who may have been listening. "What do people want living on top of each other like rats in a tunnel? Give me the back forty any day." I spat for emphasis.

Drew grinned. I marked the look on Drew's face as he had just spied a young lady walking toward town and had appreciated the view. "I'd kinda like to have a bit of both worlds, if you were to ask me." In a town the size of St. Louis there would lots of pretty young ladies. I whistled under my breath just thinking about it.

The mesa rose, and stretched out in the distance as we rode out past the county line leaving St. Louis and the civilized world to traverse through the farms that serviced it. We rode in silence both content with our own thoughts. I was retracing our journey of just the other day. Drew stayed close but trailed behind and I knew his thoughts were with Bryn, his folks and control of his own destiny, as here he was yet again doing someone else's bidding.

In the distance the mesa stood proud and tall, the dangers hidden in the slopes that brought the wary riders to the top. It starts at a gentle climb that alters quickly to a steep incline. At certain times of the year it could be very barren, but Drew and I both understood what we were facing. We climbed steadily synchronized with the rising of the sun overhead. The insidious dangers did nothing to interfere with the breathtaking beauty that surrounded us. By late morning, I had settled into my saddle, like it was an old easy chair, I was more comfortable now that I was out in the open. The city was now a blur on the horizon, the trees were becoming dense and the trail was narrowing quickly. Presently, I called a halt and dismounted to gauge the trail. "We'll keep ta the inside of the track through here," I shielded my eyes under my hat as I tried to cut the glare of the sun. "Careful, should be near that slide. Don't want to go over there or anywheres else." Drew nodded in agreement. The storm wasted land was no contest for us but we remained cautious. Shortly, we found where we had set up the blockade at the landslide. There had been no further deterioration but there was not much trail space left. So we struck a new path well back of the gaping chasm, then after a brief rest we pushed on.

A short time later, I threw a quick silent signal to Drew to halt. "Smell anythin'?" I mouthed the query while visibly sniffing the air. Drew nodded brought to sudden awareness by the whispered question. He scrambled to cover the miss. He knew I had caught him drifting. Andrew would not be pleased if he had been here. I made a note to pay more attention. His life could depend on it. His life was worth that much. Both men stayed seated, eyes alert, listening and smelling the air. "Smells like coffee to me," mouthed Drew. I nodded and signaled to dismount.

We secured the horses and quickly planned our approach. With guns drawn I pointed to Drew indicating he should skirt around to the west on the upper side of the trail. Drew nodded his understanding and crept without a sound around to the other side of the crop of trees and up onto the ledge. I went tree to tree with the stealth of a mountain lion until I was able to lay eyes on the camp I suspected was there. It looked empty, but I knew that could be deceiving. I would feel better when I knew just what the two of us were walking into; after all, I was responsible for Drew and would never forgive myself should the boy be hurt, or worse yet die, in a gun fight. But these encounters were all part of life on the trail.

~ *Sarah* ~

The others had left yesterday afternoon, Andrew and I had lazed the rest of the day away knowing it would be one of our last nights in the cabin. That evening, we had decided it was time to prepare to press on to St. Louis. Today, we had made all our travel preparations. We were ready. In the afternoon, I made a delicious stew on the wood stove. The aroma filled the cabin and there was a general feeling of wellbeing. I was content; the simple surroundings soothed me. It brought back memories of Andrew building our first home. That cabin had been not much different than this, but smaller. As it was not intended to be a permanent home, it had become an outbuilding within a year. It saw us through that first harsh winter, the wind howling like a banshee, whipping the snow in all directions around the corners of the little homestead. The tarp that covered the small square windows did nothing to keep the cold out. But we had been so happy. And then we had been blessed with Edward. How had we all fit into that cramped space? We had laughed so hard at his cute baby antics. Andrew was so careful about keeping a roaring fire going. It was amazing we did not go crazy. Then in the spring, Andrew started the building of our home. It was Andrew's gift to me and still an ongoing project. He was always doing something to make life easier or nicer for me. But our little cabin with Edward scooting around held a special place in my heart. I wiped the expected tears from my eyes amazed that I was still so emotional about losing Edward after these six years.

"Did you say something, my love?" Andrew had come up from behind and snuggled into my neck and was nibbling on my ear.

"No, just doing some memory walking, remember our first cabin?" and we laughed together. "This has been wonderful but I'm missing my own place and you're looking so much better Andrew Henley."

"As are you. Ah Sarah, you had me so worried, my love. Don't do that to me again," He ordered with more intensity than playfulness.

I turned in his arms and gave him a direct stare, "Why Andrew, you really were worried! I guess I was that sick and I must admit I was worried myself when I roused sufficiently to think about our situation." I paused for emphasis before whispering, "oh, and I love you too," as I raised my head to kiss him. "Come, dinner time."

Over our dinner we made our final decisions for our journey and the preparations to leave Aleck's cabin in good stead. We would leave early tomorrow morning. Everything was in readiness; we would make our way slowly down out of the mountains to St. Louis and all that awaited us there. We cleared the dishes together and with a reciprocal gleam in our eyes turned in early.

I was amazed how quickly we fell back into our old routines. We were up and ready to go as planned albeit a little slower on Andrew's part. He had made allowances for that. We had always been a good team and now that old oneness with each other was an asset. I urged Andrew to take some laudanum as a precaution but he would have none of it. He wanted to be fully alert and at the ready. He knew how treacherous slow reactions could be.

*T*he trail was ruined by the storm; then again, we had the benefit of five recent riders to re-strike the trail for us. It was simple to follow, I was able to concentrate most of my effort on our safety and me remaining in my saddle. We took frequent breaks to keep us both as agile as possible and I intended to stop early for evening camp.

I was about to call a halt for the day when I saw all the tracks leave the main trail. I debated whether or not to follow as it appeared all riders came back and continued on from here. Sarah and I discussed it and decided to take the detour. Shortly, we were rewarded with the entrance to the cave and obvious activity all around. We would camp here for the night as it appeared the others had before us. Sarah had bagged a pair of rabbits earlier in the afternoon; I prepared them for her and roasted them on a spit. While we waited for them to cook, we went in search of the waterfall we could hear. Sated and tired, we fell quickly and soundly asleep in the comfort of the furs and our bed rolls.

It was our second day back out on the trail and we were getting stronger and a bit quicker. We made good time but again called an early halt to our travels. We needed to set up camp for the night as we did not have the luxury of the cave. I awoke to the smell of coffee. Sarah had been up and had the coffee and porridge ready.

I was just thinking I should bring her out into the countryside with me more often when I heard the sound. Sarah heard it too and stood stalk still watching my eyes and taking my lead. I nodded to Sarah to disappear into the trees as I carefully reached for my rifle. All my instincts told me I was going to face a large animal, my nose told me it was bear. I started to whistle so it wouldn't be startled. The heavy bushy head of fur appeared first. He was coming into camp at a leisurely lumbering pace. As the bear emerged from the brush it was obvious he was a young adult male. Sarah was beside herself; however, she knew any interference on her part would end up in blood bath for both of us. With difficulty, she willed herself to stay quiet; silently she stuffed her hanky to her mouth biting it to stifle any sound and wrapped her arms around a tree for support.

A large black bear with his long black snout rooting into the air, I understood at once what I was up against. I continued whistling as I changed my posture and raised my arms in the air with my rifle held between my outstretched arms. I used everything in my arsenal to make myself look as large as possible. The pain in my leg was unbearable and sweat popped out on my forehead and ran into my eyes, the salt burning and blurring my vision, but I stood my ground. I had caught the bear's attention; I prayed that I did not look like the bear's next meal. The black's yellow teeth were sharp and malevolent looking while its claws were long and razor–sharp on powerful paws. I was now only a few yards away. The bear reared up to his full height towering over me with menacing forepaws up in the air. The bear let out a roar that sent terrifying, shivers through us. Sarah tightened her hold on the tree hoping she wouldn't faint in fright and alarm the beast. I knew if the bear suspected any weakness from me I would be done for. Finally satisfied the bear dropped casually to all fours. Snout up and with a casual sniff, he ambled to the far side of the camp. With one lazy swipe he felled yesterday's cooked rabbit that hung at the edge of camp. Taking his prize with him, he ambled off into the forest.

Neither of us moved as I continued to test the air. Finally, I lowered my arms as I called out to Sarah. I willed myself not to submit to the fear I had just experienced, more for Sarah than for myself. She quickly came to my side and stepped into my strong embrace. I stroked her hair and held her close to calm the trembling of her body against mine.

Wild animals were a fact of life but bears were exceptionally dangerous as it always took several shots from a distance to take one out. From only a few yards, I did not have a chance. I had only had encounters with the big blacks a couple of times in my life. Unless they were hungry, they usually stayed away especially if they heard you coming first.

"It's over my love," I crooned into her ear. I rubbed her back, and sure now she was stable, I returned to fixing the coffee. With the bear fresh in our minds we both moved quickly to eat and break camp. Eager to be on our way in any case, we saddled the horses and departed.

For the most part we had to ride single file as the trail was narrow and in some cases had been completely obliterated by the strength of the storm. I found that when my horse had to pick its way over some of the debris the change in gait was agonizing. It had been years since I had been down this way, so, I was pleased to find that even in the wake of the storm there were some land marks that I recognized. I could easily follow the tracks of the five preceding me but knowing the trails was essential to survival. The riding was hard and tiresome. My leg ached continuously but I stoically carried on. On this part of the trail, it was vital that both feet remain in the stirrups. We rode on quietly, each lost in thought watching the tree tops sway and listening to the rustle of the leaves as a gentle wind swept across the mountain. The cacophony of sounds were easily identified and therefore caused no alarm. The hours passed in the same way.

Painfully and with great care, I pivoted in the saddle turning toward Sarah, I felt the pull on my injured leg and could not control the grimace. "I… it's time to stop for another rest," she responded to my pain. "I agree. We can stake the horses here. It's a good spot with the stream running so clear." The horses bent their heads to the cool water and munched on the grazing that was available to them. I got off of my horse, stiff and in pain, limped to a huge rock and leaned against it. Sarah cleared a spot for the fire and quickly had it started with a coffee pot on to boil. When she turned around I had disappeared, she realized I was now resting on the other side of the rock in the shade. "Let me look at your leg," she said as she approached.

~ Sarah ~

"*I*t's alright. The saddle riding is rough but it can't be helped. I will feel better after some of your fabulous coffee," Andrew's words were short and filled with anguish.

I rolled my eyes and grinned, "Alright Mr. Henley, coffee's coming up." Stubborn but lovable old fool, I thought to myself. "Just going to get a few of those herbs I saw."

"Don't stray too far, my love, and carry your gun."

It was actually a day to be enjoyed if we had been in better health. I filled my herb bag while Andrew rested his leg. I didn't wander too far. My cough was just about finished and I was feeling more like my old self. When I came back, I found Andrew snoozing behind the rock. I gently touched his shoulder and he was instantly awake.

"I'll pour you that coffee now," as I spoke there arose a call.

"Halloo camp," called a very familiar voice. I smiled, stood and quickly returned the call, "Earley, hello, we're over here."

Earley and Drew entered the camp from opposite ends. Earley told Drew to fetch the horses while he made the coffee for all of us. I received hugs from both men before Drew followed Earley's instructions.

"Glad you made it this far," Earley said. He had been thinking he and Drew would find Andrew and I still in the cabin. "Looking much better than the last I saw you, for sure" and spat for good measure. I rolled my eyes; the men were not used to having a lady present in camp. "Sorry Sarah," Earley flushed with embarrassment. "Don't think twice about it . . ." I started, and Andrew finished with "but don't do it again!" while a smile tugged at the corners of his mouth. He too thought of me as one of them. After all, who had been beside him during the beginning years, splitting wood, cooking meals and notching cabin logs with him. They always made me feel like a special lady.

~ Earley ~

"**S**o, tell us the news from St. Louis," requested Andrew. "I assume Bryn and Aleck made it in one piece or I'm sure you'd have said something. What else has happened?" I was not worried. He could tell by my behavior all was basically well. I could see Drew out of the corner of my eye and knew he was chomping at the bit to criticize Aleck and bring attention to his interest in Bryn. "All's well. Bryn and Aleck are fine. Was a mudslide, just up yonder, you'll see. Aleck lost his horse and was pretty beat up. Bryn put his horse down with one well-placed shot, had to haul MacLaren up and get him on Tinker. Didn't think Tinker could manage a load like that, but she did. Right proud of her. Bryn I mean. Lily and John are caring for both of them now. Aleck's mostly fixed up. Bryn had some bruises and was mighty tired but she's all rested up now. Josh's been notified. Bryn's met Mr. Hall. "That's about all." My reports were usually my longest speeches but even they were succinct. Andrew and Sarah were both used to my style and knowing all was well were satisfied to wait for the finer details from the others later.

They adjusted themselves easily into their saddles preparing for another long run. Andrew's leg was throbbing with each pull on the stirrup. I knew the signs and ached to be able to ease the discomfort for him but knew there was nothing to be done but to grin and bear it. I was only too aware of Andrew's agony and called an early halt for the night. Drew and I set up camp so Andrew and Sarah could rest. With this break, we should make it to St. Louis tomorrow afternoon.

Drew and I broke camp in the early morning hours. The slope we were on was becoming steeper and we leaned back in the saddle for balance. The horses placed steady hooves gingerly on the gravel ridden side, at any moment they could easily lose their step or throw a stone into one their hooves. This trail was another disaster waiting to happen. I put my hand up in the air signaling them to stop. I dismounted with a warning sign to Andrew to also dismount but with extreme care. To approach the area of the slide, we passed the barrier the boys had built. Sarah waited restlessly upright on her horse, unsure she wanted to see what her daughter had had to endure. Andrew and I approached, staying well back from the precarious edge. As much as Andrew would have liked to have seen the actual site up close, he satisfied himself with his limited observation of the site and my description.

He acknowledged the horrific event his Bryn had faced and filled with pride at her ability to deal with it in such practical fashion. Just as he had taught her, he should not be so surprised. She was so much like her mother.

I broke the spell. "We struck a back trail. Let's be goin'. Be off of this damn hill in a few hours."

~ *Rob* ~

---

nce Drew and Earley left, Aunt Lily and I returned to the house. Aunt Lily went to the kitchen to discuss the plans for the next few days with Rose. I went to the library. I sat with my fingertips together under my chin. I realized it was my first time being truly alone since I had heard the news about my grandfather. I was used to being able to think fast in a crowd. However, I always felt I made the framework for better decisions when I had a chance to think on my own in peace and quiet. With this family, that was a rare thing and I found the conundrum perplexing: the joys and camaraderie of a family and the peacefulness of solitude.

I was surprised how easy it had been to be accepted back into the family fold. Now I understood the story of the prodigal son. The only problem was the ongoing antagonism between myself and Josh. If only Josh knew the whole story, but how to tell him, should I tell him, would he believe me? I had tried to communicate with Josh just before we headed out on the search for our parents but I was skeptical and defensive in the telling. Would Father believe me? And, what of Bryn, she was all grown up. She was a young woman now, not my annoying little sister. Drew had implored me this morning to stay between her and Aleck, but in good conscience could I do that? If Aleck's intentions were honorable as Aunt Lily and Uncle John implied and if Bryn was really interested in the man, then who was I to intervene. Still, I felt I could wear the mantle of chaperone comfortably and with good intent until our parents arrived. As the grandfather clock in the hall struck the half hour I looked up to find Bryn in the doorway studying me.

"Hey little sister, come in and sit with me. We've hardly had a chance to talk since I've been home. These last few weeks have been pretty wild," I grinned at her as I stood to seat her. Our easy camaraderie was still there; she sat with ease beside me on the settee taking my arm and snuggling into my shoulder. I was her big brother and I was glad of her unconditional love. "Yes, it's been pretty crazy . . . and scary. I'm so glad you're back. Please tell me you'll stay and not hurry away again. I hate it that you and Josh are not speaking. Can't you make it right, what could be so wrong that you can't talk it out and be friends again? You're brothers, twins no less and you were friends. The war destroyed so many families. I don't want ours to remain one of them, I don't care if you're Confederate," she paused, and then whispered. "Do you ever think of Edward, did you see him before, you know?"

The mention of Josh and Edward broke the spell. "Bryn some things never change, so many questions. How many times have I told you that curiosity killed the cat?" I arched an eyebrow at her and she rolled her eyes back at me.

"Geesh Rob, how's a girl supposed to keep track of what's going on if she doesn't ask?"

"Well here's one way, try listening. For example, little sis I happen to know you now strongly favor our Grandmother Henley."

"'I'll try,'" she said with a grimace. "And yes I know about Grandmother Henley. Thomas brought it to Aunt Lily's attention. She has two portraits that Grandfather Henley had commissioned. It's eerie but Papa really looks like his father. Grandmother, did you know her name was Emmaline? Aunt Lily took me to see the portraits; they're hanging in Aunt Lily and Uncle John's private rooms at the hotel. Personally, I see the resemblance but Grandmother Henley was truly beautiful and so elegant. I would love to look like that. You'll have to see the portraits."

"I have. When I lived here after I left home I saw them a lot. They used to hang in the hallway here. Grandfather Henley's portrait bothered me as it looked so like our father and I wasn't exactly thrilled to be constantly reminded of him. Aunt Lily moved them to the hotel on my behalf. I'm surprised they're still there. I thought she'd bring them home when I left."

They sat in comfortable silence. I was tempted to tell Bryn about my trip to India, but not yet. "I've got to get going, I want to see my horse, so I'll talk to you later." I left leaving the hall doors open.

*H*oping to catch sight of Aleck, I resettled myself comfortably by the window. I knew from here I could see anyone from the house gain access to the stables. I was glad of the peace and quiet with only the ticking of the beautiful grandfather clock in the foyer to keep me company. Movement out of the corner of my eye caught my attention. With my book resting on my lap, I had been daydreaming about my night at the cave again and the warmth of Aleck's body wrapped around me, the heat of his kisses. Then there he was, flesh and blood heading to the stables. I rose but caught sight of Rob following Aleck purposefully. I sat down again to wait wondering what Rob would want with Aleck. A short time later, lost in my book, I saw Rob return to the house alone.

~ *Aleck* ~

*I*was making my way to the stables looking for Bryn when I heard my name, "Aleck, hold up there." I wiped the eager smile from my face as I turned to Rob. It had slipped my mind that Rob might still be here. Earley had not called on Rob to be part of the journey for Sarah and Andrew but I had assumed he would go. Maybe Rob had stayed behind to keep me from being alone with Bryn. That made sense. I would not have left Bryn alone with me either! "Rob," I nodded, pausing to steady my voice. "Thought you might've gone with Drew and Earley to help with your folks."

"I'm sure Earley and Drew can handle them." He replied with a smirk, "thought I'd spend some time with my little sister. I've been away a long time and my how she's grown in my absence. We have a lot of catching up to do." I gave him a cold, black stare, but he did not rise to the bait. "Thanks for your help with my family's troubles this last while. I'm really sorry for the inconvenience we've caused, but now you're free to head out. With my aunt, uncle, and myself to care for her, Bryn'll be just fine."

So that was Rob's game. I responded, "You're welcome and thanks verra much for your kind offer but no thanks. Bryn was entrusted into my care until I hand her back over to Andrew himself. I gave my word and I'll keep it."

"She's my sister, not my daughter but just the same, I can take care of her now." Rob stood his ground, testing the waters.

"I'm verra sure you can, however, I gave Andrew my word. I am a man of my word. Aye, Bryn is my responsibility." My voice left no room for further discussion.

"Fine!" Rob acquiesced realizing he would not win this battle. I was committed to the cause. He threw his final parry as he left the stable, "well I'll be around keeping an eye on her. If you know what I mean!"

Confounded brothers! I felt I needed to vent some fury and one of John's more formidable stallions received the wrath in my ride and then my earnest currying as I muttered away about interfering brothers and my desire for Bryn. Drew was easy to handle – young and foolish. Rob was a different story, more level-headed, a businessman and definitely more calculating. I was taking the measure of the man. I could feel my romantic moments with Bryn would be seriously curtailed. It only served to wet my appetite for one of her lovely warm kisses. It also deepened my resolve to win her hand. She deserved better than me, I was sure of it. But now I faced the fact that in a few short days I had fallen in love with her and could not imagine life without her by my side. I even acknowledged I could give up my cabin and live anywhere just to be with her. Finally, content with my decisions and the condition of the stallion, I turned to leave the stable when a whisper caught my attention.

Bryn peeked out from inside Tinker's stall and beckoned me to join her. She had been there all along, I worried about how loud my muttering had been and what she might have heard. As I met her at the entrance to the stall Bryn giggled and teased, "You had Noir in quite a lather when you got back, then mutter, mutter, mutter. You had quite a lot to work through Mr. MacLaren." She pulled my face down to meet hers, I responded in kind. Her brother had other ideas. If timing is everything someone had their timing wrong. Rob came whistling into the stables. I pushed Bryn gently down into the hay in the stall. Bryn could barely stifle her giggles as I leaned in to give her a peck on the cheek, my finger over lips. Then I carefully made my way around Tinker my hand sliding gently over her rounded rump. I came out the other side of the stall carrying Tinker's tack as Bryn stepped into the corridor.

"Bryn, you wanted to go into town. Thought I'd escort you. There's some things I want." With a sly smirk he petitioned me, "Want to join us?" Rob enquired cheerfully.

"Oh, Rob, it's alright. Aleck will go with me. He already knows the stores I'm interested in. You stay and rest. You must still be tired." Bryn countered, perfectly serious.

Rob placed his hands on her shoulders and with a playful grin replied, "No little sister, it's alright, I'll take you. We need to spend more time together. Get to know each other again. Catch up and all that."

"Oh aye, things you'll be wantin'? Well, tag along if you will, we'll pay you no mind." I muttered my comments as turned into the stable to get my horse and Tinker saddled and ready. Bryn cast me a shuttered look as if to say how do we lose my brother? Then she cast an uneasy glance at Rob. Rob pretended to ignore her. So she thought she had some subtle signals to communicate with did she? Discreet! I shook my head. God save me from amateurs! Rob saddled up, "are you two coming or what?" he chuckled as he headed out of the stables.

I was at the point where I realized I would have to keep myself cool under my collar and wait for the appropriate moment to kidnap Bryn and take her out of Rob's visual field.

Rob set the pace. Bryn and I followed. I tried to keep a distance between ourselves and Rob. My frustration only increased as I realized Rob was up to the same tricks in reverse.

As we arrived in town, Rob showed no signs of breaking away to do his errands.

"Rob, why don't you go and do what you need to do, Aleck and I will go and do the same? We can meet at the hotel for lunch."

~ *Rob* ~

"No it's alright, I'll stay with you," I replied, chortling. It was all I could do not to break into an outright belly laugh. This chaperone thing was more fun than I had originally surmised. The look on Aleck's face was positively thunderous. So be it, I was having fun and would continue until I could not get away with it any longer. The tension between Aleck and Bryn was palpable and building by the minute. Bryn's cheeks were flaming red and her laughter with Aleck was forced and unnatural. I had waited a long time to turn the tables on her and now I had her just where I wanted her. I could still see her tagging along behind me, and that had been alright, but when there was a girl involved, Bryn was impossible. She would make sassy remarks and make funny faces. It was funny to think back on now. I was her big brother after all.

~ *Bryn* ~

I gave up and Aleck gave in for the moment. We set off down the board walk with me setting a healthy pace. The heels of my shoes hit the boards with a pre-emptive thump at every step. I was fuming. I was not new to double standards. The boys were always able to do what they wanted, when they wanted. Seemingly, no one had to protect Rob from a damaging social reputation. Short of murder, nobody was going to interfere. I was an adult and, as such, felt I should be able to share Aleck's company without said chaperone. It was my decision to make. I had a good understanding of my mother and what she must have gone through before marrying her father. In my heart, I sensed I had much more freedom than mama had ever had. I knew how my father would feel right now, definitely on Rob's side of the equation. In my wildest imagination, I could not fathom who had thought up such absurd rules of conduct. Sometimes, I felt so restricted I found it difficult to breathe. Trust had nothing to do with this. My parents trusted me, there was no question there, but they were so old fashioned. I was very aware of the Suffragette movements. Not as radical, I did see the necessity of equality between men and women. I had spent a lifetime observing my parents. Certainly, Mama never took a back seat to Papa. Mama voiced her opinions and Papa listened. It was the kind of relationship she would work towards with Aleck. I was innocent, not naïve. Having been raised on a ranch, there was nothing left to learn but the love that would blossom between me and my man. My feet carried me, with a will of their own, into the general store. Once inside I stopped, to give myself a moment to take-in the atmosphere. The store was bustling with business. I took a deep breath; cinnamon, peppermint and other spices assaulted my senses. From every corner, I was aware of the chatter of clusters of women congregating around the bolts of material. There were children with greedy eyes and dirty faces ogling the candy jars. The men stood around waiting just by the doors or outside smoking and chewing the fat. I wandered over to the materials and started looking. Using my fingertips, I was able to judge the cottons and finer fabrics. I was acutely aware of Aleck and Rob standing in the front of the store looking lost, wondering what to do next. At this point, I was beyond caring, let them be uncomfortable. The women in the store stared at the two handsome men who were so out of place at this time of day in the store.

I flashed Bryn a wink that did not go unnoticed by the patronage. I nudged Rob over to the guns and casings. In more manly surroundings I asked Rob, "What are ye up to man? Can ye not just leave us a few minutes alone?"

"You don't have any sisters, do you, Aleck?" I shook my head as I continued, "I didn't think so. Well here's the deal, I am having fun at your expense albeit, playing big brother. The little brat traipsed around behind me years ago; privacy was not an option and now it's payback time. I am fully aware that Bryn isn't a little girl anymore. She's a beautiful young, and I stress *young*, woman. She's not subtle about her infatuation with you, neither are you. So I tell you what. You're on notice. Hurt her, use her, abuse her, touch her in a way that embarrasses her and I will be all over you like a fly on cow flop. Then I'll kill you. Understand?"

Several hours later, back at the house, Bryn and I breathed a sigh of relief thinking we were finally alone. It did not last long. We both turned as the hall door to the library opened and Rob stepped into the room. I quickly released Bryn but not before Rob issued a penetrating look in my direction. "Bryn, I've been looking for you everywhere, thought maybe we could go for a short stroll before dinner."

"I've been with you nearly all day Rob. Haven't you had enough of me yet?" Bryn gave him a brittle smile hoping he would take the hint and leave. "And we talked this morning, remember? You've never spent this much time with me before."

"No need to get uppity little sis, I remember. It's just we haven't seen each other in such a long time and there's lots to catch up on. Don't let us keep you Aleck."

Bryn wondered if all brothers were this obtuse. "Aleck and I were . . . conversing before you barged in."

"It didn't look like much of a conversation to me. That you could do seated in a chair, each in your own chair, I might add. Not wrapped in his arms." He said testily. "But I'll be glad to join in. Have a seat, both of you. What are we talking about?"

I started to laugh. "Alright Rob, you win this battle. But be aware, I'll win the war!"

"Ah, now there's a topic. One that sets my family's hackles on edge. Were you involved Aleck?"

I guided Bryn back into her seat, picking up her hankie from the floor at her feet. "Aye, Union. And you?"

Casually, Rob responded, "To my family's deep disappointment I was considered a Southerner, therefore Confederate sympathizer. My home is in New Orleans so it came naturally I suppose."

Bryn's startled gasp drew both men's attention. "You suppose . . . you suppose it came naturally! Edward and Josh chose to fight for something that we all believed in strongly, not just something convenient! Slavery, how dreadful to own another person! Oh my goodness, did you have slaves of your own? I never once imagined it. How could you be so blasé about it? Rob if you knew the pain we went through. Our whole family has agonized over this and with you on the other side. Then Edward's death. It was so awful! How could you? How could you?," the emotion raw in her voice. Her lips quivered as she struggled to hold back the tears that welled up in her eyes.

Throughout Bryn's, rant I watched Rob's face, his eyes. No flicker or betrayal of how he really felt about all this. His quiet response, "things are not always what they seem little sis," took me by surprise, although nothing gave him away either. An unexpected response and so stoic, so guarded, perfect poker face. I was sure there was more to Rob's story. War was not natural and men rarely joined in the fray because it was convenient. I would keep an eye on this one.

William's knock at the library door and his summons to dinner broke the heated spell. Rob rose and left the room first allowing Bryn and I a few moments.

"I don't understand Aleck. How could he . . .?"

"Bryn, we all have reasons for our actions and they're never as simple as they seem and are often misinterpreted. We all have the right to our own opinion and whether right or wrong lass, we must respect each other's decisions. It will all settle someday. Put it away for the moment and come to dinner." I tucked her arm through mine and began to lead her out of the library. I stopped as suddenly as I began and with one quick movement, I pulled her into my arms and after a satisfying kiss quickly said, "Ah my lassie, now on to dinner before the nuisance has reason to chase us down again." Bryn giggled at my description of her brother, took my arm and went in to dinner.

~ *Lily* ~

They were dusty, thirsty, sore and extremely tired but they made it to our home well before supper. I fairly ran into Andrew's arms just after he had dismounted, nearly knocking him over. "Oh my God, I'm so grateful to see you two," I turned to hug Sarah. "We've been so worried about you since Bryn and Aleck arrived. And before of course! But their news of the storm and all that happened. I must say, for all the hardships, you two look wonderful, but I must insist that Doc Jones see both of you . . . It'll make me feel so much better. Come in, come in." I could not contain my excitement and pleasure at seeing my beloved brother again.

"Welcome back Drew, Earley. Your rooms are ready for you. William, please get the boys to see to the horses. Come into the house and refresh yourselves," John invited.

"You go. Drew and I'll stable the horses," Earley insisted. Drew rolled his eyes but said nothing and turned to help take the horses to the stables. When they were finished, they washed up at the water pump. The water was cold causing goose bumps to pop up on their arms and chests, but it was also reviving. Feeling somewhat more respectable Drew and Earley went in to find the others.

*L*ily was in her element. Her family was finally here in one piece. She and Rose had been busy making sure rooms were ready for our eventual arrival. William and Rose set up the bath and basin for me. Lily put out her personal lavender soaps and scented towels. After a quick sluice, I immersed my stiff and aching body into the warm water and sighed with great relief. This was my first bath in over a month and I was going to enjoy every minute of it. In John's dressing room, Andrew was enjoying the same treatment (sans lavender)! When we had been rejuvenated and finally dressed in clean clothing, we met for a quiet moment in our room. William had informed Andrew it would be at least half an hour until pre dinner drinks and he, personally, would fetch them. Andrew bent to give me a loving, reassuring kiss, then we climbed into bed for a short nap. Half an hour later, feeling refreshed and with my arm on his we went downstairs to meet up with Lily and John.

*W*hile Andrew and Sarah were resting, I made my way into town to telegraph Josh letting him know of the rest of his family's safe arrival. I was back just in time to join in Lily's excitement. The family had just taken their seats in the parlor. I gave Lily a quick hug with my hands on her shoulders and a kiss on her cheek before crossing the room with my hand out to warmly greet my brother-in-law. "It's been too long old man." Andrew tried to stand up quickly but John waved him back down. "And Sarah, it is so good to see you my dear, though the reason for the gathering is quite unfortunate," I continued, "however, it's always good when families gather together. I'm privileged to be part of yours. By the way, Doc Jones will be out here some time tonight. He'll give you two the once over. It'll make Lily and I feel better to know you really are in good health." As I sat beside Lily I turned to her but spoke loud enough for all to hear. "I caught him on his way back into town. The High's had triplets last night. All three have survived but are tiny and weak. I imagine you'll want to get some of the women out there to help. He's bringing some supplies here for them; I offered to have Rose and William deliver."

"Triplets, oh my, poor Lizzy, perhaps Rose can spare Mary for a while. She could help with the other children, cleaning, cooking. I'll talk to Rose directly after dinner. My goodness, triplets! Doc Jones has certainly been busy." After a brief pause she turned to her brother. "Andrew do you remember Thomas at all? He's really so much the same, just older. I think Father's death has been hard on him. He seems lost somehow, distant, withdrawn. He wouldn't stay here with us and wanted to stay at the hotel. He'd only been here a few days and became quite ill. This has been such a trial. Why is everything to do with Father so complicated? And with what you have all gone through. I'm so sorry, so very sorry!"

"Now Lil," Andrew interrupted. "Things will happen as they will. We're all fine and I'm sure Thomas will recover. Don't make things out to be worse than they are. We're here; we'll have a good family visit. It's been far too long and besides now I need to let this leg heal. Now we're out of the woods so to speak, I'm sure Sarah and Bryn will have a fine time at the shops with you. And the boys and I can order some supplies. I'm sure Rob would be delighted to spend some time with his mentors and the visit will be an experience for young Drew."

*W*illiam opened the front doors directing us to the family, "The family is in the front parlor". Aleck and I walked in, arm in arm followed by Rob. At the sight of us together, arm in arm Drew clenched his teeth and rolled his eyes yet again.

"Mama, papa you're here," I cried all but leaping into my parent's arms. Both returned my hugs and kisses. "How are you now? Tell me all about your ride down. We saw the most glorious waterfall and pond near a cave where we spent our first night out. It was so beautiful. But the devastation from the storm was terrible; all the trees that fell. Did you see the mudslide? It was awful. I've met Mr. Hall. Apparently I look just like Grandmother Henley. We looked at her portrait and I do," I exclaimed breathless with excitement as always.

"Bryn, for goodness sake, take a breath, child! Do sit down," Mama reproached as she admired the new blue outfit I was sporting. I looked around; all the seats were now taken. Aleck patted a spot on the settee beside him and shifted to make more room for me. Drew rose to give me his seat however smiling coyly I turned my back on him and went to Aleck. An unspoken communication registered between my parents.

"Bryn," Papa called to me with a nod to Mama. "I'd like you tell us how you fared, poppet."

I took my time to settle myself next to Aleck and gather my wits. "Oh. At first it was fine, rough going but Aleck knew the trail. I just followed him for the first two days. Lots of trees down and many more uprooted. Well, you saw that for yourself. It was rough going," I hedged struggling with how much I could tell my parents without losing my composure. I shrugged my shoulders wordlessly conveying my discomfort with the subject. "We had just spotted St. Louis off in the distance. We were making good time when all of a sudden . . ." Tears sprang unwelcomed to my eyes. Aleck subtly took my hand into his own with a gentle grip under the fold of my skirt, willing me the courage to go on. He felt the comfort of my response. I blinked a couple of times, my mouth dry as I tried to swallow, "Aleck" my squeezed his hand so hard he nearly jumped, "and his horse went over the side of the cliff. I guess the storm . . . well that section just crumbled. It was awful. I tried to grab him but I think he pushed my hand away." I was so anxious by the time I finished I was literally talking to the floor. I raised my head to survey my audience.

Papa registered several things simultaneously: Aleck's silent order to Drew, and the fact that if Aleck had actually pushed my hand away it was a good thing or I would have gone over the side with him.

After a short silence to regain my self-control, I finally continued, "I was able to pull Tinker back. You'd have been proud of me Papa. I secured Tinker and remembered to tie myself before crawling to the edge to look. It was awful, Splash was screaming in agony and Aleck . . . he was so still, I didn't know if he . . ." I choked back a sob. Aleck leaned in to calm me, "My brave, brave lassie!" "I climbed down. Once I knew Aleck was alive, I felt much better. I had to put Splash out of his misery. That was the worst part." The tears now flowed freely down my cheeks as I continued. I pulled my embroidered cotton handkerchief from my sleeve and blew my nose noisily then continued "I was able, with Tinker's help, to get Aleck back up and we rested and then came in to St. Louis on Tinker." It took a moment for me to regain my composure. Aleck handed me his dry handkerchief to dry my eyes. My story had been told. The pride in my Papa's eyes was worth the telling. He was sitting beside mama and had put his arm around her to comfort her as she listened to my harrowing adventure.

"Aleck is an awfully nice man Papa," I said reticently.

"He's an honorable man, Bryn. I would not have let you go with him otherwise. Your welfare is my main concern." I softened my tone and added. "You're my little girl and always will be." I was looking at her with a mix of fatherly pride, love and consternation. I was not sure I liked what I just heard. I would talk tonight to Aleck and to Sarah.

Immediately after dinner, Bryn and Sarah retired upstairs to look at Bryn's new clothing and to talk as they always did. They had missed each other terribly and wanted to catch up. I sought refuge in the library. I looked at the books lining the walls in the library and it brought back memories of Oakley. I recognized many of the titles. Pulling one off of the shelf, I decided it would not hurt me to open a book whether it had belonged to Father or not was no longer relevant. They were simply books. Making myself comfortable in one of the chairs by the fireplace, I noticed the bouquet of fresh flowers inside the grate. That was a trick Thomas had employed at Oakley when the fire was no longer required during the warm summer months; it freshened the air he said. Lily had taken up that housekeeping habit. I chuckled to myself wondering what other habits I might become aware of. I was noticing that my perspective on life had changed with this journey.

I rested the book on my lap. It was still early in the evening but I was tired, bone wrenching weary. My leg continued to throb and I was having difficulty pushing myself through the pain. The long hours in the saddle had hindered the healing. In typical fashion, Lily had been fussing over me this afternoon in the time honored tradition of brothers and sisters.

As if summoned by my thoughts, Lily entered interrupting my ruminations. "There you are. I'm glad to see you're taking it easy for once in your life." She sat down beside me and took my arm into hers in a possessive fashion. "I want to enjoy each and every minute you're here so that when you're gone, I'll have lots to look back on." She smiled at me. The adoration was plain on her face for the world to see. I took her hand and squeezed it. This wasn't so bad after all I thought with a fleeting feeling of guilt.

"Sarah's lying down now. It took some fancy talking but I was finally able to convince her that she needs the rest. You two can be so stubborn. Why don't you join her? I can see pain written all over your face, Andrew and I worry about you."

"I promise I'll go shortly but I can't fall asleep until the doctor's been. I think we could put his visit off for a few days. We're fine now that we're here."

"*No way...* little brother! He checks you out tonight. I want to be one hundred per cent sure that everything really is on the mend. However, I'll give you peace and quiet here then." Lily rose giving me a hug and a kiss on the cheek. "I'll get my fill of hugs and kisses while you're here. Mark my words Andrew Henley." As she left the room she softly added, "I love you! I truly do."

"Ahem," caught my attention. Aleck was standing in the doorway.

"May I come in? Aye, I have need to speak with you."

"Come in and have a seat." I rose to shake Aleck's hand. This was to be a serious discussion I registered as Aleck closed the door behind him. "Thank you for getting our Bryn here safely."

"She's no a wee lassie anymore, Andrew. She's a full grown woman," Aleck tested. "May I speak freely?" With my nod of permission, Aleck got right to the heart of the matter. "There'll be no beating around the bush here Andrew; I'm in love with your daughter. I'm asking your permission to court her in a way that will make her proud of me. I want to protect her too. The boys have been giving her a hard time because of me. Aye and I'm sure of where it's coming from. I know it is only a short time but I'm verra serious, Andrew. I love her, want to marry her. Do ya ken, Andrew?"

I hesitated, careful with his choice of words. "I understand Aleck. I'm not overly happy. Rest assured, I've no concerns about you; it's just that she's still so young. I'll speak with Sarah. She's our only girl, our pride and joy." I shook my head as if to clear the cobwebs of time that bound her to me as a child. I considered carefully then sighed heavily. Sarah was already married to him at that age. "What am I thinking? She is a young woman." Another short pause and I continued, "Yes Aleck. You have my permission to court her, if she's willing. And I get the impression she may well be. This is a bit sudden but love doesn't follow a time schedule. The boys you'll need to be patient with. Drew especially, he and Bryn are close. He's young and impetuous but he'll settle down." I registered Aleck's grimace and nod as I continued. "Rob is quite different from Drew; I think you'll need to earn his respect. Josh is already married and a father, he'll be a bit more understanding." Aleck closed his eyes and heaved a sigh of relief of his own.

"Ahh. Stay for a moment Aleck, let me reflect . . . you know Sarah and I have been married for more years than I sometimes care to remember. She's a good woman and a loving wife. Most important though, she is my friend, my best friend. We can talk about anything, we don't always agree, but we respect each other's opinion and right to it. We try to present a united front for the children but now that they are grown it is not always possible as the issues are quite different. And of course, there is that feminine point of view." I chuckled and shook my head. "She makes life interesting to say the least."

"Sarah has stood by me through thick and thin. When we were in your cabin on the mountain we reminisced about our first cabin and Edward. He was our eldest, but we lost him in the war, six years ago. When the boys were small she stood by me, even when we nearly lost the ranch. Then there was the joy when we finally had a daughter for her. It hasn't always been easy but it's always been fun. Sarah and I can laugh with each other. Sometimes we'll harangue each other then kiss good night. We never go to bed angry with one another. She is the love of my life. I imagine you want this kind of a life with Bryn and she can give it to you but you must have mutual respect and a desire to see your marriage through the bad times as well as the good."

"Aye, my own folks had that kind of a relationship from what my mother said. And that seems like what I remember. I was so young when my pa disappeared. Tell me how you met your Sarah if you would."

"When I first came out here as a very young man I did trapping and trading. That's how I knew your father. It's a rough life as you can attest, but I was doing well with it. Sarah lived on a farm with her folks just west of Springfield. I was bringing down furs that I had from three months of trapping. Both my horses were laden so I wasn't coming in quickly. On my last trap I had caught my finger on one of the metal claws. I didn't think too much of it, until I noticed in camp how painful and swollen it was. I cleaned my knife, lanced it and it was full of pus and blood. Hurt like a rattler bite. Anyway, I was feeling a little warm the next day and I was passing this ranch. I decided to see if the housewife would take a look at it. She did and so did her daughter, my Sarah. I fell for her right then and there. I had the fever for several days. Her father had passed on not but a few weeks before, so I offered to return and help them out a little until they could get back on their feet. There's been no other since. So I understand your falling fast, she's a lot like her mother. But I warn you be careful with our daughter's heart. I think that's all I have to say."

"I thank you for telling me your story. Aye, I'll do my best to make Bryn proud and happy like yourselves. And I'll protect her with my life, I swear to you. I won't let you regret your decision to bestow me this honor."

"I'll hold you to your word, Aleck. Now if, you'll excuse me I think I'll head upstairs and stretch out until the doctor arrives." With a grimace I said, "I couldn't dissuade Lily about that visit."

~ *Doc Jones* ~

his has been one long day I mused to myself, however tonight's visit was, one I was in point of fact, looking forward to. I had saved it to the last visit of the day for a reason, I would never miss an excuse to visit with Lily Wallace. There wasn't a man in town wouldn't enjoy some of her time, though all knew she had eyes for John only. Still, she was enchanting company and easy on the eyes. I was in love with my own wife who was a good friend of Lily's, but as I often jokingly remarked with the men folk, "I'm old, not dead! When I can't appreciate a good woman it will be time to give up!"

I pulled my carriage up to the front and stepped down wrapping the reigns around the post. I climbed the stairs and, before I could knock, William was opening the door. A bit eerie that chap, but I just smiled and handed William my hat. "You will be here to see the Henleys, I presume?"

"That would be correct, William. I'm sorry I'm so late. John asked me earlier to pop around to take a look at them, make sure they're okay. I understand they had quite a time of it in that storm."

"For the doctor, late is never a problem sir. The family is still up. Right this way. I'll have a drink ready for you with the Wallaces in the front parlor when you're finished. Miss Lily is waiting for a full report." I followed William up to Andrew and Sarah's bedroom.

The knock on the door was answered swiftly by a now rested Sarah. "You must be Dr. Jones," her brilliant warm smile gracing her face. "Come in, Lily told us you would be coming."

After listening to their trials and the bravery of their young daughter, Bryn, I was satisfied they were extremely lucky to have escaped with so few injuries. A comprehensive study of Andrew's leg brought a pleasant commendation. "I assure you, this leg is well set and will provide optimum healing if you are careful. I rather doubt I could have done a better job myself. How well are you moving it?"

"With great difficulty right now, like you, I'm sure the ride set it back. Not as young as I once was."

"Right you are. Just keep your movement limited and give it a chance to heal with plenty of rest. No more riding until I say so. That's the best I can do right now. There is no swelling, no redness, that's a good sign. You might want to use a cane for stability. Well, you look fine, both of you. I'll leave you some laudanum so you get a good sleep after the ordeal of the ride. If you need me for anything else just have William let me know and I'll come over." I shook Andrew's hand, picked up my bag and went out the door looking forward to my visit in the front parlor.

"You heard the doctor, Andrew Henley, don't be doing anything silly! And now you must use the cane Aleck fashioned for you, you hear me?" But Sarah smiled knowing he would do exactly as he pleased.

~ *Lily* ~

---

*I*n the meantime, my mind would not stop. There was so much to do and so little time. I wanted to meet up with Thomas. Secretly, I had to admit I had wanted to see Thomas alone before he met up with the family. My co-conspirator was just coming in the door, "Hello, my love did you get a chance to talk to Thomas? Is he receptive? Will he be here tomorrow? May I see him before hand?" John held his hand up to protect himself from the inevitable barrage of questions from me.

"I'll pour you some sherry, as I feel the need of a good stiff drink after today's excitements." He held his silence as he poured the golden liquid into the crystal glass. He handed me my glass and sat down beside me with his. There was a low fire burning in the large hearth; just enough to dry the humid air. He made himself comfortable and cozy putting his arm around my shoulder. "Much better," he said to me.

I was having none of it. "Well? Out with it then John! Why are you keeping me in such suspense? I waited patiently all through dinner."

He chuckled, "I can't help it; the fire in your eyes right now is worth every minute."

John settled his face into seriousness, "Yes, its set for tomorrow at eleven in the morning here. Thomas is more than relieved to have this over and done with. However Doc Jones wants Thomas to continue to take it easy. Seems the good doctor has been reading some new information on stress and how it can adversely affect you. Therefore you aren't able to meet with him before. However, let me confirm we are all set for tomorrow at eleven, right here. Let the devil take the hind most,"

249

and he took a long sip on his whiskey. Relief and disappointment swept through me simultaneously. I would have to wait with everyone else.

Over a pleasant drink a short time later I was reassured that my brother and sister-in-law were indeed on the mend. But no cajoling on my behalf would sway the good doctor into giving me an earlier audience with Thomas.

~ Rob ~

I was feeling restless and thirsty. I wanted a break from my family; been on my own too long I thought, just like Aleck. Poor Aleck, who appeared to be in love with Bryn and surrounded by her interfering family. Maybe I could round up Aleck for a trip into town.

As luck would have it, our paths crossed. As I came out of the back door, Aleck emerged from the stable.

"Hey… Aleck! How about a trip to town for a drink? I haven't been in the old saloon across from the Grand in years. What do you say?" I was holding out the olive branch of peace.

"Well now, I'm a wee bit dry, a break might be just fine." We advised William of our plans and saddled up to ride into town.

As we approached the heart of the city, we discussed the hustle bustle and the heavy traffic in town at this hour of the day. St. Louis was in constant motion from street vendors to stores displaying their wares. Delivery wagons with Clydesdale teams displaying their powerful grace added to the pedestrian congestion. We carefully guided our horses through the mass of energy that seemed to be bursting forth in all directions. "Organized chaos," Aleck responded. I grimaced in agreement.

We used the livery and walked the short distance to the saloon. Though early in the day, it was already rowdy with inebriated men and their hoots of laughter. Aleck and I stepped through the swinging doors and stopped to gauge the lay of the land. The room quieted as the patrons sized up the newcomers. Not sensing any trouble, everybody went back to what they were doing, the piano struck up a ditty and out came six girls, arms intertwined over their shoulders, black stockings on and legs kicking high. The spaghetti strap bodice with red and black stripes pulled our attention to the stage. The energy of movement caused the flounce in the skirt to bounce with each kick. The men started to hoot and holler, hats waving above their heads and lewd whistles erupting from their lips. The piano player started to bang out his rendition of the cancan. With the patrons eyes riveted on the stage, we had the privacy we wanted. We drew up to the bar and ordered beer. We both leaned on the bar twisting our bodies, beer in hand, so we could see the goings on.

My tension eased as I relaxed into Aleck's company. I commented to Aleck, "Won't try any tricks with you and my little sister. I've given you much more time with my sister than Drew would have allowed! And now that Pa's around, good luck!

Aleck smiled, "Quite an episode that recent storm, too much to recount. Suffice to say, she's proved to be a braw wee lassie and lovely to boot." Then he turned to glare at me.

I took the challenge explaining, "I'm finally in a position to begin rebuilding. I decided to come back to Missouri to visit my family before returning to New Orleans to head up the reconstruction."

"I've been travelling quite a bit during and since the war. I was one of the lucky ones. Most of my cargo was shipped out of New Orleans well in advance of the Yankee assault. My best captains kept those ships from harm and plied our trade in the Orient until it was safe to return. My home was less fortunate. It's an old cotton plantation north of the city and was one of the first that fell to Union occupation. Even though the interior was devastated, the structure's still sound. My slaves and those of several plantations near me were taken north and freed."

Once outside and along the boardwalk a bit, Aleck halted and glared at me. If looks could kill I would be dead.

~ *Thomas* ~

"Are you sure Sir?" I questioned Hugh as I assisted him into the carriage. "This is still the way you want to do this?" Years of servitude gave me the right to question my master's decision.

"How bad can it be? I am their father. Lily has always had a good bond with me and Andrew, well, he'll come around." I was sure of my plan as I brought the horses to a trot. Hugh was eager to see his Lily again. And for the first time, he was actually looking forward to seeing his son.

William opened the door before I could knock. William well familiar with me discreetly scrutinized the gentleman standing by my side. "Please come in. You are expected Mr. Hall. Allow me to show you to the parlor. Once you are settled, I will fetch the family for you."

I discreetly cleared my throat, "No family William. Thank you! Miss Lily, and Mr. Andrew, only. Please"

~ William ~

"As you wish," the elderly gentleman looked apprehensive and pale. He leaned heavily on his intricately carved cane as he entered the room but I gauged this was not a normal state of affairs. The cut of his coat indicated a man who was affluent, the soft wool fitting his surprisingly muscular frame. His immaculately starched and pressed shirt was of noticeably high quality, white cotton. I deemed Mr. Hall to be particularly well groomed, but he was no match to this man. The man's black silk tie hung in stark contrast to his crisp white shirt and grey suit. Funerals came to mind.

The gentleman, after choosing a wing back chair flanking the fireplace, sat down with the grace and composure of a much younger man but refrained from sitting back at ease into the chair. Rather, he sat, close to the edge of the chair with his hands, one atop the other, supported by the cane. Mr. Hall also sat in a high backed chair but close to the hall doors. That struck me as odd. Mr. Hall had gained them both admission to the house and now he virtually estranged himself from the gentleman. I wondered if they were indeed well acquainted at all. I made sure they were seated and comfortable before I backed out and closed the doors making my way down the hall to the back porch, to collect Lily and Andrew.

I heard the chatter and laughter from the back garden. Standing at the back double French doors I caught Lily's eye and went over to her.

"Your guest, Mr. Hall, has arrived." After the announcement, I leaned forward lowering my voice. "A word, mam. Mr. Hall has brought another gentleman. They are in the parlor wishing to speak with you and Mr. Andrew. Alone."

I turned to Andrew and beckoned him to follow. "Just us Andrew, we'll be back shortly." Andrew squeezed Sarah's hand. He put his arm out for me as we made our way inside. "Curious," I mentioned as we gained entry into the house, "Thomas has brought someone with him but he never mentioned anyone else coming."

I reached out to open the parlor doors just as Thomas opened them. Softly he said, "Please forgive me, understand this was beyond my control and once begun, impossible to stop. I am so sorry! Please forgive me". Once he had uttered this cryptic message, he pulled the doors open, ushering us in. I peered inside, a feeling of dread creeping up my spine. My eyes grew round as saucers as I took in the vision before me. Andrew, unaware of my discomfiture, moved behind me ushering me into the room. My legs nearly went out from under me; I leaned back on Andrew for support. My cry of shock went through Andrew as he took in the specter in the room. Thomas and Andrew swiftly moved to grab me to support me before I fell to the floor. My pale face shone with the sheen of sweat. As they moved to seat me, my mouth was moving but nothing came out as shock and disbelief annihilated any control I may have been able to muster given the opportunity. "Tell me this isn't so. My eyes deceive me." My voice a hoarse whisper, I continued. "I don't understand. Father's dead. Thomas told us so; this is not our father, is it? Tell me... tell me. . . tell me dammit," I sobbed.

T homas had taken the brunt of Lily's collapse but the act of catching my sister had aggravated my leg into excruciating agony once again. With Lily safely seated, I turned to face my nemesis. I locked eyes with Hugh while the full spectrum of pent up passion from distant past to the present flashed before both of us. Mirror images searing across an eternity of hurt and betrayal. I was stunned into speechlessness. No one heard as Thomas softly stepped out into the hall and closed the door to guard the privacy of this horrendous confrontation.

"Father. . . I might have known. That letter from Thomas. What are you up to? Do you think this is a game? You son of a bitch! My wife Sarah who has done nothing to you ever, but be kind and tolerant; my daughter, my precious Bryn, who does not even know of your existence have both nearly been killed because of your foolish actions. You selfish old man! And myself, for me I care not so much, but I'm their provider!" Slowly, I limped across the room to my father; carefully I bent over and grabbed the arms of the chair as I leaned in to face Hugh close up. My eyes were dark as coal; my rage thunderous. Hugh, in self-defense, leaned back into the chair as if it would protect him from my wrath. "You can't honestly expect forgiveness now. We came here not only to bury your remains but to bury the past. I came in support of my sister, because of Thomas' plea. I can't believe the utter gall it took for you to swagger in here. No, wait, I can believe the utter gall, you arrogant selfish, foolish old man." I spit out the words with all the fury of the man he had abandoned as a baby.

My knuckles were white as I clenched the arms of the chair. I knew if I released them my fingers, with a will of their own, would be wrapped around Father's neck choking the living daylights out of him. I was livid; my face was as florid as my knuckles were white, my heart hammered in my chest. Finally, with some of my anger and fury spent, I managed to get a hold of myself. I pushed myself to a standing position and for several silent moments stared down at Hugh. I picked up the simple cane that Aleck had fashioned for me, turned away from my father and made my way to the door. In a dangerously calm voice I said "When I come back you had better be gone." I left slamming the door behind me.

~ Lily ~

I just sat and stared at my father, trying to comprehend what had just happened. We had all been talking and laughing about different things from the past and the harrowing journey that Andrew, Sarah and Bryn had endured. And now my heart was so heavy, I felt it would drop out of my body. The shear implication of the situation magnified itself in my mind until I simply shut down. I did not know how I would survive such extreme anguish, over the current situation, but along with the anguish anger was starting to fester.

I arose from the chair and as I had done so often as a lost little girl, I dropped at my father's feet, "What have you done now? They nearly died, all of them. John and I were beside ourselves with worry. They couldn't take the easy passage. They came over the mesa to meet your deadline. Andrew's injury is grievous enough but for work on the ranch it is disastrous. It will severely impact him for what needs to be done this fall." Slowly, I stood up looking directly into his eyes, "I don't know you anymore. I knew you were ruthless in your business dealings, but for God's sake, we're your family! You really don't have a conscience. Andrew's right. You're a selfish old man who is so bitter about our mother's death that you wouldn't come to terms with it. It's been your motivation and your comfort; it supplies you with all the excuses you've ever needed. It provided emotional detachment from the ruthless way you ran your business. Your heartless demeanor gave you the wherewithal to betray and hurt the ones whose love you refused to accept. I too have had enough. I can't bear this any longer. You're not welcome here. Please leave. Get out." I shook with sorrow and betrayal.

My eyes turned to ice and the tears flowed in tiny rivers like icicles melting on a glacier.

John came through the doors coat tails flying. He caught the last sentences out of my mouth. He gathered me into his arms and over his shoulder he barked, "You heard her, get out!"

~ *Thomas* ~

*I*t was abundantly clear that my presence was not immanently required, so I stationed myself outside of the door, just in case I was needed. I was able to hear Andrew's voice, raised in anger against his father. Would those two never find peace? I heard the entire tirade and my heart was saddened. If only the old man had listened to me, this might have turned out differently. There was no stability in should haves though, we would all have to play this out to whatever conclusion it would be. I did not hesitate. I went to the back of the house to fetch John, Lily would need him.

I entered the study to find an aged Hugh sunk back into the chair in obvious overwhelming exhaustion; his eyes glazed, staring at the door where his children had left. I could not help but feel pity for the old man who had been so good to me.

In the instant that it took for Sarah to glance at me, she knew that something was wrong. Everyone arrived at once, as if an alarm had been raised, John dash into the house giving momentum to Sarah. When Earley appeared, hot on her heels, I knew things were not going well. Earley's recognition was instantaneous as his eyes landed on Hugh.

I went to help him out of the chair. "Come with me sir. We'll go back to your rooms and you can rest." Hugh took my arm. He followed me like a child in shocked disbelief, accepting the help offered to climb into the carriage.

Young Mistress Bryn was the only one who let her insatiable curiosity get the better of her. With only a moment's hesitation, she followed her mother and Earley into the house while Aleck shadowed her. Not wanting to miss out on the action, Rob and Drew followed. It happened so abruptly Bryn seeing her mother race into the parlor as Earley moved to the front door. Sarah's frantic cry, "Andrew?" obviously sent a chill through Bryn. "Sarah, he's up here," bellowed John. Sarah flew across the foyer to the stairs, stopping briefly to stare at the old man in the carriage with Thomas.

~ *Sarah* ~

I followed John up the stairs, alarmed for Lily, lying limp in John's arms. "Should we send for Doc Jones?" I asked, my anxiety evident.

"Yes, I'll have William go as soon as I have her settled in bed. You go to Andrew. I can't believe what's just happened."

I entered our room quietly, wincing at the squeak of the brass hinges as I slowly pushed the door forward. Andrew was standing by the window staring at the garden below. I went in and put my arms around him. We stayed like that for several minutes, neither of us speaking. I understood and respected Andrew's need for quiet. I would learn soon enough what had transpired downstairs. Eventually, I moved to sit in the chair opposite Andrew.

"How's Lily, she sustained a terrible shock?" Andrew's voice was flat and dull with pain when he finally spoke.

"She's alright love, Thomas came for John, and he carried her to their rooms. Doc Jones has been sent for."

"Damn him! I just saw my father come back from the dead! Treacherous old man! I told you what he was like and now you'll have the misfortune to experience it firsthand! I thought it was over. I thought the past would have been buried with him and I told him so!" I winced at his vehemence and in the same moment, I empathized the profundity of his anger and hurt. I would sit quietly with him until he was ready to talk to me of this travesty.

~ Thomas ~

*A*s I gave a last glance over my shoulder, I saw young Rob appear on the front porch. I followed the gaze of those already there. Stunned, he sputtered, "Grandfather?" The family all turned, all eyes to him.

My heart gave a lurch as I watched the first tears of remorse course down the cheeks of the man I once thought of as a giant. I assisted an overwhelmed Hugh from the carriage and into his room at the Jefferson Hotel. I managed to conceal Hugh's agitation from the interfering, gossip seeking eyes of the other guests. Hugh had been speechless the entire ride back and I found it disconcerting. This was not the Hugh Henley I had grown to know over the years. I settled Hugh into his chair facing out the window at the front of the hotel.

This fiasco, I thought, never needed to have taken place. If only Hugh could have shared his life honestly with his children. But, upon Emmaline's death, it was as if Hugh, too, had died and only the shell of the business man survived. As I settled Hugh, I noted the tidy arrangement of toiletries on the dresser, normally my responsibility, now seemingly placed there neatly by Hugh. Sometimes he really took me by surprise, as with this domesticity no doubt learned at his mother's side. Emmaline had confided Hugh's painful, impoverished upbringing to me, knowing I would never betray the trust. I had never let on to Hugh the extent of my knowledge. So it was me, not Lily and Andrew, who knew the history and the man that was Hugh Henley. Stubborn pride had prevented Hugh from sharing the hard lessons of his youth with his own offspring.

It was hot and stuffy in the room. I opened the windows that had been closed all morning. Hugh's was a large corner room and was fortunate enough to have a second window on the adjacent wall. Over the next few minutes the air in the room improved considerably as the windows let in the fresh late morning cross breeze. I picked up the sweet fragrance of the roses that were climbing the side of the house next door. The atmosphere remained solemn. Hugh's eyes were now dry but evidence of his distress was written all over his face.

"Sir, would you care for something for the shock? Would you like me to fetch Dr. Smythe?" As Hugh shook his head in denial, I continued. "You remain here sir. I'll prepare you a nice cup of tea." I quietly exited the room. Shortly, I returned with a tray of tea and some fresh baking. I prepared Hugh's tea and a biscuit and laid them on the table beside the chair. "Come now sir, you need something to quench your thirst and stave off hunger." I held the cup out for Hugh to take.

I remained speechless; I was confused by the reactions of my children. Lily was the first to regain some of her composure. I turned to face her, my equanimity rapidly falling apart. "I didn't mean for anyone to get hurt." I was deeply shocked and it came out as a hoarse whimper.

I took the cup from Thomas. My hands were shaking so badly the hot liquid resembled the open sea as it dribbled down the side of the cup into the saucer. I inhaled the soothing fragrance and sipped the hot tea. "Ahh. Serve yourself and be seated Thomas." The biscuit felt dry in my mouth and I took another sip of tea. Silence settled on the room as Thomas retrieved another tea cup, took the other chair by the window and poured himself a cup of the fragrant liquid.

Much later, with a quiet and weary, "thank you." I finally broke the silence.

"You're welcome, sir," Thomas waited. Although he had served me all these years and we had developed a strong bond, there was still the separation of master and servant. This had been tested several times recently as Thomas had taken liberty and voiced his concerns over my plan. Now I had played my hand to my family with utterly disastrous results. Friends on an equal footing we were not; so Thomas waited on my next move.

"You've always served me well, Thomas. Recently you've been so bold as to question my plan of action. Now, in hindsight, I realize you've shown much better judgment and personal insight than I."

Stunned by my admission, he stammered out his, "As ever, I'm at your service, sir."

"No . . . no . . . I see it now. More than a servant, you are a friend, a stalwart friend, my only genuine friend I would hazard to guess." I heaved a sigh and continued. "My children are right. I'm a selfish, foolish old man, Thomas. I should have listened to you in India after young Robert's visit. I know I'm stubborn and confident but it's always stood me in good stead in business. However, as you so often tried to counsel me, this isn't business. This is my family. You were right, Andrew was right, even my charitable Lily would not accept my imprudent behavior. I have made a mess of this reunion and physically injured my son." I heaved a long sigh.

"Whatever possessed me to presume they would think well of me when I had passed and then accept me when I reappeared? Did I hope to see how well they might think of me if they thought me dead? I expected some antagonism but not this . . . hatred, revulsion? My God, to think I actually risked their lives. I was so ignorant. Believe me Thomas, I tell you I never meant to risk anyone's life," I hung my head in shame. My sigh of regret shifted my body until I was hunched forward in my chair with my head cradled in my hands.

"If I may speak freely, Sir?"

"Of course man! Speak up." I snapped.

"As long as you draw breath into your body there is hope of forgiveness. Until now you have only ever considered your perspective. As you say, that works well with business. However, now with your family you must be prepared to change, accept responsibility for this travesty and, for once, be patient. I make no guarantee of the outcome. But rest assured, Lily and Andrew will discuss this; the whole family will discuss this. They are good people and with the Good Lord's help, they may be able to forgive and possibly accept. Up until now, you have been in control of the entire situation, but now you must step back, wait and allow them to resolve this in their own way and in their own time."

Feeling slightly reassured I countered, "I'll have to find a way to tell them how much I regret my actions, not just for this but everything. I just had no idea."

"Right now, sir if I my say, you really need to leave them alone. I can't stress that enough."

"I should have been involved all along. The last thing my Emmaline said before she was taken from me was to love Andrew and Lily, our children, but her plea fell on deaf ears. I wasn't ready to accept the fatherly responsibilities on my own, how I needed her, how I love her, how I miss her still!"

"Again, sir, I speak out of turn, but find it necessary to draw your attention to the fact that with Miss Emmaline's death they lost not only their mother but their father as well with your withdrawal."

"Yes . . . yes, you're right of course, I didn't honor her request . . . now it may be too late. She would be so disappointed in me if she knew."

"Yes, sir, she would be disappointed. However, with her faith and love for you, she would also expect you to rectify the situation. That would restore her pride. She believed that the good in people could always prevail. I'll never forget she gave me a chance and on my honor I believe she would forgive you with an honest effort to make amends.

Remember sir, several years ago I read a book. *A Christmas Carol* written by a Mr. Charles Dickens. During our discussions, you laughed at the Scrooge character, however, now . . . perhaps . . . you understand. As long as you live, it's never too late to change. Take heart. By the way, I saw a copy at the hotel. I'm quite sure I can borrow it for you to read. I believe sir; you'll need to lay low for the next few days. Give your family a chance to accept that you are indeed very alive and here in St. Louis."

For a while we sat in taciturnity, each reviewing the events of the last few hours and surmising possible steps toward restitution.

"I think I'd like to read that book. You're right I need to take responsibility for this mess. What do I have to do now?"

"You don't have to do anything, sir. What you should is another matter. You should do the right thing for your family and yourself," responded Thomas. "I know this is new to you but you have to eventually see this state of affairs for what it is. You're a brilliant entrepreneur. You've manipulated people and situations all of your life, now use the same modus operandi on yourself. You're not without insight. You know human nature better than anyone I've ever known. For God's sake sir, these aren't businesses to be discarded for the next venture. They're your family. Right now, I think you have to leave the next move to them. Also, anything you do now must come from your heart. Anything less and they'll know it's fraudulent. Wake up sir, time is running out!"

"Perhaps it might help you to keep in mind what Miss Emmaline would do in any of the situations you face in the next while. Let her be your conscience and your guide as you learn to think with your heart not your head. It won't be easy sir, but the rewards could be huge."

I felt I was spending a lot of time thinking about things I was unaccustomed to, uncomfortable with and felt I had no business thinking about. "Insight my foot," I growled.

"Thomas," I barked.

"Sir," Thomas replied calmly.

"Blast it all to hell and gone," and then softly, at first, I began to cry. Eventually tears of despair coursed down my face. I cried like a baby, like his son as a wee newborn in the nursing cradle beside Emma's bed. My shoulders shook and my hands tried to hide my face from the world without much success.

Recognizing this for what it was, Thomas came over and comfortingly placed his arms around me and let the tears of renewal fall. "This has been a long time coming, let it all out," urged Thomas. I cried for the loss of Emmaline, for the years we didn't have together, for the children I had ignored, estranged and ultimately lost. Finally, I wept for the pain I had negligently caused my children, Emmaline's children. Lastly, I felt sorrow for the trials I had caused in these last few months because of my egocentricity. I looked at Thomas, finally understanding that these tears were fifty years too late. "Thank you. So sorry, I think I know what I have to do."

"Yes sir, I'm sure you do. Take your time and make no rash decisions."

Thomas calmly excused himself, and as was his practice, he had dinner sent to the room for me. He also said he would have Dr. Smythe check in on me. He was right, it had been a trying day and I was exhausted. When my supper arrived, I was not surprised to see a hot toddy sitting on the tray. He promised to return the following morning, bringing the book with him.

I had only been this broken and defeated once before and Thomas had been by my side through it all. His concern for me was written all over his face. I put my head in my hands and wept.

"Ahem," with father seated I broke the silence. All eyes turned to me, "I don't want to add to the turmoil of the last few hours but now is as good as any time for me to come clean." Papa leaned in to interrupt, but I raised my hand to stop him, "please hear me out now, it's relevant and important. I've come home for a number of reasons. First and foremost, you're my family and I love you, all of you. I never stopped loving any of you, no matter what the politics were. I need to set things to rights with you, Pa and with Josh, for my own peace of mind." I took a deep breath, giving myself time to think the sequence through before continuing. "The best laid plans are sometimes the plans that fail. I had hoped to tell everyone at once, not keep rehashing the same old issues. Guess I'm a bit like you Pa; why tell a story twice when once will suffice? The few times nearly everyone was together I didn't know how to begin and then before I'd gathered my wits something would happen to interfere. I always felt a bit off kilter and kept waiting for the right time. It was never the right time; so now it appears is as right as the time's going to get."

"The second reason I came home now was, well . . . the truth is I met Grandfather Henley in India." I realized the collective gasp. When the room settled I continued, "Pa, Thomas recognized me as your son on my last voyage to India. He followed me to my hotel from the dockside. He claimed to have been at the office when he saw me and bade me to visit. I didn't know what was up. I was stunned to say the least to realize we had a living grandfather of whom we'd never heard. Over the course of my stay in Calcutta we had several long visits. During my voyage home, I had a lot of time to think about the rift between the two of you and how it applied to us. By the time I arrived home to New Orleans I had resolved not to let us repeat the same history. I finally made it up here to apologize but before I got comfortable enough to disclose my true intentions the letter arrived from Thomas. It really threw me. I was just as stunned as everyone else when we learned Grandfather Henley had died in India, except at least I knew he had been alive and I had met him." I shrugged my shoulders as if shaking off a heavy burden. "I'm sorry I didn't say anything sooner. And now this treachery, he's actually alive. I had actually liked the old man in Calcutta and really admired his business acumen. I quickly realized how his conduct had built an unbreachable wall between you; and he had absolutely no bend in his temperament. We got along quite well but then we didn't have the obstacles of a mutual history to overcome. But this deceit has thrown me. And if this is what I'm experiencing from such a brief and recent encounter I can't begin to think what you two are going through after a lifetime of this. I'm so sorry Pa, Aunt Lily." My voice drifted off.

The pain on Andrew's face was palpable. "Rob, I'm sorry. Dammit I'm as guilty as him. Guess I drove you off exactly like he did me. Now you're back and between business and politics, I can't even make you comfortable in your own home. As God is my witness I am so sorry too."

We rose and met halfway. Both spoke at the same time. "I'm sorry." We began to shake hands but as Pa expressed his sincere, "welcome home son," we ended wrapped in each other's arms. Ma, tears streaming down her face, leapt to be included in the warmth of our reconciliation. Finally, we broke the embrace.

"Rob, I'm sure I speak for all of us, we're certainly delighted to have you home." But as Ma and I sat Pa spat out. "Well now, all we have to do is decide what to do about my dang father and Thomas."

S arah looked directly at me and stated clearly, "Well, I for one, thank the old curmudgeon for inadvertently steering our son home to us. As for Thomas, I imagine circumstances were beyond his control. He's your father's servant after all."

"Thomas is a good man; he's always been more of a friend to us. He practically raised Lily and me while running the household. Of course, we were too young to understand all the details at the time. You're right, he would never have intentionally put us in harm's way. My father, on the other hand, is a horse of a different color. It's so easy to hate him and I preferred it when we simply ignored his existence. Now he's destroyed that uncomplicated state of being." I slapped my thigh wincing, "dammit, forget it, I'm tired, just forget it!"

"Andrew," Sarah countered, "this family has been through far worse over the years than your father. He's not worth this anguish, nor the coarse language!"

"Ma's right about Mr. Hall," Rob added his support. "Although I was only with them for a short time, Mr. Hall was always invited to sit and converse with us, and I do believe it wasn't an uncommon circumstance for him to be with grandfather as a companion. However, there was never any doubt that Thomas was a servant to Grandfather Henley. It is worth bringing to your attention that during the long conversations, I remember with both of them grandfather always spoke of business. It was Thomas who warmly held the memories of your mother and your lives as children in England. That's enough for me to surmise he would never willingly go along with such a cruel hoax."

"I imagine you're right Rob." With a glimmer of humor I turned and cajoled Lily. "And what do you have to say in dear Thomas' defense?"

Lily perked up and added, "I can still see Thomas in the study with Mama that first day. He held his hat behind him, worrying it, as he stood tall and proudly faced the decision of his fate from Mama. I think she loved him the moment she saw him. She nurtured him that short while and then when she was gone, I think he tried to fill that void for us. He was always so good to us, always took care of us, played with us and helped to raise us. He was a brave and true friend, really a big brother. Thomas has always been upset about the estrangement between you and Father, always trying to repair the breach. Oh . . . and just before we came in here this morning he said something about forgiveness and things beyond his control. So I guess the question really shouldn't be about Thomas at all. The real question is what we do about Father?" She looked me straight in the eye as she finished.

After a brief strained silence, Bryn stood up and all eyes turned to her. "We forgive. That's what we do. The Henley's may not forget, but surely we know how to forgive. We've forgiven Rob even though he's a Confederate. Eventually he and Josh will even forgive each other I'm sure. You're talking of forgiving Mr. Hall and I'm glad. I like Mr. Hall; he's fun even if he is a bit stuffy."

"Bryn," Mama's sharp correction hit its target. "Sorry mama. We should forgive Grandfather Henley that's what we should do. Holding a grudge against him will eat us all up and life's too precious to waste on hatred. Don't you see? We'd be hurting ourselves too. Yes, our lives were in danger, but think about it, lives are always in danger every day, even on our ranch. I say we forgive and hopefully as he gets to know us, he'll learn to be nice." She looked beseechingly at each one in turn.

"Bryn's right. My but you aren't a little girl anymore," Rob stated with pride.

"Aye lass, well stated," supported Aleck.

"Poppet, that's easy for you to say but you didn't have to live it. You're logic is sound and your argument reasonable but I for one feel I need to sleep on it at least for tonight anyway. Lily can speak for herself but I feel drained, old and tired at the moment. Sarah please! Perhaps I'll be able to deal with this better in the morning. Sorry Lily, I just can't right now. May we please have a tray upstairs later if it's not too much trouble, John?"

As Sarah rose to accompany me, John offered to have a light repast sent up shortly and two trays sent up for dinner. He suggested he and Lily would do the same as they followed us from the room. To the rest he added, "Please do as you wish. I only ask you to let William know in good time, thank you and good day and night."

~ *Bryn* ~

I had never seen Papa so angry. My eyes never left his face as I watched his barely controlled fury. He had tried to present a stoic presence but had not quite succeeded. He was almost paralyzed by shock and dismay. After they left, I turned to Aleck wanting his strong arms and broad shoulders for support. "It'll be alright lass," he cooed stroking my hair.

Rob echoed Aleck's sentiments. "Aleck's right. After, a night's sleep Pa will see the right of things. I was mighty proud of the way you spoke up just now Bryn," He winked me. "You're a real chip off the old block. Who'd a known?"

I felt the heat of the blush across my cheeks with Rob's compliment; it was uncharted territory for me to have praise from my brothers. I stood and turned on Rob; my face flushed, I gave his shoulder a shove, "What a day! I don't ever want to have another like it. Poor Papa! Poor Aunt Lily! How do you get over a shock like that? I for one can say I've never seen Papa so angry. I was worried he'd have apoplexy. Did you see the color of his face? How he kept clenching his hands? I wonder if we'll get to meet our Grandfather Henley." Some of my vexation spent; I plunked down onto the settee beside Rob, pushed him off and invited Aleck down beside her. Rob rolled his eyes then did what all Henley men do in a predicament he paced and pondered. Earley, now sure, calm would prevail, left us to our own devices. He had no wish to be ensnarled in this.

y mind was reeling, making coherent thought next to impossible. What must father be going through? Poor Aunt Lily, she was always such a sweetheart, how could her father do this to her? What had Grandfather Henley being thinking? The tension in the house was tangible. Thank goodness for Rose and William. When our parents, aunt and uncle had come back downstairs, they had discreetly served tea, scones and finger foods so the family could discuss the fiasco without the interruption of the noon day meal. The worst of the rage appeared to be spent; hopefully the more volatile emotions would begin to settle soon. What an escapade Grandfather had manufactured. I could make no sense of his plan and intentions with the added horror that the old man did not seem to realize how deceitful or dangerous the scheme was. Drew and Bryn were the real innocents in this jumble thereby being the first ones to eagerly support the notion that forgiveness was the right answer. No matter what way you looked at the problem of Hugh Henley, he was still our grandfather, warts and all. He was human and fallible like everyone else. Bryn was right. Forgiveness was the only choice.

"I think you're right Bryn, we should forgive him but it's definitely going to be the tougher road. He's the only grandfather we'll ever know. By the look of him earlier, I'd say he'll be doing some deep thinking on the situation he's created. As I said earlier, when I met him in India, I liked him. Not so much right now. But, despite poor judgment in choosing a strategy, at least he has finally tried to get back in touch. Yup, no matter which way you turn it, I'm of the belief that we'll have to work this through as a family. And he is part of this family."

"Rob, I must confess I was shocked when you told us you'd met Grandfather Henley in India. When Thomas' letter came, I couldn't put a name to the look on your face. But now I understand." She grinned back at me. "Could you tell us a bit about him, please," she coaxed. "Oh wait. Shall we have a light dinner together; keep it simple for Rose and William?" We all nodded acquiescence, Aleck left to convey our wishes to William. The three siblings dropped into discussions revolving around me, with my business in New Orleans, meeting Grandfather Henley in Calcutta and all my travels.

Bryn and I were doing all the talking so finally I asked Drew, "What do you think? You're awfully silent."

"I've got your backs on this one. The whole thing beats me. I'll accept whatever's decided. Think I'll head on over to the livery. They've got some new tack I wanna take a closer look at. I think better around the horses. I prefer the company of horses; they're less complicated and never hold a grudge." He gave Bryn a quick hug, slapped me on the back and headed out to the stables. A few minutes later, we heard the horse's hooves leaving down the lane from the house.

I chortled, "Prefers the company of horses does he? I think he doesn't mind the blacksmith's daughter either. We met her the other day. I imagine he'll give you a bit more breathing room now. You could put the shoe on the other foot now."

Bryn got out of the chair to give me a hug. Her color suddenly rosier as she whispered, "Thanks Rob, you're the best big brother. I know you've been giving us a bit of time together."

I laughed and tousled her hair, "Well I know Drew'll be back shortly. The smith's family is away for a few days, granddaughter's christening."

The conversation picked up again. The few times Bryn tried to steer the conversation to his role in the Confederacy, Aleck or I thwarted the topic frustrating her to no end. Drew returned shortly before William invited them to the dining room for a light supper. Foiled, Bryn flounced across to the dining room. I had been opening up about my life and she wanted to know everything. The dinner conversation did nothing to assuage her curiosity. After dinner, she rose giving a long stretch and announced, "Well, I think I'm feeling a little tired now myself. I think I'll retire for the evening." She feigned a yawn. Aleck walked her to the dining room doors, kissed her on the forehead and bade her good night. "Sleep well lass. Sweet dreams." He hugged her again then turned to her brothers, "Cards gentlemen?" He sensed the daggers in his back, heard her muttered "gentlemen hah!" and noted the grins from her brothers. He heard the clicking of her heels on the marble foyer and his mind's eye could see the sway of her hips in exaggerated irritation. He grinned back at Rob and Drew.

~ Andrew ~

I was feeling less tormented after talking things over with Sarah. We had talked all afternoon. She had never seen me so enraged, on the verge of losing self-control. I regretted the outburst but there was sense no crying over spilled milk. I said what had to be said and for me that would end it. Sarah shared her words of wisdom sprinkled with kindness and common sense. We managed an escape outside in the twilight without being spotted and slowly walked off some of my frustration.

"You seem to be walking much better. How's your leg?" she enquired as she strolled closely by my side. I was enjoying our private moment together. She had always had to race along to keep up with my long stride so she reveled in the ability to meander and chat.

"Better. Better each day. Don't like travelling at a snail's pace though."

"Are you calling me a snail, Andrew Henley?" She turned and coquettishly flounced off. I never let her get more than an arm's length away. I watched the sway of her skirts knowing intimately what lay beneath. I reached out in a lightening quick move and pinched her on the derriere. Sarah spun around and met the steaming desire in my face. "And just how fast do you think you can get to our rooms, Mr. Three Legs?"

"Fast enough shorty! I'm not ready to cast aside my gift from young Aleck just yet, maybe tomorrow morning."

"Perhaps you should wait 'til the afternoon you silly old coot," she teased. "You're in too much of a hurry. Give it time." We set a brisker pace home than our leisurely stroll out.

Sarah's patience chased the seething anger out of me. I was still furious about what had happened but my common sense was restored.

Now, I was unlikely to make hasty, unwise decisions; nor speak vindictively creating further agitation. Sarah understood the burden of pride all men suffered under. I appreciated our daughter's good judgment, she knew, but also understood I was not yet ready to forgive my father. She knew Hugh could not countenance humiliation either. Really what person could?

I had always depended on Sarah's insight with our ranch hands and especially when it had come to the children. Her empathy for my father was palpable. She only had a glimpse of Hugh as Thomas had escorted the old man out to the carriage, but she had seen the man beneath the fine clothing. I marveled at how often she was able to sum someone up in just one glance. However, I was irritated when she told me I needed to give father a chance, calling it a woman's intuition. "Your father's probably all wind," at the moment was her observation. Sarah also asked me to make allowance for the emotions during the war of words. "There was more than one ego at stake in the room Andrew. Just think about it, love. He's an old man. Is this the way you would want it to end with our own sons?" That effectively finished all resistance in me. I knew then I must at least try and was content knowing Sarah would be by my side through the ensuing ordeal.

The sun rose as it always does shining warm and bright into the east facing, open windows. Small dust motes floated on the rays as they crossed the floor. Rose and William had the breakfast table laid and the buffet set out when the bleary eyed members of the household appeared. Lily and John were first down. Lily was sitting with her first cup of tea as Sarah and I followed by Aleck, Bryn and the boys came downstairs. We were hungry after the events of the previous day. Sarah admitted a fitful sleep but felt much better having had a quiet chat about the events on our own. This had always been our way.

I took the lead, "With everyone here this morning, it seems as good a time as any to address the business that was started yesterday. I heard words of wisdom from my daughter. I'll think on it Bryn, but I'm not ready to forgive my father and I know I'll never forget! Forgiveness is arduous and will take time. Yes, it is better to forgive than to hate. My father and I have had enough hate to fill many lifetimes. But still, I find

I'm not yet ready to start on the road to forgiveness. I would like to take a short walk with your mother after breakfast and suggest we then meet in the parlor to plan our family's course of action. Does this suit you Lily?" She nodded her acquiescence.

~ *Rob* ~

_S_everal hours later, I sat quietly in the parlor listening to the sound of silence. I was shrouded in shades of gray as I stared into space at nothing. The hush increased my subconscious awareness allowing me access to the deep recesses of my mind. No female hysterics or drama, for the moment those scenes had been quelled. I had taken note of the calming influence and wisdom mother brought to the situation. Whereas Bryn and Aunt Lily both had a flair for the dramatic and could not contain their curiosity; continuous streams of questions flowed from them with no chance for any replies. The similarities between his sister, no longer a little kid and holy terror but a young woman, and our aunt were amazing. The bonds and traits of blood ran deep; as one of his teachers had so often said history is always repeating itself. Here was my family proving that point over and over again.

There was still no united family resolution, nor plan of action, as we wrestled to come to terms with Grandfather Henley's 'return from the dead'. It had been relatively easy for us all to agree to forgive Thomas as an unwilling pawn to Grandfather's charade. It spoke well of our grandfather that he had made the first attempt towards a peaceful resolution.

It came as a great surprise to all of us when shortly after breakfast this morning, only twenty four hours after Grandfather Henley's unexpected return, we received a Doctor and Mrs. Smythe who wished to address the entire family. I later learned they were friends of Grandfather who had wished to travel with him to America. William had ensconced the couple in the parlor and rounded everyone up. There was a distinct feeling of Déjà-vu. On the alert after yesterday's performance, and with two new strangers in our midst, we all took our guarded positions from the previous afternoon.

Dr. Smythe introduced his wife, Agnes. He explained that her father Dr. Snow, had been a long-time friend of Hugh's and therefore she knew him well enough. Dr. Snow had unfortunately passed on the previous year. The couple was considering emigration to the United States when Hugh had returned to England. They asked to travel together with Hugh and Thomas as an entourage for safe passage. The four got along very well except with regards to Hugh's charade, which none of the three approved. Then he bade her read a missive from the old man and answer any questions they might have on which she might be able to shed some light. Once in no doubt that everyone would listen she broke the seal, opened the letter and in a clear voice read out loud.

Dear Lily, Andrew and family,

I beseech you all to forgive Thomas his part in these dreadful circumstances.

I am quite sure that right now you have no desire to hear from me. However, I am coming to my senses and must plead Thomas' case. I placed Thomas in an indefensible situation through no fault of his own. The chance meeting with young Robert in India began my awakening. His visit struck within me a yearning I have not felt in decades. I became conscious that fate had provided the catalyst to start me on the path to rekindling my family ties. I know Thomas was pleased with my decision. This course of events Thomas most heartily endorsed. However my plan for how to achieve this reconciliation was challenged by him from the very inception. However, I was determined to follow my strategy culminating in the unfortunate chain of events that has ended so badly. Neither Thomas nor Robert is to blame. This disaster is totally my responsibility to shoulder.

I must impress upon you that Thomas tried to put a halt to my scheme from its very beginning. He has been my unrelenting conscience through this. Once it had begun he still pleaded with me, but I would not heed his common sense. He counseled me to stop this course of action on numerous occasions, at great risk to himself, not knowing how I would react to such insubordination. I am not, as you are well aware, a tolerant man. Of course I felt I knew best.

His loyalty to you both goes far beyond that of a servant. I earnestly hope that you will see through my selfish transgressions and recognize Thomas' inability to prevent any of the damages that have been wrought.

Once again I ask you. Please forgive Thomas for his reluctant participation in this debacle.

> *Sincerely,*
> *Your,*
> *Father*

As Agnes read, tears had streamed down Aunt Lily's face and Uncle John had moved to sit on the arm of the settee and put his arm around her. Papa assumed a mask of blank calm but I had noticed how mother had stroked his arm as his fingers had clenched in his lap. Deafening silence had greeted the final salutation. Pa shivered and murmured "unbelievable." Aunt Lily whispered, "Poor Thomas." When no questions seemed forthcoming, only stunned silence Uncle John rose, thanked the Smythes and requested a further audience with them once the family had absorbed this latest information. The Smythes readily offered to be available at the family's convenience and left.

Right now, except for the ``grandfather`` issue, everyone was comfortable with themselves. I took a deep breath and sighed. Everyone but me, I thought. I looked at the volumes surrounding me and although much smaller, I could not help but think of the parlor at my parents' home. Both parlors were well used and enjoyed, contrary to the current fashion of only using the parlor to receive guests. I put my feet up on the stool and laid back into the comfortable chair. I looked out onto my aunt's garden through the tall window. The fresh air of the country was a nice change from the heat of the city. It came as no surprise to me that I did not like the crowded city centers. I had been in many around the world with my trading but nothing beat the peaceful air of the countryside. My aunt and uncle's lawns were kept manicured with big trees providing just the right amount of shade. I was homesick for my own home just outside New Orleans. It needed rebuilding after the travesties against it from the war. I had been away a lot longer than I had anticipated. But my own return would wait a bit longer; I was increasingly desperate to clear the air with father and my own conscience. This had been coming on for a long time; it was buried deep, festering inside me through the latter war years and after. Now it all felt like a boil ready to burst, spewing its revolting pus. It was going to be messy, I knew that and I had no way of gauging what Father's reaction might be. Being welcomed home was only the first step towards our reconciliation. I desired rapport and a reconnection of the father son bond. I wanted my family back. It had been a good start yesterday but there was much more that needed to be said. I certainly did not want to alienate Pa again.

~ *Bryn* ~

*I*t was apparent that the effects of the emotional storm that had just besieged us would leave debris that would take ages to remedy. The family sat fretfully assembled in the parlor. I chose to sit in the chair my grandfather had just vacated. Aleck stood resolutely behind me. I could feel his warmth as I brought my legs up underneath me, in a most un-lady like fashion. Nobody seemed to notice so I remained curled up watching. The buzz was suffocating me so I put my hands over my ears. I wanted to scream to fill the void and alleviate my exasperation.

I managed to calm down, Aunt Lily sat on the settee beside Rob; he held our aunt's one hand in both of his. With her free hand she kept dabbing at her red swollen eyes with her embroidered handkerchief. The glass of sherry Uncle John had proffered sat untouched on the walnut table at her side. Uncle John stood behind with his hands protectively placed on her shoulders; he would take her back upstairs at the least sign of further hysteria.

Mama sat on the settee opposite Aunt Lily. Drew and Earley stood guard at her back. Mama's tension was evident as her hands were clenched. All eyes were on Papa as he limped and paced in front of the fireplace trying to vent the anger that threatened to consume him. The pain in his leg and hip must have been excruciating as he finally forced himself back into the settee beside Mama.

My mind was reeling. My whole world was topsy-turvy, I was a victim to all of the information that had been issued forth in such a short space of time. I wanted to run, to scream, to tell the world to stop for just one minute so I could catch my breath and think. The big difference was I was being included. This was a huge step forward. Maybe my family would start taking me more seriously. The worst part of this whole thing was my feeling of betrayal. I was finding it difficult to reconcile Papa's decision, with Mama's support to suppress so much of their past. This was family after all. Family had always meant more to my parents than material goods. Comfort was only comfort when shared with those you loved and trusted. That trust had been sorely tested by my parents this last week.

Late last night I had gone to the kitchen for a drink but stopped when I heard voices. Aunt Lily and Uncle John were talking about Grandfather Henley. I had stopped in the hall outside the kitchen door and listened. On tip toes I had crept closer to catch the words. I felt guilty eavesdropping but how else was anyone going to learn anything in this family; we were all rife with secrets. From that conversation, I learned that Grandfather had been moved into their hotel. Since my parents, aunt and uncle were not speaking with Grandfather, I still had not met him, only seen him in the carriage with Mr. Hall a few days ago. If my family would not introduce me, I felt my only recourse was to take matters into my own hands. I would go and meet this mysterious soul on my own. After all, he was family and I doubted very much that he would hurt me. He was not that kind of a monster. I would carry on telling no one my plans, even Aleck and I would start first thing in the morning.

Early the next morning I took great care with my toilette. I put on the lovely blue day dress with the matching reticule. My hair was its usual challenge but I finally managed to tuck it neatly into my bonnet. Bless Aunt Lily. William offered to drive me to the shops in town; he arranged to pick me up later at the hotel. As I waved to William I felt a slight pang of guilt. I had not even confided my plans with Aleck. With quick resolve and without a seconds' hesitation, I headed off to the hotel. Relieved, I found the register open on the front desk. Looking around carefully to ensure no one was looking, I turned the register around to face me. Looking up again, my eyes scanned the front lobby. This was all very clandestine and my hands started to feel damp in my cotton gloves. With determination intact, I scrutinized the entries until I located Grandfather and his room number. Relief flooded through my system as I realized I had not had to twist the information from the reluctant busy-body Frank.

Now standing at his doorstep, I realized I had no idea what to expect, or what to say so I gave myself a few moments to compose my thoughts, formulating some of the questions I wanted answers to. From the time I was a little girl, it had been pointed out to me, just how similar I was to my Aunt Lily. I was not blind, I truly recognized the similarity between myself and Aunt Lily. This was a perfect example, I was jumping into the river head first. I wanted answers. I felt perhaps Grandfather was the only person at the moment in a position to give me so I was anxious about this particular conversation. Although confident that approaching him was the right thing for me to do, I was aware this might not be a sound idea. Because Grandfather was an old man, I took time to consider my approach and whether or not he would even understand. I had no experience with the elderly let alone someone I was related to. The man Papa and Aunt Lily described would be difficult to get through to on any level let alone a sensitive one. The minutes were ticking by and I was becoming self-conscious about standing outside of his door. I was tapping my foot nervously as I clenched my hands together to steeling my resolve, then I boldly raised my hand and knocked on the door.

*I*t took me but a moment to answer. I was not expecting Thomas until the next morning and I had not made any requests for service. It crossed my mind that it may be one of the Smythes or possibly young Rob. I could not have been more astonished as I looked into the replica of my beloved Emmeline. I had gotten over the initial shock of seeing my granddaughter several days ago but still to see her up close in the flesh; the living embodiment of Emma coming to me about the same age as I had lost her took my breath away. I, was long practiced at hiding surprise, was all too aware of her anxiety and with a smile ushered her politely into the room seating her in the comfortable chair by the window. I could feel the ice around my heart melting. I could feel myself relaxing under the warmth of her gaze. Her eyes full of hope and enthusiasm, her humor wanting to bubble to the surface. There was no guile here, just honesty and genuine concern. I knew every time I saw her, Emma would be right there with me and with luck I might get to see how she would mature as a woman rather than my memory of Emma frozen in time. I felt Emmaline's spirit in Bryn and immediately felt more alive than I had felt in the years. I also felt a pang of disappointment so deep it hurt as I accepted that Emma could not be here to enjoy her granddaughter. With clarity born of brand new insight, I acknowledged all that I had missed; all of it was my own fault. The gentleman I had become bade me to sit down on the chair opposite and wait patiently for Bryn to speak.

I took my time smoothing the curls back off of my face, giving a radiant smile. I was comfortable with the silence and it struck me that even though I barely knew this man, I felt comfortable with him. It was as if the closeness I felt had been born into me and was now being given its chance to flourish. I removed my gloves and placed them on top of my reticule on the table that sat between us. The day gloves and reticule had been among the surprise gifts from Aunt Lily.

"Hello grandfather," I finally spoke. "I hope you don't mind this impromptu visit."

"A visit from any of my family will always be welcome. A visit from my lovely granddaughter is even more welcome." His manners and voice charmed me. "I'll always be struck by the amazing resemblance you bear to your grandmother. She would have adored you."

"Yes, Thomas and Aunt Lily said I look like her and showed me her portrait. I was rather shocked we seemed so alike except she was beautiful. Without being presumptuous I was wondering if you would tell be about her?"

"It would be my pleasure. You are the embodiment of her; her eyes, her hair, her build, her voice. Let me see, I am not sure where to begin. It has been many years since I have spoken of her. She was sweet, vivacious, loving and kind. Everyone loved her and would do almost anything for her. She was the love of my life. She loved books. In fact that's how we met, but you don't want to hear about that."

"Oh! Yes I would. I'd love to hear about that! It sounds so romantic. I'd love to know about my grandmother; and about you too, of course. I could have sworn my ears were on fire. I'd like to hear about when Papa and Aunt Lily were small too." I smiled nervously at him. I continued to stare, playing with my fingers and fidgeting with my skirt.

~ *Hugh* ~

I felt the beginning of a smile tugging at my face. I was terribly unused to female chatter, it was reminiscent of Lily as a young girl, "Yes I guess you could say it was romantic. I was a young lad from the poor side of town but I loved books, especially about travel. I would trudge along to the same book shop once a week. I couldn't afford the books but mindful that I was clean and careful, the owner let me look at them. One day your grandmother came into the book shop. I saw her that first time and fell in love. She was the most beautiful woman I have ever seen. My heart went into my throat. I knew she was the woman I wanted to marry. But at that time I was on my way to make my fortune. I wasn't so sure I had time for a wife. But then again, I couldn't stay away and I began to notice each time I came to the shop she would be there too. It was all too much to hope for but there it was in front of me and I took the chance. I asked if I could come calling and she consented. The rest is history." Bryn noticed the distant look in his eyes.

Bryn smiled, "that's beautiful. Were you engaged for long? Did you have a big wedding? Did either of you have family there?

"My, you sound like your Aunt Lily, so full of questions."

"Everyone says I ask too many questions and now I've seen Aunt Lily again I think they're right. But if I don't ask I'll never get to know, will I? And there's so much I want to know. I guess you're wondering why I came, I'm not sure I know myself. I'm sure Papa will be displeased, but I'm glad I did."

~ *Bryn* ~

"*I*'m glad you came too." I was so excited to be in the company of my living grandfather to notice he had not addressed many of my questions. "May I be of service to you granddaughter?" He seemed to let the word roll over his tongue.

"I'm trying to make sense of so many things. You're here. Which is wonderful, truly it is!" I paused, my polite facade melting away, as the real Bryn bubbled through to the surface with impetuous questions. "But why now? Why not when we were growing up? It's obvious you've travelled – you could have come to visit – other grandparents do. It could have been such fun. Was it your decision theirs or mutual? Although Grandmother Henley was talked about, Papa and Aunt Lily never spoke of you, yea or nay, we just didn't know. We all made the obvious assumption that you, like our grandmother, had passed away in England. What caused the estrangement? Why did it go on so long? What could have been so terrible that all communication was severed? Why couldn't one of you just say you were sorry or whatever. Why have you come with such subterfuge? Was that really necessary?" As I paused to take a breath a sudden picture of Rob and the estrangement with him popped into my mind.

"I've thought a lot about this situation. Of course we all have and have discussed it endlessly. Although it's not my position to criticize any of you, I must tell you how I feel. This is a terrible deception and hurt you have played upon Aunt Lily and Papa. Although, I don't understand why you did return this way I find it easy in my heart to forgive you. I for one am glad to have a grandfather who's still alive and with who I may be in contact at will. I hope you want to stay in contact with me, you do don't you?" I smiled at the quick nod of his head as I hurtled on.

"And Aunt Lily and Papa, they're easy for me to forgive. But how will you three make amends? Or is this merely a one last time with them? This is all so very convoluted." I closed my eyes and rubbed my forehead with a slight shake of my head as I finished. I was exhausted, I kept my eyes closed, and for the next few minutes sat, embarrassed in the silence. I had really overstepped the bounds. My parents were always telling me to rein in my run away tongue. Ill at ease, I gathered my gloves and reticule, and slowly started to rise from the chair. I was trying to convey as much decorum as possible when Grandfather finally spoke.

I sat up straight as a poker; shame coursed through me as I gathered myself for what could be one of the most important monologues of my long life. For the first time in nearly half a century, I spoke from my heart. "My dear Bryn, don't go yet, please sit. I sincerely hope you can forgive me. It has taken me a very long time to realize the terrible mistakes I've made as it came to my family. I sincerely hope one day your father and Aunt Lily will be able to forgive me. My only justification and it seems pitiful now, in hindsight, is my overpowering love for your grandmother, my Emma. She was my very essence. Everything I did was only with the end purpose of making her happy and seeing her smile. My love died with her on that most dreadful day. My dear I can honestly say I died for all intents and purposes. You are so very like her. You are the image of her heart and soul. You know, I believe she may have done exactly as you have done. Emma confronted problems head on. I can only hope that one day, dearest Bryn, you too shall fall in love." I noticed the smile that lit up her face and gathered there already was a man in her life. "When that happens, please accept this bit of advice that your grandmother tried to share with me and that I, to my cost, ignored. Love others as you do him. Let your love grow and expand you. Don't remain focused on him alone. I think she was trying to tell me that the more you give love the more love you have to give, the more love you receive and the richer your life will be."

As I finished I realized Bryn had dropped to her knees and was holding my hands in hers, just as Emma had so many times in our early life. "Oh… grandfather how sad! But you have us now. Our family's together and I'm sure it'll all be right in the end. You must see Papa and Aunt Lily; you must make them understand." Bryn's upturned face captured the passion of her belief.

"Well child, that's why I am here. Thomas has convinced me that as long as I breathe there's a chance for reconciliation. I hope he's right. I'm so very sorry. I shudder to think of what could have happened to you and your family during your travels here. I never meant to hurt anyone, please believe me? Please forgive me?"

"I forgive you, Grandfather," she smiled up at me before continuing. "The storm was awful, I'll grant you. Papa was injured; then Mama and Papa were both ailing something fierce. Aleck rescued us and they're both recovering now. I hope never to go through something like that again. Mama always says behind every cloud there's a silver lining. I believe Aleck and you are my silver lining. Please try to reconcile with my Papa and Aunt Lily. I know it won't be easy, but, I'm sure it's worth it. They're both really nice, our whole family is. Eventually they'll forgive you, I just know they will. Don't give up hope, Grandfather. Now, I best be going or I'll be late for my ride." She rose and picked up her reticule and gloves which had fallen to the floor beside her.

I rose and opened the door for her. Holding her gloves and reticule in one hand, she placed her other hand on my arm hesitantly reached up and gave me a kiss on the cheek. "Dear Bryn, thank you for coming to visit. You have made this old man happy and hopeful." I returned to my chair by the window. I felt the stirring of appeasement, now I just had to sort the rest of my mess out.

The window was open and I leaned onto the sill allowing the gentle breeze to blow over my face. My mind drifted where it would and slowly memories long buried began to surface. I covered my face with my hands pulling at the handkerchief to stave off the tears that threatened to roll. I was no better than my own father had been. Never, not once, had I meted out that kind of physical abuse but I finally comprehended my apathy had been just as cruel. The one thing I had done differently was to provide the very best for both of my children. The best of everything that money could buy. My frozen heart had bought and paid for my freedom from guilt; now I would break free of that hellish purgatory with something far more valuable than money; I would pay with my heart and soul. Would that be anywhere near enough to beg for the mercy and forgiveness I asked of my children? If only Emma had not succumbed with Andrew's birth, everything would be different. Finally, I accepted that I had burdened my own son with the responsibility of his mother's death. My stubborn determination to hold Emma as she was before she died to the exclusion of all else had virtually destroyed my ability to relate to other people, especially my children. Why did I only begin to see that now? Now when it was almost too late? Thomas, had subtly, and not so subtly, tried to counsel me across the years. Dear, loyal Thomas. I really did not deserve such loyalty from him, Emma's influence again was my salvation. In retrospect, I should have done things much differently. Whatever possessed me to think that this devious plan would work? Thomas had tried to derail this chicanery too. Not prone to this kind of introspection, I was struggling with knowledge that my neglect had caused so much pain and suffering.

My thoughts turned to Bryn, bringing a smile to my face. I had not been prepared for the intense shock of déjà vu when I saw her that first time. Thomas, although he had known, had avoided mentioning that she was the ghost of Emma; her manner, her voice and those eyes, all Emma. I understood I deserved the eye-opening jolt, in fact needed. I needed the jarring to jolt me back to reality. I had had to concentrate very hard indeed when I was talking not call her Emma. Bryn had admitted Thomas had also been astonished when he first met her. "Ah well," I sighed to nobody in particular. As I sat back in the chair to ponder my next move I noticed one of her gloves on the floor. I smiled as I retrieved it and held it for a long time in my lap…just like my Emma.

I contemplated my grandfather's conundrum and my own situation with Aleck and my brothers. It was late in the afternoon. William had picked me up as agreed and once home, I had slipped unobserved up to my room to change my clothes. There was too much to think about, I was tired so decided to focus on what I really wanted and that was some time alone, preferably with Aleck. Totally alone would certainly do, but I wanted the comfort that only Aleck could supply. The stable loomed in front of me, dark and cool. There was hide nor hair of Aleck there, so I took the time and curried Tinker, chattering away unburdening my confusion over the family dilemmas and how with all of them around, I rarely had uninterrupted alone time with Aleck. Tinker had always been a good listener.

With a burst of spontaneity, I slipped quietly into the house and up the staircase. With only a moment's hesitation I turned into Aleck's room. I explored the room quickly, for what I did not know. He did not have much here. I was surprised to see one of my hankies and several hair ribbons were on his night stand. Then I spied his cotton shirt and buckskin coat hanging on the back of the wardrobe door. I scooped them up and held them to my face and breathed in deeply. They were all Aleck. I immediately felt myself relax. I needed to get away, but where? Carrying Aleck's shirt and coat, I went back out to the stable. As I had done a hundred times before as a child in my own barn, I climbed into the loft and made a bed out of the hay. The shutters of the loft were open hoping to catch any refreshing breeze that might happen by. I tugged Aleck's shirt over my head and lay down on his coat in the hay to think. I could hear the occasional blowing and stamping from the horses, they knew I was there but would never give me away.

Several hours later I woke up with start. It was getting dark. Puzzled, it took me a few seconds to realize where I was. Rising up on my elbow I wiped my face with my hand brushing the straw away. I gave my head a good shake which immediately provoked a fit of sneezing. I sat upright and continued to pull straw from my hair and managed to wipe my eyes on my sleeve. I was not the least bit hungry but I could have gone for a nice cold glass of water. I was not feeling any happier, either feeling as though tears should flow to purge the heaviness in my chest but the more I thought about it the less inclined I was to cry so I just sat in the restive silence with my head resting on my knees.

I thought back to my wonderful Saturday evening with Aleck. I hugged my knees to my chest and smiled. Aleck was very handsome in his new suit. He looked uncomfortable, the high starched collar on his shirt had been irritating him around his neck. I was moved by all that he had done for me. The violet corsage was lost in his big, calloused hands that he somehow managed to handle with a gentleness belying his strength. I was very taken with the old fashioned thong that held his thick black hair back away from his face. His face was smooth and ruddy from the recent shave. I was so excited that night. He took my hand into his, assisting me into the carriage, then climbed in and sat beside me. William graciously offered to be our driver for the evening. It was magical, the trees stood out in the shadows created by the lamplight that guided us down the lane. We had dinner at the hotel which I was positive had Aunt Lily written all over it. Frank placed us at a discreet table that had been reserved for us. It was a quiet table with fresh wild flowers centered on it. For me, there was no one else in the room except Aleck. His stare was so intense it burned through me and I felt naked before him.

I floated from dinner to the operetta. These were the tickets he had waggled in my nose earlier in the week. While we waited for the show to start, he told me about taking his own aunt to see the famous soprano Jenny Lind in Boston years ago. I was beside myself with anticipation as the curtain opened. I sat spellbound through the entire performance. I could feel Aleck's eyes upon me. After the show we walked along the boardwalk, my arm tucked safely into his. Even though it was late, we were able to get some ice cream at the general store. We sat on a bench watching the flow of people along the street and listening to the idle bits of chatter. After we finished, we continued our walk back to the theatre where William waited for us. Aleck once again held his hand for me to step up into the carriage. Before I laid my head on his shoulder, I pulled the thong from his hair, and he responded by pulling me into his arms. I stifled a sigh of shear contentment, not wanting to give myself away. I snuggled deeper into his arms and watched the stars, crystals sparkling against the night sky. Aleck pointed out some of the constellations. It had been a long, wonderful day. William stopped the carriage at the front porch. There was a fresh pitcher of water and a basket of cookies on the front porch by the swing. We sat, swinging, enjoying the companionable silence. Aleck turned to me and held me close in his arms. He stroked my hair, slowly releasing the pins out and letting the waves fall around me. It felt so good to let the weight down from my head. His fingers stroked just under my chin and then his lips touched mine, searing, making my belly feel full of butterflies. I was aware of my legs weakening, no longer able to hold me up, as I sank into him, our kiss deepening as he sensed my consent. Leaning across him, my arms came up around his neck. I jolted back to reality as he gently pushed me away. I am not sure he understood my confusion. His deep voice whispered into my ear, "Not too much temptation tonight lass. I've nay got the strength to resist." It was soon after that he led me up to my room. I still can't believe I fell asleep so quickly when the evening ended.

Finally, I was at peace again. With the darkness, I knew I had missed dinner and my family would be worrying. I had never pulled a stunt like this in my life. Of course, my brothers did this sort of disappearing act all the time, and no one ever questioned it. Tinker's soft whinny broke through my reverie. I climbed out of the loft. Tinker was looking over the door to her stall waiting for me. I rested my forehead on Tinker's nose enjoying the feel of the velvety softness under my fingertips. A while later I heard the backdoor slam. Someone was coming. I gave Tinker a "behave, don't give me away" glance and scooted back up into the loft. I immediately recognized my brothers' and Earley's voices hearing the odd comment as they saddled up and left the stables. Off to the saloon I assumed, in no mood to deal with them I had remained silent.

When did things get so damned complicated, I wondered to myself? I was thoroughly frustrated with the double standard that women had to endure. When necessity had struck, I had been sent alone with Aleck with my father's albeit less than thrilled consent, but none the less it was there. Now all I wanted was a few minutes to myself with Aleck and my brothers were like flies to paper. My ire was on a slow burn, I wanted some cuddling time, like the boys were allowed with their girls. Dreaming again of his caress I drifted back to sleep. When I awoke again I saw the moonlight across my aunt's garden through the open loft shutters. I remembered dreaming of Aleck confessing his love for me, as if that would really happen.

~ Aleck ~

*A*lthough aware that eventually her family was going to miss her; she had no idea what kind of a fuss she really had caused. "I still canna find the lass anywhere. Something's wrong! Tell me true Andrew, this is not typical behavior for the lass is it?" I was confused by this alarming turn. I kept my missing buckskins to myself for the moment. I knew who had them and she would be returning them in short order if I did not break her wee neck in the process. I turned to Drew and gave him a blistering glare. I could barely hold myself in check, my fists remained clenched at my sides. "You could'na leave her alone could ye? You've done naught but pester her since ye arrived." I spit out the accusation. Drew held his stance but his palms started to sweat.

Andrew intervened, "Not now Aleck, we need to get back out and search for her." He put a comforting hand on Sarah's shoulder. "You, Lily and Rose see to some food. You boys and Earley head back into town and continue the search. John, William and I are going to search around here in case she went for a wander. Be on the alert for anything out of the ordinary. Next meeting is here around midnight for food and results unless we find her first."

"Watch the road sides, she may have fallen and twisted her ankle," interrupted a worried Sarah.

"She'll be fine Sarah. We'll find her. Don't go fretting. Aleck, I'll leave you to your own devices. She didn't happen to confide anything to you or you didn't upset her did you?" Andrew's direct stare carried a subtle threat of injury for the wrong answer.

"I have no guilt there. I gave you my word Andrew and I have no need to repeat it." I considered Andrew's worry to have even made such

301

a statement. It came awfully close to throwing a gauntlet. I swallowed my anger and frustration and left.

We all reassembled at midnight in the big kitchen. I was famished having not eaten for hours. The whole situation was ludicrous so I headed back to the stables. It was quiet and a good place to think. I had not realized that Earley had spotted me. It wasn't until later that I learned Earley had followed his own hunch, and followed me into the barn, keeping to the deep shadows of the barn. He told me he had heard me calling out to Bryn and getting no response.

"Ah my sleeping beauty, I've been crazy with worry over you. Aye, sob if you must love but come down here where I can hold you. We're alone."

"Honest? Are ya sure? No dang Drew?" She asked through sobbing hiccups.

"Aye, lass no Drew. Now come down to me. Jump, I'll catch you."

Earley slipped back to the house. He stood at the door until Sarah looked at him then crooked his finger. She met him at the dry sink. Andrew, watching them closely out of the corner of his eye, relaxed as his wife's happy shrug and sigh of relief to Earley's whisper told him Bryn had been found but that silence was yet required.

Bryn jumped from the loft and as promised I caught her. I moved to the side and sat on a bale of hay nestling her in my arms as I had at my cabin.

She folded herself into me, my arms enveloping her, her need for my strength satisfied. She looked up at me, with a sheepish look on her beautiful face, "I'm sorry Aleck. Did I worry you? All of a sudden it was all too much - the storm, your cabin, our cave, the mudslide, my brothers, all the secrets and now my grandfather. I just couldn't stand anymore." She hiccupped again. I smiled into her soft curls running my fingers through the silken tresses.

"Look at me, my sleeping beauty." I commanded gently. My fingers caressed her chin as I directed her gaze back to my own. "Verra worried, worried sick I was. I want you for my own, Bryn Henley. I have some asking to do, but I want to know your true feelings." Then I teased her, "I'm verra happy to find my shirt and jacket too."

Bryn pulled the jacket closer and gave a nervous little laugh. "Oops! As for my feelings for you, I gather that's what you're meaning?" As I gave her a nod of approval she opted for full disclosure. "I must have fallen sound asleep at some point, and I was dreaming my favorite dream these days . . . of you. It was so real, I imagined I was listening to your voice," she blushed. I stroked the side of her face encouraging her to continue. "I love you Aleck! I've never known anyone like you. I felt safe and comfortable with you right from the beginning. It's as if I've known you my whole life. In my dreams, you say you love me, but it's just a dream. I know that. You don't have to say anything. I don't want to make this awkward but I need to be honest with you. I just can't stand anymore secrets."

I put my finger to her lips and whispered in her ear, "Ssshhh lass. You'll never be able to make me do anything I don't wish to do. Understand?" Her proximity was driving me crazy. She shifted in my lap making herself more comfortable.

"Oh and I like the way you kiss!" she added coyly batting her eyelashes.

"Now where did you learn a thing like that lass?" The look in her eyes and the candor of her words unbalanced me as I felt myself hardening against her. The heat of her body was driving me wild. It was all I could do to concentrate on what she was telling me. Before I knew what I was doing, I pushed her off of my lap and onto the hay beside me. "Lass, I'm a strong man but I canna win this battle with ye wiggling on my lap! Yer making me want to do things you have no right yet to know about."

Undaunted and climbing back into my lap, Bryn boldly replied, "My Aunt taught me how she charmed Uncle John when she was a young woman. She told me that is how she won Uncle John." She giggled up at me. "She told me to always use my feminine wiles when I wanted something. I don't think she meant to take advantage of someone but it definitely works." She stated in a matter of fact tone of voice.

"I'm wanting to court you, Bryn Henley. Now you'll know for sure as you've heard me tell you. I love you. I do love you. Aye, its' marriage with you I truly want." With that, she twirled the rest of the way round in my lap, wrapped her arms over my neck and lacing her fingers in my hair pulled me to her for a deep kiss. As we parted, I looked at her intently, she had tears coursing down her cheeks. "I'm assuming that means you're not dismayed with my intent." I ducked as she swung a paltry mock blow. "Pleased then ye be?"

"Yes Aleck, oh yes I'm pleased. I love you."

I reached up and took the medallion from around my neck. "I've never had this off my neck. My mother put it there shortly before she died. It's the mate to one my father wore, God rest his soul. I want you to wear it my sweet lassie as a symbol of my love." The emotion thick in my voice, I reiterated. "Wear it for me."

With shining eyes she turned her head so I could place the gold chain around her neck. She delicately fingered the heavy strand and the beautiful medallion. Shyly she whispered, "I'll treasure this always Aleck."

"Ah my sleeping beauty, I'm a verra happy man at long last. I'll be asking your pa proper tomorrow. But for now lass, there are some folks that are eager to see you, ye ken? I'm with you though if it gets a bit intense." I stood with her at my side. We walked hand in hand back towards the kitchen. The night air was chilly as it hit Bryn's face and she shivered. I pulled her even closer to my side. Just before we entered the kitchen door, I gave her the glove she had dropped at her grandfather's. "I visited him tonight. He divined where I might find you. He was right."

An exhausted Sarah saw us step into the doorway first and was up wrapping Bryn in her arms. "Oh you reckless girl you've had me and Papa so worried." She used the towel that was still in her hands to wipe away her tears of relief. Bryn peered around her mother to see the look of thunder on her father's face.

"Earley, please go 'round up the rest of search party," commanded Andrew. Earley already had his hat in hand and was out the door.

"Now little missy, you've some explaining to do." Andrew would never have taken this stance had he not already known her safety was ensured. "Where have you been? Your mother's beside herself with worry. And all the men have been out searching."

Bryn went to stand in front of her father and he pulled her into his arms in a hug. She knew she had been forgiven. "Papa, I'm so sorry. I fell asleep in the loft."

I entered the private room not knowing exactly what to expect. The room at the hotel was much more comfortable than the room at the boarding house, and I was happy I had accepted Lily's offer. I was mulling the current situation over in my mind. My son, my daughter, my flesh and blood betrayed by the one person they should have been able trust with their lives. I had gambled on that trust and only now was I aware that I had lost the bet. These deliberations were running around in my head. I had totally lost control of the whole situation. My acceptance brought me closer to the final truth and part of me cringed away from the responsibility, but the other half wanted to get the whole mess over and done with. Patience was not my strong suit.

A knock on the door disturbed my planning. I was not expecting anyone at this juncture so I was pleasantly surprised when I found it was Lily knocking at my door.

Like a fish out of water, I was not in my element as Lily strode imperiously into the room. I was not ready for the final act but it appeared Lily was. As far as my imagination would let me, I figured she was here to assemble a meeting, with hope in my heart, a family meeting. After all of my consultations with Thomas, I was not expecting this quite so quickly. I could not help but think this did not bode well for me. On the positive side, they could have spurned me in an impersonal, formal missive. I walked down the hallway with Lily. How like her mother she was!

"Now Papa," easily falling back into her old self, Lily chattered on, the intrusion into my thoughts irritating. "Please consider," she turned to face me in the hall outside her private rooms, "and remember what

Andrew and his family have been through. Please give Andrew a chance! He really is a wonderful man and they are an amazing family. I know . . . oh . . . oh . . . never mind." I knew what she was trying to tell me and I would surprise her and really try. The stakes were inconceivably high.

~ Andrew ~

I spent the quiet interlude before Father's arrival thinking about my earlier conversation with Aleck. I could not believe Bryn had gone behind my back and spoken with my father. I backed up a bit; she hadn't really gone behind my back. No one had ever forbidden the children to talk to my father; it had just never been an issue before. I had said I couldn't forgive father but hadn't required any oaths to that effect from the rest of the family. Bryn had professed herself to be grown up and doing what she did was indeed a grown up thing to do. She had reached out an olive branch, possibly due to her insatiable curiosity but an olive branch none the less. And in this case as well, timing would not have been an issue as no time would have been a good time in my books. It saddened me to think she did not need my permission anymore. I would never get over my feelings of protectiveness toward her; she, in the end, would always be my little poppet. That would never change and I took heart.

Aleck too had been to visit my father when I could not find my missing Bryn. My father had pointed the way.

Lily too had always maintained contact with Father, although she had deferred to my situation and never mentioned our father to any of my children. It was only me who was well and truly estranged. And I understood that being the cause of Mother's death, was the death knell to any relationship with the old man. But now, for the sake of my wife, our children and my sister, I would try once more to bridge the gulf that lay between us. I was a confident man now; Father no longer carried the wherewithal to demean me.

Lily opened the door and the men came to their feet as she entered followed by Hugh. Once Lily was seated, we all sat. Hugh took a seat by Lily. I knew her as his only ally at the moment. Father's eyes were immediately drawn to the picture of my mother, her framed face frozen in time. The look on his face prevented me from jumping up to wring his neck.

I was not oblivious to the startling change in father. He looked vulnerable somehow, certainly not the adjective I would have used to describe the dynamic force he had always been. "Would you like something to drink?" asked John, "Anyone?"

"I could use a drop of courage, John," I said.

Father also gave a nod and John poured us a stiff dram of the single malt. It would bolster the poor old guy. The look of sympathy in John's eye irked me a bit, almost like a betrayal. I had to get a hold of myself.

We were all seated and unnaturally calm. Lily could not stop fidgeting with her sleeves and smoothing the fabric of her skirt. Everyone was searching for a place to look other than the obvious. The room was overly warm and sweat trickled down my back. God this was difficult.

I broke the strained silence first. "I understand Bryn came to visit you and had a little talk. Aleck told me this morning it was you who suggested where he could find her. I owe you my thanks. But how did you know?"

Relieved not to have been under immediate attack Hugh replied calmly. "Andrew, I told Aleck to look where she would likely find him. If I was to search for Emma, your mother, I would've gone to the bookstore where we always met. I asked where Bryn would look for Aleck if she couldn't find him. It was logic really. As you are aware personal relationships are not my forte. Aleck told me she would look in the stable; I suggested he concentrate there."

We considered each other warily, like adversaries, not father and son. Suspicion was not far from the surface, our history mandated that. But I could sense the feeling in the room thaw toward father. I could feel Sarah's influence at work. I tried to see my father through her sympathetic eyes. Shockingly, Hugh had aged, yet his eyes still held the same energetic sparkle. Intrigue was hovering just below the surface. I observed him carefully, his physical stature had been well maintained, no stooping or paunch. He was clean shaven and still had a full head of hair, although it was as white as the high mountain snow.

He proved agile as he had chosen a seat beside Lily just under the two portraits. From this I could confirm father had aged well, his vigor had not dimmed. I hoped I would do as well. However, my life had been more physical, witness my damn leg. If it would heal up, I'd be fine. But there had been other accidents at the ranch in my lifetime that would take their toll as I aged. I would need to be more careful if I were to age like father. Exactly what Sarah had been saying these last few years.

After studying my father and his portrait I lifted my eyes to the portrait of our mother.

"My God, I hadn't realized, Bryn is the image of her. It's been a long time since I've looked at these portraits. I keep thinking I should remember her. I wish I had known her but of course I couldn't," I ended bitterly.

Softly Lily said, "She loved you Andrew I know it in my heart of hearts. Are you of a mind to believe such things?"

"If you don't believe her son, you should." The word son felt strange from his lips. "Your mother loved you enough to give her life so that you should live. Her parting words were to love you, love you both as we had loved each other but I was too bereft to comprehend. It was a grievous mistake I made and its cost us all dearly. I am truly sorry and though I know I don't deserve it, I beg your forgiveness. It is too great, I know, to ask for your love, friendship, and companionship. These are the things I now realize I want most in life. But foremost I need your forgiveness. To that end I must confess. I know the rumors that ran through Oakley and by my own omission and attitude I gave them substance but as I am here before you now I swear you were in no way responsible for your mother's death. I left you alone to bear that cross all your life and only now do I realize the injustice I have thrust upon you. Lily and Thomas, yes Thomas, tried often to get me to see the error of my ways but I was too set in my own mind to see the rightness of their arguments. And now it's too late."

No one spoke, all eyes were on Father. With a quiet sob, "Oh papa, "she took his elderly hands in hers.

I moved my mouth but nothing came out. I was shocked. My father had just absolved me for the death of his wife, my mother and begged for my forgiveness. The sun could refuse to shine, stars could fall from the sky but never in my lifetime did I expect an apology from my father. Then I heard it quietly in my mind and looked at Sarah for confirmation. She was telling me with her eyes and her heart to forgive. The message was coming louder and more clearly with every passing second. She needed no words to communicate. I shook my head no, but she nodded yes. Sarah always looked forward, never back. What was done was done let the past rest in peace as life belonged to the future. I knew I would capitulate.

~ *Bryn* ~

o my relief, my parents had finally decided to have a brief rest before lunch. Except when extremely ill, I could not remember a time when either of them had done that or for that matter ever had the time. I realized in the past I'd always felt sorry that my parents were sick but now I realized that I was concerned, even worried about their health. Papa's leg and mama's illness had frightened me more than I wanted to admit; but most of all it helped me to comprehend that my parents were actually aging. They used to bounce back from any illness. Perhaps my concern about them was a sign of some of my newfound maturity. All the stress with my grandfather had only made matters worse for my father, although the air had finally begun to clear between father and son.

I remained troubled as I set about finding Aleck. In the short time I had known him my world had changed completely. I had come to rely on him and his presence which I found heartening. He was like a magnet drawing me ever closer. The naïve woman in me was overwhelmed by his charisma and his kisses stirred longings in me that no other had. I felt I had known him forever not mere weeks. There were times when I looked at him that he reminded me so much of my father. I knew that was part of the attraction but recognized it was only a part. It was his acceptance of me as a woman that drew me to him. I understood that marriage to Aleck without a doubt was in my future, something I was confident enough in my own self to wait for. I found him in the stable, sitting on a bale of hay in front of Tinker's stall.

"I was just coming to find you lass," he grinned and got up to give me a kiss. I responded in kind, setting the fires of lust rampaging through his body. He did not want to let me go. "I was coming to ask you to join me for a ride in the country side. Aye, I was so bold as to have Rose make up a picnic basket for us." And he produced the huge wicker basket.

Immediately, my demeanor changed and I grinned at him with acceptance, "Oh what a lovely idea. I need my riding clothes. I'll be right back," but before I turned away I launched myself at him for another searing kiss. It was Tinker who nudged us apart and we both laughed.

I came back out to the stable in my new riding skirt and blouse, another gift Aunt Lily had showered upon me during this visit. I felt very feminine and pretty. My hat was sitting by its thong on my back from around my neck. Aleck pulled the hat forward and placed it at a jaunty angle on my head. "There now, ready lass? Shall we be off?" We mounted and left the stable at a leisurely pace heading toward the river.

After a satisfying afternoon in the shade trees on the riverbank, I felt thoroughly relaxed as we rode up the driveway to my Aunt's sprawling home. For the life of me, I could not keep my eyes off Aleck as he managed his horse; the broad muscles in his back rippling under the shirt that was tested at the seams. His easy grace so like my Papa and brothers. My eyes drifted to the beautifully manicured lawns and gardens and wished I could do something like it at the ranch. Mama's lovely roses were put to shame by the glory of the garden surrounding the front porch here. We were both surprised when we saw the carriage my grandfather had been using tied up to the rail. We saw William out tending to the horses.

"What's happening William, is my grandfather here?" I asked.

"Yes, Miss Bryn, he and Mr. Hall are inside with your aunt and your father." He enlightened me as he gestured for the stable boys to refill the trough with fresh water for the horses. "I believe the rest of the family is due to arrive any moment. In you go, Mr. Hall said they'd not be here overly long."

I glanced at Aleck who returned the same look. He shrugged his shoulders, "No use surmising, we best go in and see what the situation is."

I was in the process of removing my riding gloves as we entered the house.

The sound of agitated voices carried from the parlor. We entered through the large double doors together. I briefly closed my eyes on a sigh as I discovered the source of tension. Papa was addressing

Grandfather. "So now you think to try to buy us off?" Papa raised his voice to his father.

I had witnessed that stubborn set to his mouth before. It was exactly the same thing Papa did when he was making a strong point. Papa was completely taken aback by the interruption and would go no further. "That's not true Andrew, sit down please," he requested.

Thomas interceded, "please give him a chance Andrew."

I spied Mama and she finally coaxed him down beside her, "Give your father a chance love. Mama caught Aleck and I out of the corner of her eye, "Oh hello you two come in and take a seat."

Grandfather smiled wanly. Everyone was present, with the exception of Drew and of course, Josh who was still out on his ranch. I had to wonder if I was the only one who could see the love written on his face. One thing was for sure, there would be no was comfort until he fully accepted the burden of guilt for the estrangement. It was uncomfortably embarrassing to see him struggling to come to terms with what he had done.

Apparently, he decided to take the high road, "We have been through all of this and I do not wish to revisit the discussion. Later I will again try to beg your forgiveness as I attempt to be the father I never was. But for now, this has nothing to do with me and everything to do with your mother. Thomas if you would be so good as to bring me the urn."

Thomas broke the wax and silk seal on the urn then passed it to Grandfather who took it and turned it around in his hands admiring the workmanship on the outside. It was typical of an urn from India, beautifully inlaid with enamel. It was not really a burial urn but more a beautiful lidded vessel. This was a memorial style urn which could be displayed with some ceremonial ashes from the funeral pyre. The workmanship was exquisite and to be admired. Thomas handed the awkward urn to Hugh with relish, not wanting to have anything more to do with it himself.

"This urn now represents so many different things. In the first place it was meant to represent my final resting place, yours do to with as you would from scattering my being from one end of the earth to the other or burying my remains in a Christian cemetery or the family plot. Honestly, I would like someday to rest in the grave with Emmaline in

England if you would care to know. It also represents my deceit. There is some tarnish, I wish to remove and replace with something a little more sterling, such as my once upon a time good character."

"I know it will take the remainder of my life to try and mend the fractures I have placed in our broken relationships, but your mother, now there is a different story. From the beginning, she loved both of you. Carrying each one of you her eyes sparkled with the mystery of life to be that only a woman seems to know about and understand. Andrew, she begged me with her last breath to love you. But selfish man that I was I only perceived that you had taken her away and you could not replace her. How wrong I was and how much I have missed. That is now my cross to bear. You became a good man; I can see that and I know I can take neither ownership nor pride for it."

"I would like to share these gifts from your mother." Aunt Lily and then finally Papa nodded their agreement. Grandfather reached into the top of the open urn and pulled out a sheath of papers, "your mother had her own money. It was a relatively small sum however I invested it for her in her own name and it has grown considerably over the years. I have never needed it to care for any of you. With your permission I would like to disperse it to her grandchildren and Thomas." He placed the urn on the floor beside him and rested the papers on his lap. He looked into the stunned faces that surrounded him and he smiled.

"To my faithful valet and friend Thomas, this will enhance your freedom ten-fold. It will provide you a good start in whatever endeavors you seek. Invest it wisely and it will continue to grow. Emmaline saw a good man in you and her judgment was sound. However, I sincerely believe she loved you as one of our own. Please enjoy this in her memory as you are one of the few who knew her so well." Thomas swallowed hard as he took the certificate. His jaw dropped when he saw the amount, "I can't sir, this is too much." Grandfather brooked no arguments, "You can and you will. It's alright Thomas, you more than deserve it. It is my understanding that our Rob has made you a business proposition. I suggest you take it. This will make the transition much easier and you'll never be dependent upon anyone but yourself."

"As for you Rob" Grandfather continued. "You have some troubles facing you not unlike what I've had over the years; I want you to take this. It is timely I think in light of recent developments at the docks in New Orleans. This should help you pave the way to a reasonable solution." He handed Rob the certificates. "I want you to know grandson, I have looked into your company and see a wise investment and growth strategy. A well run business. Should you ever need a backer or silent partner, please come to me second, after your father," he looked directly at Papa.

"Thank you very much, Grandfather. I really appreciate this. And you're right, the timing couldn't be better. Thank you again."

"Now my dear Bryn, please come here. That's right stand right beside me." He took my hand in his and clasped it with all the life he had in him. "This is for you, from your grandmother, and oh how I know she would have loved you on sight. You have put the twinkle back in my eye, young lady. I know your parents have raised you well and provided amply for you, this will afford you some extra luxuries that most young couples cannot have as they start out. Enjoy her gift. And you, Aleck, you will also have me to reckon with should any harm come to her. Do you understand?" Grandfather glared at Aleck. "Yes sir, I ken. I'm thinking to take good care of her," he chortled. "Only as it's a verra long line I'd be facing!" Everyone laughed with him.

"Lily and John, you have been very prosperous. Your instincts for investment have panned out admirably. Your hotels are second to none. You have good friends at your side. You are many times blessed. Over the years, when you were a young girl Lily you delighted me with stories imagined or other-wise. As a young woman, you ran the household and acted as my hostess. I do believe I never thanked you. I thank you now. I was always so absorbed in the next business deal that I didn't take notice of the sadness in your eyes. You tried to tell me in your own way. I never heard you. Rest assured as long as you live your mother will never be gone. I don't know how I missed it and yet I did. She would be so proud of you my dear. So for you Lily I have this."

He pulled a burgundy velvet box from his pocket. "I have given you all of the jewels from your mother's jewelry box, but not quite all her most precious pieces." He opened the box and Lily gasped in awe. Glowing on the black velvet interior was the most exquisite necklace, a large opal with a collar of brilliant diamonds. The opal was the size of a silver dollar and its fire as it caught the light took Lily's breath away. She had never seen such a beautiful piece.

Grandfather continued, "This is the first real piece of jewellery I was able to give your mother as a present before our wedding. She always said as such it was her favorite. I had met one of my captains down on the docks one morning. I knew him by sight but his name eluded me. He was a seasoned old salty though not much older than I. Desperate he stopped me to share his sad tale. He showed me this necklace. He was from down under where the opal came from and he had had it made for his love. Unfortunately, when he arrived back in London she had taken ill and died shortly before he could be with her again. He knew I was to be married. So great was his despair he asked me to take it, and give it to my love. The opal itself is priceless as are the diamonds. But for me it is priceless for a greater reason than money, her love of it. It has been with me every day all these years; it makes me feel your mother's presence and her love for me. I want you to have it; your mother always wore it." Lily took the box from him and bent to kiss his cheek. "By the way, several years later Captain Walters captained The Emmaline and then I was able to pay him fairly for the necklace. He was not keen to take the money but he saw your mother several times and always with the necklace around her neck so finally he accepted. The chain is strong and you, my little lamb, would play with the chain and pendant as if it were a mere bauble around her neck and she would laugh with the joy of it. As a babe you were always in her arms. She was loathe to lay you down."

"Now finally, Sarah, come here my dear. Not all wrongs can be righted with a bauble, no matter the value, and I would never insult you that way. As with all things special I'm learning, it is the story that makes the magic. Emmaline and I were not married but a few years and my business was prospering. She had never been to sea so I surprised her with a voyage on my newest acquisition. A beauty of a clipper I had just added to my fleet. I had never been on her for lack of time. She had been tested seaworthy and was ready to make her maiden voyage. I arranged for the christening and all was in readiness as we arrived at the wharf. She was gently swaying on a calm sea in port. Emma was overwhelmed when she realized the ship was to be named for her. She was thrilled and took the Champaign bottle from its holder. She hurled it on its ribbon and the bottle came crashing onto The Emmaline's bow. The roar of excitement and anticipation was something to be heard. I can hear the echo and see her delight even now in this room. Here I am rambling on. I'm sorry, John please bring Sarah a chair."

Grandfather waited for her to be seated comfortably beside him then continued. "The day was perfect, the waters were calm or at least to those of us who loved the feel of the keel under our feet. The sway that leads one to restful slumber in the night. The clipper was swift and trim. But poor Emmaline spent the next two days in the Captain's cabin with a bowl in one hand and cold cloth in another. Mrs. Fairchild and I danced attendance on her. My Emma was not made for the sea. When we docked at Edinburgh, she wobbled on my arm down the gang plank. She was much relieved to have terra firma under her feet, but my brave girl smiled. Her pale face indicating the depth of her seasickness.

It did not take long to gain her feet and in a few hours she was more like her old self. We settled into our hotel. Mrs. Fairchild, Emma's maid and our cook was in the next room ready to assist. We went down to the pub and got something to eat. Emma only picked at her food but her color was returning. We were staying on High Street just down from the castle. The next day the bakery shop yielded some delightful pastries for us to have in our room.

Emma still suffered from her voyage however, we wandered up and down Castle Hill Road inspecting all the shops with Mrs. Fairchild in tow. Back down near our hotel, we went into a small jewelry store. I say small and I mean tiny, the store and living quarters were very much smaller than the room we're in now. An old gentleman came out from behind the curtain that separated the store from his quarters. If he'd danced a jig I wouldn't have been surprised he was like one of the wee folk the Scots are so superstitious of. He looked Mrs. Fairchild and me over but his attention was fixated on Emma. I was a little apprehensive but no harm was portended so we looked at his cases of gems, silver and gold. The Scots are noted for their work in silver, gold jewelry is rare in the Highlands."

The old man was obviously not one for chatter; he reached into one of his cases and pulled out a beautiful silver pin. Emma gasped when she saw it. 'Aye, tis a beauty lassie, but this un,' he reached into a case behind him and withdrew the most beautiful pin I've ever seen, it was stunning. She reached her right hand out to touch it; the old man gently took her left hand, turned it over, stroked her palm and fingers several times then placed the broach in her hand. Curling her fingers around it he held his hands around hers for a moment. Once he released her hand she traced the fine engraving and her finger lingered over the exquisite stone. They stared deeply at each other for what seemed like many minutes but were really only a handful of seconds. The old man then told us it was a star ruby. He bade her to hold it to the light and her face lit up when she saw the striking stars appear in the stone. The intricately hand tooled gold shone brightly in the dim light of the shop. There was a pair of entwined hearts and in each heart was nestled a thistle so precisely engraved you'd think you could prick your finger on them. The large ruby sat majestically in the center where the hearts overlapped. Across the top spanned an elaborate crown."

You could hear everyone's intake of breath in the room. Absolute quiet. This was a Hugh none of them knew, quite possibly the Hugh their mother had fallen in love with. Open charm and his ability to spin a tale was startling and at the same time heartening. Andrew could not help himself he was mesmerized trying to link this person with the cold, detached father he had grown up with. "It was as if the old man knew something," Hugh continued. "He seemed fey and the eerie atmosphere of the store intensified the mystery. The old man continued its story, 'Aye, for yer time lassie, this wee broach is what ye be needin'. It's a Luckenbooth as made for the good Queen Mary herself. Tis a token of love, luck and fate.' I remember Emma stroked the broach and she exclaimed with pleasure over its beauty. I knew she had to have it." Hugh took a breath and closed his eyes reliving the memory.

"But there was more and the old man's voice dropped to a whisper. 'Pin this to ye lass and no take't off. When the wee bairn comes along pin it directly to her shawl. Aye, the lad too.' What an extraordinary thing to say. Of course I bought it for her, but we talked and talked of the old man and what he'd said to Emma. We had no idea until we got home that she was indeed with child. You my dear Lily. Your mother wore the broach faithfully and just after you were born the pin was placed on your shawl. We were not so lucky with Elizabeth, our next babe, Emma wore the broach once she knew she was with child but at the birthing it was mislaid and not pinned to our babe until later. We lost Elizabeth on her birthing day. But you Andrew, from the moment she suspected she was with child she wore the pin. We were all instructed to safeguard it and place it on the babe immediately at birth. Your blanket was pinned I remember seeing the Luckenbooth on you in your birth cot. Like her opal I have kept this ever with me, but my selfish days are over. I held this precious when I should have held our children. Sarah, I wish you to have it. Having spent this time with you has been a gift. You are an amazing and loving woman, much like my Emma and a man needs that love in his life. Emma would be delighted to see this go to you, Andrew's wife." Hugh smiled at her and nodded.

From a rich black velvet bag Hugh removed the Luckenbooth broach still in the original linen bag that the old Scot had put it in at purchase. He gently removed it, stroked it and laid it in Sarah's hand, holding hers as the old man had held Emma's. Sarah was speechless, and took her hankie to dab at the tears that had come unbidden to her eyes. She bent over and gave him a hug and a kiss on the cheek. Her reaction meant more to Hugh than Sarah would ever know.

"I have a certificate for young Drew which I will deliver within the next day. I also have one for Josh. I'll hold onto it and hope I get to see them some time in the near future."

Hugh settled back in the chair apparently relieved. "Emmaline, your mother and grandmother, would be so proud of all of you. It would have delighted her to give these to you herself. Besides being beautiful and a wonderful wife and mother she was kind, fair and generous. I had lost sight of that. Well, I'm satisfied I've completed my task so now if you'll excuse me I'll take my leave. Thomas?"

"Yes sir, your carriage is ready."

~ Bryn ~

After Grandfather took is his leave, the room was so quiet you could hear a pin drop on the carpet. The room was close, and I was conscious of every breathe that everyone took. My heart was hammering in my chest and I could feel my cheeks burning. I looked at Papa, and could not believe he was speechless. I could not believe I was speechless.

Aunt Lily was the first to move, calling Rose to bring tea and sandwiches. It seemed no one had an appetite, although I did manage to eat. The tea was hot and soothing. It was the distraction we all needed. Because then everyone started to talk at once.

It sounded like bees humming out in the garden. I was listening but not taking in any of the words. My main concern lay with Grandfather. He had seemed so sad when he left. He walked with his back straight using his cane for occasional support. Then I thought enough is enough.

"Well, what do we do now?" I enquired. The broken silence was astonishing. "No one has died here, but to look at us all, one would never know. I think there needs to be some sort of decision. It seems to me we have been hanging in limbo for several weeks. Yes, there have been many shocks to take in, but I think we are strong enough to meet this head on. Isn`t that what you have always taught us Papa?"

Mama came to my side and we sat waiting for Papa to answer. "Yes, Poppet you are right, and to be honest, I have seen many changes in my father. I am not too old to learn and not too proud to admit it. What do you say Lily?" said Papa.

I was paying close attention. Aleck was on my other side, silent waiting for the other shoe to drop. I went to Papa and hugged him tight. I took his hand in mine as was our custom.

320

"Andrew, it can be the only way. We must forgive him, so we can forgive ourselves. There's been so much animosity and to be honest the wish of my life is to see you two together. You are both so stubborn, but honest men.

In the ensuing days, things quieted and the family found consolation in the normal routine of life. There were exceptions of course. Papa was anxious to be on his way with round up coming at him fast, he had a lot to think about and the trip back home just added to the pressure. Resignation was not in our collective nature, but some things would take time, as they mulled over the events of the last week. Grandfather's confession of guilt, although late, was staggeringly welcome. The pace home for the Henley's would be much different and the trip would be much more enjoyable on the whole. It would be the long way around as we should have come in the first place. Human nature being what it is, and its demands on those trying to control it leads to the inopportune disasters that be felled us. Our inevitable weakness when pitted against the wrath of the storm was proof in itself of man's insane inability to admit to his fallibility. Fortunately, none were worse for the wear and even though Papa was still dealing with the constant reminder, his leg offered him, he was still in good stead to travel home. It had been hectic and nerve wracking trying to figure out what supplies to return to the ranch with. We had to take this opportunity to buy the necessities that we would normally need to order or do without.

It was getting late in the afternoon, Aunt Lily was the first to speak. "I'm sure we're all hungry. Why don't we go to the hotel for a nice lunch? Perhaps, we could ask Father to join us?" She gave a sideway glance to Papa. He seemed to take the suggestion in stride. It was a huge concession on my Papa's part. He actually nodded his agreement.

I volunteered to fetch Grandfather, and luckily he was in his room. His face lit up with pleasure at the invitation. It was a quiet repast. Not exactly uncomfortable, but not the way I was used to sharing meals with my family. Although we attempted to put on our social graces, the general rule was that we are a rowdy bunch. There was always a lot of talk, some arguments, but most of all laughter. It was Mama who maintained order at the table. It was Aunt Lily whose melancholy turned once again to enthusiasm. "How wonderful to see Thomas again after all these years," she said looking at Grandfather. "The gift you gave him Papa was priceless. Thomas never complained about his lot in life and now the world is his oyster."

Grandfather agreed wholeheartedly although he had been relieved when Thomas had volunteered to stay with him to the end of his days. Grandfather laughed when he acknowledged that losing Thomas would challenge his easy lifestyle. Only now was he beginning to appreciate the unconditional companionship Thomas always quietly extended. Grandfather heaved a heavy sigh.

Aunt Lily leaned over and patted his hand in understanding. "Oh Papa it will be wonderful to be a family again. We will be here for you should the need arise." She smiled patting his cheek encouragingly.

I overheard Papa speaking to Mama, "It's time for us to think about getting back home. I'll admit it took a load off of my mind when Earley went back to give Josh a hand. They're a good team. But I want to be there too."

Mama knew Papa like the back of her hand and she had been more than ready to leave, "I'm ready whenever you are, my love. This has been a lovely holiday but I know you want to be home to prepare and we have much to do to ready both our home and the ranch for the winter."

Rob piped into the conversation, "Pa, ma, if you don't mind I'd like to come along home again for a quick visit. I'm so close, compared to New Orleans. I want to square things with Josh in person. Then I'll head south and deal with my other problems. Once I start with that I'm afraid I won't get away for a while. Family first though if it's alright with you?" I was thrilled, this was going to be so good.

"Of course!" we all replied as one and smiled at each other.

"Andrew," I held my breath as Grandfather hesitated. "I'm sorry I put you in the situation where I need ask this question. How's your leg fairing? Will you be able to travel," Grandfather wavered before adding, "son?" The look on my Papa's face was priceless. I was excited beyond words. I wanted to jump up and down like when I was little.

"Its ok just throbs a bit at night."

Mama gave him an incredulous look. "A bit, you toss all night trying to find a comfortable position."

Papa ignored her observation while turning to address Grandfather, "Doc Jones said I could ride for a few hours then have to rest it. By the time we get home the leg'll be nearly good as new."

"And I'll see to it you follow Doc Jones instructions Andrew Charles Henley." Mama interrupted brooking no argument.

I could see Grandfather struggling with remorse at the tension that had been created, so he changed the subject, "I still need to catch up with Drew any ideas where I should look?"

That's when I took the opportunity to get a word in edge wise, "You'll usually find him around the horses. In St. Louis you'll find him at the livery, learning as much as he can. He relates better to horses than people."

"Except in St. Louis," Rob interrupted. "There's the blacksmith's daughter here, oh and horses." He added the latter with a knowing chuckle. "Yup pa, both your youngest – smitten."

Papa rolled his eyes, "Drew too? What else don't I know? Rob!" Rob looked directly at Papa, grinned and shrugged. No answer was his best answer. Mama stared intently at her son but he refused to look into her eyes.

I explained to Grandfather, "Drew has a small smithy back home that he's trying to expand. The town's grown so we could actually use a full livery. Capital is his major issue right now." Papa asked John to us back to the house, "Come on, Rob and I'll take you over there now if you'd like."

Grandfather readily agreed, 'I'd like that very much. Just remember it's your mother who'll be helping him, Andrew. I promise I won't interfere in any of my grandchildren's affairs without your and Sarah's permission or without giving you the first chance of investment and support. I'll work on earning the right to help."

The rest of the day passed in a flurry of activity, as we packed up our things. I packed my beautiful outfits from Aunt Lily admiring each piece before it was placed into the portmanteau. It would land on the bottom of the wagon and I would not see any of it until we were home again. I looked around the room and I knew I would miss being here. I loved being with Aunt Lily and Uncle John, but the fact of the matter is, I was homesick. I think Tinker was too. It had been a while since she had had a free reign. Its' funny about being away. I was impatient to know that nothing had changed without me.

I sensed the decision in my parents as well, that it was definitely time. Not just because the round up was looming in front us. It was more basic than that, this was after all, not home. The days of resting after our ordeal were over. I could see that Pa was restless, and was pacing more than usual. Mama had already started to pack their things. The bolts of material that would last until the following spring. Seed for the homestead garden, and all manner of new tools were packed into the back of the wagon.

I went to seek out Mama and see if she needed any help. I found her still lying abed. "Mama what are you doing still in bed?" Mama looked up at me from her pillow, her hair floating around her head like a halo.

"I am taking advantage of the last time for a long time that I will be able to lie in bed with no worries. It occurred to me that at this moment in time everyone is happy. Your father is on his way to reconciling with his father, Thomas has been set up financially but will stay on a while to assist your Grandfather, I am feeling re-newed, and your father is healing nicely. What else can I say." She smiled.

"Well, I rather thought you might want to go home." I said. I sat down on the bed beside her. "Yes, I want to go home Bryn. I am getting up now. I know we have a lot to do." She laid her hand on my cheek and let it linger. I smiled back. The bag holding the broach was on the bedside table. She took out the broach, and admired it gently turning it in her hand. I wondered if I would ever see her wear it.

"Bryn, so much has happened in such a short period of time. I am so proud of you. You have grown up right before our eyes. I will confide in you, and say I am so happy and relieved that so many secrets have been laid to rest. The price of reconciliation is without sum. It is the most precious ability we control, to forgive and be forgiven. Having Rob back in our lives is something my heart thought never to see."

My Aunt Lily was so much help. She is so organized and William and Rose were irreplaceable. Aunt Lily spied the Luckenbooth broach and picked it up. When she looked at me there were tears of joy in her eyes. They always crinkle when she laughs, which is a lot, and also when she cries.

"I am overjoyed that he gave you the broach. I love you Sarah Henley, and I will miss you both terribly. This has been an exciting time. It's been like riding wild horses." Then she laughed and I watched her eyes crinkle.

"Bryn dear, where did your Papa disappear to?" she asked.

"He went to the livery to find Drew. With plans being imminent to return home, he went straight to the livery. He told us we would need additional transportation and this was Drew's forte. I am sure he asked Grandfather to go along," I caught the look that went between my Mama and Aunt Lily.

When Pa returned, he had Drew and Grandfather in tow. They were talking enthusiastically about the possibility of a livery at home. We are situated on a ranch surrounded by more ranches. We know every one of our neighbors, but not because we can see them. Papa and Drew had been talking about a livery for our town for a long time. The town was small, but the General Store carried most of our needs. If not they would order it in. There had been rumors of the railroad coming through and the ranchers were very divided. Papa saw the practical value in having the railhead close by for transferring cattle. No more extensive and dangerous cattle drives to the railhead. Others were not so convinced, but be that as it may it was bringing a steady flow of new folks into the area.

It changed the whole dynamic. It was a financial boom for those willing to take the risk. Drew was on the leading edge of this growth. More people, meant more horses, more carriages, more work. I could see the fire of the challenge in Grandfather's eyes. Grandfather had already made an investment through Drew. It was whole new adventure for him.

In the end, we were the proud owners of a carriage and a flatbed wagon. "Between the three women in this family, we have a lot more to take back with us." Papa gave a false grimace and rolled his eyes. "Drew is going to acquire more horses. We will need them so we can rotate them out. You know how I feel about killing good animals."

We were all seated around the table. It would be our last meal with Aunt Lily and Uncle John. The conversation had become stilted as we tried to hold at bay the emotion of leaving.

Mama brought the topic to light that we were all evading, "What about your father?"

I couldn't believe his response, "What about him?" he snarled.

Mama snapped, "Don't take that tone with me Andrew, you know exactly what I mean. He's not a spring chicken anymore. You need to make the days count while there are days left to count. It is my considered opinion he would not refuse an invite to the ranch and I wouldn't be upset if you asked him to come and visit. At least for a little while. You owe it to yourself and to him. Give the dust a chance to settle."

Papa grudgingly acknowledged that he would, "think on it".

Mama always knew what to say and how to say it, "Andrew, whatever you do it will be the right thing."

The next morning saw more details fall into place; tools to be purchased and food to be packed for a two week journey. I managed to procure some of the newest cooking gadgets for Becky at home. I spied an egg beater with a rack and pinion movement. Truly fascinating, and what a time saver. I knew Becky would love it. We also stocked up on things liked canned beans and coffee.

Lily was concerned with Bryn's nearly empty hope chest. Her thoughts were that it was abysmally empty. In no time under her expert eye it filled up. Aleck and Bryn would be very comfortable indeed. Of course, Lily would come to the wedding in the spring. I was still pushing for a summer wedding. Aleck wisely stayed out of the debate but was secretly pulling for Bryn.

It was after breakfast that Andrew corralled Lily, John and Rob for a quick meeting in John's study. He wore his grim face as they emerged and whisked me out to the carriage and into town. I did confide to Bryn that there was an awkward moment when we ran into her Grandfather. I conveyed in a subdued voice that the meeting had been tense. It was that greeted Hugh.

The conversation went something like this, Andrew greeted him and Hugh returned the greeting. Then they were discomfited.

"Nice day" said Papa

"Yes, yes, a lovely day," answered Grandfather. To hear me talk about it, Bryn had to stop the laugh that was trying to find an exit.

However, I continued, the best part was your father asking your grandfather to come and stay with us. My heart really went out to him Bryn. It was so wonderful to hear him address your father as 'son'.

"Son," Hugh acknowledged inwardly pleased to hear the familial moniker from Andrew in a pleasant tone of voice.

"So," Andrew hesitated. "What are your plans now Father?"

"I've been asked to stay for a visit with Lily and John before I make my way down to New Orleans. You have no objections, I hope?"

Andrew took a deep breath. "Well," he hesitated. "I was. . . Sarah and I wondered . . ." He turned to me tongue-tied, the words just beyond his ability but the intent was clear. I hopped out of the carriage took his hand and spoke for him. "We're hoping you might consider coming with us to see our home and to meet the rest of the family."

Pleased surprise registered on Hugh's face. "I would like that very much. I'm sure Lily wouldn't mind. Are you sure you want me to come for a visit son?" Hugh asked him carefully.

"Yes, Father I'm sure. I talked to Lily and John this morning. They're well pleased with the idea as is my Sarah. We'll be leaving before the week's end can you be ready? But there are some things I must do beforehand." Andrew said he had never heard his father whistle before.

y the weeks end everything was in readiness. The wagons were packed and tied down. There were two extra wagon wheels tacked on the side of the wagon. The tools were in place on iron rungs that were there for that purpose, easy accessibility in case of a disaster. I refused to think along those lines firmly believing that lightening does not strike twice in the same place.

I saw Grandfather pull up in his carriage, with two people in tow. I could see it was Doctor Smythe and his wife. They dismounted from the carriage with Doctor Smythe assisting his wife.

Grandfather approached Papa and in a conspiratorial voice asked him something. Papa beckoned Doctor Smythe. He cautiously approached, "Have you any more room for two more travelers? My wife and I have come to like America, but we were hoping to be somewhere a little less hectic than Boston or St. Louis before we make up our final decision. We'd be happy to help out with Mr. Henley and any other problems that may arise. My wife is an able nurse. I expect we might find accommodation upon our arrival."

"A doctor is always welcome. Can you handle a wagon?" Papa asked him.

"Most certainly I can, although your terrain may require my learning some new techniques. Both of us are accomplished riders." He confirmed.

"Welcome aboard then," Papa said and turned. "By the way, there is always room for a doctor in town." He smiled.

Aunt Lily and Uncle John were there for our farewell. She hugged each of us in turn. "Don't make it so long next time, Andrew. I will miss you terribly. Father, be good, get to know him, you will be glad you did. Be safe and let us know when you arrive. I will worry until then."

I knew Aleck was going to be with us. We had discussed our next step. He was going to winter with Josh and Becky. They had room and could use the help Aleck would offer. For me one adventure was coming to an end with another one around the corner. I was young and in love, what more was there? My family had been through the grist mill but managed to come out whole and the stronger for it. The tests we go through in life are never of our own choosing, but the challenge must be met, for the alternative is not worth considering. I would miss my aunt and uncle, but I knew I would see them again. I was anxious to be home, in my own bed. Mama and I would have such fun over the winter planning my wedding to Aleck. My heart was full of anticipated excitement as I got to know my grandfather. I wanted him to tell me about my grandmother and the book store he had alluded to.

It was time for me to mount. I had decided to start off on Tinker and Aleck with his new horse. The fall that plagued my nights was a distant nightmare that I could control now.

Drew helped Mama into the coach that he had purchased. Mama would ride in style. He climbed into the driver's seat, the pride of accomplishment written all over his young face. Mrs. Smythe would keep Mama company in the coach.

I looked back and saw Grandfather hanging back a bit. I called to him, "Come on Grandfather. Now I can't wait to get home. I have a book I want to share with you."

THE END

About the Author

Christine Ellen Law lived, worked, and found inspiration for many of her characters during the nearly twenty years she lived in the foothills of the Appalachian Mountains of eastern Tennessee. She now resides in central Ontario, Canada, where she is hard at work researching and writing her next novel.

Lightning Source UK Ltd.
Milton Keynes UK
UKOW02f2201010317
295675UK00001B/188/P